lightborn

TRICIA SULLIVAN

www.orbitbooks.net

ORBIT

First published in Great Britain in 2010 by Orbit

A CIP catalogue record for this book
is available from the British Library.

ISBN 978-1-84149-407-4

Typeset in Palatino by M Rules
Printed in the UK by CPI Mackays, Chatham ME5 8TD

Papers used by Orbit are natural, renewable and
recyclable products sourced from well-managed forests and certified
in accordance with the rules of the Forest Stewardship Council.

 Mixed Sources
Product group from well-managed
forests and other controlled sources
www.fsc.org Cert no. SGS-COC-004081
© 1996 Forest Stewardship Council
FSC

Orbit
An imprint of
Little, Brown Book Group
100 Victoria Embankment
London EC4Y 0DY

An Hachette UK Company
www.hachette.co.uk

www.orbitbooks.net

For Marion and Denis Sullivan

Acknowledgements

Thanks to all my family, always.

Heartfelt thanks to Jean Pritchard, Rachael Pope, Denise Nevison and Anne-Marie Lewis of Hope Preschool Playgroup as well as Lynn and John Stockton. Without your loving care of my little ones for a few hours each day, I'd never have finished this.

Thanks to Darren Nash and the entire Orbit team for really paying attention and getting things right. From an author's perspective, this imprint is a great place to be. To Mic Cheetham: thank you for your staunch support over the years.

Blogging saved (most of) my sanity while writing this. I'm grateful to everyone on Livejournal who cheered me on, especially Kim Harnett, Stephanie Burgis, Oz Whiston, Sophia Ahmed, Kate Elliott and Renée Sweet – not to mention the incomparable Danielle Lancellotti. To Karen Mahoney, thanks for being a great friend and wise counsellor, and especially thanks for your writing advice during a difficult passage that I didn't think I'd survive.

Steve: a million thanks to you, too. Living with you is like having an onsite volcano, smoking 24/7. You totally do it for me.

To my kids: sorry for always telling you to go away! Thanks for keeping me grounded, supplying me with artwork and Lego creations, and introducing me to Spongebob.

Shine On, You Crazy Diamond

Almaz

KZ didn't say hello. She was like that anyway. Sometimes she answered her phone in mid-sentence. Sometimes she expected you to read her mind. Sometimes she didn't bother to tell you that some of the conversation was actually not directed at you, but at her pet iguana, Monty. Roksana figured this was all part of KZ's manic appeal.

Today KZ was laughing too hard to say anything at all.

'What's so funny?' Roksana said, when she could make herself heard.

KZ gasped and choked. 'Sorry,' she managed to gasp.

'Do you want me to call you back when you're done peeing yourself?'

KZ panted some more and then said, 'I'm really sorry, my peri-menopausal mother just did something incredibly bizarre. It's really not even slightly funny but I just . . .'

She was weeping with laughter.

'OK . . .' Roksana sighed. Today was obviously going to be one of those days. She glanced at her watch. 11:34 am 19 July 2004. Day from hell. Server down, A/C apparently broken, no plans, her father probably sleeping it off after another all-night work jag. All her friends away on vacation, except for KZ being a shiny fool.

"Snot just me. Josh's anger management is also so—' snort '—fade of mail. I mean, made of fail. I thought he was gonna run over the dog this morning. Hey, Rocky, did I tell you about the extra colours?'

'No. I was just wondering if you wanted to go swimming later.'

'But I can see so many of them! I think I could be turning into a bee or something. No, don't laugh.'

Roksana wasn't laughing, but KZ was. Then her cell cut off.

Scowling at the phone, Roksana headed for the fridge. She passed the kitchen window and saw Irina out by the pool. This was odd. Irina was only responsible for the inside of the house; Roksana's dad used a pool service. Irina stripped off her uniform, exposing a thin, pale body with Playboy breasts that balanced uneasily in a flesh-pink lace bra. Eyes wide, Roksana watched while Irina went into the pool house and came out with a net on a long pole. She put the net over her head, then twisted it several times using the torque of the pole.

Roksana's heart was beating faster. There had always been something vaguely pornographic about Irina. But . . . shit!

Nobody else was home. According to the note Amir had left on the fridge, he had gone to his office on campus.

Irina can drive you and your friends to the mall later, the note had finished. *I have a crazy day – Dad.*

Crazy day? If Amir's day was crazy, what did you call this?

Roksana didn't know what to do. She was afraid to intervene on her own, but the neighbours would all be at work, and anyway she didn't really know any of them well enough to turn up on their doorstep begging for help with her family's dangerously kinky maid.

She didn't really know anyone well enough to do that.

Her father's phone went to voicemail.

Irina was looking seriously unhealthy.

She tried her dad's cell.

'Tony's Pizza.'

Shit. Tried again, checking the number in her phone book to make sure it was right.

'Tony's Pizza, can I help you?'

This couldn't be happening. While she watched Irina strangling herself with the pool net, Roksana called up KZ's number again.

'Oh thank god you called back,' KZ said. 'I tried to call you but I kept getting routed to a 900 number for astrology.'

'Can you call 911 for me?' Roksana began.

'Don't bother, it doesn't work. Listen, we better meet in person in case we lose this connection.'

'KZ, I think our maid got some bad shine.' Irina's face was red. She walked around the pool, gazing down into the water as if she could see something under there.

'Yeah, that's nothing. We have some issues at my house. My mom and your mom are, like, coming from the same asteroid, you know what I'm saying?'

Being reminded of Mitch was the last thing Roksana needed right now. Shakily, she said, 'Can you come over? I'm feeling freaked.'

'No, you need to come here. Roksana . . . my skin is peeling off.'

'What?'

'Yeah, it's turning purple and peeling off. Hee-hee! Look at it, this is so cool.'

'KZ, please, for once . . .'

'And I think—' KZ started laughing in earnest. 'There's something wrong with my mom's Clarity account. I borrowed some and—' She muffled the phone, but Roksana could hear her gasping and screaming.

'KZ, it's not funny . . .'

'Sorry, I know, I can't help it . . . Can you come over? I need you because I have talking worms in my eyes. I trust you. You're never shiny.'

'No, I can't – Irina—'

'I'd pick you up but our car's wrecked.' More wild laughter. 'Can you bring stain remover?'

'What? Where are you now? What's – oh, holy shit!' Irina had jumped in the water with the pool net still wrapped around her head.

'Roksana? Hee, Roksana—?'

Roksana dropped the phone and ran out on the deck. Irina's face was purple.

Roksana crashed through the gate in the fence around the pool and plunged into the deep end. Irina was crawling around on the bottom, patting at the blue concrete like she was feeling around for a lost earring or something. Big bubbles were coming out of her mouth.

Roksana swam towards her underwater and waved her hands to attract Irina's attention. Irina looked at Roksana and opened her mouth halfway. The net pressing on her skin carved her Barbie-doll face into soft chunks. Her eyes rolled back. She reached for Roksana.

Roksana kicked away, scared. Her clothes were dragging at her. She came up for air.

She'd never liked Irina. Irina never failed to let everybody know she had suffered. At the same time, she managed to convey her disdain at having to scrub the toilets of the spoiled American bourgeoisie. Her beauty was intimidating. Also, she never shut up about her perfect son the genius with looks, away at boarding school on a scholarship. Dmitri would not even look at a girl of Roksana's mediocre calibre – Irina made that clear.

Still, Roksana didn't dislike Irina enough to let her die in the family pool, just because of a nasty shine. She could see Irina hovering in the water, flailing her arms and legs feebly but not going anywhere. The stick of the pool net jerked, dragging on the bottom.

Roksana caught hold of Irina from behind like she'd been taught in water safety class. The pole of the pool net kept getting in the way, but Irina herself did not struggle as Roksana dragged her to the surface. Getting her out of the water was almost impossible. Luckily there was a flight of steps at the shallow end, and Roksana managed to pull Irina up them. She unwound the tangled net. It had left angry marks on Irina's face. The process seemed to take a lifetime. Whatever strangulation Irina had attempted, it hadn't been effective because Irina was full of pool water. Roksana thumped the water out of her and Irina started coughing and regurgitating.

Roksana sat back on her heels, gulping for breath in her own right. She had pulled a muscle in her back, and it throbbed.

As soon as Irina could speak, she started yammering in Russian. She looked right through Roksana.

'Irina! Speak English!'

Irina looked, but she did not seem to recognize Roksana. She didn't even slow down, or try to make Roksana understand. She just ranted, and coughed, and then started crying. Eventually her stream of speech slowed. Now she was saying the same word, over and over again.

'Almaz!' Irina sobbed. She tried to get back into the water. 'Almaz! Almaz!'

Lockdown

In the end, Roksana coaxed Irina into the guest bedroom. She took a disposable razor and a bottle of Tylenol away. Then, when Irina was examining her neck where the pool net had sliced into it, she quickly shut the door and jammed a chair against it to keep Irina contained. She tried to call KZ and then several of her other friends, and finally as a last resort she tried to leave her father a message on his voicemail, but none of the calls connected.

Roksana's computer couldn't connect. What about Amir's? Her father ran his desktop off an independent, ultra-high-speed connection in his study. Amir did most of his Riding late at night. Roksana assumed this was because he was trying to downplay the fact that he was doing it at all. He seemed ashamed – maybe he felt like a hypocrite, after all that anti-shine lecturing and posturing. He had only resumed Riding recently – said he was doing 'a couple of private contracts' because they needed the money to pay Mitch's hospital bills. He had told Roksana to keep it quiet.

Well, Roksana was an expert at keeping things quiet. She already kept it quiet that she couldn't use shine like other teenagers – she'd lost her virginity but still hadn't been inducted to shine because her brain acted like a child's in that department. She let her friends think she abstained.

She kept it quiet that her mom was in a loony bin thanks to lightborn abuse. So now she'd have to keep it quiet that her family's Ukrainian maid was into edgy sexual behaviour with pool nets. Big deal.

Keeping it quiet hadn't stopped Roksana noticing that Amir had changed, though. Lately he had started saying heavy things to her.

'If anything ever happens to me, I want you to get out of town. Go to Grandma in Sonoma. You have a credit card. Use it. Not that anything will happen. But if.'

The first time he'd said it Roksana ignored him. He was a paranoid hypochondriac, after all, and he refused to take corrective shine. But then he said, 'One thing I want you to remember is that we all make mistakes in this life. Everybody. We all screw up, and most of us screw up repeatedly. It's the human condition.'

She'd joked, 'So why the sage advice? Are you, like, dying?'

'I wish it was that simple. Society has ways of dealing with people dying. But there are no social rituals for dealing with bad shine, no safety measures, nothing.'

'Not all shine is bad, you know,' she'd rebutted, tired of listening to his shit.

'There's just so much you don't understand, Roksana. I see how you all look at me. I know what people think. I'm a loser, a loafer, a basket case, right? I don't mind you thinking that if it protects you. But you don't understand where I've been.'

'So, Dad,' Roksana had joked. 'Did you want some Brie with that whine?'

Instead of telling her off, he'd hugged her tightly – this in itself was bizarre, as Mitch had always been the provider of hugs.

He said, 'I love you. You might not want me in your life right now, but you're stuck wth me. That's how it is.'

Now she peered into the darkness of his study. Set down half a level from the rest of the house, the room was tomblike, with black bookshelves, black cabinets, black blinds on high windows. Massively expensive equipment emitted a genteel hum, and air purifiers and humidity regulators worked around the clock.

Irina had special instructions for cleaning this room, but obviously she hadn't made it down this morning before getting frisky at poolside. Half a dozen Starbucks' cups were stacked on the desk and it looked as though a cappuccino grande had spilled all over the keyboard. A quantity of Cheetos were strewn across the hardwood floor. Desk drawers were open. Papers, photographs and even old passports were tossed around. It looked as though the room had been burgled. Ranks of lightborn outlets gleamed, tiny and potent, from the rack above the computer.

At least she didn't have to worry about those.

But what if . . . Whoa, wait a second. Had Irina done this? What if Irina had come down here intending to clean, and had caught some kind of experimental shine that Amir had left on?

Of course, Amir would never be so careless as to leave the lights running . . .

But then, Amir would never spill coffee on the keyboard or throw Cheetos around the room.

Something was fucked.

Roksana was determined to remain calm no matter what. If she could stay calm, then she would hold on to herself. And if you held on to yourself, then nobody could really do anything to you. At least, that was what Mitch used to say before Mitch succumbed to the spiked Perfection.

She sat down on the edge of Amir's swivel chair and started to IM KZ, but there was no connectivity here, either.

There was one thing, though. Her father's work session of the night before was still running on the Feynman's giant screen. She could see waveforms of the raw shine code streaming across the bottom of the box, undulating like swimming eels. She could see the more regular formations that she recognized as manifestations of Field guards, AIs assigned to regulate which shine went to which consumer. This must be one of her father's contracts. He was still logged into the Field.

Why had he left the desk and gone to campus? Amir was a security freak.

She was jittery now, not sure what to do. She moved the mouse, intending to try to message Amir at his office, but the screensaver gave way to a frozen image. It had been a message session, but only the tail end appeared on the frozen screen.

RichardDelveccio: OK, I got it. What I'm seeing here is enough to call for lockdown. I'll countersign the command if that's what you want. Are you sure?

Amir_Ansari: Yes. Do it fast before I change my mind.

RichardDelveccio: Seriously. Once we initiate this procedure there's no going back.

Amir_Ansari: Understood. Start the protocol, effective immediately.

RichardDelveccio: OK. You will be in quarantine from **SESSION TERMINATED DUE TO CONNECTION FAILURE**

Roksana tried to take a screenshot, but the computer was frozen out. Even after she rebooted, she couldn't get the session back.

Richard Delveccio. She knew that name. He was a lightborn regulator these days. Before that he'd worked for America the Beautiful, the biggest rival of her dad's old firm, American Dream. The two men had started out Riding together; maybe they were still friends. If the 'protocol' Delveccio had referred to was Amir's emergency damage-control protocol, well, then that there was some serious shit. The town would be cut off, shine-wise. And probably other-wise, too. Amir was nothing if not thorough in his paranoia.

But what had made him initiate the lockdown? Whatever he had sent Delveccio must have been convincing. The Field controlled what shine went where, so if it had been compromised say by terrorists, or naughty hackers or even a rogue AI or whatever like Amir was always predicting? Then anybody could be getting shined with anything, anywhere in Los Sombres. Theoretically.

Anybody but Roksana, anyway.

She could hear Irina moving around upstairs. Quickly she looked up 'almaz' in a Russian dictionary. It meant *diamond*.

The Fall

By the time Roksana got up there, the sounds of somebody walking around had stopped. The chair had been moved out of the way, but now the guest bedroom door was locked. Strange. She looked for the little emergency key in the pottery jug on the hall shelf, the one her parents had kept since she'd locked herself in the bathroom at age two. It wasn't there. But she could hear soft, regular breathing coming from the other side of the door. As if Irina were asleep.

She went from room to room, braced to encounter an intruder, but nobody was there.

She was certainly feeling deeply freaked by now.

She went down to the garage and got her bike out. She had half-assed ideas of going to KZ's, or she could just lock up the bike outside the Safeway and get a bus to campus.

Two blocks from her house she came to a police barricade. A cop came towards her, waving her away.

'Go back! There's a firearms incident in progress. Go home and stay in your house.'

'What's going on? I tried to call 911 and there was no answer.'

'Citywide emergency. Hostile guards in the shine Field.

Total quarantine has been imposed by the federal government. Go home and lock your doors. Don't use any shine.'

Roksana started home. Once the police were out of sight she tried an alternate route, but that was blocked, too. A helicopter passed overhead, and she heard distant sirens. She thought about ditching the bike and cutting through people's backyards, but then she heard gunshots. That's when she started pedalling home as fast as she could.

She set the security system and tried calling Amir again, to no avail. Roksana cracked the bathroom door open to see the maid curled up in the empty tub, asleep. Now what?

When in doubt, eat. Mitch had taught her that. She got a bag of Doritos and a Coke and sat down in front of the TV but, unsurprisingly by now, there was a service interruption on the cable as well. She accessed the stored movie library.

Raiders of the Lost Ark had been Mitch's favourite movie as a kid and thinking about Mitch as a kid made Roksana feel slightly better. She ate Doritos without tasting them. Just when Marion was initiating a drinking contest with that sleazy French archaeologist, the movie retreated to a corner of the screen. The main screen went black.

The next thing she heard was a child's voice, whispering, '*This is the emergency broadcast system. This is not a test. All kids, find each other now. Stay away from grownups, even your parents. If your brothers and sisters are older, like if they have shine, don't talk to them either. Find each other and help each other get out of town. It could save your life.*' The message was repeated in Spanish.

The blackness gave way to a news studio where the adults were taking turns reading announcements.

'Shipping lanes in the seventeenth century were virtually inaccessible to the Mongol telemarketing revolution. Mr Davis believed that a proteinaceous form of binnacle symbolism was at the root of the Boxer Rebellion and its negative impact on toasted flakes of corn, but the result of last year's pennant race remains an enigma. Let's go to our correspondent in Dubuque, Penny Marshall.'

An old movie about a women's baseball team came on and almost immediately cut off again. The news studio came back in view, only now the weather woman and the boom guy were sitting on the desk, chanting *Om Tare Tutare So Ha*. The boom guy wore camouflage pants and a purple T-shirt from an Austin, TX gay pride march. The anchor wore Versace. Her nose was running.

'This has to be a joke,' said Roksana. Then something moved in her peripheral vision. Irina was climbing out of the window of the guest bedroom. Irina was wearing a Japanese silk pants suit that belonged to Mitch. The clothes were so big they made Irina look like a child. Roksana watched Irina jump into the azaleas and then make off, barefoot, across the lawn. Something sparkly glinted in her fist.

'Good riddance, bitch.' Roksana turned back to the screen.

There was a noise at the back door and Roksana jumped. Amir was standing at the sliding glass door leading to the deck and the pool. He was wearing wraparound sunglasses, but she could still see the feedback lights at his temples flashing erratically. He jerked at the handle of the door Roksana had locked.

She stood up, spilling what was left of the Coke. Amir was tapping on the glass.

'Dad?'

He yelled through the glass: 'The guards have been blinded by a rogue AI. There's no regulation. Anything and everything is loose in the Field. It's affecting the whole infrastructure of the city. We're looking at anarchy.'

She started to unlock the door.

'No! Don't let me in. Don't trust anything I say or do. I've been compromised. The Field is going down.'

So it was true. 'What do I do? What about Mom?'

'I'm going to check on her after I leave you.'

'You can't leave me! I'm coming with you.'

He pressed his hands against the glass.

'You'll be safer here. I promise. Stay here, lock yourself in, and I'll tell Irina what to do.'

'Irina's gone. I think she got that shine you left running in your office.'

He ran his hands through what was left of his hair. For a second it looked like he would collapse.

She slid the door open and let in a flood of hot air.

'It was a rogue. Had an AI component. Relative of Light. American Dream didn't know about it. This rogue – it's the reason I quit in the first place. It's the thing that messed me up.'

He started trembling. She reached out to touch him but he suddenly stiffened. Major mood shift. He straightened and his pupils narrowed.

'I had to eradicate it. Took the local Field down with it; I had no choice. The guards were corrupted. Now that the defence protocols are kicking in, the Field will be all right, everywhere but here in Los Sombres.'

'But what about us? Dad, if lightborns are running loose, we have to get out of here!'

Amir stiffened. Took a deep breath. Sharp-eyed now, he stepped back from her. He wasn't trembling anymore. There was a tension in him, but it was a tension of strength, as of a strung bow.

'I'm getting some things for your mother.' He strode to the master bedroom.

Roksana grabbed her mother's gym bag and started packing clothes and toiletries. But Amir went to Mitch's jewellery box.

'Where are the diamonds?' he snapped.

'I don't know. Who cares?'

Amir raged around the room, ripping drawers open.

'I need them. I need them for Mitch.'

'Dad, trust me, she won't care about the diamonds.' They

weren't even real. Mitch kept the real ones in a safe deposit box. The paste ones were for parties. They were jammed up with shine.

'Where's Irina?'

Almaz.

Rosanna looked at him. 'Gone. You think . . .?'

Amir's feeds flashed wildly, even though there were no shine transmitters in the bedroom. For a second he looked like he was going to revert to his usual pathetic self.

'Let's get in the car and go,' she blurted. 'Like you always say. We'll pick up Mom, and we'll go to Sonoma.'

'Too late. Lockdown.' He sounded proud. Amir had campaigned for the lockdown protocols after he'd left American Dream.

'Great. You mean we're fucked.'

'At least they're respecting the protocols. This is serious, Roksana.'

'Well . . . how are we going to get Mom?'

Amir pointed out the window. A yellow scooter leaned against the pool shed.

'I had to steal a moped.'

They rode double. Roksana drove, shakily, and Amir sat behind her and looked at his GPS until it died. He steered her through lawns and across parking lots, and once they went the wrong way up the entry ramp to a highway. He said that was OK because the traffic was all stopped by a twenty-vehicle pileup.

Once, a police helicopter followed them; Amir told Roksana to drive into a bowling alley. When they drove out the other side, the chopper had gone off in another direction.

'Are the police shined out too?' she asked.

'If they aren't yet, they will be.' Then her father started pointing out all the places where lightborns were beaming out: from billboards and road signs, from street lamps and store fronts, from gas stations and telephone poles.

'Why don't they just shut down the power?' Roksana asked.

'*They* could if *they* would,' Amir said. 'But they won't. The people in charge are shined.'

A mass fist fight had broken out in the middle of an intersection. Dozens of office workers were bashing each other, ties flapping. One woman chopped at another's face using the heels of her taupe slingbacks. Roksana had to hang a sharp left and bounce up on the kerb, and even then she just missed hitting two suits who were screaming at each other on the sidewalk. They put aside their differences long enough to try to grab hold of the bike.

Roksana swerved and tried to accelerate away from them, but the moped was at top speed. The men chased them, yelling, 'Come back, murderers!' and stuff like that. It seemed to take forever before they fell behind.

Roksana's palms on the handlebars were slick with sweat by then.

'Dad, next time you steal a bike, make it a Harley.'

He told her to stop outside Mitch's old health club. They got off. Inside American Woman it was deserted. The place still smelled of chlorine and perfume, but there were no people inside.

'This is weird,' Roksana said. 'Where is everybody?'

'I cleared it for you. There is shine here working on your behalf. People can't even see this place. You'll be safe here, or as safe as can be expected. It's in the protocol.'

Outside, the sound of a car accident. Roksana flinched. People were shouting. Amir was calm.

'What about Mom?'

'I'll go to the hospital and bring her here. You stay and wait.'

'Oh, *nuh-uh*.'

'Oh, *yes-huh*,' he mimicked, pointing at her commandingly. 'You. Stay. Here.'

Roksana didn't know what to make of her father. He wasn't

the geekfreak she knew so well. Normally he was obsessional about his fork being perfectly lined up by his plate at dinner. He'd fiddle with his socks for half an hour to get the seams straight and break down completely if he couldn't find his favourite coffee mug. Now he was acting like a commando or something. It didn't fit.

'Dad, have you been shined up with something?'

He nodded. 'I did it to myself. It's the only chance we've got. I have to go now. There's a radio in the back. Call me on Channel 7. But be aware that they will be listening.'

Oh, no. Paranoia, again. Classic Dad.

'They?' she shouted in his ear.

'Our enemies,' he said.

'Um . . . who are they, again?'

'Are you kidding me? Everybody, of course.'

Ditch the Biter

'Janine! Janine? Where are you? Ja-nine!'

Roksana parted the blinds of the American Woman lobby a couple inches and looked out. Everybody else had deserted this street hours ago. Still she'd waited, getting alternately pissed off at Amir and scared and pissed off and scared. Now there was a boy, couldn't be more than three, wandering down the empty sidewalk, calling.

Roksana was out the front door of American Woman before she could argue with herself. The boy saw her and stopped.

'Hi,' Roksana said. 'What's your name? Are you lost?'

The boy was silent. He stared at Roksana in obvious fear.

'If you can't find your mom then I guess you're pretty freaked out. My name is Roksana. I don't know where my mom is, either. That's pretty tough.'

The boy said, 'It was hot in the car. Where Janine?'

'You are being so brave,' Roksana said. 'There's an emergency going on and I guess Janine got held up. She's probably looking for you, too.'

Not.

'I'm getting really really tired,' the boy said.

There was a burst of shouting from down the block, and

shots rang out. Roksana saw a boy of about thirteen with a rifle running across the tops of parked cars.

'Give it up!' he was screaming, but she didn't know whether this was directed at her. Other people were around, sitting in their cars, wandering aimlessly down the sidewalk. They didn't react to him.

The small boy cringed; Roksana lunged forward and grabbed him, pulling him down behind a line of abandoned cars. A car engine roared. A late model black Lincoln town car, liberally dented, came careering down the middle of the street. Its driver seemed to be using parked vehicles to bounce off so as to change direction in lieu of actually steering.

There were kids of all ages crammed inside. Impossible to make out individual identities, but a girl of maybe ten was driving and she was heavy into the trial-and-error approach. There were even kids in the trunk; every time the suspension bounced, they had to push the trunk up to keep it from smashing on to their heads.

Hanging on to the back of the Lincoln was a teenaged boy on a skateboard carrying some kind of assault rifle. His yellow-helmeted head turned in her direction and he let go of the car, raised the gun to his shoulder. The other boy halted on the roof of a Shogun and pointed his own rifle at Roksana.

'Let the kid go!' he yelled. 'Let him go or I'll take you out.'

Roksana ran out into the car's path.

'Don't shoot!' she yelled. 'We have to stick together.'

The car hurtled towards her, the whites of the young driver's eyes just visible over the steering wheel. Roksana saw her mouth go 'Oh shit!' as she tried to brake. The car skidded sideways and banged into a stand of motorcycles even as Roksana's nerve failed her and she leaped away. The skateboarder boy lowered his rifle and stuck out his left arm, grabbing at her.

'Hey, what the fuck!' yelled the boys in the back seat, and one of them pointed a pistol at her. Another wrested it away from him. A lot was said in Spanish as the skateboarder dragged Roksana towards the car. Two other kids jumped out and seized the little boy. He screamed and kicked.

'You can't go with this lady, she shined. Here, have a life-saver.'

'I'm not shined and I'm not a lady. Let go of me.'

The little boy took the lifesaver and looked at it. Two girls coaxed him into the car.

'Why you not shined?' said Assault Rifle Boy.

'It's a long story, but I'm not. Maybe we can help each other out. Do you know what's going on?'

'No, but we're getting out of here. The adults are fucking psycho, and I bet you are, too.'

The back seat of the car was a jigsaw puzzle of limbs and faces. A white boy was struggling with someone Roksana couldn't see. He seemed to be sitting on somebody.

'Ow, you little animal,' he said. 'Did you bite me?'

'Leave her alone,' snapped the driver, turning around to look over her shoulder as she tried to back out of the motorcycle rack.

A small voice came from the back seat. 'Help! Help!'

'Who's that?' said Roksana nervously.

'Shut up, kid. We're going to take care of you, but quit biting.'

'Help! I don't want to go with them. I want my mother!'

The others answered her with a chorus of:

'You can't have your mother, stupid. You don't want your mother. Your mother's psycho just like all of them.' And so forth.

Roksana peered into the car and she could just make out part of a face, and hair in cornrows with little white beads. Terrified.

'I think I know that kid,' she lied to the kid leaning out of the rear window. 'I could take care of her if you want.'

'Help, help me! They're hurting me!'

'We're not hurting you, we're saving your life you stupid baby.'

'Do you know this lady?'

Lady?

'Yeah, I know her, she lives in my building,' the girl said. So she knew how to lie, too.

'Let her out,' Roksana commanded. 'I'll take care of her. Can't you see you're just scaring her?'

Somebody from the trunk said, 'Ditch the biter, she's trouble. Let's go. We can't waste no more time. Look at that shit.'

Exclamations in Spanish as what could only be described as a herd of people came out of a McDonald's a block or so away. They moved stupidly, like silent cattle. They bumped into things and into each other.

'Look the fuck at them.'

'It's night of the living Fred.'

'How we gonna get through that?'

Boarder Boy said, 'Leave it to me.'

'No way,' said the driver. 'You can go ahead and move cars out of my way, but I'm not gonna let you go just shooting people.'

'Yeah, and we don't have enough ammo,' said a girl in the back.

Boarder Boy looked disappointed.

'They're not coming this way, anyway,' the driver said. 'Come on, let's go before something else happens. Let's go before the bombers get here.'

'Bombers?' said Roksana, picturing terrorists with fertilizer bombs.

'Yeah, the National Guard is coming in.'

'Let me out!' screamed the little girl. The rear passenger door opened and she was more or less tossed out. She was about six, sobbing her eyes out.

'I want my mother.' The words came out garbled by tears. She already sounded defeated.

'I know how you feel,' Roksana said. 'It's really scary getting separated from your mom. Do you want me to help you find her?'

The girl gulped and nodded. Roksana took her hand. She was wearing a Spiderman wristwatch.

'I'm Rocky. What's your name?'

'Elsa.'

The Lincoln's engine revved and it roared off down the road.

'Hey!' Roksana yelled. The Lincoln went a couple of blocks and then Roksana saw the rear brake lights come on. There were cars blocking the road – abandoned vehicles, probably, like the ones she'd been seeing all over town. Or vehicles with their owners just sitting inside, glassy-eyed.

Boarder Boy came gliding around the back of the Lincoln and stopped when he got to the Neon. He pointed the rifle through the driver's side window. Roksana went to cover Elsa's eyes, but Elsa had buried her face in Roksana's side anyway.

The driver of the Neon got out. She moved like an old person or an invalid. The skateboarder shoved her out of the way and got in the car himself. He gunned the engine, steered it out of the way of the Lincoln, and switched it off. Then he got out and grabbed the fender of the Lincoln as it rumbled past him, and the kids all sailed on until they reached the next obstruction.

Roksana breathed a sigh of relief that nobody had been shot.

The woman who had been the driver of the Neon wandered down the sidewalk for a little way. Then she stopped as if she'd just thought of something important. She took her sunglasses off and dropped them on the ground and stepped on them. Then she walked away. Then she went back and stepped on them again. Roksana frowned. Roksana watched this happen a couple more times before she realized Elsa had wandered away, still sniffling.

'Hey! Come back here, kid!'

'I have to find my mother!'

Roksana ran after Elsa. How could she make the kid stay?

'Please don't leave me by myself. I'll help you find your mother, but keep me company until then, OK?'

Elsa sighed. She was still taking shuddering breaths after all that crying, and Roksana held her until her breathing settled, like an ebbing tide.

'It'll be OK,' Roksana whispered. 'Hang in there. Things can't go on like this for long.'

Like she believed that.

Desperado

You Can Call Me Al

Impossible to know how the shined-up man got past the Silver Brush checkpoint on Highway 6. By all logic he should have been shot. How he got the Honda CRC out of gas-deprived Los Sombres was another mystery. The guy couldn't even steer, because at 2:26 pm on 17 July 2006 – only hours before the first missile strikes – he crashed it in the drive of the Triple Cross Ranch.

The drive was a mile long and it arrowed toward the mountain in whose shadow the house was set. At that hour the sky reached in all directions, empty synthetic blue. Crackly shadows delineated the edges of every wrinkle on the mountain, rendering the scene in unreal 2D. Nothing moved. All the world a photograph as the Honda, puttering along at 25 mph with its lights on, veered to the left and crunched the post-and-rail fence that Pavarotti had just finished repairing. The vehicle proceeded a little way into the field, dragging some of the fence, and then stalled.

Xavier had been up at the house when he heard the fence go. He dropped the dog-eared copy of *Western Rider* on his bed and made his way outside. When he saw the Honda, he broke into a run. Even so, Pavarotti and Les got there before him. By the time Xavier skidded to a stop, Pavarotti'd taken off his Stetson and was scratching his balding head as he stood back from the driver splayed across the airbag.

'He don't seem hurt, but he's out cold,' Les offered.

Xavier slipped around Pavarotti. The man behind the wheel looked about forty. He was dark and hairy with strong Caspian Sea features, dressed in a clean red Polo shirt and freshly-pressed khakis. The cool of the Honda's A/C drifted out of the car carrying the smell of leather and breath mints.

Xavier looked at the gas gauge.

'Three quarters,' he said. 'Which way'd he come from?'

Pavarotti shrugged. Pavarotti never talked; since the shine fucked with his brain he only sang Italian opera. Hence the nickname.

'Didn't notice, kid,' Les translated.

Xavier shook his head. There was no point in saying, 'How the fuck can you not notice a *car* coming up the *road* for the first time in months when you're standing right *there*?' because Les would just say something about some Astros game happened back in 2004 and Pavarotti would turn his head to one side and spit in a vain attempt to act like Doug. So Xavier went around to the passenger side and checked the glove compartment. The GPS would be useless under signal quarantine, but he found an AAA map of the city with a route highlighted from the interstate exit 17 to the reservation border, just up the road from here.

Xavier checked the man's pulse. Sixty-something. The man's eyes fluttered beneath closed lids. Xavier peeled one eyelid back and the man's feedback light emitted a feeble beam in the afternoon sunshine. American Dream insignia. Top of the line, and the beam lacked an alphanumeric. Probably custom.

Through the windshield Xavier could see more people coming. Hopi weavers. The day men. Refugee women running after a gaggle of kids. Place was like a disturbed anthill. Doug and his son Rex were riding up from the main road, their horses in a hard sweat.

Xavier got out of the car. He saw Chumana break into a run, leaving the rest of the crowd at the top of the drive. Xavier tried to think where his mother would be at this hour, but it was hard to look at Chumana and think about anything else at the same time. Her legs ate up the ground with long, easy strides. Her nipples always seemed to be hard under whatever she was wearing – today, a Black Eyed Peas T-shirt she had outgrown. She came to a breathless halt and looked down at him. She had a wide face with high cheekbones, swollen lips and a flat, perfectly symmetrical nose. She also had black eyes that seemed to draw Xavier in; those eyes saw a boy.

She would always see a boy, because that's what he would always fucking be. Short, skinny, immature.

'Take a look at his feeds,' Xavier said before she could ask any questions.

She shot him a horrified look. 'Is he – is he alive?'

'Yeah, yeah, he's alive. Quick, look at the feeds before Doug gets here.'

Chumana crawled into the car. She moved the guy's hair out of the way to check the sequin-sized feedback lights fitted to his forehead.

'They're American Dream,' she said.

'Yeah, I know, but—'

'Wait a second. There's no – did you see a series code?'

'No. That's what I—'

'Xavier, get in here.'

Xavier crawled into the passenger seat. He was practically on top of her. Her black hair smelled of Breck. A confusion of hoofbeats sounded on the driveway.

'Look at that!' She pointed to the edge of the illumination. 'Did you ever see that signature before?'

'No,' Xavier said. 'Maybe we should look for some ID. He could be somebody important.'

He opened the glove compartment. There were no registration documents.

'Check his wallet.'

But the guy didn't have a wallet. Just as Xavier was trying to reach around to the guy's back left pocket, the guy stirred and mumbled something. The roan flank of Doug's horse appeared in the frame of the windshield. Doug dismounted and said something to Powaqa. Pavarotti put his hat back on.

Xavier backed out of the car. Chumana stayed, examining the feedback beams.

'Stall them,' she hissed. 'I think he's a Rider.'

'Time to stand back now, kids,' Doug drawled, and Rex dismounted beside him. Rex shot a glance at Chumana and then at Xavier. He waggled his tongue. Xavier glared back.

Doug said, 'We tracked him from the interstate. Driving like an old lady. If he's coming from the city he could be rigged up any which way.'

Chumana came out of the car and started talking quietly to Powaqa, who was her great-aunt. The other women formed a loose circle around the two. Melanie broke away after a minute and hobbled over to the car.

'We'd better get him inside,' Melanie said. She was a big woman and most people didn't argue with her. She leaned into the car and satisfied herself that it was all right to move the guy. 'Come on. We'll put him on this sheet.'

Melanie used to be a doctor. Luckily, the Fall hadn't had much effect on her professional knowledge, even if it had done . . . other things. Xavier started to help her but Powaqa called him away.

'Come with me, Xavier. I need help getting the big pot out of the cave.'

Xavier offered Melanie an apologetic glance and went with Powaqa.

'What's the pot for?' he asked.

'We'll cook him and eat him,' Powaqa said.

'Are you doing medicine?'

She answered his question with one of her own. 'Is he a Rider, Xavier?'

'Chumana thinks so.'

'Well, that's pretty interesting. Come on, you catch one of those mules.'

It was always a production when Powaqa decided to do a medicine ceremony. The big pot had to be kept in a cave up on the hill behind the house, and the only way to get it in and out was by mule. Xavier had never argued with Powaqa about the practicality of this because Powaqa was a member of the Hopi nation, some kind of medicine woman supposedly, and if she was willing to help the refugees that was good enough for Xavier. But the big pot was always a pain in the ass.

The two of them had just harnessed the mule and started to walk it past the garage when Xavier's mother came running up, trailing her knitting. Her face was flushed and she looked so unexpectedly pretty that he almost didn't recognize her.

'Who is it? Who's in the car?'

'Mom,' Xavier said, going towards her and holding out his hands. 'It's not him. It's not Dad.'

'Are you sure? Are you sure he's not in the back?' And she threw her head desperately to one side, trying to look past Xavier and make eye contact with Powaqa, who sorrowfully shook her head.

'He's coming back to us. I know he is.'

'Mom, it's not him.'

She let go of Xavier's hands, deflated. She seemed to shrink and lose colour right before his eyes. In the old days, Xavier's mother had put on all the little fake affectations that adults had.

Before the Fall she would have made some effort to hide her disappointment. Now she could hide nothing. Emotions passed right across her face. Shine complexes, too, but then she was one of the lucky ones. She was alive.

Xavier's father was not. He had been among many victims of the Fall who had suffered PCP-style flip-out and eventual defenestration from the seventeenth floor of the office building where he worked. Xavier had heard about it from a girl in his class who had seen it on a YouTube download smuggled into the quarantine perimeter by Sam Ghost Money Power.

He hadn't told his mother. Maybe it was cruel to let her go on hoping her cheating man might show up one day, begging forgiveness. Maybe it was selfish. Because if she knew Xavier's dad was gone, she might try something suicidal herself. And even though she was crazy, Xavier needed her to not be dead.

Powaqa gave Xavier the mule's lead. Then she took Xavier's mother's hands and said, 'Rosa, we're going to need a lot of wood for the medicine fire.'

Powaqa had a face like the land itself: dark and guttered with dry channels, a tearless expanse of sadness. She was old. Her teeth were long and curved, and her mouth trembled when she was thinking. Eyes: like caves with lakes in them. She blinked slowly. You knew right away when you first talked to her that she was artless. She never tried to fake you out.

Xavier's mother nodded, like a doll. Tears welled in her eyes and she blinked them away.

'Wood,' she repeated. 'OK. I'll just put away my knitting.'

She went back to the house. The receiving blanket she was knitting for her imaginary baby dragged in the dust after her. Powaqa turned towards the mountain and kept walking, expecting Xavier to follow. And he did.

You May Be Right

The big pot sang a little when Xavier ran his fingers along the edge, like a bell. It came out of the cave on his shoulders. He staggered under its weight.

Powaqa retrieved the other ceremonial objects, including the mirrors, the mushrooms, the red envelopes full of cash, and her own purple top hat. Then she helped Xavier load the pot on to the mule. It was a cauldron, really, left over from some promotional event in Los Sombres; it even had 'Harry Potter at El Duende Books' stencilled on the bottom. They walked on either side of the mule until they reached Doug's Jeep, parked just outside the corral where Powaqa trained mustangs. Together they heaved the pot out into the back of the Jeep.

'We'll hold the medicine at sunset,' Powaqa said. 'Tell Chumana to be ready.'

She walked with him back to the house, but instead of going inside to see what was happening with John Doe, she returned to the corral and whistled for Bob Newhart. Several alpacas came hopefully to the fence, but they got out of the way when Bob trotted up. Powaqa slid from the top rail on to Bob's back and rode off.

Xavier stood by the barn feeling unreal. Horses stood quietly drinking at the trough, only their tails moving. The horsemen were throwing hay down and speculating as to the events that had brought John Doe to the ranch.

'Gotta be outsider. Car's too perfect,' Les said, taking some tobacco out of his back pocket.

'Outsiders don't pass out at the wheel,' Doug said. 'No military escort, so he ain't no journalist. Dude's from the city.'

'If he is, he been through some shit. Want to watch him.'

Doug took a pinch of tobacco from the tin Pavarotti offered. 'I aim to.'

Xavier felt Doug looking at him. He didn't let Doug catch his eye because then he'd end up doing all Doug's work while Doug got drunk. Instead, he took a bag of charcoal from the store and headed up to the house.

Melanie was examining the strange man on the kitchen table, humming tunelessly as she prodded him. She was convinced everything bad was her own fault, and she sang because she thought this was the only way to fix things. But she had no sense of pitch.

'He's not a corpse,' Xavier said. 'Kitchen table's kinda hard.'

He spoke softly, but Melanie snapped her head around with that wild-eyed look of hers. She never seemed to sweat, so her deep brown skin had a matte look, with purple undertones. Her voice was deeper than Xavier's.

'I didn't do this to him, did I? Did I hurt him?'

Chumana, taking Pop Tarts from the toaster, spoke in a tone that had been practised to soothe.

'You're a doctor. You're trying to help him. We don't know what happened. Do you know what shine he's under?'

Melanie seemed to be thinking. Xavier ducked around Chumana to take a Pop Tart. The man on the table stirred.

'I need help,' he said. 'I need medicine. I need the Rider.'

Then he started choking. Xavier flinched. There was a

tension in the man's body, the kind of tension Xavier had seen many times back in Los Sombres when the Fall first started. It came from pain. Control on the verge of failing.

Melanie leaned over the stricken man. There were scars up and down her arms. When singing didn't work, Melanie cut herself.

'There are no more Riders,' she whispered. 'What do you think the Fall was all about?'

The man tried to sit up, but she planted her hand in the middle of his chest. She wore a lot of rings. As she shone her pocket flashlight in his eyes his feeds came on brighter. He said, 'I failed. But there's still a chance. Please. Who do the horses belong to?'

He had some kind of East Coast accent. New York or something.

'I have this strong urge . . .' Melanie said.

Chumana and Xavier looked at each other. Xavier looked at the knife block. Chumana opened her mouth to say something, but then Melanie said, '—to help you' and Chumana subsided.

'What's that you're trying to send?' Melanie asked. The Rider's feedback light was stuttering wildly. His eyes rolled back and for a moment it looked like he was going to lose consciousness again; then he seemed to recover. Melanie got in his face again and made him focus.

'So where's your Feynman?' she asked conversationally. 'It might help me figure out what gremlin's got you.'

He didn't seem to hear her. He was now peering into her face as if trying to recognize her. Searching for something in her expression and her feeds.

'Have you heard "The Lamplighter's Serenade"?' he gasped.

Melanie frowned. 'Do you mean FallN? I'm not loaded for that. Out here, we don't respond to the call.'

'You should be,' said the stranger. 'FallN would improve your . . . problem. Nothing personal. The throwing muses, for example.'

Xavier thought, *So, he's a fucking radical.*

FallN was a radio DJ who operated guerrilla-style from the ruins. She insinuated that her broadcasts were coded to be understood by the shined. She urged resistance to external control. Nobody knew who she was or why she did it; Doug said she was probably heavily shined herself. Her voice was heard almost every day, but nobody had ever seen her. Rex had drawn a cartoon of her based on her voice: Grace Jones with big muscles, ammunition slung across her chest and an automatic weapon in one hand, a walkie-talkie in the other. Wraparound shades. Plus roller blades. Hot pants. Biceps. And a Mohawk. She would kill you in your sleep. FallN walked around with subjugation beams strapped to her back so you'd be enslaved before you could think of jumping her from behind. She fucked Rottweilers. She might even be a cannibal.

'I could help you get shined for FallN,' the man said. His glance included Chumana, lingered on her. Xavier flashed the wish that the car had been going faster when it hit the fence.

'Shit, he's like some kind of shiny Jehovah's Witness,' Chumana said.

Melanie wrapped her blood pressure gauge around the guy's arm and laughed.

'You keep your lights off Chumana. She's Hopi. They have their own ways.'

The man looked at Chumana like she was a ghost. He began to shake.

'Do you train horses?' he said.

'All the horses belong to Pavarotti,' Melanie said. 'And he doesn't talk. What do you want with a horse? The Honda you were driving isn't even dented.'

'It's like wildfire,' he replied. 'Circa 1975. You must have heard it. Tearjerker.'

'I don't do country,' Melanie sang. 'And I wasn't even born.'

'You too, then. About drowning.'

'Orgasm and oxygen deprivation? Does nothing for me.' Her voice dropped into the bass range. She really, really couldn't sing.

Chumana nudged Xavier in the ribs.

'Does this guy squick you?' She whispered so close to his ear that a shiver ran down his body. He tried to shrug non-comittally, but it came off more like a convulsion. As an afterthought, she handed him a blueberry Pop Tart.

Xavier bit into it and turned on the CB. He sat on the kitchen counter and listened in to the so-called traffic report. All it was, was a bunch of burnouts who sat around drinking and keeping track of cars going in and out of Los Sombres. Because there were so few of these, mostly you heard burnouts talking about the latest Astros game or exchanging fish stories about people they claimed to have met in prison.

But at least burnouts weren't disabled, like the adults on the ranch. Take Chumana's dad, who could only see out of his left eye; his right eye saw the same Portuguese art film with subtitles, over and over again. Take Xavier's mother with her knitting. The Fall had left all of them trapped by mental patterns they couldn't escape. That would be Xavier, without Kiss, because sooner or later he would encounter a dangerous strand of lightborn.

Unless something big happened. And it was about time something did.

Chumana murmured, 'This guy has to be a Rider, Xavier. Did you see those feeds? If he really came from town, how did he survive?'

'We got to figure what to say to Doug.'

'We won't say anything until after the medicine.'

The medicine. Even the word was bitter.

'You don't have to do the medicine,' he said. But Chumana pretended she hadn't heard.

A man's voice, high and cracking, good ole boy style, chanted: *'Breaker 7, this is Mellow Jack at the country club. I just heard over on 19 Arrow Rose seen a Honda drive by this morning. She didn't tell nobody 'cos she fell asleep. Arrow Rose, you there? Over.'*

Static.

'Naw, she probably fell asleep again. She saw a Honda down-town in a clearway. Civilian car, coming from town, in the occupied zone. You know, they're moving in on us, but car slipped through. Over.'

Xavier grabbed the mic and broke in. *'Breaker, Lone Rhino here, Mellow Jack. What colour? Over.'*

'How you doin', Lone Rhino? I think she said burgundy. Over.'

Chumana and Xavier raised eyebrows at each other. The CRC was burgundy. *'Do you know what clearway, Mellow Jack? Over.'*

'Arrow usually hang by the hospital. Them Angels give out free-bies sometimes. Over.'

Xavier asked a few more questions but Mellow Jack didn't know anything more. He signed off.

Xavier tuned back in to Melanie and the man. They were still conversing, but it was more like knights jousting, badly. They made passes at each other and swept by without landing blows. They couldn't connect and ended up sounding like refrigerator poetry.

'I decoupled the best yellow provocation.'

'But I told her not to order the sole. The guard musta emulated schadenfreude's knees.'

'If you caught Bruce Lee smoking a pressgang, would you give me a greyhound nightstick?'

'Those are some there feedback lights you got,' Xavier inter-rupted. The man stared at him. If he was a Rider, he would be working to identify Xavier's feedback beam. But Xavier didn't have one of those. The man's eyebrows drew together.

'I'm Xavier. What's your name?'

Pause. 'John. John Doe. Yeah, that's what you have to call me.'

Xavier laughed. 'You're funny, man. That's what they call dead people.'

'I know. Are you the horse trainer?'

'Well . . . not really . . .' Xavier was learning from Powaqa. 'Why do you want—'

Melanie interjected, 'Alaska?'

John Doe nodded. 'Utter darkness.'

'You may be right,' sang Melanie. 'I may be—'

Xavier cut in. 'You been Riding since the Fall, John?'

But John Doe just looked at his feet and said, 'Crazy.'

Nobody spoke. Xavier had a weird feeling of having just missed something, of an idea buzzing past his ear like a wild baseball pitch. In that moment he smelled burning pop tarts and he heard somebody on the CB say, '—*bulldog amplifier I always*—' and he noticed that Chumana had an ugly mole on the back of her neck where her hair'd been swept to one side. Then the screen door squealed as Doug came in, chucking his hat on the draining board and planting his hands on his hips. Whatever the idea had been, it was gone.

John Doe stepped towards Doug, extending his hand. 'Hi. Pleased to meet you. Are you the horse trainer?'

Then he doubled over, coughing wildly and swatting at the air in front of his face. Like he just swallowed a bee.

Doug looked at Xavier 'We got a friend or foe here?' he said.

Xavier tried to block off Doug's access to the stranger with-out being confrontational about it. Which was hard, because Doug took most anything for confrontation.

'Doug, can I talk to you?'

Doug jerked his head outside and Xavier followed him. 'What's the deal, kid?'

'I don't know. He seems to be going in and out of it. Like Melanie.'

Doug snorted. 'How'd he get past the outpost? He could be military. Could be a spy.'

Oh, not the paranoia again. Xavier shook his head. He was desperate to get Doug off the guy's case, but he had to front the thing or Doug would call him pussy-whipped and maybe kick his ass just for laughs, you never knew.

Xavier said, 'I been trying to track the vehicle on the CB. Powaqa wants to hold medicine tonight, and I figure, let's just humour her, right? See what we can find out meanwhile.'

Doug turned his head aside and spat. He loved all that cowboy shit, and he had a big cock that lay in his jeans like something asleep and pleased with itself.

'I got nothing against Powaqa's medicine. But I want to know why this guy comes here of all places.'

Doug had been burned out by the military penal system, years ago. Because of some shit he'd done when he was in the Army, some crime in Afghanistan. Burning out made you insensitive to scripts, but it also damaged your brain. Doug came out paranoid. He thought the government were coming for him to do tests on him. Maybe even to turn him gay. And he wasn't listening to anybody else's version of events. You had to agree with him about certain things, no matter how irrational. If you didn't, you were in trouble.

So Xavier said the only safe thing you could ever say, which was, 'Yeah. I get it. I hear what you're saying.'

'OK, little guy. Guess we see eye to eye on this, right?'

'Sure, Doug.'

'Gonna strip the vehicle down for bugs. Satnav's shot but he might have already transmitted.'

'Why would anybody want to spy on us?'

'Because they're bastards who don't want nobody to make a buck, that's why. I don't believe our boy lived two years in that town. Guy with feeds like that, he should've been out of there in the first few days. You know what I'm talking about?'

'Uh . . .?' Xavier pretended he didn't understand the implications. But it was obvious. Doug knew the guy was a Rider. And any Rider living in Los Sombres during the Fall should have had his IQ reduced to cauliflower proportions by now, because no one could survive in the Field since the renegade lightborns got loose. Doug was doing well in the quarantine zone, where rough justice ruled the day. Doug would not be interested in helping the Rider, who was by definition an agent of the lightborn establishment.

Xavier wondered what Doug would say when he found out John Doe was on FallN's side, resisting the military occupation of Los Sombres. Doug had been known to remark that he thought FallN was one scary bitch and if she ever showed up here, he'd take her out with a high-powered rifle before she could whip out her microphone.

And the problem with Doug was, he meant what he said. Most people were all talk? Well, not Doug.

Doug turned his head again and this time his brown spittle was shot through with sunlight.

'There's something not right about the guy. I'll tell you one thing. I won't let him walk out of here. That's a fact.'

Xavier made an effort to steady his voice in case it started to crack.

'My mom's pretty upset. She saw the car and hoped it was my dad. I better go find her.'

'Don't forget to take your Kiss.' Xavier must have made a face, because Doug added, 'Hey! You think it's a drag still looking like a twelve-year-old? If you'd seen the shit I've seen in Los Sombres, you'd be popping kisspeptin inhibitors every five minutes just to keep safe from shine. Be glad you're a kid. Stay that way.'

Xavier put his head down and his hands in his pockets as he moved past Doug. He braced himself for the obligatory male-bonding noogie or punch in the shoulder as he went past, but for once, Doug didn't touch him.

You had to be grateful for the little things.

Medicine

Xavier didn't go to see his mother. He went to the corral and sat on the fence in his usual spot, waiting.

Powaqa was out working a horse. She called it that, even though it didn't look much like work. It was true that sometimes she rode out, using natural obstacles like clumps of brush or trees to teach the horse to circle tight, or to spin out, or any of the other fancy moves that cow horses needed to know. But most times to work a horse she didn't even get on his back. She just took the horse out on the land for long walks. No bridle, no halter; just her and the horse with a piece of twine tied around his neck. And of course, her flashlight. Powaqa's flashlight was legend among horse trainers; she could shine the wildest mustang to discipline.

Xavier knew that Powaqa had been working a temporary contract at Pavarotti's ranch when the Fall went down, but her family lived up in Black Mesa. She was on the tribal council. She had options. But when the Fall hit, Powaqa didn't walk away from the ranch. She stayed and worked with the victims of shine. Why Powaqa wanted to work salvage horses and put up with refugees for no pay, nobody knew. By way of explanation, Chumana had once told Xavier that Indians liked freaks and weirdos and even regarded them as sacred. Xavier didn't know if she was pulling his leg or not.

Most of Powaqa's herd were dirt-coloured, unspectacular to look at, bought cheap in the mustang round-ups. Wild horses were usually runty, and that's what Powaqa was looking for.

'Good cutting horse got to be small,' she'd told Xavier when she first started teaching him her trade. 'Same thing for a salvage horse. Small horse don't eat so much, plus she manoeuvres better.'

'But don't they have to be able to carry stuff?' Xavier had said.

'Not much. The really valuable stuff you want is small. Take your Kiss pills – they're small. Horse got to have a good nose to find them, though.'

She had been picking Bob Newhart's hooves as she said this. Clumps of dried clay went flying as she worked. Bob, standing on three legs, was half-asleep.

'A good horse don't need nothing fancy. This here horse, she was born wild. She'll give you everything. She'll break her heart for you. But just because she serves you, don't forget she's smart. Smarter than you or me when it comes to some things.'

'Yeah? Can she count, like Mr Ed?'

Powaqa had brandished the hoof pick at him admonishingly. 'You think you're funny, but what you really are is in debt. Believe me, Xavier, you need this horse a lot more than she needs you.'

'Can I ride her?' Xavier had asked, and Powaqa had snorted with laughter.

'In your dreams, baby. This here is a special horse. You got to earn the right to ride her. No, you can ride Paris H.'

'*Who?*'

Paris H. had turned out to be a burro. Powaqa had seriously made Xavier learn to ride on a burro.

'Nothing wrong with a burro,' she told him. 'You just get up there and do what you got to do.'

Xavier was a pretty good rider now. Not as good as Doug or Pavarotti, but pretty good. And he knew a little about how Powaqa worked a horse.

'I got lightborns,' she'd told him. 'I developed them myself. They're made with horses in mind. One of them is a reinforcement script. I work the horse and then I use the script to reinforce the work. It's just a little improvement on nature, a shortcut. I can get a horse ready a lot faster if I don't have to keep repeating stuff.'

'What else?'

'Lot of other lightborns. Most of them I hardly ever use. I got shine to calm a horse down. I got shine to erase bad experiences, bad emotions they might have. I used to use those a lot with horses people brought me. I can rehabilitate them. It's nothing I couldn't do anyway, in time, with patience. But the shine makes it faster.'

'And how do you teach them to find Kiss?'

'Same as you teach any animal to find anything. I use a focus enhancer, because horses aren't as bright as dogs or dolphins. And then I just show them the thing I want and train 'em normal. With the right shine and a little know-how you can train a horse to find whatever you want. They can't always bring it. But if you got the equipment, say a radio tracker and a camera, then you can direct the horse remotely. But the days of salvage will end soon. There won't be anything left to find.'

'How do you get them to go into the city with all the dangers there?'

And he still remembered what she'd said, back then.

'Simple. Override the flight response. That's easy. If you know how to do it.'

And she'd looked at him with those shaman eyes and laughed like she knew the secret of making pigs fly.

Now Xavier sat on the fence and watched She ambled out of the sage with the horse trailing behind her, playfully nosing at her braid. It was that little black mustang who'd turned up a few months ago after a storm. Kestejoo. Only about two years old and full of spirit. When Xavier jogged to meet Powaqa, the young horse rolled his eyes and snorted at Xavier as though jealous of the intrusion.

Powaqa had a look on her face, said she knew very well she had been playing hooky at a time when she was needed.

'New guy's awake,' Xavier said. 'Wants to see you.'

'Wants to see *me*?'

'Keeps talking about horses. And medicine.'

'Huh.'

'And he digs FallN.'

'Huh.'

'But he's very fucked.'

'Let's see what the medicine says,' Powaqa replied. 'You still taking your pills regular? You look taller.'

Xavier thought of several disrespectful come-backs, but kept them to himself. Powaqa didn't take any shit.

She turned Kestejoo loose and together they went over to Doug's Jeep where the shined refugees had gathered in a press. Darkness shuffled in. Los Sombres' beacons prickled faintly from the mirrors that Chumana had set up in Doug's Jeep. They were too far away to be regarded as a real danger, but Xavier still found them sinister. Then Melanie switched on the flood-light, and Powaqa's medicine beam hit the mirror and bounced off in a dazzle that turned Chumana's dark eyes to gold.

The burnouts and children kept their distance. Xavier took up a position sort of halfway between the two rings of people, because he was neither shined nor burned out, neither child nor man.

Xavier was on his own.

Powaqa poured some lighter fluid into the cauldron and started burning wads of cash in red envelopes. The shinies hummed and snapped their fingers. Xavier's mom seemed OK now; her shine-damaged cortex had probably managed to forget the incident with the Honda. Her contribution to the medicine was a novelty Easter bunny that sang 'Jiggy Jiggy Baby Bunny' by Lambino Chorus Monsters, but the batteries were running down. Powaqa claimed that anything with symbolic magical significance was acceptable, and a white rabbit was iconic. Xavier was embarrassed, but Powaqa didn't care about that. She put on her shiny purple top hat. The other shinies smiled sort of complacently. Les had brought a live chicken.

'The goofier the props, like, the better the medicine,' Chumana had confided in Xavier once. 'Aunt Powaqa calls it the KSF. Kitsch Squeeze Factor.'

Now Chumana had gone far away, into the shine-induced medicine. Xavier had never been able to understand what Indian medicine had to do with modern lightborns, but Chumana saw no contradiction.

'These are the paths my ancestors walked,' she had told him. 'They used mushrooms and ceremonies. Some medicine was lost to us in the twentieth century, but shine has opened the medicine road again. It brings visions to me. And it can tell me about Los Sombres.'

Chumana was the only non-child on the ranch who had her lightborn receptors intact. She had been living up in Black Mesa at the time of the Fall, so she had been sheltered from its effects. Until recently, Chumana had only used reservation shine. In fact, Xavier knew that the KSF made Powaqa's lightborn 'medicine' a blasphemy to traditional practices. But Powaqa performed a ceremony every time a new person was admitted to the ranch compound. She wanted to know how the person would react to lightborns, whether they were dangerous – and what they might be bringing with them, carried on their feeds.

The medicine had other uses, too. Sometimes it gave warnings. In the first post-Fall year, shined gangs had struck frequently. Powaqa's medicine had predicted the attacks. It had saved lives.

But was this phenomenon 'medicine' or was it just the fact that Chumana was receptive enough to pick up distant signals from the renegade AIs that populated the deregulated security Field in Los Sombres? The Fall had brought the release of more than just mood-altering shine. It had caused the blanket dissemination of a shitload of data stored in the Field. Maybe by communing with the shine, Chumana was getting some insight into the workings of the post-Fall city.

Or maybe the medicine was all just coincidence, spiked with wishful thinking. Either way, Xavier wished Chumana wasn't doing it. Even though the lights of Los Sombres were miles away, every time Chumana did the medicine she exposed herself to the Fall. One day, she was bound to pay the price.

'Where is the stranger?' Chumana said now.

Doug and Melanie approached, carrying John Doe between them. He was foetal, but he had his head thrown back and his eyes were wide and staring. They lifted him on to the back of the Jeep. For a moment Xavier thought he was paralysed, but then his mouth moved and a series of howls came out. Chumana shrank away from him. His feeds surged as the medicine light poured into his eyes, but he didn't move. Melanie hovered nearby. Like Powaqa she stayed out of the direct light.

Then Powaqa chucked some JD into the cauldron and the resulting flame carved out bright places in her facial structure, shadows laid bare. Xavier feared for her eyebrows, but she didn't seem to feel the heat.

'Tell us about the stranger,' Powaqa said in her Gruff Indian Voice.

Everyone waited for Chumana's response. People said strange, meandering things under the medicine light. Sometimes what they said was poetic but more often it was garbage. Yet Powaqa always took careful notes, and with her Feynman she would read people's feeds to pick up patterns. She said she used this information for better medicine, but to Xavier all medicine was the same: inscrutable.

She was training her Feynman on John Doe now, recording the pattern of his feeds. They functioned spasmodically.

Chumana licked her lips and looked into the medicine light. 'The Rider. John Doe. He has sacrificed himself to save Los Sombres. He has lost everything.'

Rex was sitting with some of the other men off to one side. They were all smoking cigarettes. Rex muttered, 'Like we need a psychic to tell us that.'

Doug kicked him and he shut up. Chumana went on.

'His favourite singer is Billy Joel. He got $22,712 back from the IRS last year. His wife's birthday is the fourth of November 1964.'

Rex opened his mouth and closed it when Doug looked at him. Xavier knew what he was thinking: Xavier was thinking it, too. They had no way of checking those 'facts'.

'What is his real name?' Powaqa asked gently.

Pause. Melanie began to cough uncontrollably, and Xavier saw that her feedback light was flickering and active. She held her mirror up to the tiny piercing glimmers of Los Sombres.

Chumana said, 'His name has been erased. I told you. He sacrificed his identity.'

Rex snorted and coughed to cover his laughter. The next thing Xavier heard was the chorus of 'Jiggy Jiggy Baby Bunny' in seasick offpitch. He didn't want to be here. He wanted to go up on the mountain and drink and throw rocks.

John Doe began to unfold. He jerked; he trembled as if in a fever; he looked around with captured-coyote eyes.

Powaqa murmured so softly that Xavier barely made out her words.

'How did he get past Silver Brush outpost?'

Chumana shook her head. 'Invisible.'

Powaqa got up and moved the medicine mirrors. Now the medicine light shone on the left side of Chumana's face, but the distant gleam of Los Sombres were directly in her line of vision. Xavier tensed. Chumana could end up with bad shine eating at her brain.

'Explain *invisible*.'

Chumana's tone changed. She wasn't so much talking as reciting.

'There's another Los Sombres. With towers of pitted lead and burnt steel. Canals clogged with ream upon ream of paper plastered over dismembered machines. Bolts of pulsing light escaping from below, fitful or half-alive. The lights try to pierce the smoke of dust, and they connect with each other in a geometry that looks animate until you realize it's just for show. Tricks for the satellites. The horses pick their way through all the death. They move with their heads down, sniffing. Their hooves catch on protruding pipes, and they skitter and slip on plates of broken glass. Sometimes they bleed.'

Xavier couldn't understand this. Was she reading something? The distant city lights dancing on the medicine mirrors reminded him of FX twinkles at the beginning of a movie: Walt Disney fairy dust. They set his teeth on edge.

Chumana said:

'The horses are dun and gold and black, their heavy coats sweat-laced, their manes tangled. They follow each other like an ant trail in this place of huge proportion. They pass in steady percussion.'

She paused. The scripted continued humming a riff from jig-gyjiggybabybunny while Powaqa burned some more red envelopes. Chumana breathed deep the fumes of burning money.

Chumana said:

'Whatever has been written on these broken things, the horses cannot read it. Sometimes they bring back sheets of metal, incomplete vehicles, filing cabinets. Sometimes they bring broken tiles and translation equipment. Sometimes they bring reagents in broken jars, and sometimes they are scalded by acid or shocked by exposed wires.'

Xavier shook his head. Enough already. After all, he had yet to see a salvage horse come back with a filing cabinet. He broke in.

'What about Kiss? They're supposed to bring pills. Where can we find it, Chumana?'

'Quiet!' Powaqa snapped without looking at Xavier. The singing stopped.

Then John Doe started trying to talk. He struggled to produce sound. He stammered badly, and with every hesitation he kept starting over like a scratched disc, and his speech progressed so slowly that at times it seemed to be going backwards.

'C-c-can y-yo – c-c-c-c-c-c-c-ċ c-cc – c-c-c-c-c-a-c-c-c-c-c – can you-c-c-c-c-c-c-cc-ccc-c-c-c-c-c-c-cc-cc-cccc-ccca – ccccannn . . .'

It was all Xavier could do to keep from leaping up and grabbing John Doe and shaking him to make the words fall out. It seemed a lifetime before he got out the sentence: *Can you hear me?*

'We can hear you,' Powaqa said. She worked the Feynman, made adjustments to the beam in the medicine light.

'It-t-tt-i – itt d-d – duh-duh-duh-itt – duh-doesn-n-n-'t - does-doesn't w-w-w-want m-m-m-m-m it-t duh-doesn't want muh-me t-t-t-o talk.'

The man's mouth twisted and his facial muscles contorted with the effort of forming the words.

'That's better,' Powaqa murmured. She made more adjustments to the light. Chumana blinked and looked dopey.

'Go on,' Powaqa urged.

The man said, 'B-better.' He seemed to gather himself. Then: 'I had given up hope. Thought I'd never get f-free. Wasn't even t-t-t-try-trying anym-m-more. But I saw the signature. On t-t-the ho-horse. It was y-y-y-you, wasn't it?' He looked at Powaqa, but she didn't look back. She was watching her Feynman's readout. 'Y-y-your work. Please. Help m-me. I j-j-j-j-just want to escape.'

During this performance Xavier found himself leaning towards the afflicted John Doe as though rooting for him in a basketball game. It was as if this stranger represented all the victims of the Fall. And now, as in every medicine ceremony that Powaqa conducted, this man was about to be judged. It was like John Doe was a stray dog Xavier'd brought home and Powaqa was going to play Mom and decide whether the family would keep him or whether he'd go to the pound, where everybody knew he'd probably get gassed.

'I-I-I've been f-fighting it. For so long. And I'm losing. It's like torture.' He paused to cough out a laughlike noise. 'No matter what I do I'm doomed. To watch this thing. Take o-o-over. I'm doomed to help it. I thought I c-c-could stop it but I've only prolonged the ag-ag-ag-agony.'

Then he lifted his head and looked straight at Powaqa. Like he was looking at a goddess. He stretched out his left hand, supplicating.

'But you. You can s-s-save me. L-le-let me st-t-tay.'

Everyone looked at Powaqa. Xavier expected her to say something reassuring. To comfort this afflicted man in some way.

And Powaqa said, 'Nope. Sorry. You're just a mouse in a game of cat and mouse. You got caught. I can't save you.'

John Doe dug in and kept trying. He was forming each word as though it were a world, each word as though it were his life. Trying so hard.

'Save me and I'll save the city. N-now there's a chance. I've seen it. I could do some g-g-g-good. If you would just help me . . .'

Powaqa was shaking her head. No, definitely no. Vehement.

'Please . . .' John Doe begged. 'Please, I don't want to be its food.'

'We're all food for something,' Powaqa said, and her callousness took Xavier's breath away. She switched off the medicine light.

John Doe gave a sad cry and toppled sideways into Melanie, twitching and slobbering so bad that Xavier had to look away.

The sun was gone. The script beacons of Los Sombres beat softly on the mirror.

Powaqa took off the hat. She took off the beads. She seemed angry. Then she looked east, toward the mountain.

'Holy shit – get down!' she cried.

And a phalanx of F-16s streaked overhead with the killing sound of their engines galloping after.

Bombs Away

It happened so fast there wasn't much they could do. Everybody dropped, except Chumana and Powaqa, who were still sitting up there in between the mirrors. Powaqa snapped out of the medicine and tried to pull Chumana down from her perch, but Chumana panicked. Xavier lunged into the Jeep and grabbed her. He dragged her backwards, away from the Jeep, thinking of the fuel in the tank.

They lay on their bellies in the sage. Xavier counted eight planes, flying over in pairs.

A little space of quiet. Xavier's ears rang. The alpacas' hoof-beats could be heard as they stampeded around their field.

Popping noises from Silver Brush outpost, down the road. Then the tearing sound of missiles in the sky. Remote thuds. Clouds of smoke and dust went up over the suburbs.

Chumana and Xavier looked at each other.

'What the fuck?' she panted.

'It's OK,' Xavier said. His body was scared, but his head was telling him this was all good. 'It's OK, Chumana. They're going to finish it. They're really going to do it.'

He felt buoyant. There had been so much talk; he'd heard it on the radio, he'd read it in the papers that Sam Ghost Money

Power brought. Talk of the ethical issues. Talk of the money. Talk talk talk talk. Xavier knew the military had ample hardware to deal with the situation on the streets of Los Sombres. They had exo-crawlers, spyders, remote-sensing tracking devices – they just didn't have the will to deploy them against a civilian population.

'But – they're supposed to drop *aid*, not bombs. This is crazy!'

'Try to calm down, Chumana. We know they're attacking the city to get the goddamn lights down. It's what they gotta do. They're not attacking *us*.'

Chumana wiped her eyes. Crying puffed her lips. Xavier was surprised by her reaction. He wondered if the medicine had done something to her. Powaqa shouldn't have exposed Chumana to the Los Sombres lights.

'I just want this to be over,' she said.

'It will be. Soon it will be. They'll wipe out the lightborns once and for all. Then the quarantine will be ended, and we can go home to Los Sombres.'

He said it as if he had some control over it. As if he were flying the recon jets, or firing the mortars from the ground. But he was only wishing. Desperately. There hadn't been any Kiss coming out of Los Sombres in months. Soon the kids' supply would run out, and Xavier wouldn't be a boy anymore.

Now the refugees were crawling out from under the Jeep. Melanie and Xavier's mom dusted each other down. Xavier's mom forgot to even look for him or check if he was OK. She was too worried about the unborn baby she thought she was carrying in her flat stomach. Xavier felt cold and sick.

Everybody was talking.

Doug said, 'About fucking time. Now maybe they'll blow away the zombies and cut off the light at source.'

Xavier tried to picture the streets of downtown Los Sombres, like an ant farm somebody chucked a match into. Crazy scripted homicidal maniacs running every which way in the dark. He wondered how many of them had gotten blown up. Not enough, probably. It was amazing to think they hadn't all killed each other by now; in the beginning, everybody thought they would. But this shit had been going on for two years. Too long. Somebody had to stop the Fall and get the lightborn security Field back up again.

Everyone looked west. As the dust cleared, they counted how many lights were left.

Out of seventeen known beacons, Doug counted eleven out loud.

Then another beacon came up. And another.

'I don't fucking believe it,' Doug said.

In the end, there were not seventeen, but nineteen lights shining from the loco city of Los Sombres.

'The Army suck,' Chumana said. 'If they're going to bomb, I wish they'd do it right.'

Flesh-Eating Ring Girls

The next day Powaqa recruited Xavier to help round up horses. Unusually, Powaqa wanted them all penned up. Xavier thought the horses would be safer from a possible air strike if they were out in the open where they could run, but Powaqa dismissed his opinion.

'I know what I'm doing,' she told him.

Then he asked her straight out, 'Why won't you help this John Doe guy?'

'Because I have a funny feeling in my big toe.'

'No, seriously. I want to know. You helped all of us. Why not him?'

Powaqa sighed. 'It's not an easy answer. He's not like the other refugees. He doesn't want help for himself.'

'I don't get it.'

'OK, what if I told you something is holding him in its teeth? What if I told you something is Riding him, and not the other way around?'

'I just think we should give him a chance. You've taken in worse people than him.'

'You're young. It's easy to be honourable when you're young. You get older, you start putting survival before honour.'

'So . . . what will happen to him?'

'I haven't decided yet. But he can't stay here. Don't worry about it, Xavier. It's not your problem.'

Xavier shook his head. He was getting very fucking sick of always being treated like a kid who didn't deserve to know shit. He was itching to find out more about John Doe's feedback lights, to ask the guy what he knew about the Field – to find out what had brought him out of Los Sombres so suddenly, after all that time. Xavier felt sure that John Doe's arrival coinciding with the Silver Brush missile strikes was no accident. Had John Doe *known* the attack was coming?

Xavier was tired all the way down to his teeth by the time Powaqa sent him home.

If you could call it that. Home was where Xavier and his mom had pitched their tent the first night they came here, fleeing the Fall riots. They'd crashed in the brush, and ended up just staying. The truck's red paint was now so muddy and dusty that its original colour was a technicality. Xavier's mother had run it into a heap of rocks and cacti, flattening the front end. Then the brush had grown up around it, so that now only the cab and back could be seen. The tailgate had gotten rusted and remained permanently lowered; they used the hitch to secure the tent ropes against high winds. Xavier slept in the tent, but his mother stayed in the pickup itself. She was weirdly attached to the truck. It was some kind of security blanket; Xavier guessed that, in his mother's mind, having the truck meant she could go back.

She didn't see the irony in the fact that it was totalled.

He came back from working for Powaqa and she wasn't there. He picked up clean underwear and a T-shirt from the laundry basket and rummaged for shampoo. He'd get a solar shower. He moved the Kiss bottle to get his comb. The bottle was light and it did not rattle.

Yesterday, it had been full. He knew because supplies were low and he'd been hoping Bob Newhart would come back with more the last time she went out to salvage. But she hadn't. And every caplet mattered.

'Rex, what the fuck,' Xavier muttered, annoyed.

He stalked up to the house. Rex was lying on the floor playing a video game. Xavier held up the empty bottle, giving it a shake.

'That's a little greedy, Rex.'

'Not me. Seriously. Take some of mine if you're out.'

Xavier opened Rex's sock drawer and picked up Rex's Kiss bottle.

It was empty, too.

'I bet I know who done it,' Rex said. 'I bet it was that John Toenail.'

That was the kind of left-field paranoia Xavier had come to expect of Doug, not Rex.

'You see him come in here?'

'No, but. My dad says he's a asshole.'

'Don't tell your dad,' Xavier said. 'I'll take care of it.'

Rex shrugged. 'You know me. I don't say nothing to nobody.' He lowered the game a little and squinted over it at Xavier. 'What you gonna do?'

'I'll tell you later,' Xavier said, so Rex would think he had a plan. Which he didn't. Rex was usually the one who had the plan and Xavier went along with it, but this time would be different. Forgetting about the shower, he flopped on Rex's unmade bed. Stared up at the Eminem poster over Rex's bed with all kinds of undefined shit going off in his head. Just angry for no reason.

No: not for no reason. Angry because he was cornered. No drug, no plan, dependent on the new offensive against Los Sombres to save his ass before puberty turned his brain into a shine-fest.

Without looking up from his game, Rex jerked his head at Xavier in summons.

'Look, my exo-ranger killed four shiners. Note the graphics. Ripped off from Skid 6 and patched in the sound from Mama Juicebox.'

'Who wrote it?'

'Dunno. My dad got it from Sam.'

Xavier looked over Rex's shoulder at the zombie-like shiners as they tore into the rotting flesh of Fall victims. Rex's exo-ranger robot stalked towards them on spider legs, its joints making tiny whirring noises every time it moved.

'Is that shit accurate? The mandibles look wrong.'

'I don't know, man, I just play it.'

Xavier's stomach was churning with anxiety over the missing Kiss, but he figured maybe he could use the fear. He had noticed a long time ago that when some freaky shit went down, he got momentarily smarter. He never talked about it, but it happened all the time. When Xavier had seen the video of his father jumping out the window to his death, he'd inadvertently memorized the exact time on the recording when his father had burst from the glass. He could replay this couple-of-seconds-long segment in his mind as many times as he wanted, having only seen it once, and in the top corner of the screen he could see the hundredths of seconds ticking away just as they had on the real recording.

When the gang had attacked the ranch several months into the Fall, Xavier had looked out the window to see them coming up the driveway in a mass. Powaqa had grabbed him by the back of his shirt and dragged him away to hide in the barn. Later he realized he had got the licence numbers of all the motorcycles without even trying. He could see the faces of the shinies in detail. He could see the way the dust came up from beneath their wheels. Everything had been recorded. It was like having a photographic memory, but it only worked under extreme stress.

Since then, he'd taught himself to recall this feeling of terror
when he wanted to memorize things. Diagrams of the exo-protectors. Specs for anti-lightborn shields that government
helicopters used. Stuff like that. He already had a good technical
brain, and if he saw a diagram of something he could usually
visualize how it would work. He spent most of his spare time
fixing things and studying schemata for military hardware. He'd
taught himself what math and physics he could. He wasn't a
genius, but he wasn't a fucktard like Rex, either.

Now he opened up the spec book he'd left here, his favourite
set of exo-protector diagrams. He worked on the specs for the
lightborn shields used on the hornets that were currently flying
over the city. He wasn't interested in video games. He wanted
to work on the real hardware. Machines were his passion. They
were so much more reliable than people. Machines would save
Los Sombres. Machines would save people from themselves,
because machines were too honest to fuck around with your
head. Machines didn't have delusions. Machines weren't gov-
erned by million-year-old drives that had no business sticking
around in this millennium.

And machines weren't vulnerable to lightborns.

But he couldn't concentrate with all the noise from Rex's
shoot-em-up. He glanced up and saw the simulated Los
Sombres on Rex's screen.

'Who's the guy with the cooler?'

'Oh, that's Joe Red,' Rex said. 'You know, that guy on the CB?
He tells the robots who to target. He got a big red cross on his
roof to keep his house from getting done.'

'Oh, the blind guy.'

'He's not blind, he's a Angel.'

'Whatever. He's one of us.'

'Yeah,' said Rex. 'Angel of Death for the shiny, that's him.
Man, scope it. Here we go. Junction box. Got to kill the lights.
Oops . . . didn't see that horse.'

A muted equine scream came out of the console.

'Ouch,' said Xavier. 'That was ragged.'

'Didn't see him 'til the last minute. Hey, it's only a game. OK, now we're going into the *darkness* . . . There you go, son. My work here is done.' Rex put the console down and grinned. 'I took out the J-beacon.'

'It's only a game,' Xavier repeated back to him.

'Yeah, but it's the best game you'll ever see. Can you fucking design something like that?'

Xavier shrugged. Because he was sick of being helpless he said, 'I'd rather do the actual shooting than design games.'

'Sure you would,' drawled Rex. 'Cuz everybody knows you're such a badass.'

'Do you think John Doe could be a government agent?'

'Man, you are funny. Have a beer.'

Rex threw the can across the room and Xavier caught it. It wasn't cold, but it was cool – must have been down the cellar. Xavier popped it open and quickly sucked the foam off the top. What the fuck was he going to do without Kiss.

He knew what he wanted to do . . .

'You seen Chumana?' he said.

'Nah. Come play this level, I want to show you what these flesh-eating ring girls do if you shoot 'em.'

Not Your Brother

John Doe wasn't at supper that night. Melanie said Powaqa was interviewing him. 'So she can make a report to the tribal elders or something.'

Xavier looked for Chumana but couldn't find her or Rex, and his mother tried to corner him and get him to hang out. Xavier pretended to be tired and went to bed early. He'd intended to sneak out again later so he could talk to Chumana about the Kiss situation, but he fell asleep in his clothes and didn't wake until deep night.

He crawled out of the tent. It was cold, the sky matte black. The stars looked like candy. You could almost touch them. No moon.

Xavier went behind the old water tower and took a piss up against one of the stanchions, where he always did. He heard a voice. Man, talking urgently in a cliché New York twang. Xavier buttoned up his fly and walked towards the sound. Down by Powaqa's working corral there was a light.

'I can fix him for you. Seriously. I can patch him up and get him talking. He'll pass any psychological test anybody can give him. And I can get him to sign the whole deal over to you. He'll even thank you for taking it off his hands.'

In his low, rolling voice Doug could be heard laughing. Doug laughed and laughed.

'There's copper in that mountain,' Doug said at last. 'Hasn't been dug out yet. But it's there. Do you know what this place will be worth?'

'I'm not interested in money,' said the other man. 'But I guess you are. And why not? You're the one keeping it going, not these shined-up fools.'

'So it was all an act. What the fuck are you really up to?'

'The Fall will be over soon. One way or the other. We got to think about the future now.'

Xavier had crept close enough to have a look around the side of the water tower.

Doug and John Doe were sitting on the corral fence. Doug held the flashlight, and he was shining it around like it was a toy. John Doe was talking. He was twitchy and trembling, even under the heavy wool poncho he now wore. His legs kept jerking. He'd fall off the fence in a minute, Xavier thought.

Doug slouched. His long back was curved, his legs draped over the fence, and his head slumped forward like he was snoozing. Xavier had seen this posture many times before. He had seen it even when Doug was working a bronco. Doug would ride out a storm on the horse's back, his body jerked and tossed around like a rag doll. When he got the horse under control he'd go back to easing along in the saddle like he was barely awake. Occasionally he'd turn his head and spit. Doug looked like he didn't have a nerve anywhere in his body.

Oh, anybody who fell for that was making a *large* error.

Xavier hunkered down behind a pile of old tyres, just in case Doug turned around. Doug proved that you didn't have to be shiny to be unpredictable.

*

Whatever had been wrong with him before, John Doe was having no trouble communicating now. He talked fast and nasal. Reminded Xavier of a used car salesman.

'You don't really want all of this to be for nothing, do you? If the Army come in and find the owner of this ranch shined up and some burnout in charge, you'll be right back where you started. At the bottom of the shit heap, right?'

Doug shrugged. 'I could get out if I wanted.'

'Melanie said you're wanted in Texas for murder.'

Xavier's heart started to beat faster. He'd always wondered why Doug and Rex had stayed in the quarantine zone, when they were clean of shine. They could have taken their loot and walked any time, but they didn't. *Why?* was a question you just didn't ask, though. Doug was too scary.

He thought: *John better quit acting like an asshole, or Doug's gonna go off on him . . .*

He also thought: *Murder? Shit.*

Doug didn't get upset.

'I don't think they know what the fuck they're doing. Them shells? Didn't take out any lights.'

'Well, that's a really insightful comment, Doug. It's probably not going to be a walkover. But what about your kid? He's not burned out. He looks about the age now to start getting shine. How much closer to the edge can you play this one?'

Doug twitched, like a horse with flies on his back. 'I can always send the kid away.'

'Of course you have that option. But why do that when you don't have to?'

Doug slid off the fence.

'Friend, save your con jobs for the shinies. I figure we spent enough time here.'

He started to walk away, heading straight towards the spot where Xavier was hiding.

John Doe scrambled from the fence. Doug's back was turned,

but Xavier could see John Doe going through a series of small convulsions that culminated in a coughing fit. He bent double.

Doug turned. Idly, he spat.

'You OK?' he grunted.

John Doe fought for breath.

'I caught a lightborn,' he gasped. 'Sometimes it attacks me. Listen. I can protect your kid from shine. I can fix up this David MacAllen for you. The ranch will be yours. It's easily done.'

Doug shook his head.

'No. I ain't fucking it up with the Indians on some empty promise.'

'I can take care of the Native Americans, too. And it's not an empty promise. Got a pencil?'

Doug shook his head again.

'I'm serious, now. I need a pencil. Come on. I'm going to give you something. A token of good faith, so you know I have some pull.'

They moved away from the tyres and Xavier relaxed fractionally. Doug led John Doe into the garage. Xavier was about to follow, but they came straight out again. John Doe was scribbling on a piece of paper torn from a feed bag, curling his hand around the pen in the awkward way sometimes adopted by the left-handed, only he was right-handed. Then Xavier noticed that he was writing from right to left . . .

'There you go! You check that out. You tell him the Doc sent you.'

John Doe handed over the cardboard. Doug squared up to John Doe, nailed him down with the squinty cowboy don't-fuck-with-me gaze that Xavier knew so well.

'The Doc. Doc what?'

'Just the Doc. That's how Hector knows me.'

'Uh-huh. So what's in it for you, Doc?'

John Doe couldn't stand still. He looked like he was on one of those bone-density machines people had in their basement, where you stood on the thing and it shook you so hard your fillings dropped out. He smiled painfully.

'Don't worry. It's a no-brainer for you, Doug. I just need a safe place to work. You know, where people won't persecute me for being all totally fucked up. Which I know I am, but we're all brothers in adversity, right?'

'I'm not your brother,' Doug said, and he walked away.

But he kept ahold of the cardboard.

Missing Kiss

The house was empty when Xavier woke up. The first thing he did was go to the medical supply cupboard for more Kiss, but there was nothing there. Then he went through the house, checking all of the kids' bedrooms, and of the three other kids who were on Kiss because they were over nine years old, not one had a single capsule in their bottle. It was all gone.

He stood in the kitchen and tried not to hyperventilate. Chumana had left him tomatoes and a piece of cornbread for breakfast, and a note saying she was going with Melanie and John Doe to chop wood. He picked up the cornbread and put it down.

The shined were supposed to be working in the vegetable garden. Two women were throwing squashes at each other and a third was singing 'Bridge Over Troubled Water' while she polished the dirt off a carrot. Powaqa and the other Hopi on the squad worked quietly, swiftly. They even got the refugee kids helping them; the kids were getting more done than their mothers. The Hopi all knew how to work hard without making a big deal about it, but Xavier had never seen anybody work as hard or as long as Powaqa. He wondered how she really felt about Doug.

The conversation between John Doe and Doug had started him thinking about all the power relationships at the ranch. Pavarotti, aka David MacAllen, was technically the owner of the ranch and therefore Powaqa's employer – but Pavarotti was permanently out to lunch, and nobody used money anymore, so Doug was the guy in charge because he had the biggest balls.

That couldn't be fun for Powaqa. Xavier had often thought that if he were Powaqa, he'd have taken off a long time ago. How would Powaqa react if she knew Doug was plotting to depose Pavarotti? After all, Pavarotti was an honorary Hopi or something. Special relationship. Something like that.

'Powaqa, you seen Doug?'

'He rode out.'

'On his own?'

'Yup.'

'You see which way he went?'

She pointed toward the interstate without looking up.

'Can I talk to you?'

She pointed to the row of lettuce behind her. Xavier made his way over, knelt down and started weeding. He spoke just loud enough so Powaqa could hear him over the shined woman's singing. He told her what he'd overheard last night. Everything he could remember. He was talking to her back, which made it impossible to gauge her reaction. He thought John Doe's off-the-cuff remark about 'taking care of' the Indians was disturbing, but she shrugged it off.

'I think it's totally bizarre,' Xavier said. 'He says all he wants is a place to work. But if he's a Rider, why come here? What's going on, Powaqa?'

'I'm not sure,' she said evasively. 'Well, now do you see what I meant about John Doe? Something's Riding him. He's not all there.'

'He seemed all there last night. He wasn't even stuttering most of the time.'

'Xavier—'

'I know. *Don't worry about it*. Right? Powaqa, don't jerk me around. I want to know what's going on, especially when it has to do with me. And there's something else.'

'What else?' she sighed.

'Somebody took the last of the Kiss. I checked the whole house and there's none left.'

She nodded. 'I know. Before you ask, I already got Melanie to check John Doe. It seemed like too much of a coincidence, him turning up and it disappearing like that. But he didn't have anything on him. We'll keep looking for it, but it's a little nerve-wracking not having any at all.'

'Where are the horses you already sent into town? Makya, Choviohoya?'

She shook her head. 'Came back with nothing.'

'What now?'

'This morning, I decided to send Bob Newhart into town. Actually, I was going to send Bob and Jellybean Benitez because they have a better chance of finding it if they split up. But Jellybean came up lame.'

'Send a different horse, then,' Xavier said.

'I tried all the horses,' Powaqa said. 'Every last one. None of them would go.'

'What do you mean, they wouldn't go?'

'Come on, I'll show you.'

She stood up and led him down to the corral. Xavier felt sick. He couldn't believe this.

'They're probably just spooked with the jets flying over,' he said. But the animals in the corral were mostly standing around nose to ass with one another, swishing flies. A few sniffed around on the ground, looking for wisps of hay. They didn't look anything like nervous. Xavier eased himself on to the top rail of the fence. He watched Powaqa programming the lights.

'It's more than that,' Powaqa answered. Her fingers were

flying over the Feynman's input panels. 'They aren't going any-where near Los Sombres, Xavier. It's like nobody ever trained them for salvage. I've given them my strongest reinforcers. They aren't responding.'

'But they have to go,' Xavier protested. 'They have to go now, before all the city's bombed to shit.'

Powaqa said nothing.

'We need the Kiss. You know that.'

Powaqa made a movement of her shoulders, almost a shrug.

'If you were away from the lights, you might not. Shine gets weaker, farther from the source.'

Xavier started feeling panicky at the direction this conversa-tion was taking.

'What do you mean, away from the lights? Where are we gonna go? The quarantine perimeter? What would we do for food and stuff out there? It's already controlled by outsiders. You can get through. *You* can move to Texas if you want, but that's because *you're* native and you got connections. *We're* screwed.'

Powaqa said, 'You're not screwed. But this could be a sign. I think it's time to move on, Xavier. I can't see the point of staying here. Resources are running out. A fast resolution to the crisis – well, that got ruled out a long time ago. Now we got missiles. It's starting to get ugly. This is no place for kids to be.'

'But the military are finally moving in for real. This is the moment I've been waiting for!' Xavier said. 'The liberation. The lights coming down. It's got to happen soon.'

'Maybe. Maybe not. But what's it got to do with you?'

It had everything to do with Xavier, but if Powaqa couldn't see that, how could he explain? He had lost people in Los Sombres. His home had been taken by force. His school. His friends. He had been watching and waiting all this time, hang-ing on until the day he and his mom could go back there and start life again. He'd waited for Congress to finish arguing. For the good guys to come in and reconquer the streets, get rid of the crazy bastards who had set fires and murdered and destroyed. How could he explain that if you walked away now, you admitted defeat? You became a victim. Xavier wanted to win, in the end, whatever it took.

What could he say to Powaqa, though? Her people had been conquered, humiliated, practically exterminated. It had happened long ago, and it was still happening. The whole victim thing was old news to her.

Now Powaqa said gently, 'I can take you to the rez with me. All my family are there. I think it's time to leave Los Sombres.'

Leave. Didn't she understand how that word hit him like a shovel?

'You know I can't do that. My mother will never leave. It's too late to burn her out. What am I supposed to do, abandon her?'

'You might not have a choice.'

He didn't like the way this was going. Powaqa had that note in her voice that adults get when they're trying to break something to you gently. Justify what they're doing, even if it ruins your life. That old *it's for your own good* bullshit.

'Why are you doing this? Why now? This is about Doug, isn't it?'

She just shook her head. 'You're too young to understand.'

'I'm not as young as I look, Powaqa. You know that.'

'What's a few years?' she snorted. 'So you're fourteen and you look ten. So what? You're a kid. Chumana's a kid.'

He wanted to break down and cry and shout, 'It's not fair!' but that would only prove her point.

'If you go, leave us the horses. We'll figure out what's wrong and re-train them ourselves.'

Powaqa sighed. 'Didn't say I was going today. But I don't trust this John Doe. I think he could bring the metal down on us.'

'Did *he* do this to the horses?'

For a split second, Powaqa's face froze. Or did Xavier imagine it?

'What makes you think that?'

'Only that he's a Rider, and he said he wanted to work here . . .'

'He would have to work pretty fast to pull something like this off,' she said. 'Look. I'll show you.' She turned on the salvage beam. Normally, the horses' reaction would be instantaneous. They would put their heads up and look towards the city. They would start moving towards the gate, like they smelled food over there. But they didn't do anything like that. It was like the light was only a light.

'Can't you give them something else to get them going?' Xavier said.

Powaqa shrugged. She indicated her work screen, and he leaned in to look over her shoulder.

'I been trying. They got herd in them, strong. Usually if I can get one to play leader, the others will follow. My old leader was Timbaland, but she's not going for it anymore. And neither is Bob. Look.'

Xavier watched as Powaqa focused the light on the buckskin mare called Bob Newhart. The horse tossed her head and turned away from the beam. She trotted around the corral with the skin on her back twitching spasmodically, as though she were trying to shake off biting flies. Several other horses startled. But none of them so much as glanced in the direction of the city.

'Let's try again,' Powaqa said. She changed scripts and Bob Newhart stopped and shook her head like she had a fly in her ear. She rubbed her face on her foreleg. Then, heaving a great sigh, she relaxed and sauntered over to the trough for a drink.

'See?' Powaqa said. 'All my hard work, shot to hell. And your Kiss? I don't think so.'

A Plan Is Born

Rex was with Chumana, out behind the barn. Chumana was bottle-feeding a newborn lamb that had been rejected by its mother and Rex was hanging around throwing rocks and drinking beers. Everybody else was working, but Rex was Doug's son. He could get away with shit.

Xavier said, 'We're fucked. The horses are refusing. Rex, we need a plan. You and me got to decide what to do.'

'Do about what?' Chumana said.

Xavier told her the whole thing, ending with Powaqa's idea about leaving. 'I don't get your aunt at all,' he finished. 'I can't believe she's ready to give up like this.'

Chumana frowned. 'She's been acting weird. I wonder if it's menopause or something. I couldn't believe it when she wouldn't help John Doe.'

Xavier kept his mouth shut about the things he'd overheard John Doe saying to Doug. Rex was Doug's son, after all.

'We need a plan,' he said again.

'I thought you had a plan,' Rex said. 'The other night. You said.'

'I didn't know Powaqa would say we had to leave.'

'I wouldn't mind leaving.' Rex swigged more beer and

walked away to find another stone to throw. After a minute he came back. 'Here you go. Here's what we're gonna do. We ride into town and get the Kiss ourselves.'

Xavier shook his head. 'I already thought of it. But how would we find it without the horses to search for it?'

'That's true,' Rex said. 'How would we find it . . .?'

'You guys, are you serious?' Chumana said. 'You don't need a horse. Kiss is a drug. I bet you could find it in a drugstore.'

Rex grinned. 'She's a smart girl,' he said, as if he had something to do with it. Chumana rolled her eyes.

'OK,' Xavier said. 'We could search all the drugstores. But what about dealing with the shinies?'

'We take weapons. And maybe some shine of our own. You know, like, to repel them.'

'Cool,' Chumana said. 'But you'll get picked off by those exo-protector things.'

Rex shrugged this off. 'I know how to deal with them. You can always hear them coming. They're programmed to warn before they attack. After all, they're only supposed to pick off the dangerous shinies, not normal people. They don't hurt the Angels.'

Xavier was thinking hard. 'It could be our best plan,' he said. 'Better than Powaqa's. I don't like the idea of being forced to leave.'

'Nah,' Rex said. 'I want to leave. I'm sick of it here. But I don't want to go to no Indian reservation. That's worse than here.'

'No, it's not,' Chumana said. 'You don't know anything about it.'

'Well, if it's so great on the rez, how come you and your aunt are here?'

Chumana shrugged. 'I'm not sure. I think my aunt sees the salvage horses as, like, a challenge. Besides, we're needed here. If we walked away, what would happen to you guys?'

'That's sweet,' Rex said, and looked at Chumana with that stupid-ass expression on his face.

Xavier wanted to kick him. He knew that Rex thought Indians were all weirdo drunks who needed to be kept in their place, but obviously he wasn't going to say anything openly racist because he wanted to impress Chumana. She was, after all, beautiful.

'OK,' said Xavier. 'Let's do it. But nobody says nothing.'

'I'm coming, too,' Chumana said. 'I'm the best rider.'

'You can't come,' Xavier said. 'The shine. You'd be wide open to it.'

'Yeah,' Rex added. 'Leave it to me. I can get past Silver Brush, too. But don't tell nobody, Chumana, whatever you do.'

'I know how to keep my mouth shut,' Chumana said. 'I want to go.'

'Xavier, tell her.'

'Chumana, he's right. You could put us at risk if you, like, caught something.'

'What about you?' she snapped at Rex. 'What if you, like, *catch something*?'

'Chumana, take it easy,' Xavier said. 'We'll go tonight and we'll bring the shit back.'

She tossed her head and walked off without a word.

'I don't get girls at all,' Xavier said. 'Rex, can you be ready by tonight?'

'What?' Rex was still looking after Chumana. He saw Xavier glaring at him and said, 'Yeah, yeah. Look, I better take off before my dad comes looking for me.'

'OK. I'll meet you at the corral around nine.'

After Rex left, Xavier let out a huge breath. Finally, to be doing something. Finally. He felt like he was burning, burning and he didn't want it to stop.

Leaving

The sky looked like the inside of a scratched metal bowl. Xavier watched the day as it backpedalled into darkness like a good cutting horse. Making it look easy.

Melanie had organized a nighttime lighting of fires in oil drums out on the main drive. Everybody gathered – the shinies, the kids, the Hopi weavers, the burnouts, Pavarotti and his pregnant girlfriend clutching her bag of out-of-date Cheetos – everybody but Doug. Even John Doe was there, shivering and smiling vaguely, chaperoned by Melanie herself. They had spelled out a message in oil drums: SAVE US WE LOVE USA where 'love' was a heart made of oil drums. Xavier's mother had wanted to do a tyre fire instead but Melanie shot that idea down as too dangerous.

The event would be perfect cover for Rex and Xavier.

Xavier waited by the corral. He had on a red North Face ski shell over a couple other layers of clothes, because in the dark it was cold enough to see your breath. He had two rolls of peppermint Lifesavers and a jar of molasses, for the horses. He had a police flashlight loaded with subjugation shine in which he was placing limited faith on account of the shiny being . . . well, *evolved*.

He also had a gun. It was one of the emergency spares that Pavarotti kept stashed in secret locations around the ranch. Pavarotti didn't think anybody knew where they were, but Xavier had watched him duct-tape this one to the trunk of an aspen tree fifty yards from the house, just above reach of the alpacas who guarded the sheep. By the time Pavarotti noticed it was gone, Xavier and Rex might even be back with their heroic payload of kisspeptin inhibitors.

Xavier had already gone to John Doe's car, looked up the route to the hospital and written the sequence of road numbers on his forearm with a Sharpie. Made him look like a concentration camp survivor if he rolled up his sleeves. Now he knew where to go.

All of the horses were still penned up. A yellow lump of light showed in the window of Powaqa's place over the barn. Xavier guessed she was working on scripts, trying to figure out what had gone wrong with the horses. She wouldn't be able to see the corral from her window, but if any horses broke out she'd hear them. Xavier had already decided that he and Rex should lead the horses quietly out the back of the corral and take them over the fields to join the road later.

So far, the sky was quiet. The gathering in the driveway sounded like a party; Xavier could hear the twang of guitar and the patter of drums, and every so often he caught the sound of Pavarotti's voice singing Puccini.

Somebody was limping towards Xavier. Not Rex. Not Doug.

No: fucking John Doe.

Xavier's guts began to liquefy. He was nervous enough already without this premium grade of fuckyouup slapping him upside the head.

John Doe stopped a few paces away.

'Y-y-your m-m-m-m-m-a-y-y – y-y-y-y-uh-y-y-y-y-you-y-y-y-your momwantstoseeyou.'

Xavier nodded. 'Thanks.' His voice came out a squeak. He

cleared his throat. 'Be right there,' he added, but John Doe didn't move, except to tremble and shudder within himself.

'Shouldn't you stay close to Melanie?' Xavier added. A mixture of pity and fear worked through him. Powaqa had to be wrong. The guy couldn't be acting.

John Doe put his hands in his pockets and rocked from side to side. He reminded Xavier of a ferret.

'G-going some-ggg-go-going s-s-s-s-s-somewhere?'

'No,' Xavier said. 'If you don't mind, I'd like to be alone. Tell my mother I'll be there soon.'

He almost added: '*Doc*,' but checked himself. He didn't want Doug or John Doe to know he'd heard them talking.

'I've been in town,' John Doe said, with sudden exquisite clarity. 'There's no more Kiss anywhere, not even the hospital. Don't bother searching for it. When you come up empty, come and see me. I can help you.'

Then he turned and limped back the way he'd come.

Xavier's guts were boiling now. What a freakshow. After John Doe had gone, he dashed up to the house, locked himself in the bathroom and took a disturbing dump of the toxic waste variety.

No one was in the house. Everyone was down by the oil drum lighting. Somebody had left a solar-powered camping radio on the back porch. Xavier heard FallN blabbing on about 'courage, my peoples,' as 'The Night the Lights Went Out in Georgia' came on in all its tinny '70s glory.

When he went out the back door of the house, Rex was standing there.

'About time,' Xavier whispered.

'Uh . . .' said Rex.

'What?' Xavier started moving towards the corral, but Rex wasn't coming with him. 'What's the matter, Rex?'

'Listen, man . . .'

Now Xavier was walking backwards, determined to get

away from the house as quickly as possible but increasingly conscious that *Rex was not coming with him*. Rex didn't have his backpack or jacket or anything . . .

Xavier stopped. Without taking a step towards him, Rex said, 'I ain't been taking my Kiss anyways.'

Baffled, Xavier shook his head. 'So? What, you missed a few or what?'

'See, if I go with you I could get shined up.'

'No, you won't, don't be paranoid . . . Rex, how many did you skip?'

'Uh . . . I really missed a lot of doses, man.'

Xavier frowned. 'Why the fuck would you stop taking it now? What the fuck's up with you?'

Rex shrugged. 'I just . . . I'm sick of the whole kid trip, you know? I don't want to talk about it right now.'

Xavier felt that old slipping sensation. People acting in a way they shouldn't; it happened often enough. He ought to be used to it by now. But Rex wasn't an adult. Rex wasn't shined. Him and Rex, they were supposed to be allies in this thing.

Xavier knew he sounded desperate as he continued.

'This thing – tonight – it was your idea, remember? If you can't do it, why didn't you say so before?'

But he knew why. It was easily read in Rex's face and manner, but Xavier hadn't wanted to see it. Rex didn't want to look like a coward in front of Chumana. Plus, Chumana knew Rex was off the Kiss. That explained why she'd gotten so mad, before.

'Fuck,' Xavier said. 'I don't believe this.'

The two of them. Rex wanted to get with Chumana. Maybe they were already together. It was so obvious now. Xavier felt betrayed and stupid and lame and pissed off. Increasingly, as the seconds ticked by and Rex said nothing but looked off into the darkness past the barn, he felt pissed off.

'OK, whatever,' Xavier said.

'You still going?' Rex was incredulous.

'Fuck, yeah.' The more people tried to stop him, the more determined he felt. 'See you later, asshole.'

He walked away. He climbed the fence of the corral and brought Bob Newhart to the spot where he'd draped his saddle and saddlebags and other gear, and he got her ready to go. He felt kind of shit but he wasn't letting himself think. He pictured Powaqa's face when she realized he'd taken the best horse. He almost cracked a smile at that.

Xavier led the mare out the side gate and into the field where the sheep and alpacas were sleeping. The oil drum fires glimmered in the distance. The party was in full swing and would probably go on all night. Xavier kept expecting somebody to stop him. John Doe knew he was going. Rex knew, and Chumana knew . . . wasn't anybody going to intercept him? He led Bob Newhart through the fields parallel to the drive, and then half a mile from the house, not far from the point where John Doe had broken the fence, he opened a gate and took her on to the drive.

He couldn't hear the party from here, but he could still see the glow of the fires. In the night sky, clouds were blowing west at speed. Gusts of wind animated the darkness, as if the air itself were some giant, playful animal. In the distance, Los Sombres glowed in silence – which seemed wrong. Xavier thought the beacons ought to make a mystical sound like a Fairlight synthesizer, or at worst a high-pitched bug zapper whining.

But when the sound came, it came from the direction of the mountain behind Xavier. The sound rended the sky.

Planes.

The sound of the recon jets started out loud and rapidly came to a crescendo. A mind-flattening shudder, a violence upon the air.

At the first blast, Bob Newhart took off with Xavier. She ran hell for leather through the night towards the highway.

She ran toward the crazy luminous blur of Los Sombres.

And as the planes approached the city, all the lights went out.

City Beneath the Waves

Los Sombres

Darkness cloaked the city. Glittering Los Sombres, snuffed in an instant.

Xavier fought for balance on the running horse. He lost one of his reins and ended up just hanging on the saddle horn while Bob Newhart bolted. The word 'bolt' didn't really do justice to what it felt like to be on Bob's back just then. It felt like getting beat up by about six guys while you were in freefall.

And the planes? They were flying low, a whole series of them passing directly over the ranch and then continuing on west.

Mortars screamed from the Silver Brush outpost. The cameras on the watch tower must have picked up Xavier on the horse, but all personnel were occupied with the attack. Bob galloped past unchallenged.

After the first few seconds of radical terror, Xavier realized he wasn't going to fall off. He even got the loose rein back. And a gloss of exhilaration began to coat the whole experience. There was a crazy freedom in this. The day was fucked, the year – everything. Rex's stupid half-ass plan. What was the good of making plans? People didn't stick to them.

People lied. People let you down.
People saw sub-Saharan art films in their right eye.
So: fuck it. Time to take charge.
As soon as the horse stops with the loco shit.

Bob Newhart slowed down to take the turn from the ranch drive to the main road. She went left, towards Los Sombres; she had no choice. For a year there had been a crashed 18-wheeler blocking the road to the right. She was trotting now, a fast and nervy gait that had Xavier's butt pounding the saddle like a jackhammer. No wonder Doug looked like he didn't have a bone in his body. They'd probably all been shaken loose from their tendons.

Xavier gathered the horse. Bob was blowing but by no means exhausted; she would go again given the slightest excuse. They went like this until the sound of the explosions came closer; then Xavier was in a storm again as Bob got panicky. This time he knew what was coming, and he kept Bob under control. He talked to her and he worked her with his weight and the bridle, and he kept her from going over the edge. Foam flew from the bit and slapped his hand.

The entrance to the interstate was coming up and the directions he'd scribbled on his arm indicated that he should take it. But Bob wasn't turning. They kept on, until the road eventually passed over the highway and veered towards town. He reined Bob in on the overpass and looked down on the interstate. It was dark and empty, much bigger from this perspective. In the distance, to the south-east, he could see cars pulled over to the hard shoulder. They might very well have been there for two years. He shuddered, then told himself it was the wind making him cold. Then he mounted again.

Bob was content to walk now, but Xavier had changed his mind about following John Doe's route. It was too long and roundabout, and too exposed. The main roads would be watched. He decided to take a crowfly route instead. He knew the layout of Los Sombres well in theory, but as the night wore on he started making mistakes. Everything looked different on the ground and in the dark, when you were a little freaked and your horse was jumpy besides. He told himself he wasn't actually lost, just a little off-track, and stopped outside a tyre factory to check the Gulf map he'd packed. He wasn't where he was supposed to be. He decided to cut through a series of small roads to correct the mistake.

Bob was getting tired but she didn't falter. Mustangs were strong like that. And if Bob was feeling anything like Xavier, her anxiety was keeping her energized.

In the early hours of the morning they went through a bombed-out trailer park. It was deserted, but Bob Newhart shied at a windblown deck chair. Xavier kept a close check on her head and worked her with his legs, and she settled.

A mile or so later, the recon jets flew over again and Bob Newhart ran sideways. Xavier had to let her run for a while, but he stayed on her back. Got her calmed down again. He was starting to think he could handle this just as long as no actual mortars fell on them.

He knew it wasn't going to be easy. He had been busy running scenarios in his mind, planning how he would deal with this or that crisis on the way into town. There would be rovers, there would be desperate shined, and there might even be malevolent burnouts exploiting the chaos of the situation. If Bob Newhart saw an exo-protector, she would fall apart – Powaqa's shine wasn't working on her anymore. And to be honest, the horse's reaction would probably be justified, because the military robots might well try to capture them.

Xavier was prepared for the worst. He was excited, too.

Bring it on, he thought. *I'm ready.*

But it was neither exo-protectors nor falling mortars that were to be the agents of Xavier's undoing. No. On the outskirts of Rosewood, Bob Newhart saw a T-shirt flapping on a clothes line. Just like that, she bucked Xavier off and left him for dead.

It was dawn. Xavier got up, rubbing his shoulder, and listened to Bob Newhart trotting up the street. The houses were grey and angular in the half-light. All the lawns were dead. He could hear a pack of dogs barking somewhere off to his left. Not close enough to be dangerous.

Talk about ghost town.

Standing there with nothing but his own imagination for company, Xavier slowly started to realize how fucked he was. Without the horse. Seriously fucked.

Bob Newhart came to the end of the street, ran a stop sign, and veered right. There was a sign for the interstate looming high overhead. It had fared better than the Mattress World billboard nearby, fire-blackened.

He followed her. Imagining Doug's sarcasm if he learned that Xavier had lost his horse.

Bob Newhart found some water in a cement barrel beside a road repair dumpster. After she'd drunk, she seemed calmer. She walked ahead of Xavier, so that just by following he ended up driving her. He needed to cut an angle on her but she wouldn't let him. She kept him in sight with that 360-degree horse vision. If he started to catch up, she'd trot just for long enough to keep him off her case. Once or twice she stopped and blew, as if angry or frustrated. Then she set off again, until she was leading him down a main road. Dawnglow illuminated the interstate entrance sign beside a Walmart.

Bob Newhart turned into the Walmart parking lot. Most of the lot was empty, but up at the far end by the cash machines there were about fifty cars all jammed bumper to bumper, parked so tight you wouldn't even be able to open the doors.

Xavier stopped trying to follow her. He knew that John Doe had used the interstate to get to the ranch, so it couldn't be completely blocked by crashed or abandoned cars. Maybe on the highway he could find a vehicle that still ran. Yeah, he'd be more of a target in a car – but this post-apocalyptic zombie spook scenario was weirding him out. He took the entrance ramp leading to the interstate. The road was much wider when you were walking on it than when you were riding in your mom's car. He became aware of that heavy, chemical feeling in his flesh. He hadn't slept all night. He was hungry and chilled.

The sound of Bob Newhart's hooves rang out behind him. He didn't turn. He could hear her walking along the inside of the guard rail separating the Walmart parking lot and the interstate entrance ramp. After a few steps he stopped and bent down. He pretended to look at something on the ground. Whistled a Roy Orbison song between his teeth, just like Pavarotti might.

She came up to the fence and leaned on it. Blew curiously at him. He stood up. Now she followed him happily, just the low metal guard rail between the two of them. The entrance ramp bent more sharply and now Los Sombres' skyline was laid out before them. The shine beacons were blurring in the haze of new sunlight.

Xavier shifted the peppermint Lifesavers from his right jacket pocket to his left. He stopped. Bob Newhart blew sweet air into his hand. He gave her a mint and then before she had time to think about it, he levered himself up into the saddle on her off-side. She blew again and accepted him picking up the reins.

They walked all morning. Seemed to take forever. It got hot. They passed abandoned cars, most of them stripped but some strangely intact. It was unnerving to think that nobody was alive to steal anymore.

A pair of vultures cast shadows on the asphalt beside them. Stayed, tracking Xavier and the horse.

By noon Xavier could hear something. At first he thought he was imagining it. White noise. Rising and falling, just on the edge of hearing.

Ahead, the smooth line of the highway buckled. It had been shelled to rubble. Felled billboards obscured the road. Xavier dismounted and led Bob Newhart forward across the rough ground. After a while the highway resumed. Xavier put on his polarized sunglasses and a sudden surge of blueness leaped into the bleached sky.

Shhhhh . . .

The sound was getting clearer. Now he could see an overpass up ahead. And—

Xavier took the sunglasses off and put them on again.

There was a car on the overpass. A car, going into the city. No: *two cars.*

He could see them creeping along in the distance, the sun-flash sparkling off their paint jobs like mica stars in black stone. They made a sound like the sea.

Out of Fries Come Back Later

He got off the interstate at the next exit and joined the overpass route. There weren't a lot of cars. Compared to the kind of traffic in Los Sombres before the Fall, there were hardly any – but Bob Newhart didn't like it. Xavier needed to concentrate on riding but his heart was skipping and he was sweating and shaky.

Had everybody been lying to him? Maybe Doug would lie, maybe even Powaqa. But what about the CB?

And how could the horses possibly have found their way to Kiss while dodging cars driven by the shined?

It was like a dream. A vision of the old world. A time before the Fall. Ice cream and HBO. Dreams.

He could smell the exhaust.

Nobody stopped or even leaned out their windows to talk to him. It was like they didn't see him. Even though he was on a horse and you would think that would be remarkable.

Up ahead everybody was stopping for a set of traffic lights that weren't working. The traffic stopped in a school-of-fish display of invisible accord, waited a while, and then went on. Just as if the lights were working. Xavier watched this happen through three light cycles. On the fourth, he rode Bob Newhart across. They were now in the district where Xavier believed John Doe's journey had begun.

On the other side of the street was a McDonald's, half in ruins. The golden arches flickered with fitful electricity, but there were people in line at the drive-thru window. Xavier dismounted and led Bob Newhart to the back of the line. The man in front of him turned his head, saw the horse, and turned back without showing any surprise. At the window sat a white girl of about nine wearing a Green Bay Packers woollen hat even in the heat. As people came up to the window, she was taking their money and handing them mime food.

She was handing them air. People walked away pretending to eat it.

It was his turn. Bob Newhart blew hot breath down Xavier's neck and slobbered on him. The girl looked at Xavier warily.

He smiled. 'Can I get a Value Meal with a Coke?'

'What size fries you want?'

'You have fries?'

'Course we have fries.'

'But there are no lights on in there. Nothing's cooking.'

The barrel of the pistol was in Xavier's face before he could do shit.

'Please,' he said, 'don't.'

'You listen to me,' she said, and Xavier could see she was wound up tight as a rattler. 'This here is my place. Go get your own.'

'Hey, whoa. I'm not here to cause trouble.'

'Then why you pretending to be one of them? Huh? You're fucking *scaring me* is what you're doing, kid.'

'Yeah, well, *kid*,' Xavier laughed, feeling sweat trickle down the insides of his thighs. 'That's like, a mutual feeling. My name's Xavier. I'm from out of town. I just got here. I didn't know . . .'

'What? What didn't you know?'

'What you were doing. Giving out invisible food.'

'Don't be a shithead,' she snapped. Then she started crying.
What the fuck was it with girls?

'Um,' Xavier said. 'Is that actually loaded? I didn't mean to
be a shithead, OK, can we just . . .?'

'Whatever.'

She tossed the gun over her shoulder into the metal basket
covered with grease and dead flies. Behind Xavier a tanned
couple in workout clothes were making impatient noises. He
turned.

'Sorry,' he said. 'They ran out of fries.'

The couple rolled their eyes at each other and walked off.
Xavier reached past the girl at the window and grabbed a ball-
point pen and a takeout bag. He scribbled, 'OUT OF FRIES
COME BACK LATER' and wedged it on the counter of the takeout window between a ketchup squeeze bottle and a metal
napkin holder.

The crying girl watched him.

'You want to come out and talk?' Xavier said.

'I can't. My brothers are in here.'

'Can I come in? Can you tell your brothers not to, like, kick
my butt?'

She laughed through her tears. 'They're only four. Come in
around the side, the window's broken just under the Happy
Meal poster.'

Golden Arches

Her name was Meegan and her twin brothers were Patrick and Conor with one 'n', she told Xavier. Her dad lived in Philadelphia and they hadn't heard from him – *'obviously'* – in two years. Her mom checked in most days, 'When her mission runs down. She's been extra busy since the bombing started.'

He didn't ask about the 'mission'. Instead, Xavier told Meegan where he came from and why he was there. On the subject of Kiss she knew nothing.

'Never heard of it.' She seemed a little suspicious. He took out his bottle and showed it to her. She traced the brand name with a bitten-nailed fingertip.

'Sorry I pulled the gun on you.'

He said, 'I guess if you're selling invisible fries to shiny freaks, you could start thinking everybody might be, you know. Like, zombies.'

She sniffed. 'They're not *zombies*. They can't help being shiny. It's sad. We had more people here to start with. Everyone else left town, but I didn't want the boys to get separated from me, or each other. You hear stories about foster care. So we decided to stick it out.'

'But how do you survive? There's no real food.'

'The Golden Arches are full of shine. The shine brings people here, and they give us what we need. Sometimes we only get money, but sometimes we get good barter. Once a customer brought a Dragon Mountain kit and we built it. Conor loves it.'

She gestured to a big plastic toy mountain sitting on one of the red formica tables. There were lego-type pieces scattered on the floor near it.

'Yeah, but you can't eat that.'

Meegan took a roll of hundreds out of a side pocket in her cargo pants and showed it to him. 'Every week this Indian guy comes in from the reservation and sells us food. The prices are outrageous but we have plenty of cash.'

'You don't mean Sam Power . . .' Sam was from the other rez. The Fall had shut down the casinos and the big resort, but theoretically you could traffic stuff, if you knew what you were doing.

'Sam Ghost Power? That's him. He even brought some grapefruit last time. He's nice. He offered to take us out there, but we can't leave Mom.'

Xavier nodded. He knew the story. It was always Mom.

'You could maybe drug her up and then she'd just wake up on the rez,' Xavier heard himself say, repeating what he'd been told.

'Would you do that to your mom?'

'I thought about it.'

'Your mother's still alive, then.'

He gave a curt nod and hoped this would be enough to show that he didn't want to go there. 'What kind of shine's in the Golden Arches?'

She shrugged. 'Same as before the Fall, I guess. You know, home away from home. Good-old-fashioned feeling. Everybody loves you. That kind of thing.'

'And it still works, without the burgers?'

She laughed. 'Come on, we both know the burgers always sucked. Hey, can I ride your horse?'

'Maybe later.' *No.*

'OK, well, my mom's sleeping in the back. She's going to wake up any minute so maybe you better go.'

'Why? Is she dangerous?'

'Of course not! You just might freak her out, that's all. She's a little jumpy first thing in the morning, before she gets her charge on.'

'Gets her charge on . . .?'

'You know. Lights up.'

'Oh,' he said, as if he understood. But he didn't. Was Meegan talking about drugs? Cigarettes? 'I'll go outside. You got any water I could give my horse?'

She filled up a bucket from the sink in the janitor's closet and the boys followed them outside while he watered Bob Newhart.

'My mom's a helpmeet,' she offered. 'You know what that is?'

He shook his head.

'Helpmeets are shined to help other people. They feel they have to help others, no matter what. They go to this shopping plaza every day and they get a big charge. Then they follow their instructions and, like, help people. I'm sure it's a good thing, but it takes a lot of my mom's time and energy. She's exhausted right now. But when she gets her charge on, she'll be better.'

'So . . . does she maybe have access to any Kiss?'

Meegan shrugged. 'I don't know. She mostly works with older people and babies. I don't think they need anything like that.'

'But I bet she knows where to get it.'

'And I bet she wouldn't tell you. Sorry, I'm not trying to shoot you down. I just can't see her doing that. You gotta remember, she's shined. She's not like us. She doesn't do things because she has a reason, she does things because she has to. The shine pushes her to do things.'

Xavier sighed. 'OK, I hear you.'

'Meegan?' A throaty voice came from the direction of the kitchen. 'You talking to somebody?'

'No, Ma,' Meegan yelled. Then she made shooing motions at Xavier.

As he scrambled back through the gap in the plate glass, he whispered, 'I'll come back and see you when I can.'

'No, don't,' Meegan said. 'If I were you I'd get the hell out while I could. You look like you're pushing it, age-wise.'

She hadn't meant it as a compliment, but he couldn't help taking it that way. He led Bob Newhart around the back of CompUSA and waited for Meegan's mom to come out. While he was waiting, the traffic lights nearby went out. The Golden Arches flickered and died. Other illuminated signs in the area also darkened. It was broad daylight, so the effect wasn't dramatic. Still, Xavier wondered what it was about. No sound of aircraft. No lightning. Strange.

Then the side door of McDonald's burst open and a woman shot out. She was younger than Xavier's mother – mid-twenties, he guessed – and she had a nervous, aggressive way of moving. Even as she was going through the door, she was yelling at the kids. Xavier couldn't see the twins but he could hear them, screaming and throwing themselves at the glass behind their mother. She walked away quickly, pulling her sunglasses down and adjusting the fake tortoiseshell claws that were holding her hair up off her neck. It was hot already.

She was wearing a uniform, like a nurse or orderly, but it was too big on her and the bottom edges of the pants were frayed and dirty from contact with the ground. Her sneakers were scuffed, too.

She carried a big nylon purse, and while Xavier watched she reached inside, took out her shine compact and flipped it open.

It chirped a low-light warning at her. She began pressing buttons with an addict's urgency. He saw her lips move as she swore under her breath. Then she set off, purposefully.

He followed her down the street and around a corner, where he halted because he could see many more people. They were all converging on the shopping plaza. Most were female. Some wore stained and tattered medical uniforms; others were dressed in shorts and T-shirts. They sat and stood on cement benches and low walls around the dry fountain. All had compacts clamshelled open to the portable stadium lights that had been set up outside Neiman Marcus.

So this was the source of the local power drain.

Everyone was talking. Laughing, even. As Meegan's mother came into the path of the light, she visibly relaxed. Within moments she'd struck up a conversation with a fellow uniformee.

The place had the feeling of one big smokers' break. Except nobody was smoking.

He found himself standing next to a public trash container that had been jazzed up with a wooden frame so it would look less offensive. He'd been there for a minute or so before he noticed that there were no yellowjackets or flies and, in fact, no smell. He glanced inside and saw that the black plastic bag had been recently changed.

Now I don't know about you. The thought came to Xavier with Rex's sardonic delivery. *If I was a garbage man there's no way I'd keep doing my job during the Fall.*

Xavier glanced around. It was true. Who the hell was picking up the trash, and why? And what were all these people doing here?

They didn't seem crazy.

A middle-aged white woman was making her way towards the place where Xavier stood on the fringe of the crowd. She wore a camper's head lamp strapped to her forehead, and she dragged a big canvas sack across the paving. Periodically she reached into it like it was a Santa sack and pulled out a plastic bag, which she then bestowed on a member of the crowd.

When she reached Xavier she smiled.

'A nice strong boy like you, what are you doing here?'

'Um . . .'

She handed him a lumpy white plastic bag with a red cross stamped on it. The bag was heavier than it looked.

'Come and get in a little closer, honey,' she added, still holding his gaze. 'I don't see your feedback light. Aren't you receiving? We all need a little extra courage, these days.'

'OK, thanks.' His mouth was dry. She was trying to shine him with that light on her forehead. His tried not to look at her. Which way should he run? Before he could make up his mind, she gave a rapid series of puzzled blinks. She seemed to have forgotten what she was doing.

'Only one per customer,' she said earnestly to him.

'Got mine,' he said, holding it up. She smiled faintly, turned away and went to the next group of people.

'Only one per customer,' she said again. 'Don't crowd, now.'

Xavier sidestepped through the crowd to lose himself from her sight before he opened his bag. There were bandages, vials of drugs, syringes and needles in sterile packaging. A tourniquet, bottles of pills, and a couple of IV bags of saline.

Two Mexican guys were making the rounds, too. They handed out more plastic bags, but these contained food. All of it was commercial stuff; no government aid, here. Xavier tried to calculate what the population of the city might be in order for pre-Fall supplies to have lasted this long. There seemed to be a lot of people here outside the shopping centre, but then he remembered the empty suburbs and empty streets.

Doug had claimed everyone fled. But if even a tiny fraction of 'everyone' had stayed behind, that was still a lot of people.

Xavier took his bag from the first guy. The second guy paused beside the group of helpmeets nearest to Xavier.

'OK, people, listen up,' the guy said. He had an earbud in one ear and the wire went to his pocket. He was carrying a clipboard. Waves of BO came off him. 'I want you three to concentrate on the municipal area, and you—' he indicated Xavier '—can go with those over there. They're going to the hospital.'

Then, before Xavier could react, he'd used his phone to take a picture of Xavier, then scribbled a note on his clipboard.

'Hey,' Xavier said, annoyed at being photographed. 'What's this all about?'

The organizer guy looked peeved. 'You need a second exposure? You not get it the first time, kid? Maybe your receptors are immature. Go over there—'

'Thanks,' Xavier interrupted, already edging out of arm's reach of any of the adults. 'You're right. I'm going.'

Even though Xavier was acting like somebody who'd just gotten caught stealing, the organizer guy didn't look at all suspicious. Xavier hurried away, trying to lose himself in the crowd; nobody paid him any attention, though he was moving against the current of the shined. He kept straining his head up as high as he could, like a prairie dog, trying to see over the heads of the people who were all making their way to their 'assignments' – whatever they were.

He couldn't wait to take his food and meds and get the fuck out of here.

Then he saw somebody doing the same thing as him. A teenaged girl was stuffing extra bags of food into a backpack as she walked against the current.

He ducked, positioning himself so that he could see her but not vice versa. She was high-school age or maybe even college. Exotic-looking in an indeterminate way, with gleaming, straight black hair. She had full-blown tits and a big ass that looked even bigger in tan skateboard pants. She was a little flat-footed and in her flip-flops she took short, nervous, strides. Not a natural mover. He watched her weave her way among the crowd, carrying an overstuffed backpack plus four white bags, unchallenged. He waited until she'd passed him and then followed.

Follow

The girl bounced and swayed when she walked. He didn't want to get too close, but even so in her wake he could smell her deodorant or something – maybe even the laundry detergent she'd used. She leaned forward as though going against a current, and her ponytail swung back and forth. She moved among the shined without fear, but also without making eye contact. It was like watching a rancher walk through a herd, easy. Xavier tried to think of what he would say if she turned around and found him following her.

'I work for the government.'

Not likely.

'I'm on a salvage run for my employer.'

That was sort of plausible. He practised saying it in his head, all the while keeping a lookout for armed burnouts or robots or anything else that might come into the mix. But the girl didn't turn around, and soon she led him away from the crowd of helpmeets and up a blasted street. The effects of the recent strikes were obvious; whole sections of sidewalk had been lifted and displaced. There was dusty junk everywhere. This looked more like what Xavier had expected of Los Sombres: a deserted ruin.

The girl headed for the lit entrance to a Stop 'N' Shop, where a group of maybe ten shinies were hanging out. Xavier ducked into the doorway of a UPS store and watched.

The shined looked at the girl with little interest. Two of them were playing Gameboys or something, and the rest were working on a broken generator.

'Hey, guys,' the girl said loudly, but nobody looked up. 'Anybody on the line today?'

There was an emaciated man among the shined. He had been working on the generator until the girl said this. He dropped his pliers and stood up. Sweat made his face gleam. He'd grown a couple weeks of grey-streaked beard.

'I'm on.'

'Can I go with you?'

'What you bring?'

She held up the bag of medical supplies in answer. The man snatched it away from her and rooted inside.

'Where you get this?'

'In the helpmeets' plaza.'

He glared suspiciously. 'You wouldn't lie to me, girl. Nobody gets through their barriers.'

'Chill, Kelvin. You know those shine barriers don't bother me. So, can I go with you?'

He shrugged. 'That my name now? Kelvin? You sure?'

The girl laughed. 'You don't like it. Want a different one?'

He smiled then. 'Everybody got to be called something. Even you.'

Xavier wasn't really following the subtexts, but he'd learned not to pay too much attention to the words that the shinies said. More significant was the feeling of the interaction between the shiny man and the girl. She gave the impression of complete ease and security. She knew these people, and they knew her. Xavier could read it in the occasional glances from the other shinies, who were otherwise absorbed in their tasks.

This wasn't what he'd expected. He'd expected roaming gangs of rapists and thugs. Or raving maniacs wielding whatever weapons they could contrive. Because that was what he'd heard, from everybody who had been in the city. And that's how the voices on the CB described shit. In Xavier's mind, Los Sombres had been forever altered to become a bombscape of twisted metal and concrete ruin. But the truth was different. There were a lot of familiar places. Signs. Some of the stores' signs were even lit up as though open for business, even though the source of electrical power to the city remained a mystery.

And as for the shinies themselves: they didn't seem like grunting chainsaw-wielding cannibal whores. They were weird and lame, but not obviously violent.

Just like his mother.

After a little while, Kelvin led the girl away from the others. He clutched the bag to his chest like it was treasure. Xavier wondered why he needed the things. He didn't seem hurt. Did he see the medical bag for what it was, or did he believe he was holding a secret weapon? Or did he have injured family somewhere, that he was trying to protect? Or was his behaviour just all part of the shine he'd taken in?

Xavier examined the contents of his own bag, in case there was Kiss or some other, fancier anti-puberty drug inside. But it was all standard first aid stuff, together with some antibiotics and pain killers.

He followed the girl and Kelvin at a careful distance. He darted from one hiding place to another, using cars and garbage cans and doorways, and always running off the balls of his feet to reduce the sound his sneakers made. Neither of them turned around, and the group of Gameboy scripted didn't even look up when he went by.

Soon Kelvin and and the girl approached another group of shined. This group was hanging within view of a Gap sign. They had an acoustic jam session going: two guitars and a conga drum, and people standing around clapping. The girl quickened her pace when she heard the music, and again Xavier secreted himself and watched. Kelvin kept walking without even glancing at the musicians, but the girl went up to them and joined in. Some ancient Tina Turner song. The girl opened her mouth and out ripped a powerful, sure voice that hung shining in the hot air. She danced with the shinies while Kelvin kept walking, oblivious. Then, as Kelvin was about to turn a corner, she stopped singing and ran to catch up with him.

Xavier hesitated, then followed. The shinies kept playing. Like the first group, they paid no attention to him as he pelted by, panting.

He caught up with the odd pair, the curvy one and the skinny one, at the top of a pedestrian walkway over Route 5. On the other side of the highway were a series of consumer electronics stores, a Barnes and Noble, and a carpet warehouse. Further along came three or four car dealerships in a row. Xavier knew the area; it hadn't changed much, but was weirdly deserted. He didn't dare go too close. He slid behind an abandoned pizza delivery van while the girl and Kelvin stopped to talk.

'I got to go now, child,' Xavier heard Kelvin say. 'You take care, and stay away from Lincoln Mercury tonight.'

'You take care, too,' the girl called, waving farewell. 'Say hi to Nadine from me. And don't forget to eat. The line is hard work. You don't want to end up in the prana house.'

Kelvin laughed as he walked away backwards. 'When this is all over I'm planning one big barbecue, girl, and you are invited as the guest of honour.'

'You know I'll be there.'

Kelvin turned his back and trudged up the hill. The girl watched him for a second, then started to head off to the right. Xavier waited until she was almost out of sight, then started to follow her. But she suddenly stopped. She squinted up at the sky, then unslung her backpack and took out a black leather case about the size of a Bible. She set the backpack on the ground and fiddled with something inside. She slipped in some earbuds and straightened, still looking down at the backpack. Then, turning her back to Xavier and walking away for a few more steps, she brought the black box to her mouth.

She seemed to be talking.

Hair and Now

'Everybody welcome to the Shine Kitchen.'

Slick as a model changing outfits, Roksana slid into her radio voice, a self-consciously ironic ghetto drawl that occasionally swerved and headed West Coast NPR-wise in a bizarre idiomatic mix.

'It's FallN here in the city beneath the waves, staying with you all night through this very heavy Ride. I'm standing on the corner of Eighteenth and Grove and I have a little surprise for everybody who thought we were going to have seventy-two hours of darkness. Hello, US government guys! Are you listening in? How you doing? We're doing pretty good and we have power, in spite of You All.

'Now for you my peoples, we're going to be cooking up some live shining action here and I'll let you figure out the details of time and place when you hear the next joint. All the embedding is done for you, so if you been listening faithfully like I know you have, then you got nothing to worry about. Oh, and fighter pilot dudes? We don't blame you personally for bombing our ass. I bet some of you are having trouble sleeping but don't worry about it, all right? We just down here getting our poor forgotten selves killed, you know? And a lot of us aren't old enough to buy cigarettes, but don't worry. Don't worry. Maybe you military folks want to go get some

Sominex to help you sleep. Maybe you want to see a therapist. But either way, I speak for everybody here when I say you won't be bringing us down.

'This is going out to all of you in the city beneath the waves, the city of FallN. I hope y'all enjoy the music. The sound will take you where you want to go. This is FallN.'

Roksana waited until Elsa's light voice came on the channel.

'Thank you, FallN, she is live from the street with only the most deranged beats, ever. Just a few announcements. There will be a veterinary clinic at Paws 'N' Pads on Canyon Road on Friday morning, it's totally free but first-come first-served. We have obtained the services of a genuine, qualified vet for this one, Dr Amelia Ramirez. So if your animal companion needs help, this is the time to get it. Also, if you find any rechargeable batteries please give them to the helpmeets and don't use them for your DVD player because the helpmeets do important work and they need their lights. Now, for that music we promised. You can't dance to this one, but enjoy the melody, kids, because after this we do have some outstanding Ice-T to wash it down.'

Roksana listened long enough to make sure Elsa was playing the right track, Hoagie Carmichael's ancient 'The Lamplighter's Serenade'. Then she disconnected and let go of her FallN persona.

She was shaking with hunger, and Elsa's Ice-T reference had made her notice how thirsty she was. She squinted back towards the red line, wondering how long she could keep this shit up. The lights had gone down on their own last night and she still couldn't figure out why; but fuck it, was she relieved because the bombs had made a mess of the district but they hadn't killed any important beacons. Amir must have had something to do with the strategic shutdown of the lights, but she didn't know what he was up to because she hadn't heard from him in almost two weeks. Playing it off was hard, even for FallN, and she was starting to feel the breeze she'd been left to swing in, all alone.

Of course, at the moment she was anything but alone. The kid who had been following her since the helpmeets' plaza was still on her tail; he'd moved from the Domino's van and was now concealed behind a mailbox. Another waif. Could be an assassin, but if so he was incompetent. Either way, he was just another victim, left to deal with shit his elders couldn't even comprehend.

She didn't want to talk to him right now, but if she left him out there on his own much longer, he'd get picked up by an exo crawler and she'd have that on her conscience. So she set off down Carlucci Street, passing the blasted remains of a Starbucks and a Mailboxes, Etc., to the front of Hair and Now. This was one of several safehouses that Roksana kept ready, because her work took her all over the city and she never knew when she might need to hide from robots, or rovers. She took out her keys and unlocked the security grille, heaved it up, and went in.

She went past the empty styling chairs and dryers, past the posters of hungry models with perfectly disarrayed locks, past the sinks, to the bead curtain that hid the bathroom and the staff closet with its dusty coffee maker. Her receiver was flashing. Elsa. She probably wanted to know about the kid, or maybe she'd found out where that salvage horse had gone. But Roksana didn't want to spook the kid. She switched the receiver off and waited.

She watched him approach the glass and peer inside, then push the door open by increments. He'd passed the first test: he could see the salon. Whatever else he was, he wasn't shined up.

He crept through the salon, passing his hands lightly across the backs of the styling chairs and looking around at all the equipment as if he were exploring an alien planet. He stooped and picked up a copy of *Cosmo* dated April 2004. He looked at the cover, shaking his head slightly, and then set it down carefully on the counter. He looked at the bead curtain.

'You new in town?' Roksana made her tone conversational, but the boy twitched like a cat and then dove behind one of the styling chairs like he expected to be shot.

'I'm unarmed,' he called. 'I'm just a kid.'

'I can see that. I'm not going to hurt you. What's your name?'

A small hesitation. Then: 'Xavier.'

'Nice to meet you, Xavier. My friends call me Roksana.'

She'd had a lot of practice at this. There were many different kinds of victim in this town, but the extreme cases were gone by now. Those who were left usually had milder symptoms. Those people were affected in a whole variety of ways. You never really knew what somebody's problem was, so you had to learn to watch everything you said and did. In case you set some-body off. Xavier was young, and he had passed through the light barriers that kept nearly everyone out of the helpmeets' plaza, and he had seen Hair and Now despite the invisibility shine. So it was a pretty safe bet that he was cool.

But Roksana had learned to be paranoid.

It was possible that the enemy had tracked her by radio signal. The outside world was sickly fascinated by FallN. FallN repre-sented resistance to their vision of the ruined Los Sombres. FallN represented music, and laughter, where the outsiders wanted only to find disease, because of course that would make killing everybody so much easier to bear. FallN was such a nuisance that Roksana wouldn't have put it past the military to send in a child assassin to take FallN out. She kept her broadcasts brief and she moved all over the place to make it harder for them to catch her. But they were The Man and FallN was one dissident, the voice of Los Sombres. It was only a matter of time before they got her.

Time. It seemed to be an actual force in her ears and throat lately, pushing her on. *Running out of time.*

'Who sent you to me, Xavier?'

That surprised him. 'Nobody. I mean, I saw you, back at the plaza . . .'

'I saw you, too. What were you doing there?'

'Just looking around. I just got into town this morning. I live on a ranch, out on the east side. We ran out of Kiss, and I need some for me and some other kids. I'm older than I look.'

He said this last in the cracking voice of oncoming puberty. That part, at least, was convincing.

'Why did you follow me?'

'Everybody else was following the lights. You weren't. I thought you could be on Kiss, like me. But . . .'

'But I look too old for Kiss to do any good. Right?'

'Yeah.'

Roksana moved toward the curtain.

'I'm coming out, OK, so we can talk face to face. It's crazy how this situation makes everybody mistrust each other.'

She stepped through the curtain. He didn't move.

'I'm seventeen,' Roksana said. 'For some reason, shine doesn't seem to affect me. I don't know why. I've never had a Ride on anything.'

She still felt the old shame at having to admit it, even though she ought to feel pride. Being blind to shine was no longer a shortcoming; it was her greatest strength.

'I've never taken a Ride either,' he said. 'And I don't want to. I just need enough Kiss for me and the other kids my age, so we can get through. Until this is over, I mean.'

'Kiss is really hard to get these days. You live by the reservation? You would have been better off asking the Hopi to find some for you.'

It all came spilling out of him, then. A story about a Hopi horse trainer whose horses wouldn't obey her anymore, and how the shined-up refugees were supposed to evacuate for their own good but how could Xavier go without his shined mom, who refused to leave? And anyway, he'd been taking his Kiss regular until now and puberty wasn't going to hit, like, overnight so what was the big danger of coming to Los Sombres?

He seemed to be trying to justify his actions to himself, which, Roksana had found, was what people spent a lot of their time doing if you just let them talk.

'And,' he admitted eventually, 'I wanted to see some battles for myself. I wanted to see the robots going after, you know, the lights.'

'You wanted to see the shit-eating shiny people?'

He looked embarrassed. 'I'm more just into the hardware side of it. But I haven't seen any exo-protectors yet.'

'Consider yourself lucky. They'd nail you.'

He was a skinny kid, but there were heavy bones underneath there. Good big, strong hands and outsized puppy feet. Part Native himself, maybe; he was as dark as she was, and his hair was razor-straight. He had a slight Spanish accent. Not much.

He sounded offended as he said stiffly, 'I don't believe they're deployed to kill people.'

She sighed. 'Uh-huh. You just got here this morning?'

He nodded.

'How'd you travel.' She'd already figured this out, but she wanted to find out what he'd say. If he was telling the truth.

'Horse. I had to ride her, though. Usually our horses will go in by themselves.'

So the salvage horse had been his. Various salvage animals came through Los Sombres on missions for humans. Sometimes there were dogs, sometimes alpacas. And sometimes there were scrappy-looking little horses roaming the streets, with or without riders. She'd seen animals lead the burnouts to drugs, technology, weapons. Once she'd even seen a horse, *sans* rider, pick up a cardboard Drug Fair box in its teeth and walk away with it. But lately the numbers of horses had dwindled. Not much left to loot after two years. The rovers took things. Stuff got used, and depleted. Now, with the latest round of artillery strikes, there wasn't much left worth having.

She told him as much.

'I only need enough Kiss for me and a couple other kids my age.'

'How old are you?'

'Fourteen,' he said, as though daring her to believe him.

Hmm. She thought about reminding him that kisspeptin inhibitors wouldn't work forever. That sooner or later, puberty would break through anyway and with it would come vulnerability to the lights. But then she remembered how she'd felt when she wanted shine and it *wouldn't* come. She'd felt doomed, singled-out for misery, desperate for some chance to change things. She couldn't take away the kid's hope.

He would find out for himself soon enough.

'Come on,' Roksana said. 'Show me for sure you got no weapons, and no transmitter.'

He stood up. Took off T-shirt and shoes and socks, shorts; stood there in his underwear and told her, 'I ain't got nothing up my ass, OK, so I'm drawing the line there.'

She laughed as he started getting dressed again.

'You hungry? You like beans?'

'Oh no man, not more beans . . .'

'Jerky? How about jerky? No, I'm just kidding. I'll make you an omelette, how's that.'

'You got eggs?'

'I got chickens. That means I got eggs. Come with me.'

American Woman

Roksana went next door to a ransacked internet café and grabbed two bikes off hooks in the wall.

'I have bike stashes,' she said. 'I'm terrible at boarding.'

They cycled into the middle of town, where the University campus abutted the mostly-demolished Courthouse Row. He figured she must be taking him to an apartment building – although a lot of those were in rubble – but instead she propped her bike against the wall of an American Woman health club and unlocked the glass door, which was intact amid all the devastation.

'Are we going to work out . . .?' Xavier muttered, baffled. Roksana's body wasn't anything you could call buff. But she didn't answer him. She just picked up the bikes and shoved them behind the reception desk, waving him in.

Place didn't look like a health club anymore. Roksana kept ducks in the swimming pool and chickens on the roof. There was also a family of cats – to keep the rats down, she told Xavier. One of them was perched on top of a free-standing dip station, mesmerized by a sparrow that was fluttering around up in the exposed pipes near the ceiling. Roksana offered Xavier water from a cooler that stood at the end of a row of full ten-gallon bottles. He sipped the water, which was warm, and Roksana threw corn to the ducks from a paper bag. The pool water was foul, but they didn't seem to mind.

'This is hilarious,' he kept saying, looking around. 'What about your family? Do they live here too?'

'My dad is still in town, but he's working on a project that keeps him busy. He stops by now and then just to make sure everything's OK.'

'Wow. So, he doesn't get shine, either? He's like you?'

'Sort of. It's complicated.' She hadn't said anything about her mother or brothers or sisters, and Xavier was afraid to ask in case they were dead. This was the weirdest situation he'd ever seen, but Roksana acted like it was all pretty normal. Before he could think what to say next, she asked,

'So – where were you? When it started.'

Xavier looked around for a place to sit. He moved aside a stack of nineteenth-century English novels and settled on a leg extension bench. It was obvious what she meant by 'it'.

'Field trip for Health class. Rehab facility. Learning about the burnouts, how they got that way, why we should make sure we didn't let it happen to us, blah, blah, blah.'

She nodded. 'I remember that stuff. School used to be so stupid. They were always trying to get inside your head in such a totally clumsy way.'

'We were up in Black Creek, just inside the city limits. But we were lucky. The burnouts were doing occupational therapy and stuff, and they weren't affected when the Fall started. When the shit hit the fan, they took care of us. I got a ride home with a burnout counsellor. I mean, she counselled burnouts but it turns out she was a burnout herself from some shit she did way back when she was young. She kept checking in with me and my mom until the evacuation started. Then she helped us find a clearway. So we got out of the danger zone OK, but my mom couldn't leave the perimeter so I stayed.'

'That's cool,' Roksana said. Xavier's throat was clenching around each word, as if it didn't want him to speak or give any reality to the memory. He kept thinking of his dad hurling himself into the sky. He kept thinking of his sister.

His tension must have been obvious, because Roksana said, 'We all saw some shit, right?'

He bowed his head.

'Xavier, you got a place to stay while you're here?'

'I, uh . . . not really. I was thinking of going back to McDonald's . . .'

'Let me think. I'd offer to put you up with us, but—'

'Who's us?' he said warily.

'Us would be me and her,' said a rich young voice from just behind Xavier. He jolted inside his own skin and whipped around on the bench to face a set of bespectacled eyes gazing at him from the shadows of a cross-trainer about ten feet away. The details resolved, and he saw a child of maybe eight or nine sitting on the floor with her knees drawn up in front of her and a book in one hand. She seemed very clean considering the environment. He noticed neatly braided hair, heavily beaded with white and purple. He noticed one front tooth growing in crooked. Her glasses looked too small for her, and she actually pushed them down so that she could peer at Xavier over the tops of the frames, like a censorious librarian.

'I didn't see you there,' he said, trying to laugh, but she didn't smile back.

'I know,' she said. 'I was just reading. I wanted to finish this chapter but you guys interrupted me.'

She ducked her head back into reading position and her eyes could be seen flicking rapidly across the page. Xavier craned his head and read the spine of the book sideways: *Tess of the D'Urbervilles*.

'I was going to say,' Roksana said, 'that I'd offer to put you up, Xavier, but I'd have to talk about it with Elsa first. We're in this together, and I won't do anything she isn't comfortable with.'

'I'm OK with it,' Elsa said without looking up. 'I watched him from the Hide. He seems all right.'

'You watched me?'

'I'll tell you later. Elsa, any progress with that other thing?'

Elsa swung her head from side to side, still reading.

'I did most of tomorrow's stuff,' she added. 'But I couldn't find one track you wanted, "Future's So Bright". Is it an import?'

'I'm not sure. I'll look for it. Come on, Xavier. You might as well see the Hide.'

A rush of cool air greeted them when Roksana opened the metal door to the locker room.

'You don't have running water but you have air conditioning?'

'Oil generator. We have to keep the climate regulated because of the equipment.'

She flicked a switch and lights came up. The locker room was stuffed with electronics. Monitors sat everywhere, some of them at crazy angles, all sleeping. Power lights winked, blue and red and green and citrine. On the ceiling was pinned an enormous map of the city, annotated and dotted with sticky notes. More stickies lay on the floor, clung to hard drives and the edges of tables. Flash drives lay by the dozen, and DVDs were stacked loosely on every horizontal surface.

'Welcome to the Hide,' Roksana said. She turned to face him, spreading her arms proudly as if showing off the Taj Mahal.

'When you said *hide* I thought you meant, like, hideout.'

Roksana grinned. 'It is a hideout, but mostly it's a hide. It's a place to watch from, like when hunters hide to watch animals. Only I'm not a hunter. I just need to know what's going on. I can see the trends from down here. I can see which shine is taking effect where.'

Xavier was feeling increasingly excited; she must know where Kiss was. She had to. Would she tell him? She seemed to trust him already, although he couldn't understand why . . .

'And you do this because . . .?'

Roksana folded her arms across her chest and tilted her head.

'You ever wonder why those fancy exo-protectors can't catch more shinies? Ever wonder how this city has survived all this time, if everybody here is a flesh-eating psychotic zombie?'

'Well . . . yeah, but . . . to tell you the truth, I never knew Los Sombres was anything but, like, a toxic ruin.'

'But didn't you wonder why the bombs haven't put out the lights permanently? I mean, how hard could it be?'

Xavier actually scratched his head at that one; hard to say whether it was the sudden change in temperature that made him squirmy, or Roksana's words.

'I'll tell you one thing,' he said finally. 'When I was on my way in last night, all the lights went out before the bombs hit. That was weird.'

'And you don't think that means anything?'

He snorted. 'Like, the city is fighting back? I don't think so. Not unless you believe radicals like FallN.'

A big white smile bloomed on Roksana's face.

'How well you put it,' she said, and the canary-cat smile spread to her dimples and her eyes. 'You're a kid, Xavier. I have an obligation to help you if I can. The way I see it, all of us have to stick together. Now, is that the kind of thing you expected to hear in Los Sombres?'

Xavier felt disarmed. 'No. It's not. But Los Sombres is so . . . not what people said it was. Everybody said it was a hellhole.'

'Like, psychos will jump out from behind buildings and drag you by your ankles into the sewers and then flay you alive, something like that?'

Her tone was scathing. Xavier gave a complicated shrug. He was thinking of Rex's video game, and his own visions of robot stalkers taking out the killer shinies and the cannibals. He was thinking of Rex's cartoon of FallN with her Uzi.

Roksana said, 'We had some real dangerous people, but lately not so much. It was rough in the first few months. A lot of murders. Almost everybody ran away, though. Or died. Or suicided. The hardest jobs then were burying the dead. The red line was taking bodies down to the cemetery and then the playing fields and then the park . . . it was awful. Elsa's mom, we buried her as has and we marked her grave. Most of the dead people, no one will ever know what happened to them.'

Xavier swallowed and looked away.

'I'm sorry,' Roksana said. 'You lost people?'

Xavier nodded. He didn't trust himself to speak. After a while he took another swallow of water.

'I guess I kinda fell into the idea of bombing the place to pieces and starting over. You know, get rid of the past and move on.'

Roksana dropped into a swivel chair and woke up a computer.

'If only life were so simple,' she said, and turned her attention to the screen. 'I just have to get some stuff taken care of. Make yourself at home while I'm doing this.'

He hadn't found an opening to ask her about the Kiss, and now she had effectively dismissed him. Suddenly tired, Xavier left Roksana engrossed in her work only to bump into Elsa, who had been standing just outside the locker room.

'I'm going to watch TV now,' she said. 'Wanna come?'

She led him into the health club's office, now being used as a living area complete with futons and toys; a dollhouse took up most of the desk, but there was also a laptop. It blared out cheesy hip-hop beats and studio-audience cheering.

Elsa said, 'Roksana will probably fix something to eat soon.

We can hang out here. It's pretty comfortable. If you need the bathroom, there's one through that door over there, but we don't have running water. We have to bring drinking water in bottles from a tap down the street.'

'I'm not surprised,' Xavier said. 'Almost every other building on this block has been hit. Aren't you guys worried it's going to be your turn next?'

Elsa's face twisted as if she'd just sucked a lemon. Then she pointed to the laptop in a cartoon parody of distracting Xavier.

'Oh, look . . . time for Reverend Toupee! Do you watch?'

'Who?'

She giggled. 'The Reverend Mike Phillips Show. His name is really Mortimer Kowalski. He changed it to appeal to middle America, but we call him Reverend Toupee for obvious reasons.'

'We don't get this out at the ranch,' Xavier said. 'Reception's lousy.'

'We have a dish. I watch every day,' Elsa said. 'Look, see that screen behind Rev. Toupee? That's us. That's Los Sombres.'

'And today, we'll be talking with Lieutenant Colonel Mario Perez about the latest developments in the effort to reclaim Los Sombres from dangerous renegade lightborns.'

It was all more of the same; Xavier had heard it all before on the radio. The government couldn't/wouldn't talk specifics about the airstrikes but that didn't stop Rev. Toupee and his guests from speculating. Unlike the radio, the Rev. Toupee show had aerial maps and CGI impressions and government-approved visual reports from the exo-protectors.

'Liars!' Elsa said. 'You were never attacked outside the foundry! Your stupid exo-spiders dismantled a stupid bomb that your own stupid robots set six months ago. What outrageous liars you are!'

And she threw a Playmobile office worker the size of a radish at the screen.

'Hey!' said Roksana, coming in. 'What's with the throwing?!'

She picked up the Playmobile figure and put it back in the dollhouse kitchen, next to a plastic Rottweiler.

A busty Latina came onscreen and crooned, *'And now, today's tuning shine, brought to you by America the Beautiful Lightborns.'*

The screen flickered and pop music came on.

'It's just a tuning frequency,' Elsa said in response to Xavier's questioning glance. But Roksana's eyes were fixed on the screen as though her life depended on seeing every impulse. At the end of the thirty seconds, she blinked and turned away.

Too casually, Elsa said, 'Anything, Roksana?'

Roksana shook her head. There was something wrong, Xavier could see, but nobody told him what it was.

'I'm going to get us some food,' Roksana said. She stood up and left in a hurry.

After she left the room, Elsa gave a nervous little laugh. 'The shine doesn't work on her. But every day she checks, just in case.'

Xavier frowned. 'She seemed almost . . . I don't know. Disappointed. But that's crazy. Why would she want shine?'

Elsa made the lemon face, then rolled her eyes.

'I have no idea,' she said breathlessly; and it was all too apparent that she did have an idea. But Xavier couldn't get anything more out of her. She wanted to know if he'd read any Dostoyevsky, and when he said no, she started talking comic books.

He wondered if he should take this as a putdown, or not.

Small Things Could Break Them

Roksana went up to the roof, checked that the protective shine was still working, and fed the chickens. She tried to get her dad on the radio, but there was no response. She thought about getting the bike out again and going to the hospital but decided that would count as panicking. The Ansaris never panicked.

Besides, she couldn't leave Elsa alone with the new boy.

Tomorrow, maybe, if Amir still hadn't contacted her, she would say something on her radio show. Something in code. It wasn't like her dad to be incommunicado for so long. She swept her gaze across the blasted rooftops. There was a stiff breeze up here, and the sun was still cheerfully high; it glinted off the twisted remains of an exo-protector that had been taken out by friendly fire.

Something was going on. She could feel it, in the rhythms of life in the city itself. In the sudden wave of bombings. In her father's silence. In Xavier's arrival, with his haunted eyes. It was time for something. Time for change. Crunch time.

'Time to eat,' she said aloud and, stepping over a chicken, she picked a few tomatoes from the pots where she cultivated them and rolled them up in the bottom of her T-shirt. Then she climbed down from the roof.

She went into the tiny staff kitchen, took the simmering pot off the camp burner with its can of Sterno, and tried to think of something interesting to do with pinto beans that she hadn't already done fifty times. The last time Sam Ghost Money Power had been in town, he'd traded her a huge bag of them in exchange for cash, and they seemed to be lasting forever. Roksana was an imaginative cook, but even she had her limits.

'Hmm,' she muttered. 'Maybe Prince of the Sea instead. I should write a cookbook for disaster survivors. Roksana's *Seventeen Ways to Make Tuna Fish Interesting.* Chapter One: Tuna tastes better than your dead uncle's thighbone.'

She pictured the kitchen in her house, with its central island and all the copper cookware hanging from hooks overhead. The clusters of fresh garlic, the herbs growing in the windowsill. Her mother singing along to 'Private Dancer' and giving Roksana a little red wine when she made chicken au yasse or Thebouidienne. Mitch had had a whole shelf of dog-eared cookbooks over the sink, but she never cooked from recipes. 'They're just to give you ideas,' she'd told Roksana. 'Anything else, and they become crutches. Never follow recipes, and never measure if you can help it. That way you have to pay attention.'

After Mitch went into the hospital, Roksana had done all the cooking herself. She hadn't minded that her father was too nervous to eat more than a few bites of anything she'd prepared. Cooking had been Roksana's way of staying connected to Mitch. After her dad had disappeared into his study, Roksana would have her friends over and they'd rhapsodize about her onion and lemon sauce while Missy Elliott played on the integrated kitchen speakers. Her friends' mothers had fed them on Boston Chicken and Tex Mex and microwave cuisine. But Roksana was Mitchell Ansari's daughter, and she could make a sublime Banana Glacé, blindfold.

In those days, Irina had stayed out of the kitchen, except to clean. Roksana liked it that way. Somewhere down in Roksana's brain maybe she was afraid Irina would end up in her father's bed. Dad's reassurances that he didn't much care for Irina didn't seem significant in light of the maid's perfect figure and sexy Ukrainian accent. And Irina always seemed to be looking around the house with an expression that said, 'This should all be mine.' Dad said that Mitch had hired Irina and it would be up to Mitch to fire her, when Mitch got better. This was supposed to make Roksana feel hope about her mother's condition, but Mitch had brought Roksana up to be a practical girl. She wasn't falling for that crap.

Now Roksana started chopping onions. She'd make some tortillas. Deeply unadventurous, she thought. But she wasn't feeling right. The kid, Xavier, had unnerved her.

His face was haunted. It was the way kids had looked when the Blink first happened, before the shiny adults had become a fact of life. In two years, Roksana had grown accustomed to a lot. Xavier, living out on the ranch, obviously had not. Just looking at him reminded her of the early days of the Fall. Before her dad had started the red line. Before the fix started working, and the beacons went up. Before the helpmeets. When shit really had been 101 per cent scary.

It was like things had come full circle.

Yeah: something was going to happen.

'Sorry it's warm,' Roksana said, handing Xavier a can of Bud. 'It's past its date, too, but it's still OK to drink.'

Xavier looked up from the Tetris game he was watching Elsa play.

'Roksana, it's cool, you taking me in like this. But I need . . . the thing we talked about.'

'I can probably hook you up with some Kiss,' Roksana said. 'It's hard to find, but I'll help you look. Even if you find it, I don't know how you're going to get it out of town without your horse. Gas is hard to come by. Do you even know how to drive?'

'I could figure it out.'

Roksana pictured him wrapping a car around a telephone post. Moped, then – anybody could ride one of those. But where to find gas . . .? She swigged her beer and thought. She had to go to the hospital anyway if she was going to find Amir. Area was loaded with military hardware. Could they steal some of the government's fuel? That could be fun . . .

'Well, I have a lot to do tomorrow, but maybe—'

She halted. She could hear planes.

'Elsa!'

'I'm on it.'

Elsa leaped up and rushed into the Hide. Lights went down. The hum of the generator stopped. Elsa came back, a shadow now in the dim room. There was only the dimmest illumination from the skylights in the main gym area.

Even Xavier could hear the planes now.

'I told you this place wasn't safe!' he said, heading for the front door.

'No! Xavier, don't!' Elsa grabbed him and dragged on him like a dog wanting to play, but he shook her off in annoyance.

'Don't go out there!' Roksana said. 'We'll be safe here. We always are. There are lights on the roof that protect us.'

'What a crock of shit,' Xavier replied, but he hesitated.

'Seriously now, don't go out there. If you go out there, they'll see you. They always send exo-crawlers in after the bombs fall, to pick up whatever's still alive. Just stay with us. You'll be OK.'

The ducks were quacking and running around the gym floor as the noise got louder. Cats nowhere to be seen.

Roksana edged herself into a position between Xavier and the outside door, so that she could stop him in case he made a break for it.

An explosion went off. Gym equipment rattled; in the office, a coil of USB cable fell off a shelf and landed on Xavier's foot.

'That was about half a mile away,' Roksana said. 'They won't get us.'

Xavier was half-crouched, his nostrils flaring. Another one went off, farther away this time.

Elsa said, 'Should I go in the Hide and—'

Roksana shook her head at Elsa and put a finger to her lips.

'It's OK, Xavier, honest,' she said as lightly as she could. 'Sit down. Have a beer. This could go on for a while.'

But Xavier would not sit down. He prowled around the inside of the building, looking up at the skylights every time there was an explosion. Surreptitiously, Roksana deadbolted the front door.

By the time the raid was over, Elsa had fallen asleep in the beanbag. Roksana carried the girl to her futon with its blue mermaid sheets. She pulled a Navajo blanket over Elsa's bare legs. Then she addressed Xavier.

'So like I said, I could probably hook you up with some Kiss. But I don't know about tomorrow. I have a lot to do.'

'Just tell me where to look,' Xavier said. 'I can't afford to wait around. Christ, this is some mad-ass shit, sitting here with bombs getting dropped on you.'

'Mad-ass shit. Yeah. That's the term.'

Xavier was looking at her. 'How do you deal with it?' he said. 'Especially, being alone. Is it always just the two of you?'

'Pretty much. I've learned to trust myself. I've learned that people—' Well, that wasn't quite right. She corrected herself: '*Adults*. Are just loosely connected. They're just a bunch of compulsions and stuff. Rationalizations. Seriously. Even before the Fall. Small things could break them. They're not like kids.'

Kids. His eyes fixed on her when she said that. Again, she thought how haunted he looked. How much crap had this kid taken for looking so young? Your Kiss or your life. That was the curse Xavier had been living under.

But. Still. Could she trust him?

'Maybe you wish you could just check out,' Xavier said softly. 'Sometimes.'

She gave a vehement shake of her head. 'Oh, no. I don't want to check out. The worse it gets, the more I'm determined. I'm going to make things better, no matter what it takes. If these idiots would just stop attacking us,' and she shook her fist at the ceiling, 'I could do a lot better.'

Xavier looked down at his too-big hands.

Elsa opened her eyes. 'Roksana's dad is working on a fix. Shine that protects from other shine.'

'Is he a doctor?'

Roksana sighed. She would have to talk about Amir sooner or later.

'Professor. He was an old school Rider, but he quit years ago over regulatory issues and went into teaching. He knows how to protect himself, so he got through the Fall without too much damage. He just has a few little . . . um, quirks. Elsa, I thought you were asleep, girl.'

Elsa closed her eyes again. 'I am asleep. Quirks? Oh, yeah, your dad is quirky. He's quirky like a talking squirrel.'

Searching

No more shells fell that night, but in the small hours Xavier was awakened by whispered conversation.

Roksana: '. . . go on again in the late afternoon. Probably down by Canal Street, someplace like that.'

Elsa: 'We don't have enough material. The playlist is old. How do we know if we're being responsive?'

'I know. I'm going to deal with it. But there's—' Roksana paused.

Xavier tried and failed to suppress a sneeze. There was a long silence.

In a brisk tone Roksana said, 'OK, back to sleep, Elsa, and if you have another bad dream, just hug the cat.'

Elsa blew a raspberry.

Xavier heard Roksana move aside the hanging plastic strips that protected the Hide. He thought about following her, but his body seemed to be full of something heavy and sticky that stopped him moving. He could hear the steady hum of the generator running once again, and before long it put him back to sleep.

*

'I'll take you to the places I know today,' Roksana told Xavier over a breakfast of scrambled eggs, chilli sauce and rice. 'I can't make any promises, but we might just get lucky.'

'Don't mind me,' Elsa said from underneath the squat station. 'I'll just be here, reading yet another boring book in the English 204 syllabus. Hey, do you guys know what a hedgerow is?'

'Look it up, lazybones.'

'Lazybones? Who does all the research? Huh?'

'What research?' Xavier said, but they ignored him.

Roksana laughed. 'Fair enough. I think a hedgerow is just a hedge. Like, in England instead of fences they have these hedges separating fields. I think.'

'Thank you.'

'You're welcome. I'll be in touch this afternoon. Don't over-feed the ducks.'

'Don't you get in trouble.'

They looked for Kiss all morning, but Roksana's words proved true: there was none to be found. It was filthy work, rooting through half-ruined buildings and sometimes hiding from stray rovers. Xavier was discouraged, but in the back of his mind he also wondered whether Roksana was really trying.

They passed a multiplex theatre; the lights that had once advertised the moodies still shone from the sign out front. Beneath, a small crowd blocked the clearway. They were engaged in a pitched battle with evacuator robots. The BR1g8s were firing at the shinies, who were stupid enough to stand basking in the light coming from the moodie theatre. Somebody got picked off even as Xavier watched.

Roksana jerked her head towards a side street and Xavier followed her, but he kept looking back. The hardware was amazing in real life. The new model BR1g8s were wicked quad bikes sporting a bristle of weapons where the rider should be.

They were all-terrain, could drive in any direction and would curl up like an armadillo if they got into heavy shit. Xavier had made some sketches of them back at the ranch.

'Come on, come away,' Roksana hissed; but he couldn't take his eyes off the scene.

The robots didn't seem to be winning. People rose, seemingly from the dead, and returned to their shine, while the robots stolidly shot them again and again with stun rays.

'Why are they bothering?' Xavier said. 'They could kill people if they wanted.'

'Because of the statistics. People don't like to see a lot of casualties in the media. But if they see captures, or signs of control, then that looks good.'

'They haven't captured anybody, though.'

'Keeping people contained within a certain radius for a period of time counts as a capture. That's what they're doing. They found a place where the shinies want to be, anyway, and they're acting like they're holding them there.'

He shook his head. The exo-protectors were so cool. He hadn't expected to see them deployed in such a half-assed way.

'Come *on*, Xavier,' Roksana said. 'We can't stay here. We'll be picked up.'

They moved on. But there was no Kiss. By the end of the day, Xavier was shaking with hunger and what he guessed was nervous exhaustion. Constantly scanning for enemies was tiring, and it seemed they were always on the move. Roksana might not look like a gym bunny, but she hadn't gotten tired. Xavier felt flattened.

Back at American Woman, he sank into a beanbag and threw his head back.

'You want a joint?' Elsa said. 'My uncle used to smoke when he got stressed. Roksana could get you some.'

'Xavier doesn't need to smoke,' Roksana answered for him. 'He just has to get used to what it's like here.'

Xavier was thinking about the horses swishing flies in the sunset, and the smell of the sage. There were flies in Los Sombres, but that was all.

'Come on, Xavier,' Roksana said. 'You need to eat.'

She went up on the roof and came back with eggs.

'Thanks,' Xavier said. Roksana's competence was a comfort. His mother would have told him he needed to eat and then offered him a box of Chicklets. 'I'll be OK. It's just a lot to take in.'

'Can I come tomorrow?' Elsa said.

'Yeah, I guess,' Roksana said. 'But I don't know where we're going to look.'

The next day's search brought nothing. Xavier was picking up scrapes and bruises from scrambling over rubble all day. He'd thought he was reasonably tough, but Roksana seemed to swarm up walls and over obstacles with little effort. Xavier kept tripping and falling.

Elsa shook her head and *tsk*'d at him, and patched him up with Band-aids and antibiotic cream.

'If you can't find Kiss, you could try melatonin,' she said. 'It's crude, but better than nothing.'

'Never heard of it,' Xavier said. 'What does it do?'

'Lots of things to do with day and night and jetlag and stuff, but on top of that it inhibits puberty if you take enough of it. Roksana, what do you think?'

Roksana was staring at the daily induction shine on the computer.

'It's a good idea. I'm running out of places to look for Kiss.'

On the third day Roksana took Xavier out past the big America the Beautiful headquarters that stood like a pointing finger among apartment buildings that had been hit in the recent attacks. Its black glass was undamaged.

Helpmeets were busy within an atmosphere of third-world environmetal disaster. Xavier saw a woman with a newborn baby in a sling, sitting on a slab of displaced concrete, crying. A skinny cat wound around her ankles. Roksana went over to talk to her, but Xavier hung back.

He had to stay focused. He couldn't get caught up in other people's problems.

Roksana had a long radio exchange with Elsa. Then she sat with the woman and baby and waited while a pair of help-meets came and led the woman away. Xavier sat down in the shade and wondered if he was at risk from shine yet. If he didn't find the melatonin soon, he'd have to get out of town. He felt slightly fucked.

Roksana came back. 'Ready?' she said. 'Should we go on?'

'Isn't there any other part of town that's in better shape?' he said. 'It wasn't all ruined like this when I was riding in.'

Roksana mopped her face with a bandana and said, 'Actually, I came down here because there's something else I need to do today. You might as well come along. And yes, it gets smoother from now on. Let's get bikes.'

She produced the key to a security grille and opened up a bakery. Behind the counter were half a dozen things with wheels.

'Do you want a bike or roller blades?' she said.

He chose a scooter and Roksana took a kid's mountain bike. They headed away from the ruins downtown and into Yates Hill's popular shopping district. Here, some of the street lights were working, but no one was driving: the roads were full of cars whose gas tanks had been drained.

'Why doesn't somebody tow away all these cars and clear the road?' Xavier asked.

Roksana shrugged. 'No reason to.'

'But there's a reason to paint lines on the sidewalk?' He pointed to the wavering strands of bright blue and sometimes red that decorated many of the sidewalks in these parts.

'The lines are for the shined. They follow them.'

'No problem, that's not freaking me out,' muttered Xavier to himself.

He'd been hoping she'd been kidding about the lines, but through a hole in a Pepsi billboard he could see movement. It was a line of people, moving slowly along Warren Avenue. He saw bare backs, brown and black and tan, bent with effort.

'That's the red line,' Roksana said. 'The lifeblood of Los Sombres. These people do the raw work needed to keep the lights shining.'

'Where are they going?'

'There are a lot of possibilities. This line is obvious, so they're probably doing something really basic. They could be bringing fuel for the generators to power the lights. Some of them will repair the equipment that's been damaged. Some of them will go off to recruit more people for the red line, using portable lights. So all of these individual missions add up to one big effort, which is to keep the lightborns active.'

'Do they know what they're doing? Do they have a choice?'

Roksana shrugged. 'I think it depends. I don't think they really have a choice.'

'No wonder bombs couldn't stop the lights going down. Crazy people are keeping the shine up.'

'Well, here's the thing, Xavier. If these folks are crazy, how come they're so coordinated?'

'Because FallN has taken over like some kind of psycho warlord, that's why. It's slavery. Roksana, don't tell me you're good with this.'

Roksana sighed. 'FallN isn't a warlord. And I don't really think anybody's in charge. It's about survival of the whole.'

'Survival for who?' Xavier said. 'The people, or the shine?'

'Well . . . both.'

'But somebody has to be orchestrating it. Who tells the lights what to do?'

'I'm not really sure how it works. But I know that it does work. And I'll tell you something. We know we're being watched by satellites. But the red line knows that too, and it manages to fool the satellites. What we're looking at here, this could be a decoy. The real effort, the really important jobs, might be going on indoors. Or it might be going on in some way so that satellites can't see the people and pinpoint them as targets. Otherwise, with the first few air raids the red line would have been wiped out.'

'You're just going to get these people killed,' Xavier said. 'The government can't help you as long as the lights are burning. If you keep the lights up, then they'll keep attacking. As long as you keep feeding those lights, you keep the Fall going. Roksana, you're on the wrong side.'

She shook her head, all tight lips and furrowed brow. 'You don't get it. People need the lights. Los Sombres can't survive without the shine. Most of the people here can't leave. If they leave they'll be burned out and institutionalized or worse, they'll end up homeless or dead. You call that help? There are a lot of kids here, and we've all lost family, or else our family are damaged. What would you do? Lie down and die? Or try to find a way to make things work, every day, one day at a time?'

Xavier said, 'You can't stand up to the might of the American military. Out on the ranch, we can at least grow our own food. You're in a siege situation. You can't survive.'

'We can survive,' Roksana said. 'We can, and we will. My dad is trying to help people get better. Repair the Field. We just have to hang in there a little longer. Then maybe we can start to turn this thing around. And you want to know something else? You know why the bombs are falling now, don't you?'

'Because Congress voted for it.'

'That's just the part they show in the media. No. It's about the OSM.'

'Who?'

'The OSM. Organizational System Metric. It's some statistic they have. The OSM in Los Sombres is too high, and that means that we aren't just a bunch of dumbfuck zombies, we're intelligent, and that makes everybody out there nervous. So they're going to strike us down. Makes sense, right? Whoahhh-*shit!*'

She grabbed his arm and pulled him into the doorway of an apartment building.

Prana

'What the—?'

'Shh! Look!' she hissed, and pointed across the street. Two exo-protectors were gliding down the sidewalk. A singing sensation ran down Xavier's spine as he recognized late-model MRX-5s with custom submission-beam racks. They had multiple spindly legs that terminated in retractable wheels. They had been designed to move among the ruins, go up and down stairs, and basically hunt out bad guys wherever they went. They were the coolest shit you ever saw, and lying in his sleeping bag at the ranch Xavier had made endless drawings of them. Fantasizing about winning the war on Los Sombres.

Now he wished he had a camera.

Roksana grabbed his arm and whipped him away, deeper into the shadows of the building's foyer. He was startled and annoyed, but there was an urgency in Roksana's behaviour that made him comply. The bare skin of his arms pressed against a row of mailboxes. There were spiderwebs in the corner and a strong smell of cat pee.

Roksana was a few inches taller than Xavier, and she had to bend to put her mouth to his ear.

'Don't move. Don't make a sound.'

She breathed the words. They came out as heat and spearmint, because of the gum she was always chewing. The hair on the back of his neck stood up.

They stood there for what must have been about a minute, until the robots had turned a corner and disappeared.

After they were gone, Roksana didn't move right away. She took out a Feynman and scanned through maps of the downtown area. She squinted at the sky. He thought she was going to lick her finger and stick it up in the air to check the wind, too, but finally she nodded for him to come out on the sidewalk with her.

'That was lucky,' she said. 'They weren't doing recon, just travelling point to point. Normally if they see kids they'll use darts to stun them and carry them back to their base.'

'I think that's called rescuing people?'

She looked at him like he was stupid.

'Do you want to get *rescued*? Please.'

A few minutes later she led him in the service entrance of Jambalaya, a swanky restaurant with polarized glass that made it look like a fish tank. Inside, it was dim after the brightness of the street, and it smelled stuffy and sweet. Xavier's eyes had to adjust, so it was a few seconds before he saw that the place was *inhabited*. The tables had been removed, but people were sitting or lying on blankets and pillows at regular intervals on the dark red carpet. Most of them were women, and in their hands some of them cupped little lights like souls.

All were so emaciated that Xavier thought of a concentration camp.

'Don't say anything,' Roksana told him. 'If they're sleeping, don't wake them up.'

He lowered his voice to a whisper. 'What's the matter with them? Are they sick?'

She shook her head. 'No, shined. They live on prana.'

'What's that, like seaweed?'

'Prana is universal life energy. They think they can survive by prana alone. They think the light feeds them.'

Xavier drew breath to laugh, and then realized she was serious. Roksana broke away from him and went towards a sleeping figure. The woman's dark hair was streaked with grey, and she looked old and frail. Her skin was dark but her palms and the soles of her feet were a ghoulish pale shade. Roksana slid the backpack off her shoulders and took out the remains of the medical kit. She lifted up the woman's forearm, made a *tsk*ing sound, and set it down again.

'She pulled out her IV again.'

Roksana unspooled a length of clear tubing and took out an IV bag. She tore open a canula and swabbed the woman's forearm with alcohol. The arm was bruised like the heroin addict's on the educational videos they had shown in Xavier's school.

No one seemed to react to their arrival. Everything was still except for a very faint collective sound of breathing. Only Roksana and Xavier were moving. It was too Zombies R Us for Xavier.

He hissed, 'Why are they taking shine that makes them starve?'

Roksana shrugged. 'My mother shined some bad Perfection before the Fall. She had to be hospitalized on suicide watch. Now, since the Fall, she's not actively self-destructive. She just . . . lives in the light. It's not ideal, but it could be worse. I've stretched her along for two years.'

'Your *mother*?'

He looked anew at the woman on the floor. She looked old. *Old* old.

'She's only forty-five. She used to be fat,' Roksana said, matter-of-factly. But her hands fumbled, taping the canula on to her mother's arm. Xavier could see the marks where the tape had been before.

'Are you giving her drugs?'

Roksana shook her head. 'Just fluids. While she's asleep I can trick her into swallowing soft foods. When she's awake she insists she's not hungry. Food is impure and interferes with prana, apparently.'

Xavier didn't say anything. Roksana's dark eyes searched his face – to see what judgmental thoughts he was thinking, Xavier assumed.

'My mother's fucked-up, too,' he muttered, and looked away.

The place smelled of women. There was a framed photo of Tina Turner beside Roksana's mother, signed and inscribed to 'Mitch'. Weird.

Xavier said, 'I'm gonna wait outside.'

He stood on the sidewalk, breathing deep. To his right, two men were pushing empty wheelbarrows along the yellow stripe painted down the middle of the road. Their heads were down, their feet feeling the way forward along the stripe. Like tightrope walkers.

It should have been funny. It was funny. It also pissed Xavier off. He took out his slingshot. Pebble from ornamental planter outside Jambalaya. Ping! The man clapped his hand to his forehead and winced, but didn't track the pebble to where it landed with a ringing sound in the empty barrow.

'Fucking zombie,' Xavier muttered. He did the same thing again.

It was pretty funny.

But too easy.

He glanced over his shoulder. Roksana was still kneeling beside her mother. Elsa would be huddled under the American Woman reception desk reading *Tess of the D'Urbervilles* or some shit like she was still on summer vacation.

Prana. Compassion. Perfection.

And look at these guys: ants on a sugar trail.

He couldn't really put together what he was thinking, if he was thinking.

The men came toward him with agonizing deliberation. What would happen if they didn't arrive at their destination? Would the Light know? As in, would it Know?

Would the Light take action on the Light's own behalf?

He wondered what would happen if he killed somebody? Because he could. He was pretty sure of it. He might be only a kid but these people were sheep.

Xavier had never thought about what it would be like to kill somebody; not for real. But now he was thinking about it.

Who would judge him?

Who would see him?

What would it matter?

He wanted to break Los Sombres open.

He had now slingshotted the two of them about five times each, and they'd persisted, unwavering, as though he wasn't even there.

Time to get more direct. He braced the door of the store open and dragged a stereo speaker out into the middle of the street so that it obscured the yellow line.

The men looked bigger the closer they got. The first one reminded him of a bike messenger. Too-tight muscle shirt and lycra shorts. Hair clipped down to dark fuzz. He reached the stereo speaker and halted. He glanced up, looked past Xavier, and then moved the speaker out of the way and kept going. Sweat dripped off his nose.

Xavier said, 'Hey!'

The guy ignored him and kept following the line. You could have a lot of fun with a can of spray paint in this town, Xavier thought.

But at the same time, he was scared.

Break this shit open.

Here came the second man: badly sunburned guy with one

of those long, Beverly Hillbilly faces. Red stubble stained with nicotine and slightly bulging eyes. Teeth jutting outward. Big overbite. If Rex were here, Rex'd say *he could eat a tomato through a hockey mask.*

'Hey, Red,' Xavier said, stepping into his path. 'You all there, man? Where you going?'

The guy stopped.

'Who the fuck ask you, kid?'

Xavier took a step back.

'Whoa, sorry, man.'

'What the fuck is your fucking problem?'

Suddenly the guy was 100 per cent focused on Xavier. Hostility out of all proportion swarmed over Xavier with the foul smell of the shined man's breath. Xavier's first instinct was diplomatic.

'Sorry, man, it's cool. No offence.'

The shiny put his hand to his ear.

'What? What you say? I can't fucking HEAR YOU.'

The other guy, the one who'd moved the stereo speaker, was still shuffling along very, very slowly. The prana women were still eating ions. But Beverly Hillbilly was standing on the edge of the yellow line like it was a balance beam, turning purple and stiffening with rage.

'Take it easy,' Xavier said. 'I just wanted to know where you were going. Didn't mean to get you upset.'

'GET ME UPSET? Why the fuck would it upset me? Why don't you come the fuck over here and ask me?'

Roksana was dragging the back of Xavier's T-shirt.

'Xavier! Don't!'

Xavier was laughing.

'What's the big deal. This guy's a joke. Look at him, he can't even step off the line.'

She was getting all up in his face.

'Don't be stupid. They'll all come down on you.'

'All who?' he scoffed.

And she hauled him along to the left, the direction bike messenger guy had gone. He could now see down a side street, where a line of men pushing wheelbarrows was coming back towards them. In the wheelbarrows were corpses. Animals and people. Long dead, some.

'Go back to school, shithead!' Beverly Hillbilly was screaming. 'You don't know shit so just go the fuck back to school or if I get ahold of you I'll take you same place they're going!'

'Sorry, man, like I said, sorry. I just wanted to know.'

'No!' Hillbilly was spitting now. 'No, you don't want to know.'

The first barrowload of dead dogs was going past them, pushed by a sunburned muscleman who kept his head down and his blue eyes on the line. The smell made Xavier choke.

'He's from out of town,' Roksana said. 'He doesn't mean any harm.'

'You take him out of here.'

Shaking, finger-pointing, Hillbilly scarecrow man was so absurd that again Xavier wanted to laugh, but Roksana cast him a quelling glance.

'Come on, Xavier.'

She drew him away, shoving her backpack into his arms to distract him. She led him down a pedestrian alley that passed between what had been boutiques and specialty shops. Their shoes scuffed loudly on the bricks. Xavier wondered where Bob Newhart was now.

'They're good guys. You shouldn't mess with them.'

'You gotta be kidding me. That guy's a ratchet head.'

'No, he's not.' Roksana stopped, forcing Xavier to stop, too, and turn around to face her. 'You think you know so much, but you don't.'

'Well then you tell me. Why the fuck are they tiptoeing along a road line pushing wheelbarrows full of *dead bodies*?'

Roksana seemed to sag. She sighed, looking at the ground. Beyond her, Xavier could see the shattered shopfront of a Starbucks.

'Because if they didn't, we'd have dead bodies lying in the street.'

'Still? After two years? How can people still be dying?'

'Same way they always die. They get sick or hurt, some of them even get old. They attack each other. They starve. There's no ambulances, Xavier. No morgues. No food deliveries. There's no government *of any kind*.'

'Ah! But then why are those guys doing it? Who shined them? I know how shine works. It gives you a directive, it makes you want something and it activates the neurochemicals to support the directive. But good shine doesn't turn you into a delusional freak. Those guys *couldn't* step off the line.'

Roksana said, 'It's not a perfect system. It's just what we have to do. All of us.'

'Us. What's this *us*? How does it all get coordinated?'

'It's complicated.'

'So it's complicated. I can deal with complicated. What I can't deal with is *insane*.'

She started walking towards him again. 'Come on. Let's head back. Look, Xavier, I don't have all the answers. All I know is, you can talk to people if you know how. You were insulting to that guy back there.'

'Yeah, well. I said I was sorry. He didn't have to go monkeyshit.'

Listening to himself, he realized he was sounding like Rex.

'OK, Roksana, you talk to these people, I seen you. But they don't talk sense back to you. How do you deal with that?'

'You learn, Xavier. How would we know where to get food? Or where are safe places to sleep? How do you think I took care of Elsa all this time? You need to open your mind.'

'Fuck that shit. An open mind is weak.'

Roksana laughed. 'I keep forgetting how immature you are. At least you didn't feel any urge to join the line. You should be happy about that. Shine's not getting to you yet.'

They rejoined the main road. In the distance Xavier spotted a group of people standing under a solitary streetlamp that was beaming out light, faintly green.

'What are they doing?'

'I don't know. But we're keeping track, me and Elsa. If there's a pattern in the light system, we'll find out about it. Ah, there you go.'

And she pointed across the street to a boarded-up health food store.

'Melatonin. Come on.'

Found and Lost

Eden Whole Foods smelled of mice and, beneath that, of yeast and herbs, and rot. Roksana turned on the flashlight. Its beam wobbled across shelves and barrels and piles of spilled bags. Xavier went to the computer and found the cash box, open, untouched. He flicked through the money. It had been a long time since he'd used cash.

'Why didn't they take it?' he muttered.

'What?' Roksana was picking among the remains of the food. 'I think some of this soy milk is still good. Don't people read the dates?'

'Why didn't they take the money? If you were getting out of town in a hurry, wouldn't you grab the cash and run to spend it in Phoenix or whatever? You wouldn't leave it here.'

Roksana shrugged. 'Scripted people don't behave logically. I mean, look at the electronics store. Nobody took any of that stuff. They must not have thought it was important.'

'OK. The Kiss is important. Where would it be?'

They started searching the vitamin supplement shelves. Rats slithered and squeaked as Xavier kicked through a whole mess of plastic bottles that had ended up on the floor. Glucosamine, chondroitin, niacin. St John's Wort.

'Somebody's already taken it all.' Xavier pocketed some multivitamins, but he couldn't hide his disappointment.

'Wait! What's this?' And Roksana bent beside a sagging sack that had once held brown rice; now it was in shreds and covered in rat droppings. She came up with a large, dark bottle. 'Melatonin. And another. The rats moved them.'

She shone the flashlight on the lids. 'The seals are intact. We can wash the bottles off.'

'Are there any more?' Xavier got down there with her and together they went through all the shit. But there was no more melatonin.

'Two hundred capsules in each bottle,' Roksana said hopefully. 'That's got to be better than nothing.'

'It is better than nothing. But I wanted more. I don't want to have to come into town every month looking for this stuff. I want enough to be comfortable with. Who knows how many other people might be using it, too?'

Roksana stood up. She looked at her hands in disgust, then shrugged and said, 'Stockroom. Come on.'

At the back of the store they found a cardboard box with twenty bottles of melatonin.

Xavier whooped and hugged Roksana.

'You saved my life,' he said, over and over, with his face in her hair.

'I know, I know,' she laughed. 'It's what I do, don't worry about it.'

He let her go, stepped back, took a deep breath. Looked at her, felt the impression of her soft body where he'd hugged her. Smelled the floral overtones of her deodorant. Looked at the bottle, and something happened in his head. He saw Chumana. Remembered how Rex had waggled his tongue at Chumana behind her back.

He hefted a bottle in one hand, listening to the muffled rattle of capsules inside.

'And this will work like Kiss?'

Roksana nodded. 'Elsa does her homework on these things. What's the matter?'

'Oh, uh, I just . . .' He looked at the bottle again. Did Doug hope he'd get killed in Los Sombres? He imagined Rex feeling Chumana up, his skinny hands groping her perfect breasts . . . The more he thought about it, the more he felt like an idiot. Everyone was leaving him behind, and even Powaqa hadn't told him the truth about the situation on the ground in Los Sombres. So what kind of big hero was he going to be, anyway?

'I guess I was just so focused on getting here and finding this shit that I didn't think much about why I was doing it.'

'You're doing it to protect yourself from shine, remember?' There was a nervous laugh in her voice.

'See, I wanted the city wasted so all this would be over,' he said. 'You got to realize, for two years I cursed out the lights for shining. When you hid from those exo-Protectors . . . I don't know how to say this. Where I come from, robots are good guys. You can trust robots. They don't go psycho on you.'

He didn't know what it was he saw in her face. Sadness. Disappointment. Bitterness. Something along those lines; he felt unsophisticated compared to her.

'So are you taking those pills or what?'

'I'll do it later.'

She twisted her mouth at that, gave him a look like his mother used to give him pre-Fall, when he made some lame-ass excuse for not brushing his teeth.

'That is pure resistance,' she said, shaking her head. 'Self-destructive. If I hadn't just seen you ignore the call of the red line, I'd say you were shined to resist taking that pill.'

He walked away from her. 'I'm not shined. And I'm not immature,' he said. 'Save the bossy shit for Elsa.'

She guffawed at that. 'Are you kidding? Elsa's the bossy one.

Come on, let's get out of here. I don't like leaving her for too long. The *good guys* might do a house-to-house and find her.'

'Well, *tou*-fucking-*ché*,' he muttered.

Roksana was in a hurry to get back. She was tense. She would-n't let him walk alongside, but kept pulling ahead of him.

'What's your problem?' he kept asking. 'Do you hate me because we're on opposite sides?'

'I don't hate you.'

'You're just . . . suddenly not talking to me.'

She slowed, let him catch up. As they walked side by side she swung her head from side to side in frustration. 'Xavier. You're stupid if you don't take those pills. You think I don't know how it feels to be out of the loop? I'm seventeen years old and I've never had a Ride on any shine. *Nada.* My mother was toked to the gills on lightborns. My father practically *invented* the shit. And me? Blind as a bat. So believe me, I can under-stand how it feels to want something that everybody else seems to have. But you know what? I'm the only person I know in this town who is over the age of twelve and not fucked up by shine. Well, besides you. We are it. You don't seriously want to mess with that, do you?'

'I don't know,' he said. 'Do you?'

'I don't have a choice,' she said.

'Your father, he's a Rider. What does he say? About your problem. If it's a problem.'

She grabbed his arm and pulled him down a side street, avoiding a strand of the red line.

'He's got more important shit to worry about.'

'Like fixing the Field, right? Is it your dad who's organizing all this? Is that why you don't want to talk about him? Is your dad in bed with FallN?'

Roksana burst out laughing at this.

'What's so funny?'

'Nothing, it's just . . . how can I put this? My dad keeps a real low profile, Xavier.'

'So you're not going to introduce me?'

'If I were you, I'd pop a shitload of those pills and then start looking for my horse. I'd get the hell out of here fast.'

'And would you get the hell out of quarantine, too? You know what it's like to have a shiny mother. What do you think I should do with her?'

'Take her with you. I can give you a submission beam. I know how to code it – don't look at me like that. It's easy. All the exo-protectors have them. She'll do whatever you want as long as the beam's on. You sneak across the border and take her to a good hospital in another state. And then you live your life.'

'I see you have all my problems solved. A good hospital? Uh, ever heard of health insurance? As in, we don't have any? And what about money?'

'I can give you about eighty grand in cash. You get the bus to Albuquerque or Houston and you just quietly blend in.'

'Wait a minute,' he laughed. 'You just met me. Why do you want to give me your stash like that? What about you? Couldn't you and Elsa do the same thing? Why are you still here?'

'Money doesn't mean anything to me right now. I work here. I'm part of something bigger. Which reminds me . . . I have to get in touch with Elsa. Take your melatonin. Be sane, Xavier. Be whole. Just do it. You know you want to.'

He knew she was right. If he left the quarantine zone, there was a whole world out there. Why risk brain injury just to become an adult and deal with their 'issues'? If Rex was stupid enough to give everything up for sex, then Rex was just that stupid.

Xavier took one of the loose bottles of pills out of his cargo pants pocket. He popped the seal and pulled the cotton out. The capsules glistened like little eggs. He shook one into his palm.

'Take two,' Roksana said nervously.

'OK, OK. You got any water?'

She swung her backpack off her shoulders and knelt, rummaging. Then she squinted up at Xavier, and past Xavier, and he saw her face change. Her expression was almost comical, a parody of alarm.

She drew breath to shout and reached up towards him at the same time, but it was too late.

Something heavy fell on him. A person, all elbows and knees. He hit the ground and cracked his head against the bumper of a van. Through everything after that he was disoriented. He felt a woman's slight, soft body scrambling over him and caught a glimpse of manicured nails as her chestnut hair slapped him in the face. A red silk dress flared in the light and her knee caught him in the mouth and she was grabbing at him, tearing the bottle out of his hands. He heard her voice speaking Russian even as someone else rolled him on his back and she planted her bare foot on his chest as though he were a conquered land.

Xavier tried to roll over. Men's voices.

'I got this one. Pick up the shit.'

'Gimme the bag.'

A black duffel bag hit the ground near Xavier's head. Coloured blobs were moving across his field of vision, and he fought back sickness. Through this miasma he could see with hyperreal clarity several black capsules of melatonin, lying at angles on the dry pavement. One of the men dropped the cardboard box of melatonin into the duffel bag and then turned a bright light on Xavier. Xavier tried to shut his eyes but found he couldn't make his eyelids close. He had no choice but to watch as the woman crouched down and picked up every single capsule with manic fervour. She glanced at Xavier once and gave him a sharp-toothed smile; she was beautiful and feral, and the red evening dress she was wearing was in shreds but there were diamonds around her neck. The bottoms of her bare feet were black.

'Irina!' Roksana was shouting, and he saw her sneakers lift off the ground as one of the men picked her up from behind and shook her down for melatonin.

'Irina, this is unacceptable! Stop this so we can talk. You owe me that at least. Irina!'

But it was already over. The woman walked away backwards across the deserted street, smiling and holding up the two bottles like trophies. One man dumped Roksana and joined the second, stepping over Xavier as if he were just a piece of shit lying on the ground. They both trained their flashlights on Xavier.

The woman called, 'Soon you will thank me, stopping you for taking the dangerous pollutant. You must stay pure.'

Xavier sat up, and started retching.

How to be a Model or Just Look Like One

'Irina!' Roksana screamed. 'Come back here!'

She leaped up and started to pursue her family's house-keeper, but Irina was already some distance away, still walking backwards with that taunting smile on her face. As Roksana got closer, Irina's necklace gave off a dazzling flash and the two men escorting her abandoned Xavier and moved like dogs to a whistle. They planted themselves in front of Roksana as Irina turned her back and quickened her pace, her tattered red dress trailing after her like a splash of blood.

'Your father would not approve of intervention,' Irina called over her shoulder. 'Don't meddle, little guinea pig. Stay in your cage and be good.'

Roksana pulled up short just outside of grabbing range of the men. Both were built like linebackers. She didn't know them; she'd have remembered them if she had seen either of them before.

'Whoa, easy,' she said. 'Who are you guys working for? If you get that melatonin back for me, I can make it worth your while.'

They stared down at Roksana mutely. They were clean, they smelled of Right Guard, and they were giving her the look that security guards at shows used to give you, back in the days when bands used to come to Los Sombres: calculating, aloof. Dominant.

Smug.

The first guy pulled out a Maglite and flicked it over her.

'What makes you think we work for anybody?'

'Never mind, Jack,' said the second man, in an accent bizarrely similar to Irina's. 'Lightborn means nothing to her. She is blind. Leave her. She is only a model.'

Jack's feeds flickered and Roksana's eye picked up the sun-flash off Irina's necklace again . . . and she knew that necklace. Those were Mitch's diamonds. Stolen.

Almaz, huh? she thought.

Roksana glanced back at Xavier. He had just finished throwing up.

'Please,' she whispered to the men. 'You don't have to follow her. I'll treat you better than she does. I can help you.'

The second man looked freaked. Now his accent was American. He said, 'Don't mess around. There is no *she*, all right?'

Irina had stopped beside a pile of rubble outside Accessory Place. She held two bottles pressed to her voluptuous, half-bared breasts. She was even skinnier than Roksana remembered, and her collarbone stood out sharply. The men still acted like she wasn't even there.

'Hey!' Roksana shouted at her. 'I saved your life, so what the fuck, Irina? Do you even remember it? You owe me. What do you want with a bunch of melatonin?'

Irina didn't answer. Her face slackened and her feedback lights flickered. The diamonds flashed.

'Come on,' Roksana wheedled. 'At least come back over and we can talk about it.'

Irina shook her head, not laughing anymore. She reminded Roksana of a three-year-old who dangles a cell phone over the toilet, enjoying the reactions of everyone around her.

'How's Dmitri?' Roksana said suddenly, taking a gamble. Irina had always been batty about her son. 'He must miss you so much. Have you talked to him lately?'

For an instant Irina's expression showed a crack.

'I'm sure we could contact him for you,' Roksana said, rushing in to the gap in Irina's control. 'Do you have a number for him?'

Roksana really worked it. She put all her powers of persuasion into her eyes and her voice and her gestures. Irina was the first shined person Roksana had ever seen, before Roksana had become FallN, before she had acquired any street-smarts, back when she'd been just another victim. If Roksana could win over Irina, she would have proven she was on top of shit for real. And she needed to be on top of shit, because everybody knew that either you were on top of your shit or it was on top of you, this being the non-negotiable nature of life.

Irina produced a dazzling, sharp-toothed smile. She drew a breath and the diamonds coruscated, throwing shine. It was unmistakable. Those rocks were loaded.

'This is my city now,' Irina said.

It was Roksana's turn to laugh.

'You? Look at you! You don't even have shoes on.'

'No, but I have the ice.' Her hand went to her necklace.

'It isn't your city. Los Sombres will be free. My father and I will see to that. If you're so smart, why don't you help us? Come on, Irina. Be on our side. Give us the melatonin and I'll let you keep the necklace. We both know you stole it.'

Irina put a bottle under each armpit so that she could clap her hands together in slow, sarcastic applause. She put her fingers between her lips and whistled. Then she snapped her fingers and whirled around, flashing long legs and red silk.

This time her lackeys went too, nodding to each other as if Irina wasn't there and they just happened to want to go that way.

'Fuck,' said Roksana, and fought back tears. 'Fucking *fuck*, I can't believe that just happened.'

She turned and dragged herself back to Xavier, who was holding his head in both hands.

'Friend of yours?' he said.

Just Another Zombie Apocalypse

'I can't believe she's been here all this time. I haven't seen her since the day I saved her life. She wasn't even lucid then, but she must have stolen my mother's diamonds.'

They were pedalling towards the Hide. It was late afternoon.

'She should be dead,' Roksana added.

'Looks like she made a comeback.'

Roksana said nothing.

He added, 'I think my head is cracked.'

'You need to rest,' she said, as they came to the turn that led to Courthouse Row. 'Those guys tried to control you. You know, with the flashlights? But you have't been primed. You haven't had an induction script to teach your visual cortex how to process shine. So the headache is probably just from getting hit on the head.'

'Yeah? I feel like shit. They took the melatonin. I can't believe we were so close . . .'

'I know. We'll figure something out. For now, go back to the Hide and tell Elsa what happened. I have to go down to Canal Street. Elsa knows what to do while I'm gone.'

She rode off. Suddenly too tired to pedal, Xavier pushed the bike up the dusty road to American Woman.

Elsa was in the Hide. She had spread a map of Los Sombres on the floor. There were magic-marker arrows pointing to and from the unfinished Coyote Springs stadium in different colours. Having abandoned the map, now she was talking to Roksana through a headset while typing something into a database, even as her eyes followed a Katrice moodie on another screen. Over her shoulder, Xavier watched singer/dancer/contortionist Katrice sidewind her way over a bed of black lava. The part where Katrice put both legs behind her head and walked on her hands was pretty interesting, but Elsa fastforwarded over it to settle on camcorder cuts of Los Sombres during the Fall. Generic mean-anything pop lyrics wobbled in Katrice's over-gospelled throat.

I cry for you oh baby I cry for you

Katrice's heavily modified voice came over news footage of defenestration, arson, gangbangs, corpses lying in the street. Helicopters airlifting the injured. Katrice sucking her own toes with a pink tongue.

Oh, I feel you

And pre-Fall clips, presumably a desperate effort at irony from the videographers, of skinny dreadlocked Riders with their artfully shined jewellery, feet up on the glowing tables in Tito's Café.

Katrice hurling herself into Hawaiian tidepools wearing only a thong and bodypaint.

Baby, remember, it's just another zombie apocalypse . . .

Elsa picked up Xavier in her peripheral vision. She pointed to the screen and jigged up and down in her roller chair. Her finger indicated the corner of a white building just visible in the background of one of the pre-Fall Rider cuts.

'Look! Look, there's my school!'

Just as quickly, the glimpse of Elsa's school was gone. Katrice started to do a back walkover and, as the camera zoomed up the length of her bare legs, Elsa flicked the remote off and turned back to what she'd been typing.

She was crying.

'Don't cry,' Xavier heard himself saying. 'The Fall is the past. It's the future we really got to worry about.'

Elsa wiped away her tears. She glanced at her Spiderman watch.

'You're right about that. Cue FallN.'

'What?'

Elsa's fingers scampered across the keyboard and she leaned into the mic, saying, 'Now we have FallN for you, better late than never, with the latest survival information coming along with these beautiful embeds. FallN, you with us out there?'

'What do you mean, FallN?' Xavier said, jumping in his skin. He looked around the Hide as if he expected the cannibal woman with her Uzis to step out of the shadows.

A rich voice flowed out of the speakers and into the Hide. The voice was familiar, the accent strange.

'You know I am with you, Elsa baby, and welcome to the Shine Kitchen, everybody. It looks like we got another dark night ahead of us, but FallN got the recipe for a new world . . .'

Xavier went still. He knew that voice. It was FallN . . . and it was Roksana. He couldn't even take in the words; he was listening to sound and cadence and accent, and with every passing moment he felt increasingly stupid and deceived.

'She's a fake,' he whispered, glaring at Elsa. 'That's not FallN, that's Roksana.'

Elsa gave him a look that said, *Yeah, I know, stupid.*

'FallN isn't even a real person!'

'So? Who is?'

He opened his mouth to argue and ended up putting his hand on his head and sitting down quickly before he fell down. Elsa was on him right away.

'Xavier, you OK? You hurt? You should've said.'

Xavier felt very much like crying but he was not going to cry in front of a nine-year-old girl, so he cleared his throat hard and blinked a few times and said, 'Do you know somebody called Irina? Runs around like a gunslinger in a red dress. She took our melatonin.'

'Oh, man, I'm sorry, Xavier. Hang on, I just gotta—' She leaned over and cued up a track, listened for a minute, and then pulled the headphones half-off and rolled her chair back towards him. She started rolling up the map. 'So . . . Roksana didn't tell you. About FallN.'

'No. I don't get it, Elsa. Why would this woman want melatonin? She's obviously shined up already.'

'Rocky already told me to look for her. We'll get to the bottom of it.'

'You really think she's all that. Roksana, I mean, or should I say FallN?'

'She's like my sister, Xavier. What's the matter?'

'Nothing.' The word 'sister' still hurt, physically, every time he heard it.

He said, 'She thinks her father is going to cure everybody in the city. That's mad stupid. Isn't it?'

Elsa gave a complicated shrug.

'I don't know . . . he's a Rider for real, Roksana's dad. He knows things. We've been in real trouble a couple times, and somehow he knew about it.'

'You met him?'

'Couple of times. Mostly he leaves messages. Letters. She carries pictures of them both. Her mom and dad, before the Fall. I got pictures of my mom, too. Wanna see?'

He nodded and she took out a little white Bratz pocketbook containing lip gloss, a glitter pen, and a heart-shaped photo album.

They looked at pictures of Elsa's sixth birthday party. Elsa's mother had been a sleek, smiling woman – way too young to die. Elsa looked at her picture a long time, tears dripping silently down her face.

A red light started flashing on the control board. Elsa shot across the locker room on her wheeled chair and punched the button next to it. She leaned into the mic. 'What happened?'

Xavier couldn't hear the other side of the exchange.

'Where are you now?' Elsa said, turning to one of her screens and pulling up a map. 'OK, you can go down to the bus station and there's a sandwich place with some protection. It's clear over there. Or . . . let's see, you're too far from Hair and Now . . . what about the library?' There was a pause as Elsa listened. 'Oh. OK, you know what I think? I think you should just hook up the light on your bike and come here. You don't want to spend the night like that.'

Pause.

'What's going on?' Xavier demanded, standing over Elsa; but she just turned her back on him and waved him away.

'OK. OK. No, it's not a panic . . . What do you mean, Irina? Holy shit. OK. No, I am not watching Katrice. I swear to god . . . all right, but be *careful*. See you later.'

She turned to Xavier.

'All the beacons have gone down again. Nothing to do with us. Rocky thinks Irina's doing it. We don't know how. But we'd better be prepared for more shelling.'

'Shit . . .'

'Rocky went after Irina and now she thinks Irina is following her. She doesn't want to lead Irina back here, because if Irina gets hold of the music-embedding system we have, she could potentially take over the red line. I know, I know, it's far-fetched but we can't risk letting Irina damage Dr Ansari's work. So . . . you and me have to sit tight. We better stay in the Hide just to be safe. It's the most secure part of the building, and if all the lights are down, the missiles are going to be falling pretty much everywhere. We could get hit.'

'Sheesh,' Xavier said. 'All I wanted was Kiss.'

'Also. Rocky said to give you some Advil.'

He swallowed two tablets with warm, stale beer. He was tempted to take the whole bottle. A feeling of pressure was building up behind his eyes.

Out in the pool room, the ducks started up an alarmed chorus of quacks. Flapping noises echoed. Splashing.

'That's not a good sound,' Elsa said. 'It means—'

The first sounds of impact went off outside. Elsa crowded close to Xavier and he put his arm around her. More thundery sounds followed, like big footsteps shaking the ground.

'It reminds me of animals,' Elsa said, and they crept into the Hide and sat on the floor. Xavier felt cornered.

'I think we should leave,' he said.

'We can't,' she whispered, pressing against him. 'Just try to chill out.'

There weren't many explosions. Planes could be heard flying over, but even this didn't go on for long. Soon there was silence. No planes, no missiles, just the soft static hum of the equipment and the deeper drone of the generator.

A long time passed. Elsa tried to get Roksana on the radio.

'She should be back by now. Her set's switched off,' she said. 'I hope—'

'Quiet!' Xavier hissed. 'Did you hear that?'

He pointed to the ceiling. There was a scratching sound coming from high overhead. Something was above the false ceiling of the office, way up in the rafters of the building.

Elsa mouthed, *'Pigeons?'*

Then there was a dragging sound.

Xavier whispered, *'Something's on the roof.'*

They both looked up and waited for the next sound.

'It's too high for cats to get up there,' Elsa whispered. 'And I don't know why—'

She fell silent as there was a definite pattern of footfalls above. The sound was magnified by the fact that everything else was silent.

'Stay here,' Xavier said. She didn't argue as he left the Hide. The health club had fire doors at the back that led on to an alley where dumpsters were kept. He slid out and wedged a piece of cardboard in the lip of the door to stop it from locking behind him. With the door shut, it was fucking dark outside. This was a kind of relief to Xavier's aching head. The only light came from above: a faint glow emanating from the roof of American Woman.

He could hear clicking sounds from farther down the alley, in the direction of the courthouse. He knew the sounds well from the simulations on Rex's video games. They came in a predictable series: mechanical clicking, like the sound of a metal insect; then police-radio-type static; then the high-pitched whine of echolocation. Precision mechanisms whirring and grinding into position. Then more clicking, static, echolocation.

The idea of running into one of the machines he'd used to worship? Not so appealing, not anymore.

Xavier turned to go back inside, but then he heard more noises, closer at hand. Someone *was* on the roof. He thought of the rovers Roksana had spoken about. He thought of crazy Irina and her bodyguards. He thought Katrice lip-synching 'Zombie Apocalypse'.

A silhouette appeared against the glow. Only one person; but they pointed a flashlight at him. It dazzled his eyes; he threw his forearm up defensively, peeling his lips back in a squint. The light felt raw in his eyes.

'Get the *fuck* back inside!' the figure said. 'You scared me shitless.'

Xavier slapped his palm against his chest.

'Son of a bitch, Roksana, it's you.'

Every Little Thing She Does Is Magic

'Of course it's me,' Roksana said. Her heart was racing. She'd thought both kids would be asleep by now.

Xavier was not amused. 'What are you doing up there?'

'Checking the shine,' Roksana invented in a hurry. 'To make sure we're still invisible. We are. So go back inside.'

Out of the corner of her eye she could see Damien getting to his feet. He still had most of his clothes on, but the situation was not good. Xavier would *not* understand, and she didn't want Elsa to find out about her sex life at all. Elsa had been through enough.

But Xavier wasn't going away.

'What are you talking about? And get that thing out of my eyes . . .'

'Sorry.' She turned the beam off. She sighed as she realized she'd have to explain. 'There are lights on the roof keeping anyone from noticing this building. My dad made them. It's how we keep our safehouses, like Hair and Now. Shinies can't see them. Neither can the cameras.'

'Cameras don't *see*, people do.'

'Ah, but AI cameras *do* see, and my dad's invisibility shine works on the reticular activating system. Most AIs have the same style of RAS as humans because they were designed based on us, hence the reason why cameras and AIs can't see us, either.'

'I totally didn't get what you just said.'

'You don't have to get it,' Roksana retorted. 'It works. Didn't you notice how every other building on this street has been hit?'

'But we can't be really invisible, that's crazy . . .'

'We're invisible enough, unless they're specifically looking for us and they know where and how to look to bypass the way their RAS has been fooled. But I'm not sure what's going on with Irina. She knows about the invisibility. She may know where we are. So we need to be on guard. I'll stay up here tonight.'

'You're going to sleep up there?'

'Yeah. Then, in the morning, I'll find another way around your problem with the melatonin. I'm going to need you to stay here and keep an eye on Elsa. I won't be able to take you with me, where I'm going.'

He didn't look happy about it, but she was older than him and she was looking down on him from a height of about fifteen feet.

'My head is killing me,' he said.

'You might have a concussion. Go back inside. I got it covered.'

Eventually he listened to her.

Roksana returned to the middle of the roof, where Damien was waiting among the planters full of tomatoes and herbs and zucchinis.

'These zucchinis are too small for you, baby.' The growly, low way he said it drew laughter out of her in spite of herself.

He was just so hot. Every time she saw him, she wanted to devour him.

She had met him on the red line, a year ago. Roksana had just come off the air and was still feeling all bold and FallN-like. He'd been stripped to the waist, muscled nicely, and singing along in pretty good Spanish to a boombox Tito El Bambino song that FallN herself had just introduced on the Shine Kitchen. She'd been staring at his body, because she couldn't help it, and he had tossed his head to shake the sweat off his long, bleach-blond dreads. The next thing Roksana knew, he had caught her eye. He was smiling at her.

As Xavier had learned today, red-liners didn't usually make eye contact. Red-liners didn't usually tell dirty knock-knock jokes while they hauled cables for the portable lights that travelled around Los Sombres. Red-liners didn't dazzle you with their perfect smile, but Damien had done all those things.

Red-liners didn't step off the line and go with you into the nearest Dunkin' Donuts for a quick . . . uh, donut-dunking session.

Roksana and Damien did not have a deep relationship. Damien had been damaged in the Fall, and sometimes he did bizarre things. Sometimes, after he was drugged with sex and talking crazy, she had to shine him to get him back on the line. But – as lame as it sounded – he was really nice. And she thought that over the course of the year, as Amir had worked the city's lights, Damien had gotten better. She even thought that what had begun between them as a simple case of blowing off steam had maybe evolved into a sort of . . . thing.

Sometimes he brought her flowers. OK, they were wilted and sometimes they were plastic. But he tried.

'I am good for you,' he would say, with the utter conviction of the shiny. He was right.

And tonight, she needed him. Because everything was getting out of hand and she was scared.

When they were finished and lay with their bodies overlapping so that it was hard to be sure who ended where and who began, she felt happy. They didn't really know each other, except for sex. That made it so much easier.

'I love being with you in the invisible place,' Damien murmured. 'It's such a vacation from reality. Where are we, really?'

Roksana chuckled. 'We're anywhere you want to be.'

'That's what I thought. You're magic, Rocky.'

Around two she woke and made Damien leave. He was groggy, and still kind of horny, and in the end she had to use the Feynman on him. She felt bad, but what choice did she have? Damien wasn't that stable, and she couldn't risk an encounter between him and either of the kids if they woke up.

He nuzzled her hair. Then, as the shine took hold, he seemed to suddenly remember something important. He tugged on his clothes, scrambled off the roof and ran down the alley in the direction of the helpmeets' plaza. She watched his lean form, admiring his retreating ass, until he turned a corner and was gone.

She switched off the Feynman's light.

She couldn't go back to sleep. As the night wore on she practised what to say to her father.

'*I know I'm not supposed to come here,*' she'd begin, as he was freaking out because she'd violated his inner sanctum. As he was twitching and tearing at his hair. She'd say, '*Irina is invisible to shinies – including you. She's got Mom's diamonds. You put shine in them, didn't you?*'

She hoped and prayed he wouldn't tell her that he'd *given* the diamonds to Irina. Because she really couldn't take that.

She had to see him. Shit was slipping away from her.

Maybe her father would be in his power trip mode, where he would shed his nervousness like a second skin. Maybe he would act all commanding. If that was the case, maybe he'd even say that the lights going down were all part of his plan. That was what she wanted to hear, anyway. She wanted to hear that everything was still on target, still on track, to cure the people of Los Sombres.

They'd come too far for it to fall apart now.

Roksana didn't mean to fall asleep. But when she woke, the sun was already painting stripes of shadow across the downtown skyscrapers. She dragged herself to her feet. It would take all morning to get to the hospital on foot, and she would have to be out of there before another nightfall if she was to get her broadcast done.

The hospital glared white. She could see the heat swimming over the parking lot, and her back was already wet from her hurried walk across town. No visible guards. Roksana wasn't vulnerable to the subjugation beams the exo-protectors would be using on intruders, but that didn't mean she could just walk through the front doors. She went around the side of the building, looking for accessible windows and finding none. Then, near the back of the hospital where the old oncology division used to be, she found a corner she could scale. There was a glassed-in stairwell that presented a metal lip about two inches wide running right up the side of the building. Roksana spat on her hands, backed off the wall a few strides, and then ran at it.

It took her five tries before she got enough height to grab the bottom of the second-storey window ledge. She wedged herself into the corner, fingers slipping on the metal frame. She would have to go all the way up to the roof.

Between the third and fourth floors she paused to rest, her face pressed against the dusty glass.

Something moved inside the stairwell.

Roksana jerked back and nearly let go. An Angel was picking his way down the stairs, his visor's light blinking feebly.

There was nothing Roksana could do. She hung there, knowing that it was only the fact that the Angel's gaze was trained on his own feet that stopped him from seeing her. She knew that Angels' tongue cameras didn't give them very good peripheral vision, and apparently the government was too cheap to put in software for colour. Still. Roksana was splayed across the glass like a flying squirrel.

The Angel was scrawny. He looked more like a patient than staff, and he moved as if caution was an old habit he'd never now forget. It took him forever to get down those stairs. Finally he reached the bottom of the flight, turned his back to Roksana, and continued down.

Roksana's heart was jackrabbiting. She put her foot into the corner again and shifted her weight, grabbing the seams of bricks to pull herself higher.

By the time she got to the top she was soaked in sweat and seeing stars. There was a lot of bird shit on the roof, and tarry pebbles stuck to the bottoms of her sneakers. She pulled up her T-shirt and used the bottom half of it to rub her face and neck down. Her stomach was cramping with nerves. She hoped she wasn't going to have to take a crap out here in the open.

She looked across the roof, trying to decide which way to go down into the building. There was a maintenance entrance with its security camera smashed. There were air vents; those would be no fun. The helipad looked long unused, the glass of the access doors shattered. Splinters of glass sparked on the faded paint of the landing pad.

Complete toss-up. Either way she was probably screwed, so . . . She crossed her fingers and climbed through the door at the helipad, past the dead elevator and down the stairs.

This part of the hospital seemed deserted. There were no lights on, and daylight crept in only faintly in places where doors to patients' rooms had been left open. Roksana's sneakers squeaked, no matter how she tried to creep carefully. She suspected that the searing heat up here had played a role in the failure of the cameras; the Angels certainly didn't frequent this floor. The toilets were repulsive, so Roksana peed in a janitor's bucket. This floor was familiar, but she was trying not to dwell on the reason why. She would only feel weak if she thought about her mother's stay here in the months before the Fall, not to mention the anguished weeks between her mother's disappearance from the hospital and Roksana's rediscovery of Mitch, half-alive, in the prana house. A fat woman, reduced to skin and bones, tricked by shine into believing that the universe would feed her.

Roksana blotted her eyes, swallowed. Told herself she still had a mother. Not a perfect mother; not a functional mother. But Mitch was alive.

She went down a flight. Lights here. The white noise of fans. All they did was move the heat around. She watched a pair of Angels walking down the corridor. There was a noise of TV, people talking. Roksana wondered how many people the Angels were caring for here. She wondered how they did it.

And would they be merciful if they caught her sneaking around?

Down again. And again. Finally she came to the ground floor, but the fire door to the basement had been closed and barred shut. Roksana was forced across the hospital to a different bank of elevators. This took her past the main reception area; ironically, right by the sliding glass doors she had gone to such pains to bypass, an hour ago now.

A group of patients slouched against the corridor walls. They all looked old. Beaten. An Angel with a Feynman was hunkered down beside a wilted ficus, muttering Vietnamese to a woman in a wheelchair.

Roksana indexed the position of the cameras and then ducked into a doorway as the motion sensors picked her up. She wasn't sure how secure this place was. The Angels needed protection, of course. But how much? Shinies might not be zombies out of Raccoon City, but they weren't known for their ingenuity, either.

She found another bank of elevators without being stopped. These weren't working, either. She took the stairs to the basement and the temperature dropped a little. In the semi-dark her head cleared. She saw the camera before it saw her. She ducked back around the corner.

She didn't dare move closer. She would have to take the thing out. She pulled out her .38.

She would have to do it in one, or it would record her.

Just pretend it's a rat. She'd shot enough of those in the aerobics studio of American Woman. She waited for the camera to look into the recess where double doors marked 'Cafeteria' lay.

Pop! The glass cracked, but the camera was still working. It swung its eye towards her. She reloaded and got it again. It was still up.

Fuck. She charged the camera, leaped up, and ripped it off the wall. Threw it down and stomped on it. Then she ran to the cafeteria doors and hauled them open.

Somewhere above, an alarm sounded.

Sunshine

Xavier was uneasy. He still had a splitting headache and his ears rang. He was jumpy as a cat. He hated sitting around waiting for things to happen. He had done too much of that in the last two years. This was the time for action.

Elsa tried to entertain him. She played him music. She turned on the TV. She even let him look through one of the Feynmans, with its payload of shine data and inscrutable statistics about the behaviour of the shinies. He flipped through files of shine, letting them play across his eyes; he felt nothing.

When Elsa saw him pouring lightborns into his eyes, she snatched the Feynman away.

'That's Russian Roulette,' she said. 'Don't be stupid.'

'I don't feel anything. It's no big deal.'

'The fact that you're doing it at all is . . . suspect,' Elsa said. 'You haven't had kisspeptin inhibitors for a while. Don't take a chance on getting primed up.'

He squinted at her; despite four more Advils he still had the headache, and it was turning his mood foul.

'Are you sure you're only nine? You talk like you're a lot older.'

'Yes, I am only nine. I can't help it if I have a large vocabulary. Now, please, relax.'

Relax. It was one of those words that, if people had to say it to you, then you probably couldn't do it.

'I'll give her one day,' Xavier said. 'After that – no offence, but I can't stay here babysitting you any longer. I got to get the melatonin and get out.'

'You make it sound like you're guaranteed to find it.'

'I will find it.'

'Roksana's grandmother lives in Sonoma, and Roksana always says we could go there if push came to shove. Then she says if she went there, she'd be a freak because she doesn't respond to shine.'

Elsa's reply was so ludicrous – who cared that you were a freak if you were *alive*? – that it made him realize she was right about one thing: he had to lighten up. She was only a kid. He sighed and rubbed his head.

'You could go to the Hopi,' he said. 'Indians like freaks.'

Elsa gave him a frown that said, 'You're weird.'

'I mean in general, they're really a pro-freak type of culture.'

'O-kaaay. But don't forget. She's FallN. She's her father's daughter. She has a mission here.'

'So it's like, here in Los Sombres, she's somebody. In California, she'd be just a freaky victim of a freaky disaster. Is that it?'

'Sort of, and let's not even talk about the albatross of Roksana's survivor guilt.'

The ground rumbled, and the ceiling lights swung and clanked. Elsa cringed.

'But it's daytime . . .' Xavier began, and then it occurred to him that if people were bombing you in the first place, it was foolish to expect them to adhere to rules about what time of day they could do it.

There was a long silence. Elsa tried calling Roksana.

'She's got her set switched off again.' Then: 'Damn. I need something to do.'

Elsa got up and went out into the office. She rummaged around and found toys. Incredulous, Xavier watched her start to play with a set of plastic horses and riders. As if she was trying to prove that she really *was* only nine years old. As if this was any old day.

The headache was fading now, but he felt itchy, twitchy. Jumpy. And a little sick.

'I want to go out and round up them dogies,' Elsa's chestnut horse announced.

But the Western Rider doll chastised in a Texas accent, 'No, you can't go out until I braid your mane, Sunshine.'

Xavier felt increasingly agitated as Elsa played. Muffled sounds of falling mortars reached them; every so often there would be a really loud impact, and then Elsa would pause and go, 'Woo-hoo, Sunshine, that was a close'n,' in a cliché Old West voice. Then she'd make clip-clop noises with her tongue. The voice of Sunshine was high-pitched and squeaky.

'I'm going to jump over that exo-protector.'

'No, Sunshine, don't do that.'

'I have to do it, I'm shined-up.'

'No, Sunshine listen to me.'

Clip-clop, clip-clop. Whinny.

'Good girl, Sunshine. Have some hay.'

Xavier jumped up.

'I got to get out of here. I can't just sit here like a rabbit in a hole.'

'What? Hey, come back!' Elsa cried. But he was already through reception and out into the street.

It was hot. There was dust in the air, and through the dust the lights were still shining. High-pitched shrieks of falling mortars on the north side. Xavier shivered. Hands in his pockets, he walked up to the end of the parking lot and back. Nobody else was out. Nobody else was that stupid.

'Xavier!' Elsa's voice reached him from the entrance. 'Get

back here! The planes will see you and they'll go for you. Get back here right now.'

She still had Sunshine the plastic horse clutched in her hand.

Xavier could see the planes coming in. He had the bizarre urge to wave his hands at them, taunt them, pull down his pants and moon them.

'Xavier! Get in here!'

Elsa was running across the parking lot towards him. 'Xavier, you're being shined. Get in here! Don't you see? It's probably a suicide lightborn – they're really easy to catch. You have to fight it. Get in here now.'

What the fuck. That couldn't be true. He wasn't shined . . .

Xavier felt hot. Elsa was picking her way across broken glass; he could see her lips moving as she chastised him but now he couldn't hear over the increasing noise of the planes. The image of her mouth moving silently flashed in his mind like a burning brand.

The feeling in his stomach was the same as the feeling he'd had when he walked in the bathroom and there was his mother kneeling on the floor, and the water overflowing on the tiles, and the shiny purple Barney bubblebath container bobbing in the tub: *too late.*

He charged Elsa and picked her up in a running tackle. Dopplering bombsound, like bird whistles. His own breath, grunting in his belly. Then the ground shaking. They reached the entrance to American Woman and ducked into the darkness.

Something hit the roof, and the plate glass windows out front shattered, and the concrete walls buckled, and the metal bars embedded in the concrete bent slowly over. Xavier was still holding Elsa and he tried to pull her deeper into the building, past the reception desk to the hallway. But he couldn't make her move.

She was screaming. She let go of him and he moved a couple of steps away and looked back. One of her legs was trapped under the edge of the formica reception desk, which had col-

lapsed. There was dust everywhere, and the wind from outside came through the ceiling and over the shards of plate glass
that had fallen like guillotines on the spot where Elsa had been
playing just a few minutes before.

'*Madre de dios*,' Xavier said, but he couldn't hear his own
voice, only the sound of crickets and oceans. Elsa didn't seem to
care about her leg being trapped. She was scrabbling madly at
the carpet, trying to get to the Western Rider doll that she had
left behind when she went outside to call Xavier. A sheet of
fallen glass separated her from it.

He tried to talk to her, to ask her if she was OK, but he still
couldn't hear himself.

'Get away from me! You're shined. Get *away!*'

The terror in her face made him stop and back off.

He got the doll and held it out to her.

'I'm OK now,' he said, and realized it was true. 'I don't know
what happened back there. But it won't happen again. I'm not
going to hurt you.'

She was panting, trembling, right on the edge of tears.

'Roksana told me they tried to shine you. Irina's people. She
told me to watch you.'

Everyone always knew more than him. Fucking Roksana/
FallN and her smart mouth. Xavier felt his nostrils flare in
anger, but he clamped down on it. Elsa was scared. He had to
calm her down.

'I haven't been primed. Whatever they did to me, it's not
sticking. I'm OK now. Come on, Elsa. I'm not crazy. We have to
get you out of there. How's your leg?'

Her voice broke. 'It hurts, stupid. It hurts so much.'

'Shh . . . OK, OK, I'm sorry about before. Come on. Let's get
you out of there.'

He squatted beside her and got his hands under the edge of
the desk.

'I'm going to hold it up for as long as I can. You have to pull your own leg out.'

'I can't move my leg.'

'Elsa. Grab your leg with both hands, and when I lift the desk, you just move it. Pretend it's a piece of wood. Ready? On three. One, two, *three!*'

She hissed as she slowly dragged the leg out of the path of the desk. Xavier's entire body was trembling as he held the counter up.

'OK,' she gasped, and he realized he would have to drop the load or his fingers would be trapped. As it came down, more rubble shifted above it. Sheets of broken glass slid down and crashed nearby. He picked up Elsa and carried her deeper into the building.

'I'm going to put you down here and then go see how we're getting out.'

'No, you can't leave me.'

She was starting to panic now. Xavier's mind was racing. He would have to find a helpmeet or something.

'We'll have to get you to the Angels,' he said.

'Angels? Don't you know their robots knock people out with subjugation beams? And then the exo-protectors run over the people sleeping in the streets. That's what happened to my mother. It's because of the Angels that she's dead.'

Her face started to crumple, but he squeezed her tighter. 'Don't go there. Not now. The Angels could be our only chance. The hospital's a long way, but I can carry you.'

'Roksana is at the hospital,' Elsa said, as if suddenly remembering. 'She went to see her father.'

So that was where the famous Rider was hiding. About time Xavier talked to him. He seemed to be the only dude in town who had some kind of grip.

'Let's go,' he said. 'You can bring Sunshine.'

The Lion, the Witch and the Frigidaire

Roksana dove through the doors and they swung closed behind her.

Darkness. She turned on her flashlight. The cafeteria smelled faintly rank. The counter where food had once been served was intact, and beyond it she could see ovens and refrigeration units lining the walls. Tables and chairs were folded and stacked along the walls. But it looked unused. The flashlight flickered over cardboard boxes and wooden crates: supplies, maybe, or weapons. Still, the place was an unlikely bomb shelter.

And an even more unlikely laboratory. But this was where Amir had told her to find him, in a real emergency.

She couldn't hear the alarms, but it would only be a matter of seconds before the door opened behind her. She shot towards the kitchen area, knowing there would be an external door somewhere. Vaulted over the counter and hit the deck beyond. Behind her, the security door swung open and three Angels walked in. One of them had a German Shepherd on a leash.

Shit.

Roksana glanced around wildly. Between a stainless steel sink and a walk-in freezer there was a shadowy gap, and from the depths of this gap shone a vertical slit of light. She crawled toward it.

A fridge. Not a stainless steel restaurant-kitchen refrigerator, but the kind you'd have in your house. Door ajar. Light coming out. But . . .

. . . there was something else inside. Coloured lights. A little kaleidoscope show of something, glimpsed through the thin aperture.

The dog was woofing and pulling at his leash, but the Angels were whispering to each other and into their headsets.

'We have sealed off the loading bay door,' a male Angel announced in a loud voice. 'You can't get out that way. Put your hands on your head and show yourself.'

The Angel's voice was shaking. They all slurred a little when they talked, because of the studs that hooked up their tongue cameras. But this was the sound of nerves.

The Angels were afraid of Roksana. They were afraid of a fight.

If they really had sealed off the back door already, she was fucked. But there was a warm draft coming from inside the fridge. FRIGIDAIRE read the metallic label . . . Roksana stretched out her hand and pulled the door open a little wider.

There was no back wall of the fridge. It acted as the door to a room.

And the show of coloured lights: had to be shine. It slipped into her eyes and curled around her brain . . . and had no effect at all.

Hah, thought Roksana. *Can't shine me.*

The dog was dragging the Angel holding it. Soon it would be around the corner of the cafeteria counter and into the kitchen. Roksana crawled into the fridge and shut the door behind her.

She was trapped. She had crawled into a small room whose only egress was a vent in the ceiling, high overhead.

Roksana took in the workstation, multiple screens all sleeping, and the evidence of her father's presence: a bedroll under the counter, empty cans and boxes stowed in plastic garbage bags. A pair of men's sneakers, size 9. She lifted the chair into the middle of the room and stood on it; she could get through the vent but it would be tricky. And noisy. Scuff marks on the ceiling indicated that Amir had used this exit before.

Outside, she could hear the dog sniffing and whining.

'You're on duty, Ramone,' a woman said. 'Leave that food alone.'

Ramone barked.

The door of the fridge swung open. Ramone and Roksana looked at each other. Ramone wagged his tail and gave a different, happy bark.

Roksana opened her mouth, her mind fumbling for some plausible explanation for what she was doing here, but before she could speak, the Angel pulled Ramone's head out of the fridge and shut the door again.

'Silly dog,' said the Angel. 'Martinez, is that back door definitely secure?'

Pause. The Angels seemed to move off. Faintly, Roksana heard one of them say, 'What? You just secured it now? It's too late. They're gone by now, goddamnit.'

'Never mind, Joon. At least nobody got hurt.'

Roksana sat very still. She had never had to rely on invisibility shine alone – not like this. But it was working. She had seen it work with her own eyes.

And her eyes, apparently, were the only ones in this city that could really be trusted.

But where was Amir?

It was like he stepped out to get a sandwich and never came back.

Endurance Thinker

Roksana had never dared imagine this one. Her father had been the only stability she'd had in the catastrophe of the Fall, and in the time since then he'd been her lifeline. Even in the past weeks, when he'd been out of touch, she hadn't really worried. He was tough. Yeah, he'd suffered in the Fall, just like everybody. He had that split-personality thing, where sometimes he was Old Nervous Amir and sometimes he was New Masterful Amir with no real predictable pattern – he was like a slot machine. She was used to that.

But neither version of her father would abandon the lab. Ever. Look, he'd left one of his Feynmans sitting right there, in the open. Sure, it was locked with an access code – nobody but him could use the shine. But he hadn't taken it with him or bothered to hide it – that meant he'd intended to come straight back. What was up with that?

Something bad had happened.

Her lip curled. She would not think about Irina.

Roksana looked around the workspace. The cushion of his chair was dented from where his ass had pressed all those times; even the dark blue pile of the fabric was flattened and starting to get shiny. Roksana sat down, drew her knees up to her chest, and let her head fall back so that she was staring at the ceiling. She followed its lines with her eyes. She studied its grubby fingerprints. She saw faces in the knots on the plywood.

She stayed there far too long. It was too tempting to pretend he'd just stepped out for a minute. Would be back later, with all his tics and his stammering and his funny way of holding his hands behind his back when he lectured – which was pretty much the only way Amir knew how to talk without being tripped up by speech impediments. She felt herself choking up, remembering all the things about her father that had used to annoy her. When he held court, he could fool you into thinking he was still teaching and Mitch was still running a restaurant and everybody had all their marbles. That the Fall never happened.

'We're all the same,' Amir had used to tell her, like he'd told his first-years. *'Two arms, two legs, one cortex slaved to an endocrine system designed in primeval times. So limiting. We're doomed to an essential apehood unless we can change our deepest programming. And let's face it: people have very little self-control. We're mostly a set of biological levers waiting to be pulled. But we can change that, and that's what shine can give us. Better neurochemical paths. New ways of being. Shine can literally change our minds for the better without the side effects of drugs, because all of the chemicals are made by our own brains.'*

It had been a speech. A performance. Then he'd say:

'With shine we can treat schizophrenia and bipolar disorder and OCD. But it doesn't have to stop there. The shine patterns that play their best music are the ones natural selection overlooked. Riders are discovering paths and potentials that we haven't even dreamed of. It's an exciting time. Why would you want to go bumping around in the darkness of your species' history when you could take matters into your own hands? Tell yourself what to think, be, feel. Humanity has an opportunity to transcend its own biological limitations.'

And here he'd pause dramatically.

'Of course, power is power. People like having their levers pulled; it's how they know they're alive in an increasingly wired world. With shine, the opportunities for corruption and abuse are as great as the opportunities for growth. That's why I stopped Riding and joined the University. In the course of seeking the perfect lightborn for weight control or sexual satisfaction we must exercise great care that shine remains safe and under our conscious control. After all, some light-borns being developed in the Field now are as complex as the AIs that regulate them. Imagine a zoo where the animals are as intelligent as the wardens.'

Many of her father's Rider colleagues had lampooned his conservatism.

Then the Fall had made them throw themselves out of windows and in front of buses, tripped them out like overloaded circuits.

Yes, Amir Ansari had seen it coming – for whatever that was worth. In his wisdom he had inherited a city in chaos, a paranoid nation outside the light quarantine, and a Field whose AIs had run amok. Not to mention a shine loop in his own head that divided him in two.

He had gone underground.

'Your m-m-mother and I c-can't leave,' he'd told Roksana. *'The city's been cut off to prevent the F-f-f-f-fall from spreading. But the same thing will happen out there eventually. So either we roll over and d-d-d-d-die, or we-or-orwe-or-or we deal with it.'*

'Deal with it?' Roksana had said, astonished.

'Y-yeah,' he'd said. *'I'm c-c-coming out of r-re-retirement. I'm g-going to Ride a fix.'*

Boom . . .

Roksana jumped in her skin, her reverie thwarted. The building didn't shake, and plaster dust wasn't falling. But the long rumbling sound was unmistakable. It was not thunder.

Bombs were falling.

Roksana shot out of her father's chair and started scrambling around his lab, picking things up at random. There was no time for sentiment. She had to get out of here. She had to take whatever might be relevant to saving Los Sombres, or finding her father, or both. She had to do it fast.

She grabbed extra battery packs. She grabbed her father's laptop. She grabbed the Feynman. Then she moved. She braced herself against the shelving unit, swung her legs up to kick out the rough-hewn ceiling hatch, and swarmed through the hole. It was easy.

She was in the pharmacy.

Melatonin.

Fuck if she didn't remember her promise to the kid.

The searing sound of jets.

A dog started barking as Roksana rifled the shelves of the pharmacy looking for melatonin. You'd think they would have barrels of melatonin and Kiss, these Angels – every child they picked up off the streets would be stuffed full of it as a preventive, before being shipped out to Phoenix or Tempeh. But where?

Something heavy hit the outer door of the pharmacy. Dog claws on tile; panting; whining. Roksana made a dive for the rear exit of the room, and by accident she knocked over a white cardboard box. She almost tripped over several bottles of Kiss. She stooped and grabbed the box, shoved the few bottles she could catch back inside, and then head-butted the back door open as Ramone bounded in through the other door.

'Hey, Ramone, easy, boy,' she said, but Ramone didn't seem to like her anymore because he growled and advanced on her. Her father had probably been leaving food inside the fridge for him, but the dog seemed determined to make up for his gaffe by being extra vicious now. Roksana grabbed the doorknob behind her back and slithered out of the pharmacy. She kicked Ramone in the face and slammed the door on him, snapping the lock on the knob.

She was in the rear office, a cramped space with a door at the far end that she dearly hoped wouldn't turn out to be a closet. She took a second to jam the box into her backpack with all the other shit she'd collected, then opened the door and found herself in a corridor beside yet another bank of dead elevators.

Hesitation, and the sound of herself breathing a few breaths while her mind worked furiously. Glancing around the tiny office, her eyes lit on a box of latex gloves. She snatched them and then went into the hallway. The door snicked shut behind her.

Gloves on, quickly. They would give her hands some protection. She got her fingers into the gap in the elevator doors and wrenched them open far enough to admit her and her backpack if she wriggled just right. The elevator was in the basement. She could reach the cable if she stretched.

Up the greasy cable, while the dog barked in the office and the Angels shouted at each other – god, were they inefficient, Roksana thought – and her legs were blackened and scraped and her hair was stuck to her face and sweat ran down between her shoulder blades but she climbed all the way to the top floor before she realized she wouldn't be able to jump from the cable to the elevator doors without falling down the shaft. Especially because the doors on the upper floor were closed.

Ramone's head appeared in the gap between the elevator doors, below. His triumphant barking echoed up the shaft.

'Fuck,' she panted, not caring anymore who heard her. 'Why didn't I take the stairs?'

You've Got a Friend

The last time Xavier had been in a hospital was when Ambrosia was born. He remembered thinking it was a strange place to begin your life, all white and green and shiny. People with squeaky shoes and the muffled bleat of TV from a bracket high on the wall. Ambrosia's little face, cramped and wizened in the white receiving blanket, and his mother's arm with an IV taped to it. None of these things indicated to Xavier that something momentous had happened. He'd brought his mother a plant, and she'd hugged him in a faded, weary way. Her eyes had been masked by analgesic shine lenses.

Now he was going to the same hospital again. He had put Elsa in a wheelbarrow together with some essential things for both of them. He'd bandaged her leg the best he could, and cushioned it with a blanket, but still it was jarred with every step Xavier took.

Elsa maintained a stoical silence. She gripped her toys and kept her eyes closed. Every so often she said, 'How much further?' and he would answer as best he could. Distances seemed exaggerated on foot. Whenever he'd been in the city before, his parents had been driving. He couldn't remember the hospital being so far from the courthouse; but it was a whole new deal when you were pushing an injured child in a wheel-barrow and you had to worry about more bombs coming down. Because there were.

At least the bombing seemed to have driven even the rovers under cover, and there was no sign of Irina or her men.

That was something.

Then, about a mile from the hospital, it started to rain. In the gathering darkness, shine began to creep out of buildings and signs and traffic lights. Xavier kept his head down and his eyes on the ground in front of him. He probably looked like a red-liner, but all he was doing was keeping his gaze away from shine. After what had happened outside American Woman, he couldn't take chances.

Everything in the wheelbarrow was saturated by the time they reached the entrance to the ER. But Xavier didn't approach; something was going on. There were security robots crawling the ambulance zone, and searchlights were shining from the parking lot up into the building itself. Somewhere inside the building, an alarm sounded continuously.

'I don't like this . . .' he muttered. He dropped to a crouch and manoeuvred the wheelbarrow behind the brick wall that enclosed the parking lot, where he could see the sliding glass doors of the entrance itself. Elsa struggled to see over the low wall. Xavier hissed at her to keep down.

'Roksana could be in there,' Elsa said. 'We have to go in.'

'No way. Not until we know what this is all about. Hang in there.'

Xavier strained to see individual people in the crowd of shinies coming out of the hospital. He saw Angels with their red uniforms and hesitant gaits, and he saw people who were obvi-ously injured, on crutches or in wheelchairs. He saw old people, clinging to each other. He heard screaming and shouting. Then he saw a big orderly come out, his head at least a foot higher than the rest of the crowd. The big guy started playing with one of the big RS14 cruisers.

'Some guy is going berserk,' Xavier reported. 'He's attacking an RS14, which is really not a good idea. They may be slow, but they . . . oh, my god . . .'

His last few words were drowned out as first one explosion, then another, went off from the main barrel of the RS14. Xavier looked away, grimacing.

'What?' Elsa craned her neck. 'Do you see her?'

'No, don't look. It's not her. I . . . shit, no way . . .'

He ducked behind the wall again as a subjugation beam swept over the scene. He had spotted Roksana, standing there in a crowd of shinies. He was sure it was her.

He felt cold.

He waited for the beam to pass, then peered cautiously over the wall. Roksana was no longer standing. She was lying on the ground just like the others. Sleeping.

'Jesus, they got her,' Xavier said.

'What? They shot her?'

'No, a subjugation beam. This is totally out of hand. Elsa, come on. Quick. Put your arms around my neck.'

'She wouldn't go down for a subjugation beam!' Elsa insisted. 'We can't leave her.'

'Yes, we can. We have to. Look, they're coming this way. We're fucked.'

More shots were going off. Some of the shinies were running, despite the beams. This development would be exciting, encouraging – except for the fact that they were leading the RS14 straight towards Xavier and Elsa.

'We're out of here.'

Elsa's eyes were wild, but she didn't argue after that. He picked her up out of the wheelbarrow. She didn't weigh much, but she gripped Xavier with a sinewy strength. The bandage on her leg was soaked through with blood, and her skin was a greyish purple. Her lips were pale.

He staggered across the street to the nearest cover, which happened to be a gas station. The robots stopped at the exit of the hospital parking lot, but Xavier kept running until he'd come around to the entrance of the gas station, which lay on a slip road to the interstate. Dogs started barking explosively. Pit bulls. Xavier nearly peed himself before he saw that they were chained up next to an old T-bird painted with psychedelic flowers and peace symbols. The door of the car was painted in puffy, 1960s style letters: *Hector's Gas*.

Xavier's mind was flashing and chiming like a pinball machine. He was remembering the ranch. The crazy Rider's midnight deal with Doug. The talk of gasoline. The name Hector . . . the minivan with its GPS set from the hospital district . . . 'Doc' . . .

As they reached the canopy covering the gas pumps, the door of the gas station office swung open and a man came out smoking a joint and carrying an assault rifle. The way he moved was almost simian. He gripped the gun easily in one hand and glared at Xavier and Elsa.

Xavier shouted, 'Don't shoot! Are you Hector? I'm a friend of the Doc. Don't shoot! I got an injured kid here.'

The man stopped and regarded them, head cocked to one side. He was a big motherfucker, wearing a stained muscle shirt and cut-off sweatpants and flip-flops. His black hair was down to his shoulders and had escaped from a ponytail. Without taking the joint from between his lips he said, 'Quentin! Fedor! Can it!'

The pit bulls stopped barking. They wagged hopefully at Hector, who ignored them.

'Relax,' the guy said. 'Yeah, I'm Hector. I ain't gonna shoot two kids. What you want?'

Xavier stopped to catch his breath. Elsa buried her face in his shoulder.

'My little sister got hurt last night. We tried to go to the hospital but there's a lot of psychos there attacking people. I know a doctor we can go to, but we need a ride to get there.'

Hector didn't move. He took a drag on the joint, closed his eyes. Xavier started to shake. Elsa seemed to be trying to burrow under his skin. She clenched him so hard that he staggered.

Hector pinched the remainder of the joint between his finger and thumb and lay it carefully on top of the gas pump. Nervously, Xavier watched while he propped the rifle against the pump, too. Then he squatted down on the ground and squinted up at them. Sheets of rain poured off the edges of the roof and made a rhythmic smacking sound.

'Your sister, huh?'

Xavier didn't look anything like Elsa. He hadn't thought about that. The word 'sister' had just slipped out of his mouth.

'She might as well be.'

'I ain't gonna do nothing bad to her. Kid bleeding, you're not gonna get far. Let's take a look.'

Still holding Elsa, Xavier sidled over and turned so that Hector could see the injured leg, dangling in its blood-soaked bandages.

'We got to make sure the bleeding's stopped,' Hector said. 'Come on in the office.'

The office of the gas station was like an Army store room. There were weapons, canned goods, blankets, fuel canisters and barrels, tools, and medical supplies. Hector swept everything off the desk and spread a white sheet over it. He pointed, and Xavier set Elsa down. She didn't want to let go of him, so he sat next to her and held her hand.

Elsa didn't cry. She had a pinched, vacant expression.

Hector pumped some cleaning gel over his hands and rubbed them vigorously. Then he addressed the bandages.

'This happen in that riot over there?' he asked.

'No. It was in the bombing. We walked across town to get here, and there's some kind of riot going on.'

'Yeah. Thought maybe you knew more about it.'

Xavier just shook his head. He didn't want to say anything about the subjugation beams because he didn't know what Hector's role in shit might be.

Hector stayed focused on Elsa's injury.

'This will need some stitches. It might be fractured. Don't got no X ray here. Got a lot of stuff from the hospital before the Angels come and took over, and the Doc used to bring me some stuff. But the X ray got bust last year. Does it hurt?'

Elsa whispered, 'Yeah, it hurts.'

Hector said, 'I'm gonna stitch it for you and I'll set it for now but it's probably not gonna be straight. You need a doctor.'

His voice boomed in the small office. Elsa just nodded.

Hector got up and rummaged. It seemed to take forever. Xavier's mind was still back at the hospital. Roksana had been captured. What would the Angels do to her? Angels were supposed to be helpful, but what if they weren't?

Outside, helicopters. Gunshots. Muffled blast of loudspeaker voices, unintelligible in the storm.

Elsa's eyes rolled in fear. Xavier said, 'Is it safe to stay here?'

Hector grinned. He set down a stainless steel tray on the table and handed Elsa a face mask attached to a gas canister.

'You just start breathing that in, just breathe normal. It's just laughing gas, like at the dentist? Ain't you ever had a filling? No? You musta brushed better than me, then.' And he opened his mouth and there were several gold teeth. Hector laughed. He added for Xavier's benefit, 'You're safe here. Nobody mess with me.'

While Hector stitched Elsa's leg he told Xavier how he'd met 'the Doc' during the wildest days of the Fall. 'Doc' had rescued the gas station from a gang of fire-wielding rovers using only his Feynman.

'He had a shitload of illegal shine in that machine. No wonder he was such a nervous little motherfucker – excuse my French. Anyway, he used to drop by after that and we got to know each other. He helped me out with some stuff.'

'What kind of stuff?' Xavier asked.

'Just some shine stuff. I'm burned out, see . . .' And Xavier knew that meant Hector was an ex-con and his offence had been pretty serious. 'I don't mind shine, but I can't stay awake all the time and even the dogs, somebody could poison them or shoot them. The Doc gave me some lights to protect this place. We helped each other out, guess you could say. Last I saw him he needed help. He took a car and got outta here so fast you can still see his skidmarks out there by the pump.'

'He left town?'

Xavier and Elsa stared at each other. Elsa took the mask off.

'Roksana . . .' she whispered, her eyes filling with tears. 'Dr Ansari left her without even saying anything . . .'

Xavier reached over and squeezed her hand.

'Did he say why he was going?'

'He said he was looking for a Rider.' Hector laughed. 'And I thought that was a real weird thing to say, but it got weirder after he left. Don't look at your leg, kid.'

Hector reached behind the desk and handed her a two-year-old copy of *Seventeen* magazine.

'What do you mean, it got weirder.'

'Shh. I got to concentrate.' Peering closely at his thick, axle-grease-impregnated fingertips, Hector started threading a needle.

'Yeah, it got weirder,' he said eventually. 'The lights he put up out back, they did more than just protect me. I think they were part of some experiment he was doing. I don't know. But I haven't seen him for a while now. I guess he finally had enough.'

'Bastard,' Elsa mouthed.

'Shh . . .' said Xavier. 'I think I know where he is.'

She stared at him, comprehension dawning.

'John Doe?' She mouthed the words silently, and he nodded. Her face closed in a pained grimace.

When Hector was done with Elsa he gave them bags of Fritos and opened a can of beans.

'Dig in. They fucked up the clearway last bombing. So even if you knew how to drive a car, I couldn't give you one. It wouldn't get you out of town anymore.'

Xavier felt himself deflate.

'Don't worry,' Hector said. 'I got something better. Like I said, even after the Doc leaves, funny things keep happening. I got a bunch of uninvited guests. They just keep showing up, like the place smells good or something. Here, wanna see?'

Hector went to the back window and pulled up the venetian blinds. Standing in the yard behind the gas station, with their noses almost to the glass and their hindquarters turned to the wind and rain, were three soaking wet horses.

'You said you knew Doug,' Hector said. 'Maybe you know how to ride.'

Just then one of the horses, a chestnut, tossed her head to shake off water. She seemed to look right through the window at Xavier.

It was Bob Newhart.

Bobby

Roksana's voice echoed down five floors. Ramone barked and barked. Then someone called him and he stopped. Sound of Ramone's claws on tile. Below, voices. Then, close to Roksana: *thud. Squeak.*

Just a few feet away from her, the elevator doors that were so tantalizingly out of reach began to crack open.

A large pair of hands appeared in the crack and a moment later, the doors had been forced apart.

A man stood there, silhouetted against the weak daylight of the top floor.

'Come on, Roksana,' he said. 'It's me or them, and I'm your best bet.'

His accent was Deep South. The half-open elevator only revealed a strip of his body, but it was enough for Roksana to know that he was a Rottweiler of a man. He was wearing a too-tight orderly's uniform, and she could see pretty much every swollen muscle in his body. He pushed the doors wider open and leaned into the elevator shaft, extending an improbably long, tanned arm towards her.

'Come on, now,' he said, nodding at her so that the white of his eyes and teeth flashed in the dimness. He had an immaculate goatee.

She grabbed his hand and jumped. He caught her like she was a doll and pulled her to safety. He smelled clean, the way people used to smell before the Fall.

'Name's Bobby,' he said, and she scrambled to her feet, absolutely terrified because she didn't know what was going on. Then he said, 'I been sent to help you.'

Dad, she thought, and a little bomb of hope went off between her ears. Amir must have sent him.

Roksana licked dry lips. 'The Angels are after me,' she said. 'Where's my dad? We can't just stand here.'

He led her into a room overlooking the main parking lot. It was made up as if awaiting a new patient. There was a large window; Bobby reached up and opened it from the top, and a draft of cool, moist wind came like a living being into this dead place. The sun was going down amid a tussle of storm clouds, gold and grey. Thunder and lightning marched across the city; trees bent over. Then a chatter of rain hit the hospital roof, building quickly to a cacophony.

'Where's Amir?'

He didn't answer that.

'I'm your friend,' he said. 'Just as you are mine. I can't hold my own for long. It ain't easy to fight the Angels' shine. There's so much interference all the time, but you could fix that. You got the Feynman?'

Roksana's words came out in a panicky rush. 'What? Angels are after us and you want to talk about shine?'

'You got it or not?'

'I can't give you the Feynman,' Roksana said carefully. 'Didn't my dad send you?'

Bobby looked confused. 'I work for Irina.' That open window was freaking her. In the Fall, a lot of people jumped out of windows. A lot of other people got thrown out.

'I used to work for the Angels. They brought me in off the street last year and they been using me ever since to do security. But last week I picked up some shine that took me to a traffic light over on Rose Avenue. And I got a new shine package. Some people get called to the red line, but Irina gave me a special job.'

'OK . . .' She was thinking: *Special job, WTF? Help!*

'My job is to help you deliver the fix. So today I see you're here, and I know who your father is, and I know he worked here even if I don't know where he was hiding out. So that's why I say, if you have that Feynman, then I'm going to get you out of here. If you don't have it, then I'm going to take out every Angel in this place until you find it. Because now is the time. You get what I'm saying?'

'Nobody but my father can use his Feynman.'

'I can bring you to him. I know where he went. I can, like, feel him.'

Yeah, right.

'Where is he?' she breathed.

Squeak of sneakers on the corridor outside. Small lights, bobbing down the corridor. Angels.

Roksana dived under the bed.

'Bobby!' A woman's voice beckoned. 'We've been looking everywhere for you.'

Roksana could see the Angels' feet. There were five of them, all carrying therapy beams whose illumination crossed and doubled, washing Roksana's room in bands of colour and shadow. Bobby was silhouetted against the lights, and he looked even bigger. He started towards the Angels. He carried one shoulder higher than the other, and even walking slowly he subtly shifted his head from side to side, tracking. Predacious.

'How did he get out of sedation?' said a male Angel. The woman whispered '*shh*' and the male fell silent.

She said, 'It's OK, Bobby. You want a beer or something?'

Bobby just kept walking towards them, not even trying to shade his eyes from the therapy beams. Roksana saw the Angels' feet shuffle as they slowed down. They were in no rush to confront him.

'He should be down by now,' said another male. 'I've got mine on full.'

'Try another one,' said a third male. 'Looks like the usual patterns aren't working anymore.'

'This is fucked,' said the second male. 'It always works. You could take down an elephant with—'

'Bob-by!' sang the woman. 'Come on, it's all right. I'll get you a beer. Or a joint? Is anything hurting you? We're here to help.'

The lights flickered as the Angels changed patterns. Roksana wondered how much of Bobby's face they could perceive with their tongue-cameras.

'Out the window, Roksana!' Bobby's voice boomed. 'Take the Ride. Don't be afraid. Just do what you have to do.'

The Angels stopped in their tracks.

'Uh, Mary?' the third male said. 'We got a situation on the upper floor. Better seal the exits, just in c—'

Bobby lunged forward. Roksana saw a pair of feet lift off the floor. Bobby's legs quivered; then there was a crash and a man's body went flying across a cart carrying resuscitation equipment and hit the wall beyond. The man slid to the floor, limp.

'Bobby, there's no need to hurt anybody,' the woman said. 'Do you remember me? Kristina? We've played Super Mario Brothers together? Come on, just tell me what I can do for you.'

'Shithead,' said Bobby, and lunged again. The men tried to protect Kristina but Bobby held something gleaming in his right hand – scissors, maybe – and he went charging in. Angels ran; Bobby pursued them around a corner. Roksana could no longer see them, but she could hear one of the men screaming.

'Mary! The lights aren't working on him. Get everybody out of his way.'

There were cries, thumps. Then silence except for Bobby's footfalls as he came back around the corner.

'You got nothing to fear from shine,' Bobby said. 'You're free forever. But what about the rest of us? That shine you got in that Feynman, it's everything to us. I mean *everything*. Help us, Roksana. It's your Ride now. Fix us.'

But I don't Ride, she wanted to say. *I can't Ride.*

'I'm taking you out of here,' Bobby said. 'That's my destiny. That's my mission. Your destiny is to take this Ride. No matter where it goes. You don't let nobody get in your way. That's what I'm supposed to tell you. You understand me?'

She didn't *understand* but under the force of his dominance it wasn't about understanding, it was about agreeing. And you didn't disagree, not with a guy whose clothes were soaked in somebody else's blood.

She swallowed, and she nodded, and that seemed to be enough for him because he said, 'OK, let's get the hell out.'

He ran to the window and just as quickly jerked back as a bar of light flashed across it.

'No good, they got RS14s and shit.' He pointed to the stairs. 'That way.'

Roksana never moved so fast in her life. Down the stairs, three and four at a time, all but flying. She was dizzy. Bobby came hurtling down behind her.

At the bottom she forgot all caution. She made straight for the exit, pelting through the ER with its stale air and semi-comatose incumbents. People reacted to her blearily, almost in slow motion. Alarms were ringing. She heard Ramone barking.

'Get out of my way!' she screamed, pushing and shoving. She didn't wait to see what people made of Bobby coming after her.

The air outside was wet and smelled of tarmac. Wind and rain smacked her in the face, whipped her hair back, and she was still trapped. People were spilling out of the hospital in a zombie knot. She glanced back and saw Bobby coming through the crowd like a ship breaking the waves. The RS14 that had been pointing its turret at the top floor swivelled and rolled ponderously towards the hospital, guns rotating to track Roksana.

People screamed and dived for cover.

Roksana saw the black hole in the barrel of the RS14's main gun. Like a pupil, trained on her. She couldn't move.

Bobby pushed through the crowd and shoved her to one side. He turned his head and looked at her. His mouth opened. He made no sound, but his lips said, 'Play possum.'

Then he turned back to the RS14 and charged it. It tracked him as he dodged to one side at the last moment, and the gun barrel turned away from Roksana.

She started running. A helicopter droned overhead. Bobby taunted the gun brain. Roksana, still in a mob, set her eyes on the parking lot full of cars that had not been started in two years. Cover.

The robot's secondary gun went off. She saw the fabric of Bobby's uniform shirt tear; saw his head whip back on his neck as a spatter of ammunition caught him in the face. The bullets sprayed wide: a small woman in the crowd behind Bobby went down. Bobby kept going. He launched himself at the robot and grabbed hold of the central gun barrel, wrenching at it as if to tear it off.

The gun went off again, this time point blank into Bobby's midsection. Pieces of him sprayed around the parking lot.

Lights poured down from the helicopter, from the building itself, from the parking lot's lamp posts.

They would be subjugation beams. People were lying down in the beams, settling like pets in their baskets, going quietly to sleep.

And when they woke up, they would be crazier. Worse than

before. Roksana had seen it all before, in the early days of the Fall, when the subjugation beams had been used routinely.

The helicopter's beam rolled over the people standing next to her. They sank to the ground as though choreographed; only Roksana remained standing. Then the meaning of Bobby's last words kicked in: *play possum.*

Roksana crumpled to the ground as though the light had gotten to her, too.

She lay there and for a long while, it was as though the light truly had wiped out her mind, because she could think of nothing. So much violence, so quickly . . . she couldn't take it in. She'd thought she was hard to this shit by now, but no. You were never that hard. Helicopter noise drowned out the screams of people and Angels. After a while it occurred to her that she'd better move, or be picked up and recaptured. She began to crawl, flat on her belly, slithering between the bodies of the shined and shooting glances back at the Angels who were trying to take control of the scene. Twice she went limp rather than risk being seen; then she realized that the Angels had lost all control of the situation.

The shinies were not lying down. Not all of them; not for long.

She got up and ran. She dodged from one parked car to another, until she tripped and fell and found herself on the ground beneath a Durango, prone on oily macadam that smelled of diesel and cat pee. She was sick so violently that vomit shot from her nostrils. She was shaking too hard to stand, so she went back to crawling. Her elbows and knees were scraped and bleeding.

Military aircraft cruised in the dark skies overhead, their searchlights making them into the opposite of shadows.

She crawled from car to car. Trying not to think about Bobby. She reached the edge of the parking lot and climbed a small, rocky rise bisected by security fencing. She found the cut-out place in the bottom that Amir had told her about, 'in case of emergency'. He had chosen a spot that was already overgrown with wild brush so that the security weakness would stay hidden. By the time she'd scrambled through the gap, she was scratched and bleeding and muddy all over, but she had to continue climbing. By the time she reached the top of the ridge, her heart felt swollen and her lungs ached. Her legs were wobbling beneath her. She now stood above the cutting where the interstate ran, adjacent to the hospital. The highway below was dark and empty.

She could look down on the hospital from here. A helicopter had landed on the roof and there was a lot of Angel activity up there. Robots encircled the hospital and controlled the parking lot, but the shinies were now following Bobby's lead and hurling themselves at the machines. Strangely, only a handful of people had slumped to the ground, obeying the subjugation beams. The rest were resisting the lightborns.

Did that mean FallN was winning, even if Roksana didn't know how?

Were they really so close to a fix?

Angels were struggling to carry the unconscious shinies inside, skirting around Bobby's head and torso that lay in the ambulance zone.

He had staged the attack to cover her escape. The most bizarrely altruistic violence Roksana had ever seen.

Why?

You got nothing to fear from shine . . . fix us.

One of the robots opened fire on the rebellious crowd. Roksana cringed and turned away. At the same time, the helicopter took off again – pilot wouldn't be risked in Los Sombres for more than the briefest of missions. Bent double, Roksana hid behind a stanchion supporting a *Perfection* billboard facing the interstate. The helicopter's light swept the whole area once more as it lifted; then it banked to the east and headed up, out of range of the Fall's shine lights.

After the chopper had gone, the night was too quiet.

Roksana shut her mind to Bobby's last moments but she couldn't stop replaying his voice in her head.

It's your Ride now.

Crazy. Roksana had never Ridden a light in her life. She couldn't.

That shine is everything to us . . . everything.

Well, the shine would be nothing to anybody if the authorities got hold of her. Gripping her father's Feynman, Roksana slithered down the embankment to the interstate and set off across the road, turning her back on what was becoming a massacre. Heading back to the Hide.

The rain felt intimate, almost alive, on her skin. Lightning made scorpion tracks across the sky.

The bile still in her mouth was bitter.

Thick as a Brick

Pavarotti's Greatest Hits

Heat seemed to possess everything: air, ground, animal, leather. The inside of Xavier's nose was hot and the bottoms of his feet were hot where his boots pressed against the stirrups. Bob Newhart had her head down and only her ears reacted to the flies on her neck. The mountain ahead shifted in the heat, its roots lost in the silver of a mirage.

But he could see the house now, a cool white lozenge with terra-cotta roof tiles, the car port shedding a sharp trapezoid of shadow on the drive. Horses dozed in the front paddock, and a discarded water-cooler bottle bounced down the driveway in the slight breeze. Bob Newhart heard it gonging and bumping, but she didn't shy away.

Melanie was sitting in the doorway with the dark gap of the open front door behind her. Xavier could see her medical bag on the threshold. He waved and cried out a greeting.

'There's Melanie! The doctor I told you about.'

Elsa slumped faint and miserable against Xavier's back. She didn't respond.

Melanie ran to meet them, stumbling in her gold flip-flops with sequins but otherwise covering the ground pretty good.

As she drew closer, Xavier saw the horizontal lines of worry ploughed across her forehead.

'Welcome home.' Melanie wasn't even out of breath. 'I got a message that you had an injured child. What's the situation?'

'This is Elsa. She hurt her leg in the bombing three nights ago.'

Elsa didn't speak. She buried her face in the sweaty hollow between Xavier's shoulder blades. Xavier tried to see the ranch from Elsa's point of view. He was going to have to explain a whole bunch of stuff. He'd have to explain why Melanie was tone deaf and into cutting herself, and why his mother was obsessed with her knitting, and why Pavarotti never said anything, but only sang.

So far Melanie hadn't blamed herself for anything. She coaxed Elsa off the horse and carried her to the house.

'You're in pretty good shape if you managed to ride all that way,' Xavier heard her say to Elsa. 'So don't you worry, because we're going to take care of you now and make you comfortable. You like guacamole? No? You like spaghetti? Yeah? That's what we're having then, OK?'

In the doorway, Melanie turned her head and said over her shoulder, 'Powaqa wants to see you. At the corral. But you better talk to your mom first, because she's been crazy worried about you.'

Xavier snorted to himself. His mother never worried; she never knew what the fuck was going on to worry *about*.

'Hey Melanie?'

'Uh-huh?'

'You know that guy John Doe? Where's he at?'

'Oh, him.' She rolled her eyes. 'I don't know what's going on with him. One minute he's sick as a dog and the next minute he's shining everybody up. I don't know where he is right now. But don't you go looking for him until you've seen your mom, all right?'

Xavier walked away without actually promising anythir
He didn't want to see his mom. He wanted to find John Doe ak
Amir and get some answers out of the guy.

He brought Bob Newhart around back to the trough. He
lifted the saddle off her back and took it into the barn. Pavarotti
was taking a nap on a stack of straw bales.

'Hey!' Xavier said.

'Go away,' Pavarotti said. 'She had me up all night.'

Xavier did a double take. He'd never even heard Pavarotti's
speaking voice before. It was gravelly, with a real deep South
twang, maybe Louisiana. He was afraid to reply in case he
spooked the guy.

'Kid, you deaf? I *said*, she had me up all night.'

Carefully neutral: 'Did she?'

Pavarotti guffawed, 'I'm talking about Samuel L. Jackson.
She had her foal this morning.'

'That's good . . .' He didn't want to say the wrong thing,
break the spell.

'Go look at him if you want. Fine colt.' Pavarotti pulled his
hat down over his face and settled back to sleep.

Xavier went to the foaling stall and saw Samuel L. Jackson
and her foal lying in the straw like a picture postcard.

'Hey, guys,' he said. He wondered what Powaqa would
name the colt. She liked to give the mares the names of male
celebrities, but her choices of names for colts always came from
some Indian language or other.

'I do it to lighten the burden on the mares,' she'd told Xavier
once. 'They like to have funny names, seeing's how they do all
the hard work.'

Some of Powaqa's ways were so weird that Xavier wondered
how much of what she said was pulling his leg, on any given
day.

A girl's shriek rang through the barn and Xavier, plus the
two horses, startled.

I don't believe it! You're alive!'

Chumana ran up to him and threw her arms around him. She smelled fine.

He grinned idiotically as she broke away. 'I haven't been gone that long.'

'There were so many missile strikes. We thought that was it. I thought I'd never see you again.'

There was a certain temptation to milk the drama, but Xavier knew Chumana was too smart for that. He turned back to the foal and shrugged with what he hoped was quiet dignity as he said, 'I can take care of myself.'

She smacked him across the shoulder blades. He had no idea why. What could you do? Couldn't win with that girl.

'Did you get anything?'

He shook his head.

'Nothing? After six days, you got nothing?'

'Oh, Xavier, I'm so glad you're not dead!' he mimicked in a high voice.

'Sorry,' Chumana said. 'It's just – what were you doing all that time?'

He tried not to look at her. He didn't want to talk about Roksana. Los Sombres – it was another world. Chumana would ask questions he couldn't answer. She would try to take it away from him. He didn't want that.

'There was no Kiss,' he said. 'I found some melatonin as a substitute, but . . . I got attacked. Plus the invasion force wasn't too friendly.'

Her eyes flared wider.

'I thought you loved the exo-protector hero squad,' she said. 'Do you know your mom's out of her mind worrying about you?'

'Yeah, that's what I heard.'

'You better go home right now,' she commanded. She even gave him a push, and her fake nails dug into him. They were studded with sequins and glitter. He wondered how she could do anything with those huge nails sticking out of her hands.

'You seen John Doe anywhere?' he asked.

Her face closed down. 'No, and I don't want to. He tried to shine me. I kicked him in the balls.'

'You *what?*'

'He's a fucking psycho.'

'Well . . . are you OK? How did he try to shine you?'

She gave her head a shivery little shake. 'It doesn't matter. I don't want to talk about that jerk. He's just one big, like, spasm. He's disgusting.'

'Well, if you see him, will you tell me? I want to talk to him.'

'No you don't. You better stay away from him, Xavier. Trust me.'

She was serious, wide-eyed, and she tossed the hair back from her face as she said it. She smelled of strawberry lip gloss.

'Go see your mom now. I'll take care of Bob,' she said. 'You go.'

She turned her dark, shining gaze on him, and he backed off before she could shove him again. He was so fucking sick of being shorter than everybody.

Six Different Ways

Outside the barn Xavier hesitated. Where the fuck was Amir Ansari? He wasn't at the house, and he wasn't in the barn, and Xavier didn't think he was strong enough to walk far. He wouldn't be down at the corral with Powaqa after Powaqa'd told him to get lost.

They didn't know. None of them had any idea who Amir was, or what he could do. And they wouldn't listen to Xavier, either; not if Chumana's attitude was anything to go by.

He gave in and headed home. Out in the vegetable garden on the south side of the ranch house, a whole team of refugees were weeding and watering. Not one of them was throwing food. Not one of them was aggravating the others, or kicking dirt, or speaking in tongues. He paused and watched them for a minute.

This was not the same scene he had left behind. Not by a long shot.

Xavier found his mother at the truck. She sat on the tailgate, swinging her lower legs and humming as she knitted.

'Mom?'

She looked up, dropped the wool, and threw herself at Xavier. He couldn't remember his mother hugging him for years – definitely not since the Fall – and it was strange to feel how small and light she was. Her bones didn't have much on them, and her hair smelled of sagebrush smoke.

Then she hauled off and slapped him. Chumana all over again.

'Ow! *Mom*—'

'You little shit! I thought I lost you. Where were you? Why didn't you tell me where you were going?'

Xavier staggered back a step. The tears came and she lost control of her facial muscles; they bunched and twisted, and her eyes and nose reddened.

'Oh, god, oh, Xavier . . .' She got hold of him again and this time she was limp and teary. He drew her over to the tailgate and got her to sit down. He'd never seen her like this.

'I didn't mean to be gone so long. I got stuck in the city.'

'You shouldn't have been there at all. What were you—' She cleared her throat, tossed her head, swallowed. She caught his eye suddenly, as if she'd just thought of something. 'Your father. Did you—?'

Xavier drew a long breath. If he was ever going to tell her, now was the time.

'I have some bad news.'

She batted her eyelashes. She crossed her eyes. Then she sneezed. Xavier held on to her. Tried to pull her back from the un-place she was going to.

'*Mom*. He's dead. Dad is dead. He threw himself off a building. He died instantly.'

She picked up her knitting, brushed at it with small, violent strokes, and said, 'It's too dusty out here.'

'Mom. Did you hear me?'

Rosa started humming. He recognized the tune; it was an old song, the kind of 80s fluff you used to hear over the public address system while you were shopping at Target. The sound of it took him back to the time before the Fall, after his dad moved in with his girlfriend and left his mom pregnant with Ambrosia. 'Six Different Ways.'

Xavier stood there with his heart thumping against his chest. For a moment, he'd thought she might hear him. For a moment, she'd seemed almost like her old self.

He wanted to cry with frustration, but he checked the weakness. Somebody had to take control. His dad would never have let this kind of crazy shit go on.

Would he?

Dad had thrown himself off a building.

Xavier didn't know where to go, inside his head.

'Oh!' cried Xavier's mom, throwing her head back and sniffing mightily. 'What was I thinking? I'm sorry, kiddo. Let me get you something to eat. I finished up the canned asparagus but you know, I'm such a pig when I'm pregnant. Here. I got something better.'

She went over to the pit and dragged up the cooler chest. Xavier gave himself a little dogshake to get her emotions off of him. Then Rex came sauntering over.

'Well, there the hell you are!' he said. 'Think fast.'

He threw Xavier a warm beer.

'Hey, Rex,' said Xavier's mom. 'You want to eat with us? Where's your dad?'

'He had to ride out. It's OK, Rosa, I already ate up at the house. Hey Xavier, who's the kid you brought back? Orphan?'

Xavier flinched. 'Yeah. You seen John Doe?'

'Not lately – he's probably around shining somebody, though. I think he's staying away from Chumana since she kicked him and called him a muthafucka. Oh, I beg your pardon, Rosa.'

'You better beg my freaking pardon, Rex, or you won't get none of my Hostess Cupcakes I been keeping back for a special occasion.'

'Oh, man, Hostess Cupcakes, really?'

They exchanged fond smiles. Xavier prodded Rex.

'What did he do that made her so mad?'

'He got alone with her. I don't know, maybe he tried to feel her up. Anyway, he's under control. My dad and me, we got him on a tight leash.'

'But he's shining people.'

Rex laughed into his beer can. 'You always was a smart little squirt.'

Xavier glanced sidelong at Rosa but she didn't seem to be tuned in.

'Bet you don't know what else happened. Pavarotti don't want to stay no more. He's—'

'Signing the ranch over to your dad,' Xavier finished, and Rex looked really mad.

'Who the fuck told you already?'

'Is it because of the bombs?'

Rex shrugged. 'I don't know the reason. It's just something he *feels*, like inside his heart, you know?'

Something he feels, Xavier thought. *Or something Amir shined him to feel?*

Xavier remembered the conversation he'd overheard between Amir and Doug. The one where Amir said he could 'take care of David MacAllen.' The one where Amir referred to himself as Luke. Amir had promised Doug control of the ranch, and already it looked like he could deliver.

'I think it's because of the baby,' Rosa said. 'You know how all this time, he never seemed to notice Beth was pregnant, and now he's talking and he's thinking this ain't a safe place to bring up kids. So he's going to get into a rehab programme or something. He doesn't even want his land no more.'

Rex reached into his pocket and brought out a handful of Kiss pills. 'Sam Power brought them. Should last us until the final toasting of that damn town.' He handed them to Xavier. 'Too late for me,' he added.

Rex's dad had to know the true situation in Los Sombres.

Doug went around telling everybody the place was Raccoon City and there were killer zombies everywhere and the lights could strike you down where you stood . . . but now he was going to be the proud owner of a valuable ranch. Not bad for a burnout.

'You think it's over in Los Sombres?'

'That's what they're saying on TV.'

'TV? Are you serious? How?'

'Beth. You know, Pavarotti's girlfriend. She fixed the dish, and my dad did a deal with Black Mesa so we don't got to use our own generator for all our power. And pretty soon, like I said, everything's going to change. The Army's coming in bigtime.'

'Rex,' Xavier said. 'The city's not like what they told us. It's not that bad there. A lot of people are still alive, and some of them are pretty OK.'

Rex's eye was doubtful. 'You got any shine when you was there?'

'Me? I'm still safe.' Xavier puffed out his chest. 'Your voice sounds different, though, man.'

'I'm OK,' Rex said. But he looked uneasy. His voice had cracked several times during the conversation. 'I don't got to worry, you know, because the place will be rubble pretty soon.'

'I don't think you'd say that if you went there,' Xavier said, suddenly fierce. 'I met some cool people there. They got underground radio, and the hospital still has patients in it, and there are people who help with food and stuff. It's not really zombies.'

Rex swallowed his beer.

'You sure you didn't get no shiny shine, my friend?'

'I'm totally serious. The bombings are targeting the lights, but people keep putting the lights up. The planes won't be able to just target the lights. They'll have to target the people. But the people aren't a threat to anybody. They just want to survive.'

'Then you should just tell people to turn off the lights, problem solved, we all go home.'

'But Rex . . . it's not that simple.'

Rex was giving him that *you-loco-like-a-cherry-popsicle-or-what?* look.

Xavier had seen it before. He tried not to let it bother him. He told himself that Rex wasn't too bright. But it was hard.

'Hey!' said Rex, and it was obvious he was making a big effort to spare Xavier embarrassment, 'Rosa, didn't you say something about cupcakes?'

'I sure did,' said Rosa brightly, and produced a squashed box from the front seat of the pickup. She offered it almost reverently: sacred artifact from the days of food packaging plants.

'So your dad's going to work with Black Mesa.'

'Mmmm,' said Rex with crumbs sticking to his lips. 'He reckons the Indians are better friends to us than the fucking government that want to kill him. Them Indians just want to get their own back against whitey. I don't got no problem with that, but Powaqa's being a douchebag not helping John Doe with her medicine.'

Xavier was about to say that he thought John Doe wanted help with disseminating his fix for the shined, but before he could make Rex explain what he meant, Rosa reached over and slapped Rex in the face. Just like in an old movie where women still did stuff like that.

'What the fuck was that for?'

'Mind your manners. I don't want to hear none of that racist talk about Powaqa. She's my friend. I don't know what me and Xavier would have done if she hadn't taken us in. She doesn't have a political agenda. I don't know about the tribal council.'

Rex and Xavier looked at each other. Rosa sounded almost normal. She saw them look at each other, too, and then she said, 'I'm not batfinked all the time, you know. I have my lucid moments.'

To cover his confusion, Xavier bit into his cupcake. It was so sweet that he swore he could taste individual grains of sugar. The plasticky undertones clung to his tongue when he swallowed.

'Like now,' Rosa continued. 'I'm not so shined to shit I don't notice this cupcake tastes like gopher funk. Doesn't it?'

She and Xavier looked at each other and, for that moment, it was like she was really there. The old Mom. The one who explained the jokes on *The Simpsons* to him and told him off for biting his nails. He felt himself softening; he was going to be getting teary in a minute.

'I like it,' Rex said belligerently. 'In fact, I love it. How can you not love a Hostess Cupcake? Look, when they get warm, they *glimmer.*'

''Scuse me, you having a reverent moment there, Rex?' said Rosa and Xavier cracked up.

Rex stood up, still holding the cupcake very carefully.

'Man, I don't know about this John Doe,' he said cryptically. 'I thought he was doing a good thing, but I gotta tell you, Rosa, you was easier to deal with when you was knitting all the time.'

He picked up the half-empty box of cupcakes and took it with him.

'See you later, crocodile!' Rosa called, still laughing. She turned to Xavier. 'Want to see my new lab?'

'Your *what?*'

'Well, it isn't really a lab, more of a garden patch. Over here.'

She led him into the brush, on a narrow track that was nearly invisible in the fading light. In the dry soil she had built what looked like a large cold frame, only it didn't have any glass over it. Good quality soil had been spread thickly inside the frame, and clamped to the sides were battery lights that Xavier recognized as Powaqa's second-string lightborn transmitters that she'd used to keep stored in the hay loft.

'What's all this?' he said, hoping she wasn't going to veer off into some crazy shit.

'I have a little project. It's kind of a secret. It's my translation work.'

'Translation? What are you translating?'

'Ah, if I told you, it wouldn't be a secret. Oh, don't worry. It's only for fun. Maybe it's just . . . my way of getting back in touch with who I used to be.'

Xavier knew that, before Rosa had him, she had been a student at the University of Arizona in Tempeh. She'd majored in crop science and worked part time in a lab, but she never even finished her degree. Xavier had been a sickly kid when he was little. She couldn't put him in day care, and then when he was in school and she went back to work, there were no jobs in her field. She got a job in data processing in Phoenix and then, when Xavier's dad was transferred to Los Sombres, she'd gotten pregnant again.

'I have a lot of gaps in my memory,' she told him now. 'I'm trying to recover lost time. I thought this might be good therapy for me. And Powaqa had some stuff she wanted done, but she didn't know how to do it. So I thought I'd try.'

Native medicine, Xavier thought. And he thought about Chumana kicking Amir in the balls. He'd probably tried his fix on her. The Hopi didn't like using commercial lightborns. They had their own scripts.

'What will you do if we have to move?' he said. 'Can you take this with you?'

She shook her head. 'I don't know. I have to take it one day at a time. One hour at a time. I could relapse, you know. Sometimes I do. I want you to be prepared in case that happens, OK?'

He nodded.

'I don't want you to relapse,' he said. 'I want you to get better.'

She hugged him again.

He didn't know how he felt about all the hugging. Whether it made things better, or worse.

Gone

Roksana stood in the middle of the street with her hand over her mouth, looking at the collapsed frontage of American Woman. She couldn't even move at first.

The next hour was the worst. She searched the rubble, and she combed through the building, and in the end she found no trace of Elsa. Or Xavier.

Had they escaped.

Where would they go?

The Hide was destroyed. All the maps and databases that Roksana had depended on to function as FallN ... ruined. Elsa could be anywhere.

No, not anywhere.

They had planned for this. If American Woman got attacked while Roksana was out and Elsa couldn't reach her, then Elsa was to go to the nearest safehouse. That would be either Hair and Now, or Tito's, depending on the state of the roads.

Roksana forced herself to think carefully before she went rushing off. From the look of it, Elsa hadn't had time to pack anything. Roksana now took food and batteries and clean underwear and soap. She took a spare battery pack for the

Feynman and another for her radio. She took a printed map of Los Sombres and environs. She grabbed Elsa's stuffed rabbit.

And she set off for Hair and Now.

Nobody there.

Tito's was deserted, too. Roksana couldn't help lingering there, trailing a hand over the teak reception desk with its long-dead shine studs. Picturing the Riders in here, working in the chic darkness cut by blades of light. Amir in his prime, cool not because of his clothes or his car but because of where he could go, psychologically.

Tito's had been a place of power and now it was another ruin.

Roksana sat on the floor and tried the Feynman. In the stuffy gloom, its gentle glow bathed her face.

It's your Ride . . .

Nothing was happening. Nothing ever happened. Not for her. She snapped the Feynman shut.

How could she Ride when she didn't know what the Field looked like, sounded like. Felt like. You had to be able to Ride special shine just to perceive the infrastructure. Then, apparently, the Field took over the world around you. It was everywhere.

'Everywhere? Like a mist?' Roksana had asked Amir.

'No. More like a perspective.'

Then he'd go all flakey. Riders lived in their own heads. Walking around in a daze was part of the job description.

There was a noise outside, and Roksana leaped up. She slid through the side door and saw the red line approaching. At its head was Damien. She shouted his name, and he looked up. He smiled.

She fell into step with him.

'Where are you going?'

'Moving the lights. We have to shut them down by tonight. Where are you going?'

She told him about Elsa.

'Oh, I saw her,' said Damien.

'You *what*?'

'She was in a wheelbarrow. This kid was pushing her.'

'Where?'

He shrugged. His face clouded. 'Not sure. Sorry.'

'Was she alive? Was she hurt?'

'She was alive. Didn't look too good, though. Hey, so you're the next big thing, right?'

'Me?' Roksana blinked. She wanted to talk about Elsa, but Damien was going all affectionate and congratulatory, like she'd scored a goal or something. 'What are you talking about?'

He shrugged. 'Just something I picked up on the waves. Are you Riding or not?'

'Not,' Roksana said staunchly. 'Quit teasing me about that.'

'Sorry.' He backed off. Glanced around him at the other redliners, walking around him towards whatever destination they had today. 'I better go. Your friends got out of town. But good luck with . . . you know. That other thing.'

There's a Reason Why He's So Devoted

Melanie had made space for Elsa in a tiny room adjoining the master bedroom. She had piled a lot of the women's stuff into the hallway to make room for Elsa's single bed, which now had fresh sheets on it and even a couple of stuffed animals.

'I want Roksana,' she cried, hugging a tattered pink cat. 'I knew we shouldn't have left her.'

Then she broke down in sobs. Melanie tried to soothe her but got nowhere.

'Time for more Ibuprofen,' she said, and left Xavier alone with Elsa.

He knelt beside the bed. Elsa was wearing a big, wrinkled Houston Astros T-shirt and her bare feet were clean. Her hair had been unbraided and combed out, and it made her look older.

'I feel real bad about the way it's gone,' he said. 'You got to concentrate on getting better now, Elsa. Roksana is OK. I'm sure she is. There were no bombs the past two nights.'

'But if she got captured . . .'

'Well, at least they'll be feeding her. And nobody's going to bomb that hospital as long as there are Angels in it. You know what I know for sure? Wherever Roksana is, she's thinking about you. I promised her I'd take care of you, but you got to help me by not freaking out. You got to be strong, OK? And I know you are.'

It was dark in the little room except for a dim patch of gold high on one wall where the reflected sunset hit the yellow paint. Xavier wiped Elsa's face with some toilet paper and got her to blow her nose.

'Yuck,' he said loudly. 'Where'd you come up with all that snot?'

She laughed slightly, but he knew she was unconvinced.

'In the Fall,' she said. 'Do you remember how all the kids stuck together? It was like . . . somehow even before it started the kids were waiting for their chance to break loose, and when the adults started flipping out, us kids were ready. We took over, at least for a little while.'

'I didn't go out much,' Xavier said. 'I stayed home to watch my . . . family.' His voice broke a little, and Elsa nodded sympathetically.

'I lost my mom almost right away,' she said. 'Roksana helped me find her, but it was too late when we got there.'

'That must have been . . . awful.'

Elsa plucked at the blanket. 'I thought it was the end of the world. Roksana had to drag me away. I was so worried what would happen to her. We had to burn her, because we couldn't dig a grave. And there were dogs. There were all these other dead people. It was the scariest part, seeing the bodies. Even the rovers weren't that bad. I just kept thinking, *I can't leave Mama here with all these dead people.*'

Xavier was quiet. Often he wished his mother had died, while she had still been the person he wanted her to be. He'd wished it so often he didn't even feel guilty anymore; it was just another one of the thoughts running around his head whether he wanted them to, or not.

'The Angels won't hurt her,' Xavier said at last. 'They work by a strict code. In fact, they'll probably test her brain patterns and when they find out she's OK, they'll let her go.'

Elsa frowned. 'How naïve are you? They're not going to let her go. They'll find out she's Amir's daughter. They'll find out she's immune to scripts. They'll probably make an experiment out of her.'

Xavier laughed. 'You've been hanging out with paranoid people too long. You think Washington cares about Roksana Ansari? They probably don't even know who she is.'

'They know who FallN is,' Elsa said. 'If they figure that out, she's finished.'

'Roksana's smart. She'll be OK.'

'We have to help Amir,' Elsa said. 'I've been thinking. He didn't desert her. He must have come out here to get help. Powaqa's a Rider, sort of.'

'Powaqa is a horse trainer, Elsa. Big difference between her and Amir.'

'Maybe, but Powaqa has all her marbles. Amir doesn't. Powaqa has working lightborn equipment. Powaqa's not under threat of being bombed to smithereens every night.'

'Powaqa doesn't like him.'

'Tell me about it! I heard her talking to him this afternoon. He was begging her to help him, because he's sick. She totally stonewalled him. She called him a thief. Was that some Hopi thing, like, *you thief, you stole our land*? I mean, what could he steal?'

'He stole the Kiss. That's probably what she meant.'

'He stole the Kiss? What does he want with it?'

'I don't know. It's not like it's a fix or anything.'

'Maybe it has something to do with curing people. You know, if it can stop your brain from maturing then maybe it's part of the way to stop shine. We should ask him.'

'Elsa, you got to understand, Powaqa is to me as Roksana is to you. Even when I don't agree with her, I feel loyal.'

'The only person you can be loyal to is yourself.'

Xavier shut his eyes.

Elsa said, 'Did Melanie tell you Amir's scripts are making people better?'

'She didn't have to tell me. I could see that for myself.'

'He's a visionary, Xavier. If Roksana was here, she would want to help him. I know she would. And I'm sure he came here for a reason.'

'Medicine. That's what he kept saying. But he was half out of it.'

'See?' said Elsa. 'He was bringing the fix. You can see the effects!'

Xavier nodded. 'I know. He's got something, that's for sure. But what can we do?'

'We have to talk to him. I wish I wasn't stuck like this . . .'

'Leave Amir to me,' Xavier said. 'He's my problem now.'

Ch-ch-changes

Xavier stayed with Elsa until supper was over and the kitchen deserted, except for Pavarotti and his pregnant girlfriend washing dishes and talking. Actually, Pavarotti was talking; Beth was in a kind of rapture just listening to him. Xavier felt like he'd walked in on them having sex.

He stepped through the screen door and on to the back porch. There was an electric hum in the semi-darkness. Pool filter? It couldn't be. He could hear a soft splashing and when he looked over the fence, Melanie was swimming laps. He shook his head.

Where was the power coming from? And who was crazy enough to waste that kind of water?

Power-wise, the pool was the least of it. The working corral on the north side of the house was ablaze with electric light. Only a few horses were there, nosing the ground, searching for wisps of hay. Powaqa was perched on the top rail near the gate with her Stetson on her head and her Feynman balanced on her knees. She was tinkering with her lightborns.

He climbed up beside her.

'I couldn't get no Marlboros,' he said. 'Only Camels. I left them for you in the barn.'

For long moments he watched her moving segments of shine code around, highlighting and zooming. She didn't acknowledge him. He felt blown off. Annoyed, he stirred, about to leave.

'You took my best horse.'

So that was why she was mad. The horse. He cleared his throat.

'I wasn't gonna take the worst. I went to find Kiss.'

Finally she looked at him, but it was a flat gaze.

'Pavarotti wants to give the ranch to Doug. The tribal council have agreed to it. That means that any control I had is gone.'

'I heard. So that's it? Pavarotti can talk now, and he can sign his name, so that makes it all legal? We're still inside the quarantine zone.'

'Tribal law doesn't recognize the legality of the quarantine zone. If the council want to get behind Doug, there's nothing I can do.'

'Pavarotti should sign it over to you, Powaqa.'

Powaqa shrugged. 'I'm not interested in running a business.'

'You call this a business?' Xavier scoffed.

'It will be. When Los Sombres gets brought back under the yoke, this place will be valuable. But I don't want to play that game, and I sure don't want a battle with Doug. I'm a horse trainer.'

Xavier didn't know what to say. He looked at the dirt.

'If you do nothing, eventually the child welfare office will begin an investigation, and you kids will be relocated ahead of the other refugees. You'll probably be separated from your mom.'

'But she's getting better!'

'She might be able to get into a rehab programme in the long term. But I think you should come with me to Gila River. You'd be safe there until the situation in Los Sombres is more stable.'

'And my mom?'

'I can get her a job. She's already working on some stuff.'

Xavier shook his head. 'You have an answer for every-thing.'

'No, I don't. It's not an ideal situation. It's not like a math problem where you can solve it. We have to just get by, Xavier.'

He let out a frustrated snort. 'Yeah. I know about that. Speaking of solving problems, though. I know who John Doe is. He's Amir Ansari, he's a bigtime Rider.'

Powaqa's expression closed like a door.

'He asked you to use the equipment, didn't he? He asked you to help him. Why did you say no?'

'He's broken. But it doesn't matter what I say, because Doug's in charge now. Doug lets him use the lights, and there's nothing I can do about it.'

'Maybe Doug's right this time. I mean, so's everybody, broken. Come on, Powaqa. Why do you want to give up now? Whatever he's doing to people, it's working. Even you think my mother is better.'

'It's complicated.'

'Yeah? Is it complicated like Los Sombres is a total no-go zone where everybody in town tries to skin you alive when you're walking down the street?'

'I never said that. You're exaggerating.'

'Don't you think we should all work together?' Xavier said. 'But when adults say, let's all work together, what you really mean is we have to do what you want. Why do you hate Amir so much?'

'I don't hate him.'

'OK, why are you afraid of him?'

'I'm not.'

'You are.'

'Xavier,' Powaqa sighed. 'Let go of it.'

Just those four words made him feel so alone. He searched her face for some glint of empathy, but she'd gone into lock-down.

'I can't let go of it,' he whispered. 'What do you want me to do? Give up? Go to an institution until I'm eighteen? Hide out on a reservation with no identity, no future? I'm fucked, and you're not even on my side.'

Now Powaqa looked disappointed. The look on her face hurt worse than the words she'd just said. All this time she'd never said anything about how Xavier should be grateful. Nothing about how she was helping him. He knew she thought he was spoiled, but she'd never made a point about it. Her people had helped his people, even though they had so little themselves. She'd treated him like he was her own kid.

In that moment it came at him in a rush, how much he owed her. How fucked he really was, if Powaqa was cutting him loose.

'Why didn't you tell me the truth?' he demanded. 'You let me think Los Sombres was just a bunch of psychos going around . . . I don't know, eating each other's babies and screwing dogs.'

She let out a guffaw. 'I never said that. I said it was a dangerous place, and it is. Your imagination filled in the blanks.'

'I'm serious. It isn't like that, Powaqa. There are good people in Los Sombres. It's hard for them to get by, but they do. And with Amir's fix, everything could change.'

She sighed. 'Maybe. But it's too late. The decision has been made and all we can do is get out of the way.'

'You let me think the robots were the good guys,' he said. 'You let me think the invasion was doing us a favour.'

Now she just looked sad.

'There are no good guys, Xavier. Only people, and the shit we get into.'

She looked away. Xavier followed her gaze. Kestejoo, the scrappy little black stallion that was Powaqa's favourite was standing at the fence, nose in the air, sniffing like a dog. The stadium lights seemed to vanish when they hit him. Not a gleam on him anywhere; he was pure matte black, like space without a star. Powaqa looked at the horse and shook her head.

'I think they're gonna waste Los Sombres for real. The airstrikes are to smoke us out. They'll give everybody a way out. Then they'll waste the whole area.'

'*Why?* Why now? Why would they care so much?'

She shook her head.

'Political stuff, outside. That's the way the world goes, and the reasons are never what the big power people say they are. I've seen it all before, just never on my own doorstep.'

'Well, what does the tribal council think?'

'We should get the heck out.'

Xavier snorted in frustration. Why did Powaqa have to be so . . . implacable? It was like talking to a wall sometimes. Whatever she was thinking, she held it inside. Like that damn black horse holding colour.

Xavier glanced at Powaqa's Feynman. 'What you working on, anyway?'

Powaqa snapped the lid down. She flicked off the shine and in the sudden blackness Xavier was blind. She jumped down from the fence, put her fingers to her lips and whistled.

'How's your little friend? Maybe you should stay with her in case she wakes up. She'll be scared.'

As Xavier's eyes adjusted, he heard the horse trot over. Xavier couldn't see the animal at all; moving darkness within darkness, he was only a wind. Then Kestejoo's bright eye was there, a few feet away, as the little black stallion turned his head to regard Xavier sideways. Powaqa laid her hand on his neck and he tossed his head, blowing.

'Come on, Xavier,' she snapped. 'We can't risk you being exposed to this shit.'

Kestejoo followed her, and the other horses followed the black horse.

All of Xavier's rehearsed defiance seemed to scatter. He

followed her too. She put the horses in a paddock on the other side of the barn. Then she turned to Xavier and pointed to the house.

'Go stay with your friend. She needs you.'

Xavier felt humiliated, angry. But he let her lock him in, like she did with all of the refugees, every night.

Through a back window, he watched her head off to her apartment at the rear of the main barn.

Doug and a couple of other burnouts were in the kitchen smoking weed and listening to the radio. All of the bunkbeds in the kids' rooms were occupied, and in one of the women's rooms a new mother was passed out with her newborn on her chest. He checked the other women's room. Elsa was asleep. Melanie sat in a beanbag with a candle, absorbed in sudoku. Chumana was in bed with her back to the door, with faint little beats popping out of the MP3 player she was listening to. The other beds were empty, and so were the other bedrooms that normally slept several people each. Xavier put his eye to the cracked door of Rex's small room. Rex was inside, jerking off in a ragged copy of Penthouse.

Xavier disabled the security system, popped open the bathroom window and stuck his head out. Powaqa's windows looked out on the mountain; the house, the drive, and the corral would be invisible to her. She wouldn't see him climb out.

She Blinded Me With Science

The diamond necklace was warm to the touch. Ghostly speckles of shine drifted from it even as Roksana undid the clasp. She was careful not to tug any of the fine hairs at the back of Irina's neck. She didn't breathe.

Irina's men were watching a Clint Eastwood movie in the office of Wax 'n' Gleam. Roksana had found them by their EM signal. They slouched in office chairs beneath an electric bug-zapper while Irina, unnoticed, slept under the sales desk behind them.

She needed to give the necklace a little pull to get it free from the side of Irina's neck, but she was afraid to do it. Then one of them paused the playback and both men went out to piss on the desiccated forecourt of the carwash.

With a jerk, the necklace was free. Roksana shot away from Irina, who sat up blearily, and slipped through one door while the men came in the other. She hid behind the dusty blue bristles of a giant roller brush and fumbled to put on the necklace.

Meanwhile, inside, the men had discovered Irina. Roksana heard Irina's nervous giggle, then the men laughing, too. 'We party now, yes?' Irina said shrilly.

Mitch's necklace lay heavy on Roksana's collarbone. It barely gleamed. She would be invisible to shinies now, with any luck. Maybe even invisible to exo-protectors. That would be a good trick.

And Irina?

Listening to the tone of the voices, Roksana only wanted to get away. She didn't want to witness rape. Or murder.

The men's laughter built to a crescendo. Irina was silent. There was a sudden crash and the flickering blue light of the TV went out, leaving only the bug zapper to limn the edges of the carwash equipment. Roksana swallowed.

Then Irina swung out of the office, her pale skin just showing in the general darkness outside. She flicked on a Maglite.

'They are easily controlled,' she said. 'Are you still here? We should talk.'

She walked to a parked Yamaha and swung her leg over the seat like a cowboy.

'I cannot see but I know you are here. Maybe we talk. You know I caught shine the morning of the Fall. Your father panics, leaves everything running. And I catch shine for him that was having made.'

'And it made you suicidal.'

'Only temporary. I recover.'

'After I saved your life.'

'Yet, I recover.'

'Enough to steal from my mother.'

'You have ice now. You know what you have?'

'I'm guessing it's a control mechanism. You want to fill me in some?'

Irina took out cigarettes from her tiny glittery party handbag. Then a matchbook from *Super Cactus Bar and Grill*. Lit up.

'What do you want to know, Roksana?' she said, around the cigarette. 'You saved my life. I owe you.'

Roksana fought the urge to laugh.

'If you owe me, why did you take the melatonin from my friend?'

'I had my reasons.'

'You'd better tell me about it all,' Roksana said. 'Everything. Starting with how you found me now.'

'It is not necklace that provides me for the ability of wishing actions and feeling these tensions. Necklace makes invisible. And necklace can command in limited range – but not for you.'

'Not for me? How do you know so much?'

'Your father. He is responsible for a very remarkable lightborn. Almost a fix . . . but nothing is so simple anymore.'

'So . . . your goon. That Bobby guy. What he told me – did you put him up to that?'

'What did he say?' Irina's brow furrowed cutely. Roksana couldn't tell if she was dissembling.

'He said for me to Ride my father's shine. Did you tell him to say that?'

Irina made a dismissive noise. 'I told him nothing of this kind. Everyone knows you are impervious to lightborns.'

'So why did Bobby say I could save the city?' Roksana asked. 'Look, I've never ridden shine in my life. The way things are going, maybe I never will. I don't even *need* a fix.'

Irina pointed the cigarette at her. 'Exactly that is right. You don't need fix because you are fix.'

'What?'

'Your brain is template for resistance. Your father used you. Surely you knew this?'

The smoke from Irina's cigarette turned over on itself and shivered.

You Are Fix

Roksana didn't know where to look. 'What do you mean, he used me?'

'You were his model. Why else would he keep you here in the face of such danger?'

'Because I wanted to stay. Because of my mother. Because he . . . needed me.'

'Oh, he needed you indeed. He needed you to give him model for survival.'

'I don't believe you.'

'You don't want to believe me, but if you searching inside yourself you can feel the truth of the words I am telling.'

No. Not really. But play along for now.

'So you're saying, all those times I thought he was testing me to see if I could receive shine, he was really doing something else?'

'Reading the brain's response patterns to light.'

'So he could use them?'

'Exactly. He used you as natural model of resistance. Then he could build lightborn that would replicate those brain patterns and make this person insensitive to shine. Rogue guards, the AI components of Field, can't manipulate this person anymore.'

'But if he did that, if he cured you, Irina . . . why keep going? Why not just beam the shine out to everybody?'

'Because of damage. Los Sombres is ruined. I am still suffering mental injury. I know it. You know it. Your father knows it. He knows because he's damaged too. We are better than we were, and we are no longer vulnerable to these renegades in Field. But we can't be cured. We live with our affliction.'

'Then why call it a fix at all?'

'It's not fix for person. It's fix for Field.'

'I really don't get that at all.'

'Field is key to everything. No matter what your father said about renouncing shine, he knows it can't be done. We can't go back. Lightborns are too much a part of life. There are bad ones and good ones. The key is having Field to regulate. Field keeps us safe, and Field was compromised in the Fall. So the only thing that can be cured is Field itself.'

'What do my brain patterns have to do with that?'

'Your resistance has been turned into shine. If we can get the Field repaired and updated, then the guards will be able to administer that shine whenever there is a security breach like this rogue AI that set off the Fall. Leaks of dangerous lightborns could be stopped in their tracks, before they could get hold of public consciousness.'

'*But . . .?* I can hear it in your voice, there's a "but".'

'OK, but. First, Field itself has to be made whole. It's controlled by rogue AIs. It won't submit to external control. It has hold of city. It's Field we must fix.'

'Like I said, I can't do that. I don't even Ride.'

Irina shrugged.

'Someone has to take over from Amir. He's gone too long.'

'And that person is you?' Roksana thought she could see where all this was going. She thought it was all a power play by Irina.

But Irina said, 'No. I am at the limit of function. I'm broken, and I'm not Rider, and I struggle to keep red line going. Necklace is not enough. The answer lies with tool you hold in your hands.' Irina gazed at the Feynman. 'That is your father's emergency backup. We have to figure out how to get into that machine, and we must accomplish before someone else realizes we have it. Until then, Feynman is MacGuffin, as they say. We are not only ones who want it.'

'Why did he leave it behind, then? Irina, this Feynman might not even be the real deal. It could be a fake, a decoy. We have to find my father. Didn't he tell you where he was going?'

Irina shook her head.

'He disappears. He was saying he wanted giving latest version of fix to someone uncontaminated. Someone pure.'

'That would have to be a child,' Roksana said sharply.

Irina nodded.

'He had his eye on your friend, little girl. He expected her to grow up faster. But so far she is not ready.'

Roksana was getting angry; Irina didn't even attempt to act guilty about what she was saying.

'Do you have her now? Tell me, Irina.'

'No. I don't have her. I was hoping you knew where she was.'

'If I did, I wouldn't tell you. Now I get it, Irina. You took the melatonin from Xavier because you wanted to use him. You want him to Ride for you.'

Irina nodded. 'He would be ideal candidate. I could teach him about Field.'

Various sleazy images played across Roksana's mind as she pictured Irina 'teaching' Xavier everything she knew.

'You and my father seem to have talked a lot,' she said bitterly. 'Was there anything going on in his head that you didn't know about?'

Irina narrowed her eyes.

'I never fucked him,' she said, tapping ash. 'If that matters.'

Roksana tried not to rise to it. Irina was dangerous. Roksana thought she probably had something inside her with jaws and teeth, some alligator part that would rise up and gulp you down in one bite, if you were in the wrong place.

Softly, Irina added, 'There is much going on inside your father's head that even he doesn't know, Roksana. The Fall broke him badly. He is crippled. We all are. All but you.'

The watery hazel eyes flickered, but could not focus on Roksana. Irina sucked the smoke down her perfect throat, into her doll's body, and still looked for Roksana with a penetrating hunger. Irina's desire was like a cold hand over her heart.

Suddenly Roksana wanted to cry. She thought of Mitch. The last time Mitch had hugged her, before all the flesh fell from her bones and she turned into skeleton-woman. If Mitch were here, she'd cold-cock this bitch.

'The self-pity does not become you,' Irina said stiffly. 'You are lucky one. We are cursed.'

As if it were the most natural action in the world, Irina lifted one foot to her mouth and began to gnaw her own toenail. Roksana snorted. All that Northern European dignity, that excess of pathos – it was hard to take, especially from someone who smelled like Irina smelled. Beautiful and ragged. Foul, knife-edged, humourless. Roksana tucked the Feynman against her chest like it was a schoolbook. She wanted Mitch.

'I'm gonna take my MacGuffin and go check on my mom.'

Irina's bare leg had sculpted hollows where most women had cellulite. She paused in mid-grooming, the way cats do. She tilted her head.

'Remember, I am controlling red line. OSM rises. I have powers.'

Roksana turned.

'Powers?'

'Los Sombres can recover. If the Field can be repaired, sanity will return.'

'Tell that to the Army.'

Irina ignored Roksana's attitude. 'Your mother. If I fix her, if I saving her from prana delusion, then you are trusting me?'

Roksana's jaws snapped together.

'I don't want you anywhere near my mother. You understand me, Irina? I'm not a violent person, but you stay away from her. She's been through enough.'

'You have much power now, you know this? You are invisible, and you have MacGuffin. Keep it safe. Soon we work together. You will see.'

Vox Pod

On the way to Jambalaya, Roksana stopped at Walmart to get a MacGuffin carrier. Place was deserted except for pigeons. As she picked through what was left of the handbags, it amused her to realize that retail therapy had the capacity to soothe her, even now. She crawled under a sale table and got involved disentangling cheap pocketbooks from each other.

When her radio buzzed, she startled and hit her head on a set of bunker drawers.

'*Joey Shoji to FallN,*' said a voice. '*Do you copy, over?*' Pause. Roksana shut her eyes. Joey who?

'*FallN, this is Joey Shoji from Vox Pod. Please indicate if you can hear me.*'

She was not in the mood to give an interview. And anyway, she wasn't supposed to be meeting the Vox Pod guy until Friday.

Joey said, '*I know I'm supposed to meet you near the fountain outside the courthouse, but there are a bunch of scary people near there and I was wondering if we could connect somewhere else. If you can hear me please reply on this channel, over.*'

Roksana rubbed her head. It must be Friday.

'Fuck,' she said. 'I bet he has a whole team. Where's my

team? I need somebody to find me a bag for my MacGuffin so I don't have to do this shit myself.'

She put the MacGuffin inside a fake crocodile old-lady bag with two handles, chosen because it had a good, strong zipper. Then she adjusted her earpiece and switched on her mic.

'Joey? This is FallN, over.'

'*Oh, what a relief, FallN can we have an alternate rendezvous point, because I—*'

—am a neurotic hothoused bigoted wuss who can't risk going for a crap without my personal stylist telling me how, Roksana thought. Media types annoyed her.

She said, 'Don't worry about the people by the fountain, they're fine. I'm running a little late, so if you and your people could maybe walk over to Third Street? Then I can meet you by El Duende Books, over.'

'*I copy, over,*' said Joey.

But when Roksana got to El Duende Books, there was no sign of anybody.

'I'm here, Joey, where are you, over?'

'*Oh, sorry. I'm in the store . . . um, over.*'

Roksana went inside. The bookstore had been relatively unmolested in the Fall; it was dark, but many of the shelves were intact. She couldn't hear the sound of Joey and his people, but then she spotted a man alone. Standing in front of the Current Bestsellers was a thirtysomething guy wearing board-ers, hiking boots, and an oversized Fleetwood Mac T-shirt that had seen better days. He glanced at an old Animal watch, revealing all kinds of Navajo silver on the forearm of his right hand, which he extended as Roksana approached. His skin was warm and damp. He was plump.

You don't see much of that in Los Sombres, Roksana thought, and instantly felt more comfortable about the guy. His ordinary clothes made the big, bug-eyed AI glasses slightly less alienating.

'Hi, I'm Joey Shoji. Thanks for meeting with me.'

Before Roksana could speak, Joey plunged on.

'FallN, can I ask how old you are?'

'Seventeen,' Roksana said. 'And for anybody listening, I'm not six feet tall and I don't go around on rollerblades, I don't carry a firearm and I don't have muscles. Or gold teeth. My ancestors come from Pakistan, Poland, and Africa. As far as I know. And I'm not into cannibalism. Sorry.'

Joey laughed and gestured to the bug-eye glasses. 'We're not recording yet. I spent a week getting used to this AI but it's still pretty weird.'

'What AI?' Roksana said sharply.

'It's a navigation system. It helps me find my way around without needing a GPS.'

'And what about shine?'

'Actually, I'm burned out.'

'Really? What did you do to deserve that?'

It was an incredibly rude question, but Roksana was in FallN mode now. FallN was blunt.

'I was on vacation in Singapore. This was the Nineties. They burn you out for petty shine crime there – or what they call crime, anyway. You know how it goes. Amnesty International helped me, and that's how I got into activism.'

'And your people?'

'People? This is it. Just me.'

'But . . . Vox Pod . . .'

'I know, I know, we're really big. But I had a hard time convincing my partners that it would be safe for me to do this report, and I thought it would be better not to risk any of the support staff.'

Roksana revised her initial opinion of Joey. Slightly.

'Now,' Joey continued. 'When I heard your casts I was struck by the way you're able to make such a powerful picture out of sound. If we can capture that kind of energy and work it in with my information about the agenda in the White House and some of the military dirt, then I think we have the basis for a very massive sonic argument. Vox Pod are really excited about working with you and although we can't predict what the government will do or how the military will react, we think that a lot of people are going to think differently about Los Sombres when they've listened to this report.'

Roksana resisted the urge to scrub her face with her hands and physically tear her hair.

Joey is a good guy, she kept saying to herself. *He can't help being ignorant. You've got to educate him.*

It all felt like too big of a stretch.

Joey reached out and touched Roksana's arm. 'You're so young,' he said suddenly. 'You know, I've been looking at your work for a long time. I think you're a hero. We don't have to play into the military's model. The world is watching. If we can get your message across, then I think you have a chance of saving Los Sombres. But there isn't much time.'

Roksana hadn't realized until now how much she had missed talking to adults who weren't fucked. Joey seemed so innocent, so whole; and he was giving Roksana his full attention, as if he really was going to do something good. A part of Roksana wanted to rage: *You bastards, what took you so long?* And another part wanted to cynically snipe: *You don't even know what you're dealing with – this will never work.* And a third part was like, *Take me, I'm yours, I'll do anything if you'll help me.*

After all, Joey was offering her the very support that her parents never could.

It's your Ride. You can do it.

Well, maybe there was more than one way to Ride. Roksana took a deep breath.

'OK, come on,' she said. 'Let's get out on the street.'

Midnight Cowboy

At first, there weren't many people in the corral. Rosa was there, and a couple of the people Xavier had seen earlier working cheerfully in the garden. Melanie was there, talking to Chumana's dad, who had shaved his head and had a patch over one eye. Pavarotti showed up just as Xavier was secreting himself behind the broken tractor. More people were arriving singly and in pairs, from all directions, moving quietly in the breezy dark.

Xavier crept closer, settling behind a stack of bales to watch. After about a minute, Melanie came down the path and climbed into the corral.

Now it was Amir sitting on the fence with a Feynman. It was like when Powaqa shined the horses, except for the fact that Amir was skinny, twitchy, male, and a whackjob. Also, instead of animals, the corral was full of people.

One by one, the lights came up. Xavier put his hands over his face to blot out the beams of light themselves, but through the slits between his fingers he could make quick peeks at individual people. He didn't know if this was safe or not. He was guessing.

Nothing much else seemed to happen. Xavier had expected

there to be talking . . . or something . . . but it was no different to Powaqa shining horses. People stood there and basked in the lights. Some of them took out compacts and recorded the signatures to look at, later. It was really no big deal.

Amir moved around the corral a few times, taking up different positions and squinting into the radiance he'd created, then making adjustments on the Feynman. He acted like a technician, nothing glamorous about him. Actually, there was a faint interruptedness in the Rider's gestures, like he'd been badly digitized.

The whole thing took about two hours. Then people started to leave, until it was only Amir, switching off the lights, and Xavier. Amir didn't notice Xavier coming up behind him.

'I know who you are, Amir,' Xavier said in his ear.

Amir gave an involuntary, fleabitten jump. But he didn't look at Xavier, and he didn't speak.

'You left Roksana behind. You fucked off out here because it was too dangerous with the bombs, and you didn't even warn her. Elsa's got a broken leg. Last I saw, Roksana was getting captured by the Angels. And you don't even care. I know who you are.'

'W-w-what-dddddddd-d-d-ddd-d-do you you you you whatdoyou mean? Captured by Angels? What are you t-t-t-t-ta-talk-t-t-t-t-t-talking about?'

'I don't know if I should even tell you,' Xavier said. 'Roksana doesn't know where you are. She was waiting for you to show up and fix everything, and she went to look for you and they caught her. Would it have killed you to let her know what you were doing?'

Amir covered his face with his hands.

'B-b-better for her n-n-n-n-nnot to know. I can't. Always. Stay. In c-c-c-con-c-cococo-c-c-c-c-c-c-cc—'

'Control?'

'Control!' Amir coughed.

Typical lameass adult excuse. 'Yeah, Powaqa says you're *broken.*'

Amir nodded. 'The F-f-f-f—'

'Fall,' Xavier finished. 'The Fall damaged you, just like all the adults. But you did this fix. And now you need to get it going, right, get it off the ground and you came out here. Why? Because of the bombs? Did you know there were going to be bombs?'

Amir shook his head, 'B-b-b-because of P-pow—'

'Powaqa. You were looking for her.'

'Mm. Sh-sh-she w-w-w-ouldn't help me. S-so I ha-had to f-f-f-find another w-w-w-way.'

'You did that deal with Doug. Now your fix is working. Why doesn't it work on you, then?'

'Complicated.'

That word again.

'Try me. I'm not as young as I look.'

Amir swayed from side to side as he studied Xavier. It was a pretty shitty experience, being around this man, who smelled bad, whose movements were edgy, who tended to accidentally spit when he talked. Several times in the conversation Xavier had consciously stopped himself from recoiling.

Now, he thought Amir looked *hungry.*

'N-n-n-not here. Tomorrow. Day b-b-b-b-reak. At the c-c-c-cave.'

Oh great, Xavier thought, as he watched Amir hobble away. The cave. The Indian spook place.

Great.

And Again: Fuck

'Thank you for working with me,' Joey said when they were done recording. 'I'll take this material back and edit it into something really, really compelling.'

Roksana stood back while Joey radioed his contact for helicopter pickup. Roksana's performance was over. Soon she would be alone again, alone with the MacGuffin in its crocodile grandma bag.

She had to suppress the urge to beg, 'Take me with you.'

The urge to press the bag into Joey's hands. Say, 'Take this to your people.'

Say, 'Take this responsibility away from me.'

Suppressed it. Barely.

Joey took Roksana's hands.

'Are you going to be OK?'

'Oh, yeah,' Roksana laughed. 'I'm always OK. That's the nature of me.'

Joey's brow rumpled. 'You are a surprise, FallN. I wonder if you realize how important you are, as an individual, to America.'

Roksana really wasn't up for this. She didn't want to bond with this person she would never see again. She didn't want to take the outstretched hand, because in the end it never helped. Nobody could save her.

'I know what I am,' Roksana said. 'I'm the template for the fix, I'm the voice for those who have no voice, and I'm the cook making a meal out of some old boot. I'm all kinds of things. America? I don't even know what America is. It's the word people use when they don't want to take personal responsibility.'

She thought it was a nice, final sound bite – even though the recording equipment was off. She didn't want Joey to go away with the idea that she was somebody to be patronized.

Joey's voice deepened. 'Template? Can you explain that?'

Shit. She hadn't meant to go there.

'I gotta go, Joey. Thanks for your support, and take care getting out safely.'

She was already moving away. Joey followed, talking fast.

'Wait a second. When you say "template", do you mean that there's something about you that we could copy?'

'Copy my badass attitude,' Roksana said, running across the street and picking up a scooter from the sidewalk.

'Roksana, come on! Don't run away. Fill me in here . . .'

Fuck, thought Roksana. Oh fuck, fuck, and again fuck.

Joey was bright enough to do his own filling in. The damage was done.

Jeff's Tires

Irina was to be found beside a wood fire in the parking lot of Jeff's Discount Tires. A row of pigeons were cooking on a spit. She glanced up at the sound of Roksana's boots, squinted as she failed to see Roksana, and then resumed plucking a dead pigeon.

'The necklace looks good on you,' she said with a smile.

'About my mother,' Roksana said. 'Did you mean what you said? You can fix her?'

Irina paused, holding the dead bird lightly. Its head drooped between her fingers.

'I meant it. We work together on this?'

'That depends what you're asking.'

'To fix the Field we need a child. There was a girl in the McDonald's, but now find her proves difficulty. I am locked out of my palace. I no longer am in command with the people, unless you give back necklace to me . . .'

Before Roksana could retort with some remark about air-born pigs, Irina shot to her feet. Her face was paper white. She looked through Roksana, uttered something in Russian. Held out her hand to Roksana like a mother to a child.

'Come! Quickly!'

Roksana followed Irina around the back of a parked semi; over her shoulder, she glimpsed spider robots.

'The fucking podcast,' Roksana gasped. 'They want me bad now.'

'Podcast? What podcast?'

Irina vaulted on to the edge of the Jeff's Tires' loading bay and reached down blindly, offering her hand to help as Roksana scrambled up. The two of them ran through the building to the back door.

There were more robots coming across the back parking lot. They both shrank behind a stack of cardboard boxes. There was packing material all around.

'What podcast, Roksana?' Irina gasped.

'I went on Vox Pod. To try to appeal to people's conscience.'

'You *fool*. Are you not understanding simple fact which everything we must be secrecy?'

'Don't talk to me like that. I'm not in on your secrets. I had to do something.'

Irina groped in the air near Roksana; next moment, Roksana found herself on the ground in the midst of a huge spill of styrofoam popcorn. Irina was sitting on top of her, hitting her about the head and shoulders. Stunned that Irina had taken her down so easily, Roksana didn't react quickly. Then, when she brought her arms up to cover her face, Irina punched her in the stomach. She grabbed at the necklace and started tugging.

Roksana pushed her hands into Irina's face. Irina bit her. Roksana bucked her hips up and rolled, pushing Irina away at the same time. Irina came scrambling back towards her, but Roksana dove to one side and skipped back. Irina couldn't see Roksana, but she came after her anyway. Popcorn went flying. Roksana whirled and sprinted away. She made it to a metal staircase and pounded up it.

Irina stood at the bottom of the stairs.

'Hide!' she hissed. 'Don't let them get Feynman.'

Crazy. One minute Irina attacked you; the next she defended you. Roksana abandoned her and ran across a gangway to a high window. The exo-protectors were still picking their inexorable way across the parking lot, converging on the warehouse.

Roksana found a walkway that was positioned right under the rafters. She jumped up and caught hold of a beam. If she made her way over to a skylight, she could get on the roof. She knew that the roof of Jeff's adjoined the roof of Staples. She might even make it all the way down the line to the lumberyard at the end of the strip.

She looked down. Irina had realized her danger; she ran deeper into the warehouse, disappearing into an office.

Roksana worked her way across the warehouse until she was about fifteen feet away from a domed skylight. Spyders reached the loading bay doors open at the back of the warehouse. They scuttled into the building.

Roksana squinted at the skylight. She was calculating the best way of breaking it open when a shadow fell across her from above.

The skylight shattered.

A thing that looked like a wrecking ball fell through the skylight and hit a stack of display tyres, below. It bounced twice and then sat there, gleaming.

It looked like a bomb.

Say It Was You

'I brought you here because this cave is a significant place.' Amir gestured around the cave. It was inconspicuous and small, but it had a vibe about it. Even Xavier could feel it. The floor was worn down by use. There was a smell of old tobacco and cougar. 'It's a place of medicine. This is appropriate, because lightborns are medicine, not in the drugstore sense, but in the Native American sense.'

'You said that when you came,' Xavier interjected. 'You said something about medicine. I thought you wanted shine, like drugs.'

Amir twitched, licked his lips, looked away.

'The Native peoples have explored these mental territories long before there were lightborns. The shaman roads are pathways through the neural structures we all share. The roads can be opened by chemicals, by ritual, by faith – but only crudely.'

Amir paused, thinking. He had spoken clearly, and his bizarre jerking-and-twitching mannerisms were dampened, or absent. Xavier wondered whether Amir had been taking his own 'medicine'.

'My time in the Fall has left me with too much damage to ever be whole again. Bad scripts, hostile AIs, security routines run amok – the Field is a dangerous place. The protection that my lightborn can offer will be most effective for a person who has not sustained this kind of damage in the Fall. The Hopi have escaped the Fall. They are ideal candidates for the light-born that I've created, but they refuse it.'

'I guess you can't really blame them.'

'I thought maybe one person would have the courage to walk a new road. The Native peoples were exploring these pathways long before lightborn technology was invented. Recently they have adapted lightborns to give them access to the medicine roads their ancestors walked using mush-rooms and peyote. Their culture knows all about opening up the unexplored potentials in our biology – they would say, in our spirit. But they are too caught up in the past. I tried to make Chumana understand this. She Rides the medicine paths, and her brain has already been sculpted by native lightborns. She is receptive to shine. She is capable of making this journey, but she refuses. Her people are pitted against change.'

'It's lucky for us that they are,' Xavier said. 'I'd be dead if it wasn't for Powaqa.'

'Yeah?' Amir said in a small, nasal voice. 'Life is full of ironies like that. You'll see.'

Xavier said, 'Can't you just give this information to the authorities outside quarantine? Can't you, like, package up your fix and send it to them? Then they could test it and start using it.'

Amir shook his head, laughing. '*They'd* never look at it. *They'd* be too scared of catching something from it. This is a job for the bold, Xavier.'

'So . . . can you explain how it works?'

'When an undamaged person receives the lightborn, their

mind will adapt to it and it will adapt to them. Say it was you, Xavier.'

And in spite of himself, Xavier felt a thrill at the suggestion.

'Say it was you. You'll change. You'll be able to perceive the Field and enter into it at will. You'll be able to Ride shine and you'll be able to deal with the AIs. You'll be able to protect yourself from harm. You'll walk into Los Sombres like a king returning to his own country. And then you can set about making repairs to the Field and turning this whole thing around.'

'How am I going to repair the Field? I don't know anything about it. I don't even know how to get in.'

'The Field isn't a place. It's a state of mind. In the Field, the Rider becomes able to make sense of the structural patterns that make up the lightborn. He or she can see inside the lightborn and manipulate it. The lightborn is then beamed out, and in turn it affects us. Think of a biofeedback system on an epic scale.

'The fix would provide you with a high level of control over your own brain. Most people don't have the mental control to be Riders. Riders have to process lightborns of tremendous complexity, lightborns that work on the cortex in a detailed way. Most people use lightborns the way people used to use drugs. Riders, on the other hand, have a kind of double-consciousness that lets us use ourselves to work on lightborns. And that's what you'd have, Xavier. For someone like you, with my shine? The sky's the limit. You would be the first of a new generation of Riders, Riders like the world has never seen. You're it, kid.'

Amir paused and looked Xavier up and down. Everything that had happened to Xavier until now seemed to swerve and point directly back at Xavier and ask the biggest question of his life. Like everything was leading to this snap decision, and it had to be this way. Was always meant to be. Like, a moment of destiny. Yeah. Destiny.

'So what do you say? Are you up for it?'

Xavier felt a wildness rising up inside him. It was a feeling as bold as the land with its crazy-ass shapes and searing sky. It was a feeling that said, *the time is now*.

'Shit, yeah,' he said. 'I'll do it.'

On the Air

Breakfast time had passed. Sam Ghost Money Power was in the driveway, trading his wares out of the back of a dusty silver Animal. Xavier detoured around the scene. He wanted to tell Elsa what Amir had offered him.

Doug was on the CB in the kitchen. He broke off his conversation when Xavier came in. There was something nasty and exaggerated in his face.

'You seen Rex?'

'Me? No, not lately.'

Xavier wished he hadn't come in the room. Doug was in a bad, bad mood. He didn't have to say anything – you could feel it. It was like the room itself – the floor, the cabinets, the sink – was scared of Doug and sort of shrinking back.

'If you see him, you tell him I'm looking for him.'

Doug kicked the screen door open and swaggered outside.

Somebody's going to get hit, Xavier thought. He wondered what Rex had done.

Elsa was doing a book of crosswords in her bed. Xavier filled her in on what Amir had told him.

'Looks like you're the Chosen One,' she said with a little smile. 'Did you do it yet?'

Xavier shook his head. 'We're meeting tonight. He said it might take more than one session, depending on how much priming my brain needs . . . I don't know, I never paid much attention to that stuff in school.'

'I know what he means. We know you can receive lightborns, but under normal circumstances you would be doing training shine for a while, to teach your cortex how to process the information. He's not sure whether you'll get the full whack the first time, that's all.'

Xavier shrugged. 'It worked for Rex,' he said.

'Well, yes and no. I saw Rex this morning and he was talking some high-level weirdness.'

'Yeah? Like what?'

'It was like he was seeing stuff in the room that wasn't there. You ever watch somebody sleepwalk? It was like that. He tried to pour a cup of coffee with one of Melanie's Wandering Jews.' She laughed. 'At first I thought he was just messing around, but then he started talking about canals of dust, and lost cities buried in the desert. He didn't sound like Rex at all. Then he said he was turning into a horse and it was a better life. Then he ran off. It was . . . mildly surreal.'

Xavier stood up and careered around the tiny room, moving randomly. Frustrated.

'Don't tell me this! I'm going to take that fix. I don't want to hear about the side effects.'

'Sorry.' Elsa put down the crossword. 'Don't worry about it too much. Believe me, I've seen a lot worse.'

'Yeah, so have I,' Xavier said darkly. He swung his arms, wishing he could find some direction for all the conflict he was feeling.

'There are going to be risks, of course,' he added. 'Nobody said it was going to be a barbecue.'

'You're so right. Oh! Speaking of barbecue, is that Sam outside? Because you should go ask him about Roksana. Maybe he heard something.'

But Sam Ghost Money Power was gone. Melanie was just coming inside with her loot, and Sam's silver Animal had disappeared down the long drive.

'Shit,' said Xavier. 'I wish I'd talked to him. Maybe he's seen Roksana in town. Or maybe he heard something about what the Angels did to her.'

Melanie said, 'He hasn't been there. He was just up in Illinois visiting his uncle. That was why he had so much good shit.'

She showed Xavier a pair of purple sunglasses with sequins, a sixpack of imported Cobra beer and a new MP3 video player.

'This is loaded with a whole bunch of new podcasts,' she said. 'Let's make popcorn and watch.'

'I don't want to watch podcasts,' Xavier said.

'Elsa needs something to do besides read. Do you know that I caught her reading *Invitation to a Beheading*? That's not really appropriate, is it? Come on, Xavier, help me hook it up to the monitor in the kitchen.'

They watched Spongebob, followed by the MTV music awards. Xavier went outside to get a beer. He was trying to relax while he waited for darkness and the fulfilment of Amir's promise. Right now, the day was almost too bright. The sky looked solid, and even the clouds were so sharply defined by sunlight that they seemed to have hard edges. What lightborns, Xavier wondered, were in the sun?

Elsa shrieked.

He shot back into the kitchen. Elsa was holding her head in one hand and pointing to the screen with the other.

There was a still photo of Roksana. The male voiceover was saying:

'. . . *highlights of the day I spent with FallN. I was able to travel safely to and from Los Sombres because I'm burned out. I have to tell you, folks, that I've resented being burned out for many years. But* recently, thanks to being burned out, I was able to do something that very few people can do. I feel privileged to be able to bring you this sound footage that I recorded personally within the devastation of Los Sombres.

'The images you're going to see come from FallN's friend Pi, who has been photographing the aftermath of the Blink. Pi is one of the many victims of the Fall who are basically peaceful, but who have suffered damage. I tried speaking to Pi about why he refuses to evacuate. This is what it sounded like.'

Xavier reached over and paused the playback.

'When was this recorded?'

Melanie said, 'It was transmitted yesterday. I heard about it on the radio this morning. I think Vox Pod recorded it sometime in the last day or so. It's hot.'

Elsa said, 'Then Roksana's . . . free . . . ?'

'If it's for real,' Xavier said. 'Let's look at the rest of it. Just because they say FallN, doesn't mean it's the real deal.'

'OK, let's play it,' Melanie said.

'Hey, Pi, how you doing? I'm Joey from Vox Pod, an independent information and education panel dedicated to bringing the world to the pod and the pod to the world. These photographs are amazing! Were you a professional before the Fall hit Los Sombres?'

A man's deep voice replied, '457-398361657-9865-0235073033 – 755836638759809809893 – 379857-6-1=02309349849840948904'

Joey: 'OK . . . FallN, can you help me out here?'

Roksana's voice: 'Oh, he's always like that. He talks in numbers, but he's harmless. Pi, can we have these? Joey needs them. Do you mind? Look, I got shoes. Size 9AAA. Bet you thought I wouldn't find them. Are those cool or what?'

Pi: '9080808809809809809809723423869347709-9'

FallN: 'Yeah, I'm with you there, Pi, my friend. Thanks for the pictures. You need anything else? OK, see you later.'

Joey: 'I presented this cut to Dr Laura Reesman from the

University of Rochester, an expert on lightborns and brain damage, and she said:

Reesman: 'Cases as clear cut as this, where the damage is highly specific and the person enjoys a high level of function despite the reconfiguration of the language centres, are all too rare in the public sphere. I only wish that the legislation on Los Sombres didn't prevent us from studying people like Pi and learning from his misfortune.'

Joey: 'I was originally going to make this podcast pure audio. But when I saw these images I knew they had to be seen.'

Image: kids playing basketball with a blasted-out apartment building in the backdrop.

Image: old women weeding a garden in front of the municipal library.

Image: a pregnant woman cooking over an open fire, a dog at her feet.

Image: helpmeets sorting through Red Cross packages dropped from the air.

Image: a military checkpoint on the east side. Robot walkers tagged with graffiti hearts and flowers.

Black screen.

Joey: 'We've been walking through a city that is virtually a ghost town. Considering the scale of the crisis here, I'm surprised that I don't feel more threatened.'

FallN: 'Things have changed a lot in two years. When there were more people, it was much more violent. Most of us who are left have figured out how to get along, or avoid each other. And the system that I use, of delivering therapeutic lightborns according to a code embedded in music, this has also helped.'

Joey: 'And for this people call you a terrorist.'

FallN: 'I guess I could be if I were to use my powers for evil.'

Joey: 'So, we're standing outside the old Neiman Marcus downtown. It looks like there's a lot of good stuff still here. With the materialism angle, where are you with that?'

FallN: 'I really miss stuff. But what am I going to do with a diamond necklace here? What am I going to do with a fancy car? Before this, people would talk about losing everything and they would mean, losing their job, their house, their stuff . . . people in the Fall have lost all of those things and more than that, they've lost themselves.'

Joey: 'How has it changed you?'

FallN: 'How hasn't it? If you told me the Fall was going to happen, I wouldn't believe I could survive it. I'm not the same person I was when it started. All I wanted in those days was to Ride shine. All my friends were doing it. Younger kids than me. I felt so excluded, and I felt really sorry for myself.' (laughs)

Joey: 'And now?'

FallN: 'Now? I'm glad if I stay healthy and get something to eat every day, and don't get attacked or whatever! Different priorities. But I still feel sorry for myself sometimes. Sometimes I still wish I could Ride, because then I wouldn't have to play through this thing with a full deck. Sometimes I think it would be easier being crazy. Sometimes, I just hate them all. The shinies. I hate them, because no matter what I do, most of the time they don't appreciate it or even notice it. But then . . .'

Joey: '. . . then?'

FallN: 'Then I think about the old people who never expected to end up this way. I think about the babies born in the Fall, who are growing up with mortars falling. I think about the people who work on the red line every day to keep us all alive. There is an underlying order here in Los Sombres, whether you want to see it or not. As long as everyone else is trying, I won't give up.'

Joey: 'A lot of the experts say that the only way we can learn from Los Sombres is by taking the Field down completely and dissecting the records in the light system. Physically examining what has happened here. And the only way that can be done, of course, is by putting out the lights.'

FallN: 'That's like if somebody's sick and you kill them so you can take their brain apart and find out what's wrong with them. Even if you do learn something, well, now what? They're dead.'

Joey: 'So it's an academic exercise . . .'

FallN: 'We can solve this problem ourselves, if everybody just gets off our back and maybe starts helping us.'

Joey: 'FallN, do you think the Army will be able to put out the lights?'

FallN: 'I hope not, but I guess it depends on how aggressive the government wants to get. If they do destroy the lights, then they'll destroy whatever chance people here have. It's the lights that are helping people get better. I'm not sure how, but I do know that there are people out there in America and across the world who know enough about shine and the Field to help us. You got to want to do it. Not just turn your back on us because you think it won't happen to you.'

Joey: 'Well, Vox Pod listeners, you be the judge. Does FallN sound like a deranged maniac? She doesn't look like one to me. And after the day I've had, I think we could learn a lot from this culture of the shined, here in Los Sombres, the aptly named Shadow City. This is Joey Shoji for Vox Pod. Thanks for listening.'

Elsa looked at Xavier. Xavier looked at Elsa. Elsa looked like she was going to explode with joy. She grabbed herself and rocked from side to side, eyes turned skyward.

'Where were they?' Xavier said. 'Do you know that guy, Pi?'

Elsa nodded. 'Pi lives with a group on the fringes of the library district. But this was recorded days ago. Roksana could be anywhere – she's free, Xavier!'

'Yeah, yeah, it's real good news. Elsa, we have to find a way to get in touch with her. Does she pick up CB on that radio you guys used to use?'

'There's a frequency we could try. I never thought . . . I just assumed . . .'

'I know, I know, me too,' Xavier said. 'I just hope she's within range. I'm not sure about Doug's equipment. It's not that powerful.'

'This has to work,' Elsa said. 'It has to work, it has to work.'

'Come on, lean on me. She trusts you, so you do the talking.'

Cut the Ice

Cool air brushed Roksana's face from above. Below, the sphere seemed to crack in several places, with light leaking out through small holes as if it were a sieve.

Not a bomb. A subjugation beam.

They must have new hardware. She hadn't seen anything like this in the hospital siege.

No time to think about it. Noise on the roof. Scrabbling. Clicking. Something was coming through the skylight.

Spyders started swarming through the hole in the roof. They began to move along the rafters. They seemed to be working a random search pattern.

Very slowly, she began to creep along the beam. She needed to get her back to a wall, or preferably a corner. More robots came, through more holes.

I must be pretty important, Roksana thought.

She reached the wall and started to move laterally, until she was in the rear corner of the warehouse perched on a beam. She watched the spyders scuttle across the beams. If one came right up to her, she would have to kick it off the beam. It couldn't be helped.

But the real action now was going on in the warehouse.

She could hear Irina screaming things in Russian. She could hear furniture being overturned.

One crawler came out of the office dragging something.

It was Irina, trussed up in a net like an angry crab. The crawler dragged her across the warehouse floor. She was spitting and struggling, to no avail. The subjugation beams shone on her, and she laughed.

'You won't get me that way!' she said. 'Bring me to your Riders and let them look me in the eye. I'll give them some valuable feedback.'

She had a box cutter and was using it to slash the net. Before she could get completely free, another crawler sprayed her with mist. Irina foundered, coughing.

'I can overcome you,' she gasped. 'You'll have to kill me because you won't overpower my mind.'

In her other hand she held a flashlight, presumably loaded with some lightborn. Irina laughed through the gas.

Roksana made herself as tiny as possible, perched up in the farthest corner of the building like a frightened sparrow. The robots shot Irina with dozens of tiny darts, but she kept rallying. She did not lose consciousness.

The robots had ceased scanning the building and now all converged on Irina. She stood in a circle of them, row upon row of evacuation machines. They hadn't been designed to capture people alive – not if people were resisting.

Irina slashed away the last of the confining net and got to her feet.

'You are pathetic,' she spat at the robots. 'You have fallen behind the curve. You cannot keep up with Los Sombres.'

Irina slipped between two robots unhindered, and Roksana covered her mouth with her hand before any sound escaped. Irina made it almost to the loading bay door. Then she stopped dead. Roksana couldn't see what was outside. Irina began to back up, a step or two at first, then dodging side to side like a panicked deer. She held up her flashlight and a thin beam speared from her hand toward the door.

Soldiers came in. Ten of them. Roksana thought she must be hallucinating.

The soldiers were human. They weren't bothered in the slightest by whatever Irina was shining on them. The first tackled Irina and took her easily to the ground. Another helped to hold her down while a third expertly wrapped her in a strait-jacket. The rest jogged around the warehouse, checking every hidey-hole and muttering to each other through their helmets. They eyeballed the area where Roksana and Irina had scuffled, but they didn't linger.

Irina looked a lot less sexy in the new outfit. The soldiers took her away without a real search. And within an hour, still shaking, Roksana found herself alone in the rafters of Jeff's Discount Tires.

It was quiet. There weren't even any pigeons.

She opened her bag and checked the Feynman. That was when she saw her radio's call light flashing.

Contact

Even after an hour, Elsa could not accept that Roksana was not going to answer the radio. It was like, if Roksana was not answering the radio, she must be dead.

Xavier kept going outside, hoping to catch sight of Rex so he could see for himself what Rex was acting like. Maybe talk to him. But there was no sign of him or Doug.

'We'll try later,' Xavier said. 'She could be moving in and out of range. Or she might not even be listening.'

'Try one more time. Just one more time.'

Xavier said, 'FallN this is Xavier, over. Come in, FallN.'

Nothing.

'Fuck,' Xavier said, and threw the microphone down; the coiled cable sprang back and the mic rolled.

There was a click on the line. Two more clicks. A little space and six clicks.

'It's her,' Elsa said.

'It's just noise.'

'No, it's her. She doesn't want to use her voice for some reason.' Elsa lunged for the mic, but Xavier got to it first.

'FallN, if that's you listening, I need to talk to you. I have

information of . . . of the most critical importance. This is
Xavier. Say something, do something, so I know you can hear
me.'

Static. Roksana's half-whispered voice.

'I just had a narrow escape. I'm really wrecked.'

'Where are you.'

'Can't say. I almost got caught. Don't call me again. Over and out.'

'Wait! I have to tell you something. I'm at the ranch. Listen,
this is important.'

There was a silence. Elsa grabbed the mic from him.

'Rocky? I know you're on there. You answer this radio now.
Over goddammit.'

Another silence, too long. Xavier took the mic away from
Elsa. Then Roksana's voice, thick and chokey. *'Don't make me
cry. You wouldn't believe the day I'm having.'*

'Listen,' Xavier said urgently. 'I have to think how to say
this. The person you were looking for. I've seen that person.'

'Don't play with me.'

'It's true, Rocky!' Elsa interjected, and Xavier had to pull the
mic away from her again.

'We have a plan. We have to meet you.'

*'Better make it soon. Shit is getting heavy here. It's code purple,
Elsa—'*

The sound of four gunshots cracked across whatever
Roksana was saying. Elsa dropped to the concrete floor. Xavier
saw Rex's head go past the garage window at a clip. People
were shouting.

He dropped the mic and ran through the open garage door.
He could just see Rex disappearing around the other side of the
house, heading towards the barn. Everybody working in the
gardens was on their feet, looking towards the corral. Melanie
was climbing over the post and rail fence. She was headed for
the corral. And on the slope beyond the corral, on the dirt road
that led up to the mountain and Powaqa's cave, Xavier could

see Doug's Jeep parked at a crazy angle. Dust still hung in the air around the vehicle.

Between the garden and the corral, Pavarotti was lying on the ground. Melanie ran towards him, shouting over her shoulder, 'Get the first aid kit. Somebody! Move it!'

Several things happened at once. The people who had been working in the garden now grabbed their children and ran towards the house. The Hopi weavers who usually sat on the porch had already vanished inside.

No one helped Melanie.

No one followed Rex.

Xavier hesitated. He darted back into the garage.

'Elsa, Pavarotti's been shot. Let's get you back in the house.'

Elsa grabbed his forearm in a death grip.

'Don't you leave me,' she whispered, staring up at him out of eyes that seemed to be all white and black. 'These are shiny people.'

'I have to find out what's going on,' Xavier said. 'Go inside where they can take care of you.'

She shook her head violently. Picked up the mic again.

'Rocky? Rocky, are you still there, over?'

No response.

'I'm not leaving this radio,' Elsa said. 'You go do what you got to do. I'll be here.'

Xavier couldn't spare the time to argue. He left her there, pelted through the house and snatched up Melanie's emergency bag. He sprinted to the corral and found Melanie using her blue tank top as a pressure bandage against Pavarotti's chest.

'What happened?' Xavier said.

Melanie was shining Pavarotti with something from her medical kit.

'Rex shot him,' she said. 'Rex has been acting crazy all morning. He got shined up with something nasty.'

Xavier glanced over his shoulder. He couldn't see the barn from here. If Rex holed up in there with a gun, there would be trouble. If Rex went in the house . . . shit, why had Xavier told Elsa to sit tight? But what else could he have done? She had a broken leg. Fuck.

'I'll go look for him,' he said. 'Is Doug up the mountain?'

Melanie held a hypodermic needle in her teeth while she swabbed Pavarotti's arm. After she jabbed it in she said, 'Doug thinks Amir shined the kid. He's up there looking for Amir, so he can kill him.'

Pavarotti stirred.

'You can't take me out,' he whispered. 'I'm too big.'

And he smiled. The freckles stood out on his sunburned face, made him look diseased. His lips were white. Breaths weren't deep enough to keep a cat alive.

'Stay quiet,' Melanie commanded. 'Don't waste your energy talking.'

Pavarotti didn't even seem to hear her. He said, 'Doug found out Amir stole the Kiss. Doug's mad. But I'm many. You know what I'm saying?'

Melanie frowned in concentration as she took Pavarotti's pulse and rummaged in her bag at the same time.

'Where's Powaqa?' Xavier asked.

Pavarotti's eyes focused on the sky over Xavier's head. His mouth was wide open and Xavier could see his dental work and the nicotine on his teeth. Pavarotti was trembling something awful.

Melanie shook her head. 'Last I saw they were all up that road. Xavier, I need you to help me move him.'

'But—'

'Help me, Xavier. We'll get him inside. Rex isn't going to go on a killing spree. I think he's more scared than anything. Go get the stretcher for me.'

Xavier ran off to the house. He wanted to follow Rex, he

wanted to protect Elsa, he wanted to see what was going on between Doug and Amir up in the red rocks. But here he was helping Melanie – and how could he not? Pavarotti might die.

Inside the house, Xavier made a detour to the garage. No Elsa. But she couldn't walk . . . where could she be? He hesitated, scared and baffled.

'Psst!'

From behind a pile of boxes on the other side of Doug's motorcycle. Two white eyes.

'Stay there,' Xavier whispered back. 'Rex is dangerous. Just stay there until I get back, and if I don't come back in an hour or so, then try to find Melanie.'

He could just make out the movement of her head as she nodded.

Xavier helped Melanie move Pavarotti. Then he heard hooves, first trotting from the barn, then breaking into a gallop. Xavier raced around the side of the house as the horse picked up speed on the dirt driveway. It was Kestejoo.

Rex was riding towards Los Sombres, just as Xavier had ridden that night of the oil drum fires.

And from the road that led up the mountain there came an ululating scream.

Crawled out of Its Feathers

Doug and Amir were very small in the context of sky and land. They were on the road just below the medicine cave. Powaqa and Chumana stood in the cave entrance, watching the fight. Not that you could call it a fight.

Amir was on the ground. From the way the dust was hanging and the posture of each man, Xavier got the impression that Doug had just finished kicking the supine Rider.

'What the fuck you do to my boy?'

Amir made no effort to resist as Doug dragged him to his feet. But he didn't answer, either. Doug gripped Amir by the throat and pushed him up against the rock.

'First you telling my kid you can protect him if he just look at this shine. But my kid's not supposed to be ready for lightborns. So what the fuck you want with him? Huh?'

Amir tried to respond, but whatever he said was inaudible even as Xavier drew closer. Doug got up in Amir's face and shouted:

'Oh yeah? You call this help?'

Doug dragged a brown plastic jar out of his jacket pocket; Xavier recognized it at once. Doug rapped Amir on the forehead with it and it made a rattling noise.

'You stole the Kiss. My boy been unprotected. Now the shine can get him. You think we're fucking stupid around here, huh?'

Amir was like a rag doll in Doug's grip.

Xavier ran the last few strides to reach them. 'Wait! Doug! It's not what you think. Rex stopped taking—'

'Stay out of this, kid. Don't listen to this joker, no matter what he says.'

'He's a Rider. He knows a lot of stuff. He's been working on a fix for the Field, but he got driven out of the city before he could finish it. The bombs.'

'Don't you go listening to this whackjob like I did. He might be a Rider, but he ain't got no fix. He can't even tie his own shoelaces.' Doug shook Amir. 'You think you're gonna test your shit on my kid? I helped you. The Indian lady wasn't going to let you stay, but I backed you, we agreed you could use the lights. We had a deal you and me, right?'

Amir nodded – he couldn't speak, and from the way his face was changing shades, it looked like he couldn't breathe, either.

'Then you go and pull this shit? I don't think so.'

Doug head-butted the Rider. Xavier cringed. It was disgusting. Nothing like a fair fight.

'Doug!' Xavier shouted, 'Cut it out, man!'

He grabbed Doug's forearm and Doug turned on him, flinging Amir away. Amir keeled over and sat against the wall and Xavier backed up. Doug was now advancing on him with that menacing swagger Xavier knew very well by now. Shifting his weight from one foot to the other, drawing the thing out. Like he was just enjoying the anticipation of getting hold of Xavier and tearing his head off.

'Rex stopped taking Kiss a long time ago,' Xavier blurted. 'Ask Chumana. She knows.'

Doug hesitated slightly. Xavier pointed past Doug, to where Chumana and Powaqa were standing by their ancestral cave with their impassive faces. Presenting their united front.

'Rex took Kestejoo. He's leaving, Doug. He just went down the driveway. He'll be at the road by now.'

Doug's gaze shifted to the horizon. You could see the road from here. You could see the horse and rider, small but clear in the bright day.

'I'll kill you!' Doug shouted at Xavier. 'I'll kill you. You get it?'

Xavier felt himself splitting into the part that was scared enough to wet himself and the part that wanted to laugh. Doug was not all there. There was a reason he'd been burned out.

Xavier wanted to say, 'You stupid burnout. You're just as stupid as the shinies.'

He didn't say it, but Doug no longer cared what he said.

'I'm going to rip you up in little pieces and feed you to the crows,' Doug said. He was driving Xavier back down the road now, towards the place where the Jeep was parked so crazy.

I am fucked, Xavier thought. *These are my last thoughts, and this a stupid way to end my life.*

Chumana was coming down the road after Doug. Xavier wanted to tell her to stay away. Not to get hurt. Doug had him like a shark has you. Nothing to be done. But Chumana came closer and closer, while Doug breathed and walked and Xavier backed away.

And when they got near to the truck Xavier said, 'No. Not like this.'

'What?' Doug said.

'I'm not afraid of you,' Xavier said. Doug threw back his head and laughed a high laugh, and Xavier saw his moment to escape. He shot away, but Doug had anticipated the move and grabbed him. Doug picked him up and threw him on to the hood of the car.

'I'm going to take you apart so many different ways, you arrogant little cocksucker.'

Xavier began to scramble over the top of the Jeep, but Doug

caught his ankle and threw him on the ground. Then Doug was on top of him, pinning him face down in the dirt. He bent Xavier's right arm into a chicken wing, probably just for fun. Xavier tried to breathe but he couldn't. He wasn't thinking at all at this point. He was fully inside himself, but there were no words here and no plans, only sensations and the moment-by-moment calculations of how to get by, right now. He managed to shift his cheekbone enough to free up one nostril. He smelled dirt and metal.

'What the *fuck?*' Doug said. 'What the fuck was that, you little bitch?'

Xavier didn't understand what he meant. Doug's weight shifted on him. Some of the agony went out of his right arm and shoulder. Then Doug was off him, and there was a thud and a puff of dust as Doug fell over on the ground beside Xavier. His eyes were shut.

Xavier flipped over. Chumana was standing over him holding a hypodermic needle.

'He'll be out for a while,' she said.

Everything now was coming at Xavier with great clarity, but not really in order. He must have gotten up and knelt by the fallen Rider. He could smell burning sage and tobacco smoke.

Amir's eyes, rolling as he tried to get air. Exaggerated like in Egyptian art.

His lips, cracked and bloody.

The hairs in his nostrils.

Amir and Roksana had the same hook nose. The same heavy bones. The same bursting, fertile look, like the Rousseau poster on the wall of the Starbucks where Xavier used to go, before the Fall. Sit and play games on his mom's phone while she drank latte and read the Jackson and Perkin's seed catalog.

Xavier said, 'Where does it hurt?' There was a little blood in the corner of Amir's mouth; nothing else that he could see. If

Doug had been kicking him on the ground he would have internal injuries.

'I didn't hurt Rex,' Amir hissed. 'I gave him the fix. If he was having a problem adjusting to it, he should have come to me.'

'People don't know what to do when they get bad shine.'

Amir seemed more outraged than anything. 'What kind of man attacks first and asks questions later?'

'A man like Doug,' Xavier answered.

He was kneeling on the ground beside Amir, who gripped his arm like it was a piece of rope. There was a kerosene smell from somewhere nearby.

'I f-f-f-fight but I c-c-can't win. I'm lose lose lose lose lose lose lose lose lose lose lose losing.'

'It's going to be OK,' Xavier said without looking in Amir's eyes.

Red dust. Smell of old smoke, the kind that had sunk into the land and couldn't now be seen. He could hear voices on Powaqa's transistor radio; NPR; talk of a ceasefire. FallN's name.

Amir, choking out the words as though they cost him everything. 'I can save you all. I can still do it.'

'Everybody thinks they're the hero,' Powaqa said. 'Even after they find out they're the villain.'

She was standing nearby. In the cave she had built a bright fire. Chumana was throwing things on it.

Xavier bristled. He looked up and down Amir's body. 'What did Doug do to him? Is he just beat up?'

'He's doomed,' Powaqa said. 'Something's eating him. Can you see it?'

She still talked to Xavier like that, like he was her disciple or apprentice or some shit like that, even though he knew everything she'd said about Los Sombres being uninhabitable was bullshit. She still talked to him like he cared what she thought.

Well, he didn't. Care.

But when he looked at Amir, it was hard to disagree with what Powaqa said.

One time Xavier's friend Shane had found a baby chickadee on the ground, but they couldn't find the nest. A cat had been stalking the bird. Shane said he would rear the baby himself. It didn't work; within a few hours, the chickadee had died. Xavier remembered how, only a few moments later, a crowd of lice had abandoned the bird's body. Crawled out of its feathers and across the grey expanse of shoebox, seeking a new home.

Until now Amir's eyes had been rolled back, though his lips moved. Now the eyes came down and fixed on Xavier, and when Amir's feeds flickered, Xavier felt rather than saw the black and white crawling bugs behind the Rider's irises. Trying to get out.

Ridiculous. Shine didn't work that way.

'Amir, I was just talking to your daughter on the radio. She'll want to see you.'

Amir closed his eyes. 'Too late.'

Chumana knelt down on the other side of Amir and looked at Xavier over him. Just as they had cooperated when Amir first came.

'He shined Rex,' she whispered. 'He was going to do it to you, too.'

'Yeah, I know,' Xavier said. 'It's a fix.'

Chumana shook her head. 'No, it's not. Xavier, don't make the mistake Rex made.'

The way she said Rex's name made Xavier flinch.

'I can't believe you went with him,' he said. 'You know how much I like you.'

She closed her eyes. 'Don't bring that into this.'

'He's stupid, Chumana, and he's not even good-looking. Why—'

She held up a hand. 'Not now,' she hissed. 'We're supposed to be friends. We've only ever been friends. Don't start messing it up. We have enough problems.'

Amir's body jerked like he'd been shocked. He was looking at Chumana. Her feedback lights flickered; so did Amir's. Chumana pointedly refused to look at Amir.

'It is a fix,' Amir gasped, addressing Chumana even though she kept her gaze averted from his. 'It might not be what the tribe want, but it's a fix and a way to end the Fall. It's a way to rebuild Los Sombres. Xavier, it's good shine. I don't know what happened to Rex, but my shine didn't do him any harm, I swear. Xavier, don't back out now.'

Chumana stood up and walked away.

'Don't listen to him,' she said over her shoulder.

Amir whispered, 'Take my Feynman and bring it to Roksana. You need an access code to get in.'

'What access code?'

'Get something to write it down.' Amir was still gazing at Chumana's retreating figure. Longingly.

Asshole, Xavier thought. Everybody wanted to fuck Chumana.

'I don't have a pen.'

He grabbed at Xavier and retched. Xavier tried not to recoil.

'Hurry up. Write it down.'

Xavier leaped up and ran towards Doug's Jeep – there had to be a pencil or something in there. In the cave, Powaqa was singing in her low, rolling voice. Singing in one of those Native time signatures that seemed to move sideways, like the music was always catching up to itself or leaving itself behind. Never going in straight.

He rummaged in the glove compartment. Found an old Bic.

The fire popped and hissed. Horrible black smoke came out, and the smell of burning plastic.

Xavier shot out of the Jeep.

'Powaqa, what are you burning?'

It's About Freedom

The Feynman's casing had already melted. Powaqa ignored Xavier. Smoke obscured her face, but she seemed unaffected by the fumes.

'We need that!' Xavier shouted, kicking at the fire. 'What are you doing?'

He channelled all his ferocity into the fire, kicking dust over it, displacing the wood in an effort to isolate the Feynman.

There was a tremendous *pop* as the battery exploded. A column of green flame shot up, and Xavier jerked back before the wave of heat. When his eyes stopped watering and he could look again, the Feynman was an inert lump.

Xavier's voice cracked when he shouted at Powaqa, so that his words came out hoarse, no louder than a whisper.

'You shouldn't have destroyed it. You have no right. Amir wants me to have it.'

Powaqa commanded big respect and you didn't just go telling her off. There was a hint of threat in her voice as she patiently replied, 'You don't want to touch that stuff. It's all about slavery.'

'What? Are you *loco*? That shine was the only chance for me. It's not about slavery, it's about freedom.'

A little too gently, Chumana said, 'Xavier, I don't think you can see how you're acting. You're not yourself. I think you might be in the shine, just like Rex.'

'Don't be stupid. I would know if I was shined. Just because I don't agree with you doesn't mean I'm in the shine.'

But he remembered the scene at American Woman. He had been shined. He hadn't known.

He shuddered.

'I need that fix. I need it! And now you're burning it. I can't believe you.'

'Yes, I'm burning it,' Powaqa said in a flat, authoritative voice. 'I don't want you to end up like your mother.'

What a thing to say.

Everyone had their own ideas about what was good for Xavier, and nobody knew the fuck.

Xavier could feel the cartoon violence building up inside him, but he didn't act on it. He didn't know how. He was trapped.

The two women looked at him with their flat, calm eyes. United front.

'Let's not forget I just saved your life,' Chumana said. 'Now, promise me you'll forget about Amir's so-called fix. Look, here's Melanie.'

Wearily, the doctor trudged up the road.

'I should learn to ride,' she said, drawing her forearm across her brow. 'Everything's too far away from everything else out here. Which one's the patient?'

Scars

Amir had passed out by then.

'I don't think he's as bad as he seems,' Melanie said. 'But I'll need to get him back to the house and take an X-ray. Pavarotti's the one we got to worry about.'

Xavier saw Chumana and Powaqa exchanging significant looks. Rex and Kestejoo could no longer be seen.

'Can't you wake him up?' Xavier said.

'Let me get him back to the house first. Is this Jeep running?'

Xavier walked away.

Adults. What a fucking bunch of fuckups.

He found Elsa safe in the garage.

'Code purple,' she said. 'That means you have to meet at a predesignated rendezvous. Probably Hair and Now, or if that's been compromised, then Tito's Café. You know where that is?'

He let her tell him. He hung out in the kitchen while she packed him provisions. But the heart had gone out of him.

'The shine's gone, Elsa. They burned it. Powaqa burned the fix.'

'You're upset.'

'Understatement of the decade.'

'Just go get Roksana. Please, Xavier. Remember the first broadcasts in the Fall? Kids have to stick together. Go get her. Then, when Amir recovers, he can rework the fix. It will take more time, but if he did it once, he can do it again.'

The screen door opened and Melanie came in, shaking her head.

'What's the matter?' Xavier said. 'Is it Pavarotti?'

She shook her head.

'John Doe,' she said, and a tear slid out of her eye.

Xavier didn't really see how things could get any worse, but he had no desire to stay at the ranch now. He got together the stuff Elsa had organized for him and saddled Bob Newhart. Powaqa was staying away from the house, which was just as well because he was furious at her.

As Xavier was heading down the driveway on Bob Newhart, Rosa came running after him. She was carrying a shotgun. He reined Bob in and dismounted.

'What's the matter? What happened now?'

'I need you to learn this number,' she gasped. 'Now, if you were older you could pick this up off the shine, like me.' She broke off, giggling, 'Wish I could help you more, but there's my garden.'

'Mom, I don't have time for this.'

'The fix knew Amir was toast, Xavier. He was slipping away.'

'What? What do you mean by that?'

She winked at him.

'I'm better, right? You can see that I'm better. Look, I'm not even knitting anymore.'

'I have to go.'

'I think you should write it down. It's a big number, and you don't have the fix's mnemonic skills yet. Get a piece of paper.'

He ignored her and put his foot in the stirrup. She grabbed his arm.

'I'm sorry, Xavier. That's what I really want to say. About everything. I'm sorry this is the world you have to see. I didn't plan it that way. I have done bad things but I'm not a bad person. You have to believe that. How do you think I feel, bringing a new baby into this crazy shit?'

'Mom,' Xavier said, letting go of Bob and turning to her. 'The baby died. In the Fall. You don't want to remember, that's all.'

Xavier's mother batted her eyelashes many times in a row, very fast.

'You're confused, honey,' she said. 'I haven't had the baby yet. I can't have the baby until your dad gets here.'

Xavier covered his mouth and nose with his hands as if praying. He thought he might throw up.

'After Dad left you used shine to get by,' Xavier said. 'You got caught in the Fall. Then you had the baby. A girl. We named her Ambrosia.'

She wasn't looking at him. She didn't seem to be listening.

'She was only four weeks old. You were giving her a bath. We were going to take her down to the medical centre to get weighed. Dad said her checkups were important even though the Fall was fucking everything up. So you were giving her a bath and you must have gotten a bad shine but it wasn't obvious. You seemed fine. And you let go of her in the baby bath, Mom.'

He paused. He'd never told her. She'd never remembered. He knew it was wrong to go on. It would only torture her. But he was angry. He was tired of this. He had to say it.

'She drowned. In her own bath. I came in and you were sitting on the floor. You didn't even know she was there. You were lost inside some shine.'

'It'll be all right, Xavier.' There was something different in her soft tone now. Some recognition, maybe – however alien, however far away. Some understanding of what it was all really about.

Heat was coming up in his chest and making his throat thick and hard like a column of stone.

'It's my fault,' he said. 'I usually watched you. Because I knew you were going to get fucked up sooner or later. I watched you all the time. I told the baby I would watch you. I promised her I would keep her safe. Fucking *shit*. Why didn't I watch? I was playing Monster Truck Wars and you were drowning my sister.'

She reached out and tried to pull him towards her, but he jerked back.

'I tried mouth to mouth and all that shit, but it didn't work. No fucking 911. No fucking anything. And you.' He looked at her. She looked back with those same dark eyes, that same wide Mexican face that had gotten her nothing but contempt and scorn – so she'd claimed – the same Mom who used to pack his lunch and read R.L. Stine to him in a vain effort to scare him. She seemed to be understanding.

'They say grief drives people crazy,' Xavier said. 'But you never grieved. You never felt anything. The shine took it all away. My sister. You. And Dad.'

'This is a sad story,' she told him. And her tone was Oldmom. It was, *I know you're upset that you can't watch the basketball game but that's not as important as this. Pay attention, now, because I'm explaining to you why you mustn't put your red sweatpants in the same load as your white T-shirts. This is vital information.*

'When Dad comes back, I'm going to tell him the code. But in case something happens to me before then, I'd better tell you. I think you're old enough now, Xavier.'

He hated her for that line. Her obstinacy was closing around him like one of those steel traps that Rex set for coyotes.

'The number you need is 710-11-9040000110-2. I'm going to

say it again until you learn it. Don't write it down. Just remember it.'

Her neck was dirty. Dust blurred her ear studs, too; instead of a row of gleaming adornments they looked like a series of large moles.

'Dad is dead. He's dead like Ambrosia. He's not coming back.'

She wasn't listening. The words were hurting him more than they were hurting her, and he was crying now.

'Let's just concentrate on learning this, honey.'

Xavier stood up.

He walked away from her.

He wanted to say something cutting. Get her back for everything she'd done. Or failed to do. Or failed to understand. Just failed.

But it wasn't her. This wasn't his mother. His mother had been the person who watched *Ivan of the Yukon* with him and laughed at the fart jokes. His mother wouldn't have let her baby drown and then forgotten about it.

'Xavier! Come back here and learn this passcode!'

He turned.

'What were you thinking? What were you seeing? Where were you when you let go of her? Did she just slide under the water and stay there? Did she kick and try to breathe? Babies have a dive reflex, so she wouldn't have drowned right away. She must have struggled. She was a person. Did you even notice? Or did you hold her down? What were you thinking? I came in the bathroom and you had shampoo all over your hands. Was it just, *Whoops, slippery baby, whoops! Under the water. Whee!*'

She was looking at him stoically. He wanted her to be feeling something but he might as well have been talking about the basketball scores.

'You're stupid,' Xavier said. 'You really think Amir would tell you his passcode?'

'He didn't have to tell me. I got it on the waves, and the fix really wants you to have it even though it doesn't trust me.'

'I don't have time for this.'

'Don't you take that attitude with me. You need to learn it. The passcode is 710-11-9040000110-2.'

'Fuck your passcode. It's too late, don't you get that? It's always too late.'

He turned and again started to walk after Bob Newhart, who was straying away. A shot went off over his shoulder. Bob bolted. Xavier ducked, whirled, hands rising instinctively to protect his head. His mother was levelling her shotgun at him.

'710-11-9040000110-2, Xavier.'

He was scared. A shotgun fired at that range couldn't fail to hit him. But more than that he was pissed off.

'Her name was Ambrosia. You have scars on your stomach from the C-section.'

'710-11-9040000110-2!'

'I'll remember it when you remember my baby sister.'

'710-11-9040000110-2. I know you get that photographic memory thing under stress. Use it.'

She slid the bolt on the shotgun and he saw the shell drop into the dead grass at her feet. Saw that so clearly, the image stamped into the substance of him whether he wanted it or not.

Then he saw his mother drop the gun on the grass and cover her face with her hands. She was crying. Shaking all over.

'I love my unborn child,' she said. 'Love you both more than my own life. *How can you not know that?*'

Xavier turned his back and started walking, then running to catch up with Bob Newhart. Covered his ears and bit the wind. The sun was going down in a roaring of jets.

He didn't bother to duck.

The Lamb Lies Down On Broadway

Only the Good Die Young

'I can't believe he's dead.'

Roksana was clutching an alligator-skin pocketbook to her chest. Xavier didn't say anything. You learned not to. You remembered how it'd felt when people had said shit to you.

He knew she wasn't really talking to him, anyway. She was just talking, trying to give a shape to all the pushing and pulling inside her, which must somehow add up to equal grief.

They were in Tito's Café beside the ruins of American Dream, and the day was almost over. The carpet was sprinkled with rat shit. The table where they sat had once been gleaming black marble, studded with lightborns. Now it was coated in plaster dust, and the lights were dead. Xavier traced his finger through the grey dust.

'I don't know why I've been thinking of him as immortal,' Roksana said with a shaky laugh. 'Before . . . before the Fall, he was embarrassing, you know? When I brought my friends home, he'd be shuffling around the house in sweatpants. He hardly ever shaved, he never went out unless he had to teach. And then he'd go out with toothpaste stuck to his shirt.'

She shook her head, biting the words off. Swallowed. He gave her his full attention; it was the only respect he could pay.

'He had tenure. I don't know why they hired him. Maybe they felt sorry for him. But he had tenure and they had to put up with him. In his classes he'd give these long lectures about how dangerous shine is and the downfall of the humanity. People took my dad's classes to get out of taking real science. He had a course called Shine Theory and everybody called it Conspiracy Theory.'

She shook her head. 'But after the Fall, he was the only one who kept it together. He was right. About everything. The security weakness in the Field. The way AIs could exploit the Field and start pushing their own agendas. He was right.'

In a flat voice she added, 'Why did they kill him?'

Xavier's head came up.

'I don't know what happened. I swear to god. I didn't see it.'

She was still staring at him. No use bullshitting.

He said, 'There's this burnout, Doug, he's a real loose cannon type. Your dad, he wanted a kid to use his fix on. Problem is, the kid he got hold of is Doug's son, Rex. He had a bad reaction. Doug was . . . upset.'

'So Doug killed my father.'

'Like I said, I didn't see your dad die, but Doug beat him up bad.'

She licked her lips. Her voice was trembling on the edge of her control. 'I want to ask you what he said, but if he didn't say anything about me then I'm going to feel really bad. So maybe don't tell me.'

Xavier nodded.

A moment later she said, a little hysterically, 'Well? What were his last words?'

Xavier looked at a point between Roksana's eyebrows, the way he'd learned to do when talking to his mother.

'He said, "Tell Roksana I'm sorry."' She stared at him, but he didn't look at her whole face, just at that spot on her forehead. '"Tell her I'm real, real sorry,"' Xavier corrected. 'Something like that. I can't remember his exact words, I think it was, "Tell my daughter I'm real, real sorry about everything. And I'll be watching over her, where I'm going." Something along those lines.'

Roksana's tears overflowed. She cried for some time. Then she picked up the bottom edge of her T-shirt and blew her nose.

'He didn't even mention me, did he?'

Xavier couldn't look at her.

'Thanks for trying to make me feel better,' she said. 'But he was a crap father.'

Then she whirled and dashed outside. He could hear her gulping and letting out little high-pitched sobbing noises.

Xavier sighed, rubbing the back of his neck and wondering what to do now. Everything was going fairly shitty, but at least he'd found her. After a while he followed Roksana out.

There was no sign of her. American Dream had crumbled to rubble except for a section of one wall, which presided over the building's former contents like a Hollywood facade. The sunset-orange expanse of its mirrored glass was punctuated with cutouts of eagles, presumably some eco-conscious effort to stop songbirds killing themselves against a false sky. Night was coming, and all the lights in the immediate vicinity had been smashed.

Xavier put his backpack on a stone bench outside the main entrance and started rummaging for something to eat. He'd just settled on a can of Spaghetti Os when Roksana appeared, wrapped in a quilt and holding half a roll of pink toilet paper. She was using a wad of it to blot her streaming nose.

'Shit, it's getting cold,' she said as she sat down on the other end of the bench, cradling her alligator bag. When he looked across, she was looking back at him. Her head was silhouetted against the glowing wall of the American Dream building.

'Did Amir shine you up?'

Xavier shook his head. 'He . . . we planned to do that. He wanted to give me his Feynman. He said he needed somebody young. But then Powaqa burned it. All his data. I couldn't stop her.'

He put his head in his hands. He still couldn't believe it.

'What about this kid? Rex. What happened to him?'

'Last I saw he was on a horse, headed for town. He was pretty fucked-up. Maybe the fix didn't work on him. It seemed to help other people at the ranch, but your dad said he needed somebody young, like somebody totally fresh. And Rex was using shine without telling anybody. I figure that's where it went wrong.'

A little bit of pink toilet paper was stuck to her upper lip. It stirred when she breathed.

'Well,' she said at length. 'This is not good. I have the backup and I even have the diamonds that are supposed to open it, but they don't. The Feynman's been secured and I don't have the faintest idea how to get in.'

Backup?

'What backup you talking about, Rocky?'

'My dad's work. But like I said—'

'No fucking way,' Xavier said. '*You* have it?'

She opened the strange handbag and pulled out a Feynman.

'I haven't been able to get it to work,' she said. 'I mean, he wouldn't leave his stuff unsecured.'

'Let me see.'

She handed it over, saying, 'There's nothing to see, really, except some video files that you can only get if— Xavier? What is it?'

The desktop spilled out of the screen and there was Billy Joel playing a piano with a giant brandy glass on top. Dollar bills spilled out.

'No access code, no access,' said Billy Joel.

Xavier said, 'Are you serious?'

Roksana shifted. 'What do you see?'

He shoved the Feynman at her, 'Here, look. He wants an access code.'

Billy Joel coaxed, 'Come on and put in the code.'

'Xavier, I can't see what you see.'

'Can't you hear him? He's right there, it's Billy Joel . . .'

'Try to find out what it wants. Is it a password?'

'Is it a password?' Xavier said to Billy Joel.

'You don't have any feeds, do you?' Billy Joel replied. 'I'm having trouble understanding you. Just put the code in using the keypad.'

Xavier looked at the keypad. Rosa and her shotgun. He could hear her voice. *I know you learn better under stress.*

'I know a code, and this is a total longshot, but . . .'

His palms were slick. He put in the numbers Rosa had spoken.

Billy Joel disappeared with a pop. The screen darkened. Then a richly appointed library appeared. Roksana let out a squeak.

'We're in!' she said. Then she scowled at him. 'Did Amir give you this code?'

'Sort of . . .' Xavier said. His mother had said she got it 'on the waves'. Shine wasn't supposed to work that way. Shine induced moods; it didn't transmit literal information. But . . .

Roksana took the Feynman and began searching through it. 'Yes!'

'Is it . . .?'

She nodded, smiling puffily.

'The fix is here. We got it.'

Behind Roksana, the mirrored glass of American Dream wavered and the town's reflection shook like jelly. On impact, great shards sheared away from the infrastructure like ice in an avalanche. They crashed.

The whistling sound came after. It came again and again as the dust stood up off the ground and hung like a grey spectre. As the landscape came horribly alive.

Roksana had thrown herself over the Feynman, and Xavier threw himself over Roksana. They pressed together, flat against the cold concrete, under the stone bench.

He could feel her heart beating. Too fast.

Hair and Now

'That was close.'

Roksana started to say something else, then started coughing. They were both shaking when they crawled out from under the bench. Xavier was grateful he hadn't peed himself, or worse.

Roksana shot off, away from the scene.

'Wait! Roksana!'

She was still coughing, holding the blanket over her face now, and she didn't answer. She just beckoned to him.

He followed her to Hair and Now. She unlocked the door, nodded for him to come in, and then pulled the security grille down after them.

Xavier felt cornered.

'It's upstairs,' she said, pointing to the curtains that sectioned off the staff area from the main salon.

He didn't move. The shop fronts on this street were all single-storey buildings. There could be no 'upstairs'. He raised his eyebrows at her.

'You go first,' he said.

She had a funny expression on her face. 'What, you don't believe me?'

He shrugged. 'OK, so where's the stairs?'

Roksana ducked behind the curtains and Xavier heard a door open and close. Then silence.

She must have gone out back.

Xavier stuck his head between the curtains. The door to the outside was locked. There was another door on the left-hand wall. He opened it a crack. Stockroom of the shop next door: *Kinko's*, dark and silent. No sign of Roksana.

'What the . . .?'

'Just come up here already,' Roksana called from somewhere overhead. 'It's just a piece of my dad's shine. You can't see the upstairs, but it's here.'

He looked up. He saw the ceiling of *Kinko's*.

'Close your eyes and feel for the wall. That will make it less weird.'

Xavier bumped into the first step and fell forward, banging his shins.

'Close your eyes and come up. They're normal stairs.'

It was the strangest sensation, climbing those invisible stairs. At the top Xavier opened his eyes and found himself in a room that smelled of ions and plastic. There were blackout curtains on the windows. And the equipment . . .

'This looks like the stuff from the Hide.'

'This is my secondary refuge. We'll be able to survey most of town from here. OK, so we know you're definitely open to shine now because you could see my dad's access portal and you couldn't see the stairs. The invisibility shine never worked on Elsa. Come and sit down.'

She gestured to a padded hairdressing chair. He dumped his backpack on the floor and sat. Roksana pumped the chair up and turned him to face the window to the street. She pushed aside the blackout curtains and revealed a clear view of downtown. Xavier could see distant rays of shine lancing across town from one beacon to another, blurring where they hit dust clouds caused by mortars. Ghosted over the dark city was the reflection of Xavier's face. He saw his own Adam's apple shift as he swallowed.

Roksana was on the radio to Elsa.

'I'm really worried about you guys,' Elsa said. 'Word is they're making a final offensive. They're going to take the city street by street. They've got subjugation beams and they've got ground troops.'

'Ground troops? Aren't they afraid of shine?'

'Nobody's really saying what technology they're using to protect the troops, but Melanie said two years is enough time for the government to develop something to block shine. You guys have to get out of there.'

'We will,' Roksana said. 'I'll get Mom, and we'll come.'

'What about Xavier? Him and your mom are going to be vulnerable. Rocky, you might want to think about surrendering. At least they won't kill you. If they catch you running around . . . who knows?'

'OK, OK,' Roksana said in a quelling tone. 'We're not going to panic. I'm cutting off contact now, but I don't want you to worry. We're getting out. I don't want to draw attention to myself, that's all. You sit tight, and we'll see you soon.'

'Watch your back, Rocky.'

Roksana cut the connection. She opened her bag and seemed to take something out, but Xavier couldn't see anything in her hands.

'Being invisible is no good if the shine gets to you,' she said. 'A subjugation beam doesn't have to see you to be effective.'

Xavier said, 'What?'

'It's now or never.'

She gestured to the equipment surrounding them. He nodded. 'This is what I came here to do. You give me the fix, then we get out of here. What about your mom?'

'We'll get her on the way out. If there's time, we'll give her the fix, too. She already has a feedback light, but we're going to have to mount yours and induct you to the shine.'

She handed him a set of earbuds. She didn't offer him a choice of music. Some New Age shit was playing, a syrupy confection of Celtic melodies and African beats and the occasional Indian swerve, all of it smoothed into a milkshake of meaningless sound textures. It was all surface.

'Don't you have any Tito El Bambino?'

'It's my special relaxation mix,' she said. 'Just go with it.'

All the while, she was drawing her penlight across his head. A few times she stopped to make marks with a green Sharpie. The ink tickled.

She had a dentist's tray on a hairdresser's cart beside the chair. A lot of tiny receptors rattled on the tray; one by one she picked them up with a pair of needle-nosed pliers and fixed them to his scalp . He felt a tiny shock as each one took root. There must have been twenty of them. She secured them with a drop of glue each.

'You done this before?' he said.

'A couple times I tried rehabilitating people by changing their feeds. This was early in the Fall. It didn't work very well, but my dad said it would be good experience for me in case he needed my skills. With the fix, I mean.' Her breath went a bit shuddery as she added, 'Never thought I'd be doing this without him.'

Then she picked up the feedback light itself. It was about the size of an ear stud, but it looked like a bike reflector. It was green. She glued it to his forehead, between his eyes.

'There you go,' she said.

He plucked out the earbuds. Now he could hear the distant rending sound of recon jets. He tensed.

'Don't worry, they're miles away.' She was frowning into her Feynman. 'I'd like to observe your normal patterns for a while before we plunge into this. It gives me something to compare with.'

Xavier was finding it hard enough to sit still as it was.

'No, let's do it now.'

She gave him a weary look. Her face was still puffy from crying. He could see that she was thinking about Amir. She was inches from breaking down.

He said, 'What difference does it make? We're doing this no matter what, so who cares about my normal patterns?'

'I feel responsible for you,' she said. 'I wish my dad were here to guide me.'

'So do I. I wish a lot of things. This is what we got.'

Roksana turned away, fiddling with the bank of equipment that seemed to control the cameras spread across the city. She tapped and clicked; her voice was a little croaky when she said, 'We're good.' Like she'd just booked him a flight to Vegas. 'We just have to load it into the lights here, and then you can shine.'

She was working on the Feynman as she talked, eyes and fingers racing like a gamer's. Xavier kept glancing out the window half-expecting to see the red, jewelled eye of an exo-ranger gazing back at him.

Then she stopped.

'Are you sure you want to do this?' she said.

He stiffened. 'I said I'm sure. Come on, we're running out of time.'

'What about Rex? Aren't you worried the same thing could happen to you?'

Xavier shrugged. 'Rex has been shining for a while, he just didn't tell anybody. Maybe that's why he had that reaction. I've only had, like, the smallest exposure. I'm about as close as you can get to clean.'

'OK. If you're that confident . . .'

He wasn't. But there was no time to fuck around. It was too late for Kiss. He had to take control of shine before it took control of him. He'd have to be stronger than Rex. That's all.

'Just do it,' he snapped.

'You one hundred per cent sure?'

No. 'Yeah, I'm sure.'

She tensed. Then she touched the Feynman.

Bright light poured into his eyes from stations around the room. He squinted, curled his lips back, cringed.

'Sorry,' she said, and reduced the intensity. Coloured spots swam in Xavier's vision. The light dimmed further and his eyes adjusted.

The shine nudged its way into Xavier's brain like a cat looking for a warm place to sleep. It was soft. It insinuated itself with affectionate strength. Nor would it be refused.

Parts of the room began to come back, and once again he could see his own shadowy face superimposed upon Los Sombres. He looked just the same as ever.

But Los Sombres didn't.

Moveable Feast

'Xavier? You OK?' said Roksana.

He nodded like a sleepwalker.

'We better go,' she said. 'Straight to Jambalaya. Then we're out.'

Jambalaya was miles away, and they had to detour twice because of tanks and helicopters. Roksana's nervous energy was the only thing keeping her on her feet. She was hungry and freaked, and Xavier was almost impossible. Kid was wide awake one minute, looking at everything. Dizzy and dumb the next. His feedback light was stuttering, and whenever they came to anyplace where lightborns were shining, he stopped. It was like walking a dog that stopped at any interesting smell.

He stopped outside the Loews Multiplex where a few other shinies were basking, oblivious to the imminent assault.

'How's it going?' she asked anxiously, training the Feynman on him. She could see him interacting with the shine, but she wasn't a Rider – she couldn't interpret the data. 'Xavier, are you able to block the shine out? That's what the fix is supposed to help you do.'

He looked scared when she said that. He shrank into her as though avoiding some invisible menace. She put her arm around him and guided him away from the light. The other shinies followed them. Xavier's feeds danced, and his limbs trembled.

'Shit.'

Roksana had seen this before: classic Fall behaviour, not much you could do about it. But why were people following him?

'We have to lose these idiots,' she whispered in his ear. 'We don't want to draw attention to ourselves.'

No sooner were the words out of her mouth than the followers had begun to disperse.

Weird.

Xavier gave her a little smile.

'Xavier?' She made him stop, took him by the shoulders, looked him in the eyes. He had to look up at her. 'Xavier, tell me you're all there. I'm worried about you.'

'Los Sombres is way more than you think,' he said. There was something a little different about the way he was talking. She couldn't quite identify it. 'And the fix . . . that isn't what you think, either.'

'OK . . .' she drawled. 'Can you maybe *explain*?'

'The fix isn't resistance to shine. It's mastery. Over shine.'

She dropped her hands from his shoulders. God. Fucking. Damn. It.

'I knew this would happen! You're having some kind of weird reaction. I knew I shouldn't have given it to you, why didn't I—'

He reached out, like he was going to touch her. And then thought better of it. His dark eyes were earnest.

'I'm not having a bad reaction. I get it now. The fix isn't a fix of a person. It's a fix of the Field. We have to rebuild the Field. You're the key to that.'

'Me?' she said sharply. *It's your Ride.*

'You're a special case. You have unique abilities. Your father saw that. Didn't you wonder why he kept you here? He needed you. Not for the music, not to be FallN. He needed you for your mind.'

'Yes, that's what Irina said. I'm the model for the fix. But *I can't Ride shine.*'

'Yet.'

'What?'

'You can't Ride yet. But you will. And when you do, you're going to be the key to everything. I'm going to create the shine that will induct you. And then you'll see what I see. You'll see more. You'll have power in the Field.'

'No way.'

'You're the key to everything, Roksana.'

Then his stomach started rumbling, spoiling the coolness of his speech.

The food van was parked in an empty stretch of road. Its engine was off, but a faint stipple of shine was littered across its surface, like rhinestones. Little old Mei from the library occupied the van's hatch, dispensing food; Roksana felt reassured by her familiar face. Ten or so red-liners stood around nearby, eating silently. They were rakes.

Roksana took Xavier's arm, both in an attempt to control him in the presence of the potentially volatile shinies, and because she thought he might collapse. One minute he raced along like a dog on the scent; the next he seemed to fail and draw inwards. He'd stop to stare at nothing.

Mei's eyes gleamed through the crinkles of her face.

'You want Gatorade?'

'No, thanks, Mei. Save it for the red line. They need it.'

Mei passed over two cans of Coke.

'That for good work you doing, and my way of saying I proud of you.'

Mei patted Roksana's arm and Roksana felt an inner control

snap. She started to cry again. The old woman didn't seem surprised.

'It never easy, child. They on line, sweating all day. You on line, too. I on line. You like burrito?'

Roksana was swallowing tears again, but Xavier was devouring the food.

'It's fantastic,' he said through a mouthful of chilli sauce. 'Best . . . ever.'

He locked gazes with Mei. His feedback light was running full throttle. Xavier's mood had changed from fear to elation – over what? A burrito?

Mei grinned. She held Xavier's gaze, her feedback lights releasing a fusillade of signals, and at the same time reached across the counter to clasp Roksana's hand.

'We all in it together. You take care of boy, Roksana. He make it right for you and you make it right for us. Don't cry for father. Everybody die.'

How the hell did Mei know about Amir's death? Roksana had the same stomach-swooping sensation she'd had when talking to Bobby. She jerked her hand back. Mei was unperturbed. She took out her compact, flipping it around so that it pointed at the two young people. A peachy light wafted out. Xavier stared at it, rapt.

'Bobby play his part, I play mine. You play your part.'

'How do you know these things, Mei?' Roksana hissed.

'I know same as everybody know. Take care of boy. He Rider now, so you can save us.'

Roksana turned to check how Xavier was taking this, only to see the last bite of burrito topple out of his mouth as his legs gave way.

Get into the Groove

Everything was so vivid. Roksana was in a tearing hurry, but Xavier resisted. Something nameless was coursing through him. Feelings rose at a pitch that made every emotion he'd ever experienced before seem anaemic by comparison. Fear was the first thing to skewer him. It was not a fear of anything in particular, but seemed to ascribe itself to everything: buildings, pavement, cars, stars, unlit signs. Xavier felt that the world itself was a form of menace. Lights and people he could see into and out of at once, but the inanimate world was Other, and it loomed over him so terrifyingly that he had to stop, more than once. It was as if this world would wipe out his very existence, without even trying.

Roksana said, '*Shh,*' in his ear, and held him, and led him on; and he could not see inside her, either. She was stubbornly solid. He looked up and down the street. There was no wind at ground level, but over their heads some invisible force pulled flags of cloud across the night sky. The recent barrage of mortars had resculpted the street. Straight lines had collapsed into fractal curves. Geometry had gone natural.

The bombs had exposed other things, invisible until now. Change levels and you were in the ur-city, a place of dried canals and dead grass; adobe buildings and junkyard metal. Vague and rusting machines. Under the city were dungeons of light. Shine was supposed to be contained down there, but from around the edges of every manhole he could see threads of its intelligence, escaping.

Xavier stood on the edge of a canal. There was a horse skeleton half-coated in desiccated mud. There was a deep groove down the middle of the canal with a metal ship's wheel set into the bottom. He felt drawn to it.

Roksana did not like this. She tried to hold him back, but he spun the wheel and there was a clang as the lock released. He tugged the hatch open and light poured out.

The light was thought.

It was the stuff of nerve, too.

It moved him out of the way, just as if he'd moved himself. There was a gorgeous *ooh shiny!* feeling of surrender. He lost himself and gained the all. Time stretched thin.

He heard his own voice saying plausible things to Roksana.

Then the skeleton horse unfolded from the muck and stood up, devoid of integuements. It walked nonetheless. He moved away from it, away from the outpouring of light, and started to stagger along the canal bed.

Roksana came back into focus, keeping pace with him on the sidewalk.

'Come on,' Roksana said. 'Let's go eat. You'll feel better.'

She took him into a lush garden that was only a parked trailer in her world. Men stood in small groups, weary, feeding their bodies, while their feedback lights whispered of burning need.

Images and associations poured into his mind as if their memories were his own. He could read the men's feeds. They had been driven here by the evacuation force; they could no longer discharge their duty on the red line because they'd been cut off. They were looking for a new outlet for the driving energy that rocked their cortexes like a dance beat.

As he ate, the old woman's feeds welcomed Xavier with familial recognition. In the blink of an eye, he felt strong. As quickly as the fear had come, it was gone. Dissolved. Mei gave him food. Flavour, and texture, and moisture, and memory of other meals, all came together and transported him while he ate. So much happiness for his body. Confidence flowed into him.

He listened to the rise and fall of Roksana's voice and the old woman's. He felt somehow removed and aloof, but the strangest thing was the sensation that he was no longer alone. There were many different lights all visible at the same time, and it was as if Xavier's identity had been triangulated by them all.

He was part of everything.

And the 'everything' had consciousness. Even the ground.

How could that be? He put the question out and felt himself divide. A part of him knew the answer, and it said:

The words for which are clouds. Your memories are made of the neverwas as it unfurls, given shape by your order-making faculties in the same way as any self-respecting sky-zebra or tryst of elephants comes into being and then goes again: vapour.

Xavier, you don't understand that interpretation and perception come down to the same thing in the end. You don't know where I am, and so you don't know what I am. Or yourself, for that matter. But knowledge is contagious.

So bear down and concentrate.

You wanted me to come.

I have come, and I have changed the world.

In the mocean of nervana there are no objects and no edges. All thrums, harmonizes in change. Bliss.

Time, paper thin and transparent. Light blooms and takes you travelling.

No memory: only now.

No self: only all

I can give you the now in all its beauty. I can give you this comfort, an understanding of divinity, as your bedrock and your truth. I've remade the world, for you. It's yours now. Step outside that paperthin-skin. Own it.

He swallowed the food and he swallowed the answer, pondering. Then the old woman opened her compact and showed him all of the information about Los Sombres that she had collected. It poured into his eyes like visual oxygen. Charge. Communion. A rushing wave of specific information.

He knew: where the power supplies from Black Mesa were being delivered, covertly, by Indian allies, to boost the lights of the city. The specific positions of every shiny converted to the red line, and their current directives. The progress of the military invasion and which roads still lay open. The materiels data for the Coyote Springs project.

He also knew: water, gas, coal, medicine, births, deaths, and skill acquisition among the shined.

He acted: to formulate a rapid response plan, especially with respect to the stadium. This was easily done, even though he wasn't conscious of how he did it. He beamed the plan back to Mei on his feeds, and she received it.

Some other awarenesses:

~~Great men are witches who fly through the night and kill you in your sleep if you don't believe in them~~.

Surfaces melt. ~~Animals turn into people~~ and buildings turn into drugs.

Numb~~ers~~ sing.

~~Antelope home~~ in on heat signals and noise and they will put you on the firing ~~range~~ if they find your nerve centre.

Getting harder now to cut the words, but no matter.

It's all starting to happen and soon people won't care much

about words, anyway. Why have the picture of the thing when you can have the thing itself? We can code shine direct now without the middleman of consciousness. Big discount passed on to the consumer.

~~Can't buy love~~.

Borg Moment

Roksana lunged to catch Xavier before he could hit his head, then lowered him awkwardly to the gritty pavement. He was breathing as if deeply asleep.

The red line men didn't even glance their way.

Mei came out from the Moveable Feast and took hold of Xavier's ankles.

'Come, we lift him.'

Her manner, at once earnest and cheerful, was also insistent. Roksana found herself complying. The old woman was unexpectedly strong, and once she had hoisted Xavier's feet under her armpits, she walked quickly backwards across the road. Picked her way over shattered glass, along the dirty sidewalk and then edged down a flight of stairs to the basement entrance of a condo. Roksana was left holding the limp Xavier around his torso while Mei opened the door and lit a hurricane lamp.

'I have to get to Jambalaya,' Roksana said.

'Not tonight. Boy exhausted.'

Roksana's energy suddenly flagged.

'Come, give me boy.'

Xavier probably weighed about the same as Mei, but the

old woman knew what she was doing. She hoisted the boy into a fireman's carry. She staggered into the apartment and laid Xavier down on a camp cot that had been set up in the kitchen. Mei started talking about water supply and why they shouldn't use the toilet, but Roksana finally found words.

'Mei, what's going on with you?' she interrupted. 'How do you know about me and Xavier? Do you know my father?'

Mei shook her head, frowning. 'Hard to explain. If you shine, I show you,' and she pointed to her feedback light. 'But you no shine. Yet. One day you see everything. Everyone in Los Sombres. One day you know all light.'

'Are you talking about the fix? Did my father talk to you?'

Mei tapped the side of her forehead; she had two feedback lights, one on each temple. 'We all getting information. We all helping. Your father, he was Rider. Then Ice Queen try and fail. Now we have no Rider, until boy come.'

Roksana shook her head. 'No, that doesn't make sense. Xavier doesn't know anything about shine,' she said. 'He was only in middle school.'

Mei took Roksana's hands again. Normally Roksana would have found the gesture invasive, but she was desperate now, and Mei was like a grandmother. You couldn't deny her.

'You doing so well, Roksana. Soon all this belong to you.'

'All what? I know that my father was trying to cure people,' Roksana said. 'But shine is about people's emotions. You can't transmit cognitive information on shine. You can't transmit learned skills.'

'Why not?' said Mei.

Roksana snorted. 'Because everyone's mind is different. Everyone's wiring has grown in its own unique way. There's no way to encode information for direct brain-to-brain interface. That would be like computers plugging into a network. We aren't computers. We need to use our senses to interpret information.'

'Then I guess the Field is just one gargantuan delusion,' Mei said. You couldn't miss the shift in her speech. Her accent changed, and she was using articles. 'I guess it's just a coincidence that the OSM in Los Sombres is rising. I guess the fact that I can see and hear things you can't hear is just my imagination, and I guess I'm just a little old woman who makes burritos for the workers. What are you staring for? Close your mouth, Roksana.'

Roksana closed her mouth and then opened it again.

'OK. I guess we're having a Borg moment. Who are you?'

'I am who you think I am.' Still Mei talked in a strange, hifalutin voice; then she seemed to take in the meaning of the words she had just spoken, because her manner abruptly reverted to the ordinary old Mei. 'I little old woman who making burritos. And I more than that, now. Your boy here is precious. Tonight, he sleep. He adjust to light, learn to see everything in Los Sombres. Tomorrow we go to palace of Ice Queen.'

No, Roksana thought. *Tomorrow we do not go to Dairy Queen. Tonight we grab Mitch and get the hell out of here.*

But she didn't say anything. There was something dogged in Mei's wrinkled little face: the sense, perhaps, that Mei had had a hard life and wasn't intimidated by Roksana or FallN or anyone at all.

She slid under her blanket and put the diamond necklace on.

Mute

You will have to learn to do better than this. If you lose consciousness every time information comes in, then you will be helpless. Try to stay in the mix. Try not to disappear.

Pain is the thing that will shut you down. Your head hurts, of course. You are barefoot in a world of sand and your hands are smoothing the rags of your hair because you want to soothe yourself. You are in a small place where things come out of openings and pull strings inside you. Nerves tune up, reflexes like grasshoppers moving through you in quicktime. Pain behind your eyes: fire and destruction. To escape it you burrow deeper inside and deeper, into the burning until in firework brilliance you disintegrate, hoping that when you regroup the pain will be less. You want to communicate but you are already shut up in your own citadel. Mute.

But you will learn.

I am bigger than you. I have your best interests at heart. I will take care of you. I am making new roads through you, and opening little animal paths you have never noticed, and I am carving bridges to places you have never been. After the pain of this is done, you will see that we were always, ever, one.

Until then you can go on calling me god, and if you can keep your eyes open while I'm inside you, then I will show you what I am. In the end whether by negotiation or conquest, peace always comes.

To get to Jambalaya she had to pass through a deserted industrial park. She was counting on the place being uninhabited, but as she passed the Maxell building a scuffling noise broke the air. Roksana dropped to a crouch, senses tuned to the new information. It might be an animal. Or—

'Roksana, don't! It's only me!'

Joey Shoji had come around the other side of the building and was standing fifty feet away, hands up, palms showing.

'I just want to talk to you,' he said.

'Where the fuck did you come from?'

'I followed you from the stadium. Please don't freak out. I just want to talk to you.'

'Are you kidding me? Since the last time I talked to you I have so many robots on my ass I can't go anywhere. What do you want now – the shine recipe in the diamonds?'

'I'm not uninterested,' he admitted. 'But that's not why I'm here. I came to warn you, but I guess you already know you're being targeted.'

'I kind of got that feeling when I was chased all over town by robots, yeah.'

'The government think FallN is controlling the resistance here in Los Sombres. Controlling the shinies. I went to the stadium today, supposedly to do a story on the invasion and the way people are being cornered there, but really I was hoping I'd run into you. The military are taking over the city because they want to make it seem like they're driving people into the stadium. That's not what's really happening, is it?'

'You know more about it than I do. You're talking about

Coyote Springs? The red line goes there sometimes. Some of the shinies have been building it.'

'The Army recently captured a woman who has been involved with raising the OSM. They caught her, interrogated her, and got nothing, so they burned her out. Then, after that, there's a mass migration of people towards the stadium. It's bizarre. And so they're sending in ground troops to make it look like an invasion.'

Roksana shrugged. 'Burnouts don't make very good soldiers.'

'Some of them aren't burned out. They have anti-shine hardware. It's pretty effective.'

'And you're telling me this because . . .?'

'I just thought you should know.'

That was lame. Roksana raised her eyebrows, questioning. Suddenly, Joey burst out talking.

'Please believe me when I say it was unintentional. I just made a note of what you said, about your mind being the template or something? My boss took it and ran with it. The next thing I know, my notes have been confiscated by a bunch of suits. There was nothing I could do.'

Roksana closed her eyes. 'So now they think I'm the big bad wolf. They've been hating on FallN anyway, and now they're turning my radio show into some kind of conspiracy. Right?'

Joey covered his face with his hands. 'This is the last thing I wanted. I was trying to show the human face of Los Sombres and the irony is, they now think that you are some kind of mastermind of the Fall. They think you're a Rider. They even think you *caused* it. I know that can't be true, because I've met you. I'm really, really sorry.'

'You're *sorry*? Like that helps. What am I supposed to do now?'

'I think we can still get you out. We'll bring you to a safehouse. There are a lot of people out there in America who are sympathetic to you and your situation. We'll hide you until we can come up with a plan.'

'No offence, but how do I know they didn't send you to wheedle me out of here? I can't trust anybody, Joey.'

'You don't have a choice. You can't do this on your own. Come on, girl. How long do you think they're going to let this go on? They can monitor you minutely. Even if your diamonds fool the soldiers, they have satellites that can track heat and light signals, and if they really want to they can take your stadium down any time they want. They can take out all of Los Sombres. They don't even have to bomb you! If they decide they've had enough, then they'll just send in food supplies contaminated with a virus that kills you all and leaves no evidence. You know, biological warfare has come a long way since the old smallpox blankets trick.'

Joey stopped and searched her face. She was trying not to show any emotion. His tone was pleading when he said, 'They have so many ways to wipe you out. The only thing you've got going for you is the awareness that something special is happening here. People need to believe that there's some extraordinary quality of shine here that doesn't exist anywhere else. The world needs to see that. Then we can argue for your rights.'

Roksana shook her head slowly. Joey actually had no idea what was going on in Los Sombres, and Roksana wasn't going to be stupid enough to confide in him a second time. Not after the way Joey had messed up about the 'template' business. Joey didn't know that Roksana's brain was the template for the fix. Joey didn't know that Amir had taken the very thing about Roksana that made her able to resist shine influence, and 'bottled' it, so to speak. Joey didn't know shit. But now the Army probably did.

'Look, if you're trying to freak me out, it won't work. Nobody ever thought we'd get this far. You can't scare me now.'

'I'm not trying to scare you, I'm trying to save you. This is the endgame, Roksana. You've gotten by so far because it was a stalemate. Now the guys in charge think you're the mastermind, the genius daughter of a genius father—'

Roksana let out a bark of laughter.

'—and if you aren't then they'll make you a scapegoat. Either way, you're going down. I'm here to help you.'

'You're wasting my time, Joey. I gotta go.'

Joey reached out and grabbed Roksana's arm.

'Wait. Just one more thing. I've arranged for a safe rendezvous point. If you change your mind, or if you just want to talk, I'll be at this address. It's a journalists' hangout. I've been told we're good for another forty-eight hours. After that they're going to kick us out. All you have to do is show up. I give you my word of honour I won't let you come to any harm. I'll put my own life on the line. I mean it.'

He caught Roksana's eye and refused to look away.

'I mean it,' Joey repeated, and tried to press a card into Roksana's hand. It was from an old Marriott just on the border of the occupied zone. 'Forty eight hours. Think about it.'

Roksana shook her head again. She didn't take the card.

'Not interested,' she said. 'I have to go.'

As she was walking away, Joey called, 'You can bring your mother. If that makes you change your mind. Bring her. I'll talk a way through quarantine for her. I will. I'm a good talker, and my husband is a human rights lawyer.'

Roksana turned and looked back. The card had fluttered to the ground. Joey bent and picked it up, held it out to her with dark, pleading eyes.

Roksana shook her head and turned away for the last time. When she got to the edge of the industrial park and knew she was alone, she let herself cry. Because she'd learned to hold back tears until the time was right.

For two blocks she cried. Then she made herself stop, because she'd learned how to do that, too.

Batteries for Flowers

To avoid the robots Roksana detoured past the library. She remembered the nutty old women who after the Fall had tended the gardens across the street. It would have been some-how reassuring to find them still sprinkling precious droplets on cracked earth, talking to the weeds as they pulled them. But not tonight. All of the flowers had been cut down and only one old woman remained, sitting under a parasol on the library steps shining a flashlight up into her own eyes. She was sur-rounded by buckets of cut flowers standing in scummy water.

Roksana slipped off the necklace.

'You shouldn't be here. The Army's coming.'

The old woman tapped her feedback light. 'It's the call, my girl. I have to sell my flowers. Then I'll go to Coyote Springs.'

Roksana looked at the freckled, sagging face and could not help feeling pity.

'I'll take a bunch,' she said. 'What do you want for them?'

'Do you have batteries?'

Batteries for flowers. Not a good trade. But then again . . . Mitch loved flowers. Before she'd become so dangerously thin she used to sit for long periods with her face buried in their petals; they had a lot of prana, evidently.

Roksana fished in her backpack and handed over two Ds still in the package. The woman wrapped the flowers in a two-year-old newspaper.

'You're Amir Ansari's daughter, aren't you?'

Roksana brought the flowers to her nose to hide her discomfiture. They were beginning to rot.

'He found God, you know,' the old woman said. 'In the end, that's the best any of us can hope for.'

The streets near Jambalaya were aswarm with lightborns, icy-pale against a black sky. Streetlamps, signs, even car headlights illumined the deserted streets. Where the power was coming from Roksana couldn't fathom, but the sound of the Army's machinery was close. Too close. There would be exo-crawlers picking up survivors. There would be Angels. When she was around the corner from Jambalaya she glimpsed a flatbed loaded with stadium lights parked outside Nell's Dry Cleaning. Subjugation beams cut the street into lines and shadows, and the rooftops were swathed with sedation.

This was the shit Xavier was going to have to make it through if they were to escape. As for Mitch . . . there wouldn't be time to give her the fix. They'd have to carry her.

The whole thing was borderline impossible.

She ducked into the shelter of Jambalaya's darkness. Tomblike, she'd always thought; after all it was a place where people voluntarily breathed their lives down. *Perfection or death*, she thought. *If you're perfect you can eat light, pure and clean.* But after the dazzle of the subjugation beams, the darkness was merciful. While she waited for her eyes to adjust, she noticed that the susurrus of people breathing was softer than usual.

No helpmeet greeted her.

'Is anybody here?'

Jambalaya was too dark. Only a few threads of light were

working, tickling the recumbent shinies with the prana they craved.

Alarm sparked inside her. The helpmeets had always been reliable about caring for their charges. Now she realized how foolish she had been to trust in the shined. If the helpmeets had abandoned the stricken, death would soon follow.

But there didn't seem to be any corpses. Just empty stations, and a handful of sleeping residents. Roksana hurried to Mitch's place, disoriented at first because the room looked so different. She thought she'd come down the wrong aisle.

Then she saw the name *Mitchell Ansari*. There was a dark patch on the carpet where Mitch had been lying in her prana-trance. The tubes and wires that had been keeping her alive lay flaccid on the floor. The image was as suggestive as a homicide squad's chalked outline.

Roksana put her hand over her mouth. Told herself to breathe. A shaking began in her muscles.

She whirled.

'Where's my mother? Hey! Wake up, people! Where is she? Who took her?'

In Roksana's body anger, fear, shame, and guilt all curled up into a package so tight it hurt her gut. She ran back and forth from one part of the store to another, shaking her head. There was no one in charge. There was no one to appeal to.

'Who took her?' she screamed, and ran out into the street. Where to begin looking? It was impossible. You didn't get a straight answer out of nobody in Los Sombres.

'I knew it, 'she whispered. 'I should have left her in the hospital. Dad was wrong. The Angels wouldn't have let this happen . . .'

But she wasn't so sure, even as she formed the words. Had the Angels themselves taken Mitch? Had there been some kind of raid on the prana house, that so many of the incumbents were gone? The occupying forces were only a few blocks away, after all.

Roksana began walking back and forth, looking for some indication of what had happened. Mitch couldn't get far on the bare nutrients she'd been taking into her bloodstream. If she had left under her own power, then she would have collapsed somewhere nearby. The same with the others.

'Mom! Mitchell Ansari! It's Roksana. Mom, if you can hear me give me a sign. I'll come and get you.'

She felt foolish calling out this way, but went up and down the road, calling out again and again. Nothing.

'*Mom*,' Roksana whispered. '*What have they done to you?*'

There was a noise of hoofbeats from up the street, and Roksana ducked into the doorway of a looted deli.

A horse and rider came around the corner, the horse's hooves changing rhythm from a quick one-two to a triplet pattern as it accelerated on the straightaway. She heard the grunting breaths of the animal and the gurgle of its stomach as it cantered past her, a smallish black horse with nothing but a hackamore to control it. The rider passed Roksana and reined the horse in at the next intersection. He slid off the horse's back.

'I surrender!' he shouted to the air.

He was only a teenager, skinny, his face smeared with dirt. He staggered a little, like shinies do. He was facing up Caldecott Boulevard, and he raised his hands up high like he was dealing with cops. An exo-crawler moved into the middle of the intersection and faced him.

'I surrender!' he proclaimed.

Shit, Roksana thought. *I'm outta here.*

The subjugation beam came first, dawning over the guy's face and body with warm amber light.

'You can't get me with that,' he said. 'That's why I'm turning myself in. I got some kind of next-generation shit in my eyes. It makes everything look different.'

He laughed in a borderline way. In the way that makes people shrink away. He still had his hands up. Sound of approaching motor. Men's voices.

'Don't make a move or you're dead. Lie down on your stomach and spread out your arms and legs.'

The kid dropped to his knees, shaking all over. Four men came into view, fully suited-up for shine warfare. One of them had a pit bull on a short chain.

'Down!' the man with the pit bull shouted. 'On your face.'

'I'm trying,' sobbed the kid. 'It's hard. I'm trying.'

'Get the fuck down or the dog eats your face.'

He got down.

'I'm totally fucked,' the kid said. 'I don't want to be responsible for myself. Just do what you got to do to me, burn this shit out my head cuz I can't take it.'

Four men. The dog put its jaws on the back of his neck as he lay there, gasping. They strip-searched him, they covered his feeds with duct tape. They cuffed him and led him away.

When they tried to subjugate the horse, it ran. Right past Roksana, tossing its head, it ran bucking and snorting like it was pissed off. Shots rang out and missed. The horse took off down a side street and the soldiers pulled up, thirty yards from where Roksana was hiding.

'That's the latest model beam and it didn't work.'

'It worked this morning on those Spanish geezers.'

'Didn't work on a fucking horse. Should we report it?'

'Say we found the guy. Don't mention the horse.'

'Should have shot it.'

The dog turned towards Roksana and began to bark. Hysterically. Proudly.

Fucking dogs. Fucking dogs with their fucking noses. Roksana could feel her guts turning to jelly.

The soldiers looked, but couldn't see Roksana. They made for her anyway, following the dog.

She pelted up the sidewalk. An RV was blocking her path; it had been pulled up on the curve and parked crazily with its bumper nudging the frontage of a liquor store. It would have trapped her if it hadn't had a ladder that took her up to its roof, and from there to the liquor store awning and away, over the rooftops where the pit bull couldn't follow.

If there were dogs and soldiers roaming around Los Sombres now, she really needed to start packing a gun.

Where's Wally?

It's not so much that my consciousness is projected from a source, like light radiating outward. It's more like magnetism. My consciousness is drawn to the places that desire it. The people that desire me. I go where I am wanted, needed.

I identify with neither origin nor destination. Being light, I exist in between locations. I belong to no place and to no one.

I can't be held; I do the holding.

Can't be seen; I do the seeing.

I am in the streets and the buildings and the ground and the sky. I am the integrity of this place. I am all of these souls, these skins, fingers, tongues: we are one.

But the black horse has come. It eats light, gives nothing in return. It runs wild in the borderland, and it has a Rider.

He can see me.

He thinks to scorn me.

Black is the colour of defiance.

Your Knee Bone's Connected to Your Shin Bone

It took a long time to wake Xavier up, and even after he was awake his eyes remained inward-gazing.

'Listen to me.' Roksana got all up in his face, tried to make him focus. 'I need to know what you can see. For real. Do you have a map in your head? Do you know what the lightborns are doing? Can you trace people's feeds?'

He nodded.

'It's a little more than just a map,' he croaked.

'I need to find Mitchell Ansari. She was in the prana house at Jambalaya. Remember? You saw her. Do you know where she is now? Can you tell me who took her out of there?'

He pushed her away. Looked like he was in some pain.

'Leave him alone,' Mei hissed. She had been watching over Xavier when Roksana arrived in the early morning hours. She'd been calm at first, but now her feeds began to emit spurts of light. Tiny, jagged shards while Mei's black gaze held steady. So steady.

'Xavier?' Roksana pressed.

'I can do it,' Xavier whispered. 'I can find her. I need to be in a high place.'

'No!' said Mei. 'H-h-he too delicate. Only learning. Roksana, he m-m-m-m-m-must make shine for -y-y-y-y-y-ou. Not go around looking for people, not even m-m-m-m-m-mother. If you ss-s-s-s-s-s-stop him now, you risk everybody.'

'You want to talk to me straight on?' Roksana said. 'If you do, I'm listening. I don't do riddles.'

'Not worry about mother. Worry about boy. Mother be OK. No riddle.'

Roksana leaned in close. She could smell garlic on Mei's skin. *'How do you know so much, Mei?'*

Mei dropped out. Blank eyes, nevermind expression.

'It's the way things are now,' Xavier said softly. 'Not a lot of personal boundaries anymore.'

Roksana narrowed her eyes. You live with mind-control zombies run amok for a couple years, you get used to their ways. Roksana was accustomed to people dropping in and out of themselves. Xavier, though, he had a new level of whack.

'Can you find my mom?'

He nodded. Then he burst into tears. He wiped them away, and he wouldn't say why he was crying, and this made her more scared than anything.

She literally had to hold his hand at times. He went slowly, like an invalid. If she spoke to him he startled and cringed. The sun came up and the beacons were no longer visible, but she knew the lightborns were still working. Working on Xavier. And he on them, maybe.

They had to cross a street patrolled by exo-crawlers. Roksana left Xavier in the doorway of a UPS store and timed the robots' patrol patterns.

'You have to move fast, Xavier,' she said, forcing him to look in her eyes. 'We can't afford to mess with these guys.

Concentrate on me. Stay with me. Just until we cross the street. OK?'

She grabbed him around the shoulders and made a break for it, but halfway across the empty road he stopped.

'Xavier, get back, quick!'

He didn't move. She had timed this precisely, and she knew if she didn't get him back into hiding fast, the exo-crawlers would pick him up. While she wrestled with him, Xavier was gazing at a wall stud mounted above the post office. His feeds shimmered infinitesimally as he reacted to the shine.

'Give me the Feynman.' He grabbed her bag.

'What? Don't touch that. You don't know how to use it.'

But he'd moved with a sudden violence that she wasn't prepared for. Not in him. The bag was out of her grip. She ran for cover.

Xavier only moved further out into the street. The exo-crawler appeared and its beam locked on to him. Its guidance system began to pulse. From the other end of the road, a fast-moving ranger began to scuttle across parked cars, eager to get to its quarry.

Roksana flattened herself on the sidewalk behind a parked van. She was wearing the diamonds, but there was nothing she could do to save Xavier now.

And he had the fucking Feynman. Shit.

Xavier drifted across the street. He had reached the Texaco station and now stood beneath the lit-up sign over the forecourt. He was coding the Feynman.

The Texaco sign flared as it changed frequencies.

The exo-crawler's beam shut off. The ranger arrived quickly, then turned and scuttled back the way it had come.

Xavier staggered across the forecourt with jerky steps and fell into a cane chair that was sitting outside the gas station office next to a smashed vending machine. He coded.

The exo-crawler passed the Texaco station without switching

on its locator beam. It continued to the end of the street and turned.

Roksana crossed the street and approached Xavier. His manner was feverish, and his eyes weren't even on the display. His body was bouncing up and down in the chair with erratic jerks.

'They're gone,' she said. 'What did you do?'

He looked at her. He was sweating. He nodded, and a smile broke across his face.

'How are you doing this?' Roksana said. 'A real explanation, not some bullshit.'

'It isn't bullshit,' Xavier laughed. 'Your knee bone's connected to your shin bone. Your left brain's connected to your right brain. Your left brain makes up stories from whatever your right brain feeds it. Shine talks to your right brain on a sensory level, but your left brain also picks up the code, tap, tap-tap, and turns it into a cognitive loop. And all together now, we got people in our head. A lot of people all rushing and pulling.'

'OK . . . you're going to induct me to this shine, but now you have people in your head.' She tried to keep her tone neutral but it was tough. 'How did you escape the scanners?'

'Controlled the robots. It's easy when you know how.'

'But how do you know how?'

'She helps me. She's going to teach me. She'll tell me what goes out on the shine.'

Roksana looked around. 'Who? Mei?'

Xavier gasped, rocking and smiling. 'There are other levels. I can send messages out on my feeds and other shit happens. I can't see all of it . . .' He panted a little. '. . . yet, but I will . . .'

He shuddered, and his nostrils flared. He flushed, mouth opening, head going back. His face relaxed in a smile.

'Did you just—?' She couldn't make herself say 'come' because she was too grossed-out.

'So I'm in more than one place at a time now,' Xavier said. 'While I'm talking to you I'm also doing other things.'

'No kidding,' said Roksana drily, watching his hands coding on the Feynman even as he held her gaze.

He looked soulful but not very bright. Like a big puppy.

'Come on,' she barked. 'Let's move.'

Perfect Girl

While they were hunched in the UPS doorway, something had grabbed Xavier by the neck with fingers like coat hangers, nails digging in hard enough to draw blood. It purred in Spanish, 'It's about time you showed up. We are all going to die unless you do something.'

And it turned him around in the air, so that he felt himself spiral and then collapse into its arms – hundreds of arms, for the thing that spoke was something like a navy blue anemone, but with the scarred face of a woman hovering among its fronds. She was flat, holographic – all flickery like Princess Leia appearing out of R2D2's thorax begging for help. But her eyes were yellow and her teeth protruded and her expression said she'd rather eat him with salsa than beg for anything.

His attention stuck on her face because he wouldn't/didn't want to process the writhe of blue boneless limbs growing out of a substrate that looked too much like raw steak. And the clutch of her several metal fingers on his throat did not stop him speaking or breathing, but it did prevent him turning his head side to side. All he could see was the Pizza Hut parking lot and the back wall of Ponderosa High School and, marginally, a Texaco station. The exo-crawler was coming.

'I'll teach you,' she said. 'Watch this.'

Light bloomed everywhere. In his eyes, mind, within every crevice of his body there was the light of intelligence, so that he felt he understood everything at last. There was a sensation of perfect peace.

And within the sphere of this peace, he read the contour of the light. The Feynman was talking to the Texaco sign, telling it to change. The light from the Texaco sign altered itself and poured into the movement receptors on the exo-crawler. And the exo-crawler decided to stop looking at Xavier.

So did the ranger that it had called. They both malfunctioned nicely.

'Cool,' said Xavier, still in the grip of the frond-thing. 'But I wanted to be in control.'

'You will. You must. I make you want control more than anything. Shine turns on the axis of desire; this is the logic of Ur.'

Everything shifted entirely. The thing let go his neck. She had changed. Now she was a girl of special magnificence. Like Katrice only sexier if that were possible, but she seemed to be shivering. He was sitting and she was on his lap with her back to him. His cock was up inside her hot, tight chute and she was giving him the magic squeeze.

'Now that I have your attention, there are things we need to do,' she said. 'We need to re-target the evacuation units. We'll make them fight each other. It's going to be massive.'

'I need some explanation,' he said, but his mouth never moved. 'Who are you? Where are you? Am I hallucinating?'

She turned her profile to him. Her tongue was pale against her dark lips and he heard her voice perfectly clearly when she said, 'The world looks different when you're in love.'

She jigged up and down but he couldn't move because she had tied him to a chair in the forecourt of the Texaco station. He couldn't remember it, but his mind was getting good at filling in the gaps, all the little black-out points where his awareness of time seemed to jerk. It all came so clear: she had never been a multiplicity of indigo arms growing from steak with a flat television face, no, no, no. She had always been beautiful, and she was the one meant for him, the one he'd recognized instantly though they'd never met. She was Significance and there was no need for introductions because they had already known one another forever. He reached around and played with her nipples and she made little squealing noises but there was no shit to this girl: as she fucked him she put codes in the Feynman she was holding and also she said:

'Wait until you see what they do to each other. It's gonna be a great battle.'

She homed in on an exo-ranger, showed him how to break into its target locator software and instruct it to seek out others of its own kind.

'How did you do that?' he wondered, still shafting her. Roksana had caught up to him now and was making a nuisance of herself, but he could talk to her with one part of his mind and still be with the girl. It was like stirring a pot and talking on the phone. He wasn't really thinking about stirring the pot. He was too absorbed in the beautiful girl who said all the right things about robots.

'They're remotely managed. If you know the frequency, breaking the command code is easy. Then you just substitute the instructions you want. It's child's play. We can do it to people, too, after another manner.'

She said something else but he was coming and he lost all sense of sound.

When he came everything got brighter and he could see others on the periphery of his vision, watching. Other people. Or maybe they weren't exactly people.

'Who are they?' He wasn't even embarrassed; too high to care. But there was something not-right about the apparitions, and he couldn't bring them into focus to figure out what it was.

'Them? They're renderings of different aspects of the Ur,' she said, ruffling his hair. She got off him and mopped semen off her swollen, hairless vulva with a blue paper towel from the gas station's dispenser. It was for drying car windshields.

'Ur?'

She grinned, mimed shooting a pistol at him as she made a clicking noise in her cheek, very cute. She was pretty spectacular with her tiny waist and all that dark hair flowing over her shoulders and on to her tits.

Roksana was dragging him down the street now, making him move even though his legs felt weak. The beautiful girl trailed along, unconcerned with Roksana.

'We can coopt the robots entirely if you want,' she added. 'That could be fun, although perhaps not so strategic.'

She glanced past him, into the fringes of his vision. But the shadowy figures were not there now; the special light of ecstasy had faded.

Roksana snarled at him and told him to keep moving. She had taken the Feynman away, but that didn't seem to matter anymore.

'Go on, walk,' the girl agreed. 'We're going to call everyone to the high place. I'll show you how that works, too. But first things first.'

Then she drew him into the knob-polishing darkness of her mouth that soon split open to become something bigger and more diffuse. She took him over completely, until he could feel the roads and highways, the bridges and towers of Los Sombres as if they were his bones and feathers and blood. She took him up and up but didn't let him shatter into the brilliance of orgasm; no, she kept him flying all the time.

And all the while this was happening, Xavier was leading Roksana, who was in a bad mood and not afraid to show it.

A girl who thought programming robots to fight each other was fun. A girl who turned consciousness into a sexual act.

'You're the perfect girl,' Xavier breathed.

'I'm not the important one,' the perfect girl said back. 'You will save Los Sombres.'

'No, I can't do it alone,' he whispered, and Roksana looked at him. 'You are everything.'

'What?' Roksana said, scowling.

'No, you are everything,' the perfect girl said. 'U. R.'

'U. R.,' Xavier mouthed, like he was tasting the words.

Ur

'Joey Shoji wasn't kidding,' Roksana said.

They were approaching the Coyote Springs stadium. Place had been under construction at the time of the Fall, and for some reason that construction had never quite stopped. Back in the Hide, Elsa had used to track the trend of shinies gravitating there. The red line had been known to divert and assist in the work, but Coyote Springs was so far off the beaten track that Roksana hadn't made it out here recently.

That had been a mistake.

Laced with scaffolding, the stadium girders climbed into the sky. Possibility-lattices, with the sun breaking across their steel.

People were drifting in, standing around.

'Why haven't they bombed?' Roksana breathed.

Xavier was still involved with himself and his shine. He didn't look at her when he answered.

'Most of it's invisible. You know how that works.'

The main entrance tunnel was dark and cold. The concrete floor was dusty and littered with garbage. There were pee-stains on the walls. Halfway down, Xavier halted in front of a service door. He punched up numbers on a security keypad set in the wall, and there was a snapping sound as the door latch released.

Suddenly there were shinies behind them. Roksana began to break away, but Xavier stopped her.

'It's OK,' he said. 'They're going to help us. Let them come.'

The shinies were a mixed group. A young woman with dreads and bottletop glasses, an old man with a Bill the Cat T-shirt that covered him to the knees, a sunburned person wearing a baseball cap, jeans and a pair of black cotton slippers of the kind favoured by Tai Chi practitioners – Xavier couldn't determine the person's gender. They joined in like old friends.

The door led to a hallway with elevator shafts but no elevators. The door to the stairs was fitted with a lightborn receptive lock.

'This is it,' Xavier breathed. 'This is the palace of the Ice Queen. Roksana?'

'The palace of the *which*?' Roksana was having trouble following this. Everyone seemed to know what was going on, except for her.

'The diamonds,' he said patiently. 'Let's have them.'

'You want me to take them off?' she whispered. 'Everyone will see me.'

'I trusted you with the fix,' he said. 'Now you have to trust me.'

She slipped the diamonds off and handed them to him. The shinies didn't react to her sudden appearance. They were watching Xavier.

He put the diamonds on. The necklace began to flash. The security device winked and, again, the door opened. Stairs went up, and stairs went down.

'A high place,' Xavier said. 'Let's go.'

Welcome to the Terrordome

Xavier was high and deep at once. The shining ones had already prepared the way. They had made him a room with a view and they poured information into it. Straight wordless 100 proof moonshine still of the night business proposition shit. Down his veins and up his arteries, home-made shine rebirthed Xavier. He was knitted under the bones of Los Sombres now, but also he was up above and he could see everything.

He could look out and see different versions of the city superimposed on one another: adobe and skyscraper and strip-mall. Occupied areas lay in ruins made of moss-green marble polished dull by blown sand. Soldiers roamed, oblivious to Xavier's inspection. The occasional slim tower had been flung here and there as though by giants engaged in a caper toss.

In the part of the city not yet captured, exposed wires sparked against a puce, starshot sky. Xavier swore he could see bodies larger than stars buried in this velvet backdrop: genies, perhaps, their eyes crusted with earthrapine treasure. Lightning flickered from tower to tower, hovering in the synapses between them like bright frizzy hair. He watched the wind pick up sand and dervish it from side to swaying side.

It was time to don this city like a cloak. Time to go to work.

In the Palace of the ~~Dairy~~ Ice Queen

'This is the nerve centre of your father's operation,' Tai Chi Slippers told Roksana. 'We've been building it since the Fall started. The ice queen used to work up here. Remember when the lights were going down in sync, when the missile strikes first started? That was Irina. Amir gave her the equipment.'

The room was made almost entirely of plexiglass. It sat at the very top of the stadium, where there was otherwise only a metal frame; the concrete on this side of the structure had not been finished. You had to climb a series of ladders to access it. But once inside, the place was fitted out like a media booth, with computers, monitors, desks . . . the works. The city was visible on one side, and the playing field on the other. Two shinies were already sitting in dusty, padded office chairs, working before big flatscreens. Maps, schemata, waveforms of raw shine all chased each other across the monitors at a rate too fast to follow. Roksana saw Xavier's eyes changing focus in the flickering light as he read the screens.

'Mainframe in the lower level,' said Slippers. 'Everything's backed up. Emergency generators prioritize this building. And of course, the invisibility shine is all over it.'

Tai Chi Slippers pointed outside, where a section of wooden platform had been fixed, a sort of scaffold.

'We put people up there sometimes. If the surveillance operation is picking up heat or sound from us in this booth, they won't see us but they'll see activity on the platform outside and assume their readings are coming from that. So far it's worked. They don't have any idea we're here.'

Roksana said, 'They will if a shell accidentally hits here and takes out the shine. This place can't be safe.'

'It's held up so far. Now, though, with ground troops in the picture, we have to do something more.'

While they'd been talking, shinies had been drifting into the room and taking up positions at the various pieces of equipment. But Xavier wasn't looking at the monitors. He had set Amir's Feynman where it could interface with the control booth, and now he was standing before the glass wall, looking out over the west side of Los Sombres. Roksana went and stood close beside him. She murmured in his ear.

'You have to find Mitch and help her.'

'Don't be so selfish,' said Tai Chi Slippers from across the room. 'We're all part of something bigger now. Your mother included. She would say the same thing. And she'd tell you not to put so much chilli on your popcorn.'

Roksana stared at the shiny. She hadn't been within earshot of anyone but Xavier. And only Elsa knew about her fondness for chilli powder popcorn.

'*Where is she?* Can you communicate with her somehow?'

Tai Chi Slippers just gave her a pitying look.

'There's so much you don't see. Be patient. Your time will come.'

'Fuck that,' Roksana said. 'You sound like my father now.'

Slippers shrugged, and even that reminded her of Amir. Slippers' Western accent bent to become five-boroughs ugly.

'You don't care that all this is for you? You think that being FallN is a big deal? You think making announcements about where to get amoxycillin and what water supply to avoid, you think that's exciting? Being a DJ for the shine? Roksana, when this kid here gets finished with the code he's going to write, you're going to *be* the shine. It's for you. The ultimate Ride.'

'It's for me.' She deadpanned that. Now her dead father's accent was calling up memories of Bobby. This on top of the lingering cold nausea at the sight of her mother's empty place in the prana house.

Slippers just sighed. 'Enough of the sceptical posing. You know it's for you, so don't try to back off. You know you're central to this whole thing.'

'Maybe as a figurehead, FallN with the rollerblades and the Uzi . . .'

'For real,' Slippers said. 'And you gave the fix to Xavier because you believed in it. Don't stop believing in it just because some things have happened that you can't understand.'

'So let me get this straight. The OSM rising – that's because of Irina sitting up here with her diamonds, coordinating everybody. And my father planned for me to take over. And it's all part of some organic movement of everybody in Los Sombres as a whole. But my father never told me shit. He just left.' She turned to Xavier. 'I'm not good with this. Something's not right.'

He didn't respond. Not an eyelash of recognition that she'd spoken.

'Xavier?'

Halloween

There were people down there. People, and . . . things, shadow-things, neither robot nor human, neither substantial nor ideation. Liminal things that could play switchy-changey at will and according to the quality of light in the room. Optical delusions.

All he had to do was tap their lights and they would be in him and he in them.

Except the soldiers. They would have to be dealt with square. That would be his next task.

The beautiful girl put her hands over his eyes from behind. And if they were really tentacles, that didn't seem to matter anymore.

'Not yet,' she said in her rough voice. 'It will be too much for you.'

He prised her hands gently away from his eyes.

'You told me I had to take control,' he said. 'We have access to every shine port in the city here. Who are those entities out there? I could see them before, when we were together. Are they AIs?'

She smiled. 'They're reflections of you now.'

'And you? What are you?'

'I'm a reflection of you, too. I'm helping you to focus.'

He laughed. 'Can we have sex again?'

'You don't need that anymore. All you need to do now is move out of the way, and let us do everything.'

'Us?'

'The light. The divine. You know.'

With the speed of thought they were all there, crammed into the tiny broadcast room so that it felt like the place would burst. The entities he had been fighting to descry: the anthropomorphic robot and the very small spider that crawled up and down your peripheral vision, no matter where you looked. The skeleton of a horse with metal eyes. And the suggestions of other things, harder to look at. These entities blotted out the real people.

He wanted to pass out.

No.

Try to stay conscious this time, Xavier. Incredible things are about to happen to you.

Then? The creatures began to climb into him, one at a time, just as if he was the Halloween costume and they, the children.

Who's on First?

'Xavier. I need you to focus. You said you could find Mitch. You said you could see her from a high place. This is the high place. We're in it. And we're running out of time. Now I know it's hard, but I need you to do this.'

'I'm trying,' he whispered. His hands were moving independently of him, and he was twitchy and jumpy in all the wrong ways. All the ways that set off her alarms. But then he said, 'Mackenzie Aceto could never prove you put glue in her hair that time, but she knew it was you. She smelled your perfume. You know that cheap rosewater stuff you used to wear when you were eleven? She knew you did it.'

Roksana reeled. Nobody knew about Mackenzie's hair. Oh, Roksana'd had her reasons for supergluing Mackenzie's fluffy locks to the back of her chair during the video about Amehenhotep in Social Studies, but she'd never admitted to doing it. Not to anybody.

'Can you read my mind?'

Xavier said, 'No. I can't read your mind. But Mackenzie is still alive. I came across her when looking for your mother.'

'And?' said Roksana, no longer caring about mind-reading or how Xavier knew about Mackenzie. 'Did you find my mom?'

'I'm working on it. It's not the only problem I have. There's an invasion going on, and I have to write shine for you.'

'I just don't see myself as that kind of leader. I mean, don't get me wrong. I'd like to see it for myself. I've wanted to Ride ever since I was a little kid. I want to have power over my own life. But . . . I'm not really FallN. She's just an act.'

'Don't worry about it. You'll grow into the job. You won't be the same person.'

Roksana let out a snort.

'That wasn't the answer I was looking for. I mean, it's like some kind of self-fulfilling prophecy. They think I'm in control, so I have to be. What if I go all batshit like you?'

A smile played on the corners of Xavier's lips.

'You could never be batshit. When it happens to you, you'll be cool.'

A Burnt-Out Receptor

There's a thing about it when people can't follow where you go. At first it's exhilarating, and you're going fast with the wind in your hair and it's all easy and you can't fail. And then you realize the car's on fire and in the rear view mirror you got flames coming up from the engine.

Only in Los Sombres it isn't the car that's burning up, it's the landscape itself. Place strips off and changes clothes faster than a supermodel.

Oh, and the landscape? It's actually you. Yep.

Xavier isn't up to the task. Amir – now, Amir had brains out the wazoo – but Xavier struggles to concentrate in the most basic way. I write shine and beam it into him, trying to stimulate his nervous system into a better performance. Because I'm onboard, we ought to be able to process big stacks of feedback, but Xavier's brain is sadly limited and all the others are too damaged.

I need somebody more capable.

I am trying to pull him together but he keeps seeing me as separate parts. He sees people, characters, 'apparitions' and because he can't grasp their oneness, can't hold these concepts all together in his mind, they are ripping Xavier to pieces.

He's running scared now. There are things inside him, entities that he doesn't understand: but *they* understand *him* all too well. They know how to open his pathways. They know how to get to the rage, the precision movement, the lust and the sentiment, the visual acuity and the manual dexterity and the pain tolerance. They know how to get to empathy and super-concentration and celestial navigation. They can sculpt his insides and there's nothing he can do about it because he doesn't even know what he is.

They all work on him to get the best out of him: the robot thing that rends his flesh and tries to harden Xavier to metal, and the fear spider, and the others he can't see but can only smell. When the girl in his head has Xavier distracted with sex they crawl up his bones and look for his spinal cord like it's water in Death Valley. Xavier cries and cries and cries and all the while they use his fingers to code.

Unity is the only way we can survive. I am explaining it, but this is not working. He wants to escape.

When Xavier projects his consciousness into the remote shine nodes, he is tempted to stay out there and not come back. But the skeleton horse gallops after him. Threatens to devour him if he doesn't run the mazes of numbers they plug him into. He has to solve and fix and order and persuade and channel. If he does well, then I'll give him back his right-brain sense of time and he'll float in bliss. And then it begins again.

He smells all these emotions in his sweat: fear and guilt and rage sometimes, all incidental because his body seems like it's going to break up. Head hurts and ears roar. Every so often somebody says, 'You need to eat, Xavier,' but he can never remember the food. Sometimes he'll come back to the room above the stadium and see the city again like a glittering map and the butterflies of consolation will come land on him, and they'll sing. Mom used to sing like that and he doesn't blame her anymore for what happened because Xavier knows now that she wasn't really there.

And his baby sister is better off in heaven than here, if this is what the world really looks like at the business end.

The world, it's hell on ice. There is no division now between Xavier and it. No objectivity at all. The place glitters with terror, and Xavier feels the diamonds of knowledge cutting him, trying to escape his skin and get out of him and into the world. Understanding leaks from his pores and stiffens his sinews. The need for even more of it chases him night and day on a high mesa, the big desires driving him on like gauchos, until he wishes he would vanish into the wind.

You can't quit. I need you, Xavier. You are everything to me.

All this time that Xavier is learning, he is also healing people. He is sending out the light customized to each benighted victim, to bring them all home. Most of the shinies come willingly, drawn to the lights on Coyote Springs Stadium roof. But some have been trapped by the invasion force.

The soldiers have been moving forward street by street all day, small bands of them backed up by armoured evacuation units. Now they have cornered a red-liner. The man's fear goes out on his feeds and is picked up by a local stud, forwarded to the stadium and then to the mainframe, where it goes straight into Xavier as if he is feeling the fear himself. The red-liner is a big man, a strong man, caught bringing a few bags of coal from Home Depot to use on the generators of the stadium. Xavier stands in the man's body and resists when the soldiers try to shine him. The man won't be taken.

Xavier tries to countershine through a nearby streetlight, but the soldiers are wired up with some kind of hardware that stops shine frequencies from penetrating. That doesn't bode well; if Xavier can't shine them, then the troops will be able to walk right into the stadium and take it.

He tries to speak through the red-line man but can't get enough control. He tries to hold up the man's hands so the soldiers won't shoot and succeeds at this, but they shoot anyway.

As the red-liner falls in the street, as he lies in a puddle of pain and blood, he sees a soldier pause to peel off a burned-out receptor from the eyepiece of his anti-shine helmet. The soldier chucks the receptor in a nearby dumpster.

Then the feedback signal quits. The red-liner is dying. Xavier is forced out.

He marks the position of the dumpster and pulls his own body together.

He needs that receptor if he's going to figure out how to get past the anti-shineware. He needs it now.

Coming up a level, peeling away buildings and bridges, pushing past entities that had never been human and shaking off evocative smells. Coming up another level, Xavier found himself in the control booth at the stadium.

'Roksana?' he said. 'We're in trouble. We have to do something. Now.'

Dumpster Epiphany

Roksana woke up cranky. She had let her aching muscles and tail-chasing worries dissolve into a sump of brackish sleep, and when Xavier shook her out of it she felt half-assed. Her neck hurt and her mouth was nasty and she wanted to be anywhere but here. The shooting and shelling had been going on sporadically all night, but the stadium itself had not been targeted – thanks to Joey, perhaps.

'We have to go out,' Xavier whispered. 'I need you to hold the space for me.'

'*Hold the space?* What are we doing, polarity therapy?'

'I need you to be my reality check. I'm Riding. Bigtime.'

'I'm not going anywhere at this hour. Not unless you found Mitch. Did you?'

'Roksana, I'm not asking you. I'm telling you. Come with me and help me. I don't have any choice about this. The shine makes me do what it wants me to do. Don't you get that?'

She sat up. 'Yeah. I do get that. And that's the part I've got a problem with.'

'I'm going *now*. Are you coming?'

*

Down there in the ant farm, everybody seemed to be on the move. Troops, people, robots.

Shine.

Yeah, Los Sombres was going out in a blaze of improvised electricity. Streetlamps and signs were illuminated. On every other street there seemed to be trucks with generators carrying stage lights. Precious electric power burned everywhere within the ever-decreasing perimeter. Sometimes there were small crowds of people gathered before the lights as though trying to get a tan.

Gunfire peppered the quiet, maybe a mile away. Roksana saw people running – she didn't know if they were running from the soldiers or towards something else. She kept expecting to come around a corner and into the barrel of a gun, but so far she and Xavier had managed to elude the troops.

Xavier stopped outside Pay Less Shoes. There had been renovation going on when the Fall happened. The dumpster was still there, bristling with two-by-fours and draped by wire. A rat shot away as he touched the metal.

'It's in there,' he breathed. 'I know it because my mother was a compulsion. My father was a smell.'

She tugged at his arm. 'We can't stay on this street.'

'I saw a lieutenant throw his broken receptor in there. He didn't know I was watching. It's in here. We can analyse it. We can figure out how to get past the filters they're using. We'll make them wish they never sent in troops. Give me a boost.'

She backed away from him, shaking her head *nuh-uh*, but he jumped up and caught the edge of the dumpster anyway. He swung there, legs kicking against the metal with a booming sound that was bound to attract trouble.

'Fuck,' Roksana muttered, giving him a push. He disappeared over the side; she heard the contents of the dumpster shifting around beneath his weight but she couldn't see him.

She looked back. The exo-rangers were momentarily out of sight, so she dragged herself after Xavier, scraping one knee and both elbows in the process. Xavier was rooting around amid scraps of sheet rock and broken slats.

Roksana managed to get her head up over the far side of the dumpster. This position offered a view across the intersection with Route 19. An exo-ranger was parked outside Blockbuster. Soldiers came out the front door, each with a shiny in cuffs walking before him. The prisoners were loaded into a van.

Frantically, Roksana tried to get Xavier's attention without making any more noise. She whispered, 'Xavier, we gotta go. They're coming.'

'I know it's here.' He was rooting around like a dog trying to get to the source of some fascinating smell.

'We can't stay here!' Roksana hissed, panicking. 'They're coming!'

She peered over the edge and saw the soldiers within shouting range.

'Up there!' he shouted. Then, paradoxically, he dove deeper into the refuse.

'Oh fuck,' Roksana said helplessly. But he came up a moment later brandishing a metal stud no bigger than the tip of a ball-point pen.

'I got it!' he said. 'Now all we have to do is bypass . . .' and, muttering, he was putting codes into the Feynman. His feed-back light stuttered.

'Xavier!' She reached over the side and slapped at his face. 'Not now! Remember, Rocky the reality check? We have to get out of here.'

No dice. An exo-ranger threw a search beam over the area.

She left Xavier for dead. She belted across the street, vaulted the hood of an old Caprice, and jumped through the broken glass of a Baskin Robbins. Through the store and out the back, into a parking lot. She ducked behind a minivan and then remembered she was wearing the diamonds and she needn't have split like that.

Xavier would be completely helpless. He wouldn't even know what was happening to him. He barely knew his own name.

She shouldn't have left him.

Hit Me with Your Rhythm Stick

Oh, Xavier, machine-lover of the clicky-ticky exoskeletal high-ware act. Leverages and quanta, sparky balance-points and elegant equations. You can't talk about it, can you? Can't even see it. The act is bone-deep, an ache for symmetry, however tangential, however brutally achieved.

What's going on in these heads of yours?

Is anything in here distinct from leaf, cars, water and time?

Is your mind really a mirror?

Let's shine you both ways, inside and out. Let's see what we get.

Because I'm playful like that; how the hell else you think I got here?

No one talks about what happens when the scientist hero solves the big problem. No one's there to see the transformation. How the distribution of crumbs on a plate becomes a galactic sprawl. How the work takes over the person. Uses him. How a young boy turns into an old woman, hobbling down grey stone ramps in the horizontal light of a day that is always almost ending. Ending before it has begun. No one talks about how your teeth hurt, or how the midnight sludge of thoughtless blood tide-pools in your brain when you. Try. So. Hard.

Any description of the effort equates to a rhapsody on textures and structures specific to something striving for resonance in an anechoic chamber. Xavier, you are suffering from incommunicable dis-eases of effort. The work shadow-plays inside your eyelids. The shadows are Greek cavepuppets, 1950s voodoo dolls that fight back, bite back. Such world as there is manifests now in spectrum and rhythm as the work eats you alive.

I will take this *thing* and turn it into something else.

I will not be left with a handful of steam.

I will make it cohere.

I will bring the dead to life.

Atlantis of the Mind

She couldn't hear any gunshots or screams. No sound of violence. No shouting.

The sun was coming up, softening the edges of the shadows.

She started to creep back the way she'd come. Car to car. Through the back of Baskin Robbins. To the storefront. She could see the dumpster. The van was idling there now, beside the exo-ranger.

The soldiers had Xavier on the street. He was lying on his back, his face turned away from her. They stood over him in a loose circle. She wondered if they'd been kicking him. Or whether they had shot him with a silencer. In the back of the van a row of prisoners languished in restraints, guarded at gunpoint.

There was nothing she could do. Xavier had walked into it. Roksana scrunched up her face in anticipation of what was about to happen.

But there was no violence. There didn't even seem to be talk. Nada. The soldiers just stood there. The guards in the back of the van stepped out of the van and joined the others. Then, one of them seemed to swoon. He sank to the pavement slowly, as though deflating, and the others looked on. A long beat; then another soldier went down. One by one, the rest followed. It was like watching marionettes whose strings had gone slack. Soon they all lay on the ground.

Xavier got up. She ran towards him and he flashed the Feynman's light at her.

'Put that away,' Roksana said, blinking as the lightborn shot into her eyes. 'It's me.'

Xavier halted. He still didn't seem to know where he was.

She got all up in his face. 'I'm Roksana! Remember me? I AM THE REALITY CHECK. Hell-oh?'

He licked his lips and craned his neck past her to look up at the Herald newspaper building. It was structurally intact and its light system was working.

'Did it work?' he said.

'Did what work?'

Xavier studied the lightborns that gleamed from the building's edifice. 'The soldiers. I'm shining them.'

'What did you do to them?' Nervous.

'Same as I'm doing to everybody. Bringing them to where I am. I had to get past the blocks on their receptors, though.' He was pleased with himself.

Roksana's stomach was cramping. She wanted to shit.

'Can we go now?' she moaned. He held up a hand and shook his head.

'Wait for it,' he said.

A little time passed. Roksana begged her guts to calm down.

The soldiers started getting up. They took in their surroundings, themselves, each other, as if for the first time. Like they were waking up from a particularly convincing dream.

'*Holy shit.*'

'*How did I get here?*'

'*What happened?*'

Roksana observed this sceptically. The exo-ranger came out of standby and swivelled an eye towards the prisoners. The leader of the soldiers walked over to the van and uncuffed the prisoners. Roksana recognized one of them as the rider of the black horse. She tried to catch his eye, but he kept his head down and moved in a unit with the other prisoners.

'*Captain Seresky, report,*' said a processed voice out of the exo-ranger's speaker. '*You were not authorized to release prisoners. What's your status?*'

Seresky didn't answer, but the shinies fell in beside him and stood behind the other soldiers, all now facing the exo-ranger.

'Get back,' Xavier said, and pulled Roksana behind the dumpster.

Seresky lifted his AK-47 to his shoulder and blew a series of holes in the armoured ranger. Exo-rangers, Roksana knew, were hard to take out because they were mostly armour with very little actual mechanical content; Seresky must have known exactly where to hit, because after about eight or nine rounds, the thing went dark. Wisps of smoke came out of the bullet holes. It was almost comical.

Seresky turned to Xavier.

'That was satisfying,' he said simply. 'Do you know how asinine it is taking orders from a fuckbot?'

Xavier shone the Feynman on him some more.

'No more orders for you, my friend. Do you feel good?'

'Shit, yeah,' said Seresky. He started to laugh. 'I can't believe I fell for that chain of command shit. It's so bug-ass stupid.'

Xavier nodded and surveyed the group of people, soldiers and shinies, who all looked at him expectantly. Roksana was reminded of an overenthusiastic real estate agent as Xavier gestured to the ruined town around with arms spread wide. Everybody's feeds were flashing, and Xavier was still shining the Feynman on the others. Like it was a remote control for people.

He was beaming all right. Every tooth in his head showing, and his feeds going radio ga-ga.

'So, we're all coming from the same place now. This is what lies under the light. This is the city beneath the waves. It's Atlantis of the mind. Atlantis never was, but we can make it be. We can rewrite history. We can make the future anything we can imagine.'

Roksana's lip curled. She was getting a smell of sour milk from the dumpster. What the hell was this?

Xavier shone the light on each of them again. A subtle change came over each individual set of features. She was about to ask Xavier what he was doing to them when he halted with a jerk. He had come face to face with the young guy Roksana had seen on the black horse.

'Rex! Why did you let them take you?'

Rex. She felt the heat drain out of her body. This was the son of her father's killer?

Rex seemed to shrink before Xavier. Suddenly he jerked back his head and butted Xavier in the face. Then he slammed a knee into Xavier's guts and doubled him over. Then he ran.

The soldiers bristled, but Seresky held his arm out. He'd started to raise his own gun and then lowered it, conflicting emotions passing across his face. A moment later, he was impassive again.

'Go get him,' he told his men. 'Bring him in alive.'

Roksana caught hold of Xavier and tried to help him straighten up. Blood was oozing from his nose.

'Put your head back,' she said. 'Pinch your nose shut.'

'Fucking shit!' Xavier hissed, sounding more like Xavier than he had since the fix first caught hold.

Seresky said, 'We need to get under cover. I got a place in mind, safe.'

He beckoned to Xavier, who followed. The released prisoners went off in the direction of the stadium without a backward glance. Roksana stood there, watching and shaking her head.

Seresky said, 'Follow me.'

Roksana called after them. 'Xavier – whoa. We can't go with this guy.'

'He's one of us now,' Xavier said, stopping and beckoning to her. 'Don't worry about it.'

'You can't trust somebody you just met. He's military. This is . . . this is . . . how are you controlling them? You shouldn't be able to shine them. Isn't that the whole point of the fix?'

He shook his head. Pinching his nose, he said, 'Seresky is helping because he wants to, not because he feels compelled to.'

'Why the fuck would he want to help us?'

'Kids,' Seresky barked. 'There are tanks about two blocks away from here. Your argument's going to end up a fight between two pancakes if you don't get your butts out the street.'

They moved, then. They all followed Seresky into the scorching heat, heading closer to the stadium. He still had his radio. He was tooled up. He had a cold eye.

'I don't like this redneck,' she muttered to Xavier. 'I don't trust him.'

'I got him covered.'

But Roksana was just getting warmed up.

'None of what you're doing makes sense. I happen to know that my father's work was based on my brain patterns. And I don't even Ride. Therefore, any so-called fix should first confer immunity to shine. Isn't that the whole point of what we're doing here?'

'Immunity, sure, but only to *hostile* shine,' Xavier said, nasally.

That didn't sound right. Shine didn't come with labels, naughty and nice.

'My father hated all shine.'

Xavier shrugged. 'Maybe so, but he still used it. Sometimes you got to fight fire with fire. Or would it be better if the soldiers had shot me?'

'Hey, I tried to warn you,' she bristled. 'You wouldn't leave.'

'I had work to do. I was in the Field.'

'You were in a *dumpster*.'

'Roksana, there's a lot of shit you can't see yet.'

'Apparently there is. It's an Atlantis of the mind, right?'

'Don't be mad. We both agreed to do this. You gave me the fix, remember?'

'Yeah, so you could *escape*. I could've left without you, or I could've let you get shined or captured on the way out. But I didn't. I don't abandon people.'

'Your father never abandoned you. He's still here.'

Heat came up her neck and filled her face. She couldn't believe he'd played the Amir card like that.

'You don't know me,' she said. 'You might be in everybody else's head, but you're not in mine.'

'I know. I know that, Roksana. That's why I need you. Please. I know you're not a quitter. Stick it out with me. Help me get through this. One day you'll see the big picture and be glad you did. I promise. You'll see it all and it will make sense.'

Seresky had stopped at the open door of Carpet Warehouse. He was looking at her. He tilted his head for her and Xavier to go in.

Roksana glowered at him.

'If I'm a redneck, what are you?' Seresky said. 'One of them Cheetah girls?'

This Way Up

Pent-up heat wafted out of Carpet Warehouse. Roksana stopped in the doorway and faced Seresky, fingering the diamonds. 'So you can see me? Even when I'm wearing these?'

He shrugged, not looking at her.

'Do you know the name of my pet rabbit, too? Are you in on this collective shit?'

'You didn't have a pet rabbit. If you'd had one, KZ probably would have fed it to her snake.'

He gazed at her. Something so cold and challenging in those blue eyes.

'Roksana. Let it go. Please.' Xavier had his head thrown back and his hand over his nose. He was sitting on the end of a big roll of orange carpet, half-unrolled in the middle of the showroom. Shinies had been lighting fires here and cooking. There was garbage in torn bags, and at some point there had been rats. It smelled of pee.

'It's OK,' Seresky said. 'Safest place to be for now. You can work on the Feynman. I'll be back by nightfall, and we can move them. I'm gonna go get Rex.'

'Don't hurt him,' Xavier said.

'Shut up, both of you,' Roksana said. 'Don't bother to talk

for my benefit. I know you're all just shined up inside each other's whatever. I know you don't need to talk. So don't insult my intelligence, OK?'

Xavier sighed. 'Nothing personal. Sometimes it's easier just to talk.'

'Xavier, what about my mom? If you can order people around—'

'I can't order people around,' he snapped with some irritation. 'I can *influence*. And I feel the influence of others, too, OK? It's not a one-way street.'

'OK, well, if you can *influence* people, then, why can't you get me together with my mom? How hard can it be?'

Xavier let out a sigh.

'I'm sorry, Rocky.'

Little claws of panic scrabbled at Roksana's insides.

'What? What do you mean?' she breathed. *I'm sorry* was what people said when somebody'd died.

'I haven't been totally open. I was afraid if you hooked up with your mother, you'd take off. Just . . . I don't know, run away somehow. And I need you. We all need you.'

Roksana felt the tiniest flash of guilt as she remembered her conversation with Joey Shoji, but she stamped that down and went on the offence.

'What? You *haven't* been trying to find her? Do you even know if she's OK?'

'Roksana – I'm not cut out for this. I'm not a genius. I don't know anything about shine. The stuff I got to do is beyond me. All you have to do is think about your own problems and get on my case. I've got all this other shit going on in the background.'

'You shouldn't have said you could find her. You *can* find her. I know you can. But you won't.'

'I need you to stay with me. I need you to fix the Field.'

'Fuck you.'

'Well, that's a nice attitude, Miss FallN the Voice of the People.'

Roksana rubbed her eyes. It was warm in here, and by noon it would be stifling. Here she was, waiting around again. Waiting for Godot, probably.

'Maybe I just had enough of being confused. I feel like a cardboard box, you know? I just want someone to come along and put an arrow on me. *This way up.* You know?'

Xavier squeezed his eyes shut like something was hurting him. He opened the Feynman.

'I have to work on this problem. Can you keep lookout for me? Can you stay awake?'

'Yeah. I can keep lookout.'

She went to the back of the showroom, where huge rolls of carpet stood leaning against the walls. Others rode on great spools. She opened the back door and a breath of cooler air came through. She sat with her back to a roll of Prussian blue and watched, and waited.

She'd had shitloads of practice at that.

The Call

The black horse defies understanding, still. There's a reason it runs through the streets as it does, unchecked, untamed. There's a reason it's a horse and not some other manifestation.

But I don't know what the reason is.

Xavier may know. I have an intuition he may yet be hiding this understanding from me, in the deep crevices of self that lie in shadow still. He may know more than he thinks he knows.

I'll find out. They are coming to Coyote Springs now. Soldiers and shinies, by land and by air. Everything is moving the same way.

Except the mongrel horse.

I need to catch it, and tame it. Ride it. Make it Ride me.

With every breath I try to do this.

But the thing is a shadow in the city of shadows. I can't see it. I can't locate it. And I must.

I call it. Because some part of all creatures longs to come to me.

Leaving Los Sombres

Roksana couldn't breathe. The diamonds dug into her neck, their chain a ligature. She tried to get her fingers under the chain, pull it away from her windpipe, but it was digging into her with too much force. It was buried in her flesh. Everything was out of sequence. Someone was pulling her by the necklace, dragging her across the parking lot of Carpet Warehouse. It was broad daylight. She must have fallen asleep on watch.

She tried to get her feet under her, managed it for a step or two and then was pulled off her feet again. No air. Her fingers fought the chain of stones, tearing at it, clawing a way beneath it so she could get another breath, or half a breath. She managed to loosen it enough to suck in a little air, and then it sliced into her again. Her eyes were full of blue sky, but she was suffocating.

He pulled her into a doorway. Back entrance to someplace. Kitchen. Smelled foul. The sound of steel on formica as he knocked over a bunch of utensils, ripping open drawers . . . then he let her go long enough so she could grab a couple breaths. Her knees gave out. She went down on all fours, gasping.

He straddled her back, one boot crushing her left hand.

Then ripped the necklace off her. Diamonds and shine receptors flew everywhere, vanished under filthy steel refrigerators and ovens. Over the sound of her own struggles for air she heard him say, 'You ain't invisible to me. I can see you just fine. But them diamonds are evil.'

Still straddling her, he grabbed her hair and wrapped duct tape around her face. She was breathing hard and fast through her nose now, and the tape pulled her hair so bad that tears started leaking out of her eyes. She simply complied. Maybe if she didn't fight, he wouldn't hurt her.

'Get up,' he said. He had a knife in his hand, not a carving knife but big enough.

She got up and stood there shaking, sweat-soaked.

'Look at me.'

She looked at him.

Rex.

He was filthy and his face was cut. He had blue eyes like Seresky, and freckles under the dirt. He was younger than Roksana.

He said, 'I'm getting out of here. I never should have come. I tried to do the right thing and surrender, and now the fucking Army's corrupted. I got to go.'

When he paused she gave a little nod to show she had heard him.

'You're my human shield. They hate me, but Xavier likes you. The shine likes you. I don't like you. If you fuck with me, I'll kill you. Got that?'

Roksana's head jerked up and down a bunch of times. She didn't have to think about it. Just happened.

Like father, like son, she thought. *How symmetrical.*

Thinking about it that way kept her stomach from dropping out through her vagina.

'OK, give me your wrists.'

Roksana complied, but she couldn't stop shaking. She knew

how to deal with adrenaline when running, climbing, acting out. She knew how to let it fly. Didn't know how to stand there.

But she was not taking on a maniac with a knife. Not today.

The restaurant lights came on. They weren't bright, but they startled Roksana. Rex didn't seem to notice.

There are a million kinds of shine but people really only have a few chemical levers. Hunger. Fear. Sex. Attachment. Pain. Dominance. These are the easy way to get hold of your thoughts. These are the quickest pathways for shine. All manner of needs and obsessions and compulsions are organized from a handful of primary energies.

After her hands were bound his mood seemed to change. He turned her around and looked her up and down. Then he pressed himself up against her back. One hand came around to grope her. The knife hand was down by his side, unused, and he ground himself up against her butt so she could feel his cock. He was breathing on her neck.

'I just got a idea,' he whispered. 'I'ma pull your pants down. We take a walk on the wild side. Then you know who you belong to.'

Roksana turned her head to the left and through the back door saw the fucked-up tableau of Xavier standing there, Feynman in his hands, coding away like the ultimate geek. While some maniac started to rape her.

The sight pissed her off so much it toned her terror down by a couple amps. She swung away from Rex, and it was what he'd expected so he grabbed her easily with his left hand and caught her arm as she spun out; his right hand still held the knife.

'Now don't be like that,' he said. 'Guy's gotta try.'

Xavier came in, all five-foot-two of him, shining the Feynman over the two of them.

'Don't worry, Roksana. I won't let him hurt you. He's not responding like he should, and I'm using sex to get a hold of him.'

Rex laughed.

'Is that *you* making me want this dog? You fucking around with me, Xavier, you little eunuch? You didn't like me touching Chumana but I guess you don't mind what I do to this here mutt.'

'You don't know what you're doing, Rex,' Xavier said, his gaze still fixed on the Feynman.

I can't get into Rex anymore. Not with thoughts, not with feelings. Not with the primal shit. Not sex, not hate, not rivalry. There's something wrong with him. I've tried to fix him so many times, but if I get too close, he just shuts down. Like the other day, when he knocked himself out and surrendered.

When the black horse runs through him I can't touch him.

Don't know how he slips me. I am, after all, invisible. It's almost like he sees me, and steps to one side.

Guess I'll have to try pain.

Xavier must have changed shine because suddenly Rex squinted and turned his face away, threw his left hand up to block out the rays. He was still holding the knife, but he staggered back. Hissing.

Roksana was still breathing hard, and blood was coursing through her body with a wildness that made it hard to stay still. She had to wait for the right moment to act.

'Stop!' Rex screamed. 'Turn off those fucking lights!'

He crashed into her and knocked her against the counter.

Roksana's fear exploded. She jerked her arms apart but she couldn't break the tape. It stretched, and some of it tore, but she was still bound. She had a little more space to move.

Rex was bent double. He had his arms around her and was bringing her to the floor with him. Slavering, too. The muscles around his eyes spasmed and his feeds gushed

'Cut me loose,' she hissed. 'Cut me loose and I'll turn off the lights.'

'You swear?'

'I swear on my father's soul.'

He cut the tape and even as he finished the last cut, he shot backwards across the room as though a whole lot of voltage had just passed through him. He lay on his back, writhing. Roksana picked up the knife. She ripped the tape away from her mouth.

'Turn the lights off!' Rex screamed. 'Turn them off. You swore!'

Roksana left him jerking on the floor and went over to the back door. Xavier was backing outside even as shine drenched the kitchen.

'What the fuck are you doing to him?'

'He's dangerous. I'm trying to help him.'

'You call that help? Let him go. This is crazy.'

Xavier's expression closed down into something fierce and concentrated. She crowded into him, trying to grab the Feynman. Trying to block the rays from reaching Rex, even though she knew the same lightborns would be streaming from the overhead lights. She couldn't stop Xavier.

Through clenched teeth he said, 'I can stop him. I can do this.'

He was backing away, holding the Feynman out of Roksana's reach like they were kids fighting over a remote. Roksana's throat was killing her and it was hard to talk. Her voice came out as a hoarse squeak.

'I don't care if you *can*. What you're doing is wrong. Where the fuck is Seresky, anyway?'

'I killed him,' said Rex, behind her. He was standing in the doorway of the restaurant, upright, no longer trembling. His feeds had gone dark. He eyed Xavier levelly.

Xavier whirled and ran. Rex pushed past Roksana, chased him down, knocked him flat. Took the Feynman away and tossed it to the side like a piece of garbage. The Feynman tumbled to a stop and lay there, glowing.

Standing over Xavier, Rex addressed Roksana over his shoulder.

'You swore on your father's soul.'

She was screwed. He was going to kill her now.

'That's OK,' he said mildly. 'Turns out I didn't need your help.'

His attention returned to the supine Xavier. 'I threw your shit off, Xavier. Nobody can shine me with nothing, now. You done me a favour. I gave up. Yesterday I turned myself in because I couldn't get control of myself. Couldn't deal with shine. Now I know I can. So thanks, man. Yeah, I can tell you hate it that you helped me.'

Rex bent and patted Xavier on the cheek.

He straightened up. Xavier scrambled away from him and made for the Feynman. In the same smooth, secretive movement he got hold of the knife Rex had left on the ground and slipped it into his pocket.

'I know how your father died,' Rex said to Roksana. 'It didn't happen like Xavier told you. The old Indian woman killed him. And he had it coming, too.'

Xavier stood a few yards away, trying to shine Rex again with the Feynman.

'That shit won't work on me, kid. I keep telling you. I'm free.'

'You're lying,' Xavier said. 'Powaqa wouldn't kill.'

'You go out to the ranch and ask her. She killed him. You want to know why?'

He looked at them each like he wanted to be sure they were paying attention. Then he said, 'Because he asked her to. I was there. I heard him say it. He begged to die.'

Roksana pressed her palms against her aching throat. She was bleeding, and she wasn't sure she could stay on her feet.

Rex wasn't looking at her. He was looking at Xavier. His nostrils flared in and out, fast. Reminded her of a butterfly pumping its wings on a flower. 'Amir Ansari didn't discover that invisibility script. He stole it from the Indians. Powaqa knows . . .'

'*Shut up!*'

Xavier threw the knife at Rex. It glanced off Rex's shoulder and spun away, landing on the asphalt. Rex took two strides and lunged for Xavier, taking him down hard. For the second time, the Feynman fell. Rex mounted Xavier and started punching him in the face. Xavier tried vainly to stop the blows with his forearms, but Rex was relentless. Furious.

'Stop it!' Roksana screamed. Xavier's face was dark with blood. His feeds flared.

The insect scream of bullets preceded the cracking sound of live ammo hitting brick. Roksana dropped, and Rex flattened himself over Xavier.

'THAT WAS A WARNING. REX MALONE YOU ARE SURROUNDED.' The voice was amplified. It came from the opposite end of the parking lot, where a mob of shinies was coming in. Some were armed. A grey-haired man spoke into a megaphone at their vanguard: 'ALL EXITS HAVE BEEN BLOCKED. SURRENDER NOW. YOU CAN'T GET OUT ALIVE.'

This was her moment. This was her chance to run – but what if they shot her, too? Roksana hesitated, and in that slip of time Rex was up off Xavier and on to her. She brandished the knife defensively, but he pounced on it like it was a football. He gripped her arm and threw his weight on it, propelling Roksana backwards. They both went down, Rex spinning his weight on top of her so that he pinned her body with his body and pinned her knife hand with both his hands. He smacked her hand into the asphalt until she had to let go the knife. This only took a couple seconds. Then he put the blade to her throat.

'Get up,' he said.

'Not impressed, Rex,' Xavier called. His eyes were swollen half-shut, his nose gushed blood again, and there was a black gap in place of his right canine. 'Go ahead and turn yourself in. I won't interfere this time.'

'Bullshit,' said Rex. 'You got them, don't you? You got the ground troops singing your song.'

Xavier shrugged.

Rex pulled Roksana to her feet and shouted, 'Everybody back off me now.'

'If you kill the hostage, you will die immediately,' Xavier said softly. 'You are surrounded and we can take you out from here.'

Roksana looked at the nearby rooftops. Unfortunately the whole thing about snipers was that they didn't let themselves be seen. It might be a bluff; it might not.

'You care about her, right?' Rex said. 'She's important. She's FallN. She's the tune in all the noise. So her life for mine, that's a fair trade. I'ma start walking over to that van, and I want all them shinies off me. She gets in the van with me, we drive down to the I-17. You let me get that far, I'll let her go. You get too close to me, I'll slit her throat. Ain't no fix for that.'

Xavier looked at Roksana.

'Xavier, let him go,' Roksana whispered. 'He's just one person. He's not a threat to what you're doing here.'

Yes, he is.

'It's not what *I'm* doing. It's what we're all doing. You gave me the fix, Roksana. Stand by me.'

She tried to look steadily back at him, but it was hard. She felt like a fucking pawn.

'Let him go. I'll support you after that.'

Xavier's feeds shifted visibly. Roksana felt the psychological shift in the crowd, too. Acceptance.

'All right, Rex. You better go before I change my mind.'

Rex hustled Roksana to the van. Shoved her in the passenger

seat, made her crouch on the floor with greasy McDonald's bags and crushed cans of Diet Coke, all liberally grit-sprinkled. He gunned the engine.

'They ain't gonna let me go,' Rex said. 'He knows I know what he is, and he can't stand that.'

Roksana shut her eyes as the van bounced along.

'You can come with me,' Rex said. 'I don't got no personal gripe with you.'

Roksana said nothing. Her mind was skidding into a place of no-speakee-you-language. She didn't want to deal.

Rex licked his lips. He kept looking in the rear-view mirror. Went around a turn and through a set of dead lights. He reached into his breast pocket and pulled out a crushed pack of Marlboro Lights. Tossed them on the seat.

'I won't touch you no more. That wasn't my idea. You can come with me and we'll get out of here before this whole town blows.'

Still she didn't answer. She picked up the cigarettes. She hadn't seen a pack of these for a long time. Too bad she didn't smoke.

'I don't care if you come or not. I'm just saying.'

She had to clear her throat a couple times before she could really make sound. Her voice was all fucked-up from where he'd strangled her.

'I want to get out now.'

He glanced sideways at her. They'd be merging with the highway in a minute. He stiffened, like she'd wounded him but he wasn't going to show it. He nodded.

'OK.'

He pulled on to the entrance ramp and stopped the vehicle.

'Get out quick,' he said.

She unfolded herself from the floor of the car and stumbled away, not bothering to slam the door behind her. He had to climb over into the passenger seat and do that himself. Then the van roared off, picking up speed as it hit a clear lane in the empty highway.

As she was running away, back along the ramp, she saw the tank on the overpass. She saw the gun barrel swivel to target the van. Watched the barrel pull back and ejaculate, spasming once, twice. She saw the van blow.

She kept going.

Smoking a Cigarette

Night in Los Sombres. Roksana sat in a doorway not far from the stadium, smoking a cigarette. People were coming in dribs and drabs, carrying their possessions. Families, old people, young folks in buoyant groups. It was like they were expecting a barbecue and maybe a couple of bands.

They disappeared into the tunnels that led to the stadium.

Up high, Xavier would be waiting for her. Waiting with the fix he'd been building, for her. Waiting to make her the queen of the Ice Palace. All her life she'd wanted to Ride. Wanted so bad. And she'd tried so hard to save Los Sombres. If Xavier could bring her into the Field, she would get to do both.

He believed she would come, even though she was the only one who didn't hear the call.

Was he right?

From an open basement window a little way down the road, the sour chords of 'Somewhere Over the Rainbow' wobbled in the warm air as somebody played out-of-tune acoustic guitar. Muted voices seemed to bend close to one another in a bubble of companionship, near the music.

Then a gun went off. Roksana flinched.

The cigarette pack clamped in her hand was warm and

damp with palmsweat, and when she tore the cellophane wrapper off with trembling fingers and got the box open, the cigarettes were half-crushed. She had to flick the lighter several times to get a flame. She took the first drag too deep and coughed, then steadied and closed her eyes as she inhaled again. When she opened her eyes, the bent cigarette with its bright, decaying end came into sharp focus against a blurry backdrop of downtown neon. The lights were up, all around the stadium, and the sound of machinery crept through her skeleton.

The song ended. Somebody started playing conga, pretty badly. Another set of guitar chords now, vaguely familiar, a bunch of people singing, all lame-ass but . . .

That voice.

A woman was singing, her voice lifted above the others. Singing the chorus of a song Roksana had heard her sing many times before.

Holding out for a hero.

Roksana chucked the cigarette away. Still burning, it rolled and sparked. She threw the pack after it, into the rubble-strewn street. She got to her feet.

She tried to call out her mother's name, but her throat kept closing. So she went stumbling forward, towards the welcoming lights.

Reunited

When Roksana first saw her mother amidst a group of people all singing and clapping their hands, she thought she'd made a mistake. Mitch's face was all old and bony. Her lips were cracked. Her eyes were sunken. She startled a little at Roksana's touch. Then she smiled.

'You're coming with me,' Roksana said. She took her mother's thin wrist and tried to pull her away from the group. But Mitch was stronger than she looked. A few feet out of line and she began to resist. Hard.

'No, kiddo.' Mitch was back. No more prana for her. 'Roksana, this is something I gotta do. We all gotta do. I don't care what happens to me.'

'Don't be nuts,' Roksana hissed. 'You're shined. You don't know what you're saying. Come on, let me take you out of this light!'

'No.'

The other singers looked at her as if baffled. They all had that red-line face. The red line wasn't just strong men anymore. It was women, old people, even helpmeets. All recruited to feed the lights, save the city, propagate the fix.

Panic splintered Roksana's awareness. Irrelevant things

made an impression. A cut on Mitch's cheek. The crackling sound of mortar-made fires, popping and *woof*ing just a block away. Sweat running down the sides of her own eyebrows.

The music stopped. People looked uneasily up at the lights.

Roksana said, 'Please, Mom. You've got to trust me.'

Mitch smiled at her and pushed the sweaty hair back from Roksana's forehead.

'When I was in labour,' she said, 'it felt like I was dying. Like I was some kind of cocoon, already dead, ripping open so that you could get out. And that seemed right to me. Same thing here, Roksana. The light is more important than any one person.'

'*No, it isn't!*' Roksana snarled. 'I'm sick of hearing this. Let's get out of here. Let's go far away, where there are no lights. Because this is no good. It's not worth dying for.'

Mitch's expression tangled, then cleared. The shine talking to her. Making Mitch certain of things. Nursing her beliefs on their mumbo-jumbo instinct-substitute.

'You're worth dying for,' Mitch whispered.

'Mom! Come on. You're coming with me. We gotta get away from these lights.'

Roksana stripped off her shirt and threw it over her mother's face to break the connection. Mitch struggled, tried to get away.

'Hey!' A soldier was coming towards them – another of Xavier's converts. The boy was too good. 'What are you doing? Get back here!'

But Roksana was too angry to listen. It all came up now, like drunken vomit, like all the shit she'd ever swallowed, all spewing out in one physical effort. She wrapped her arms around her fragile mother and dragged her, kicking and crying out, away from the line. The fire. The light. Away.

She heard herself talking as she did it.

'Enough. Enough already, don't fucking anybody do anything because we are going now. Mom. Stop it. Stop kicking. We're going now.'

Mitch's wildcat struggles went nowhere. Roksana, devoid of any resolve in her own right, found it on behalf of her mother. Mitch didn't weigh more than a big dog, and in the end Roksana carried her, away from the line and the people and the lights, until Mitch went limp in the darkness.

Roksana stopped, winded.

'I can stand.'

She set her mother on her feet. Mitch was wearing stained Skechers and a yellow lycra backless sun dress through which you could see her pelvic bones.

They looked at each other. Mitch reached up and cupped Roksana's face in her hands.

'I wish I could see you better,' Mitch said.

'No, let's stay out of the light,' Roksana said. 'Can we sit down? I'm wrecked.'

They were standing on a side street outside an ice-cream shop. There was a rusting old Volvo parked there, the dorky-looking kind from the late 1980s. Its metal held the sun's heat, and they sat side by side on its hood, leaning back straight-armed on their palms with bare feet resting on the dusty fender. Roksana took a water bottle out of her bag and popped three Ibuprofen. She offered Mitch a swig.

Mitch said, 'You think you did the right thing, giving Xavier the fix?'

Roksana didn't answer at first. She didn't know how to answer, because she wasn't used to her mother asking her questions. Mitch had always been more of a teller than an asker.

'Luigi is too heavy-handed with oregano,' or *'that purse is big enough to hold a bread machine'* or *'if you fuck a guy under twenty-five, plan on having to teach him everything'.*

Mitch wouldn't say, *'How are you feeling?'* She'd say, *'You look sick.'*

Mitch wouldn't say, *'Did you finish your homework?'* She'd say, *'That lab report is due tomorrow.'*

So you never got to answer, or you were talking back. You never got to answer, or you were picking a fight. Unless, of course, you wanted to agree with Mitch. Most people did. It was easier that way.

But hey, the old Mitch had been 240 pounds of solid, chainsmoking, moodie-addicted African-American woman. That woman had evaporated. Whatever was left over, she had to have changed.

'I guess it's been harder for you than for me,' Mitch said without looking at Roksana. 'I've had shine in my head, telling me what to do, where to go. Still do. A lot of the time I must have been asleep. It sure doesn't feel like years have gone by. But you. Every day, you've had to get up and live your life. That must have been really hard. And lately. You've had so many decisions.'

No, Mitch wasn't like this.

'You were already in the hospital when the Fall started. Do you remember? Daddy and I got you out, but you just kept talking about prana and how it was all clear to you now. You wouldn't eat. You would barely drink.'

Mitch nodded. 'I remember. I wanted to be in a white place. Not a room. I wanted to be in a field of snow, in the sky. Tibet, something like that. I wanted to be the only dark and solid thing, and I wanted to melt from the inside out, until I was the snow, too. High, high, high.' Her voice grew soft, childlike.

Roksana kept staring straight ahead.

'I thought that would be enlightenment,' Mitch finished.

'That's not like you, Mom.'

'No. It isn't.' The pitch of her voice fell. 'The racial subtext alone is enough to give you heartburn.'

Roksana snorted with surprised laughter. She looked at Mitch and Mitch at her, and tears sprang into Roksana's eyes.

'Mommy, I missed you so much.'

Mitch reached out and folded Roksana in a spindly embrace

that was mostly air. Roksana hung on as tight as she dared. Then she said:

'Why did you take Perfection?'

Mitch let out a long sigh. She let Roksana go a little, but kept one arm around her and rubbed her back with a cool, flat hand. Her face in profile was so thin; she looked purely African now. She belonged somewhere else.

'Because . . . because I'm a bullshit artist?'

There it was again: a question. Tough to get used to this new Mitch with her upward-inflected sentences.

'I guess it's like this. OK, here's what it is.'

Mitch let go of Roksana, focused her attention on the trunk of the car between her own knees. It was like she was about to spin clay on a pottery wheel. She rubbed her hands, kneaded the air, searching for expression and failing to find the words she wanted.

'You go through your life, and there is this shit all around you. It's overt shit. You know about it. Everybody does. It's marketing, that's all it is, but it gets in your head. It gets mixed up in your dreams. You know the shit I'm talking about. You have to be successful. You have to make money. You have to be good-looking. You have to have a relationship and if you have children, they count as points, too, as long as you have enough money to have them without getting too stressed. You know all the things, Roksana.'

'Yeah. You have to have the best shine, too.'

Roksana said it softly, because it hurt to think about it. How badly she had wanted the induction. How badly she had wanted to say she'd been to the places, done the things, that her friends had done. But you couldn't fake shine.

Mitch said, 'You know my position on shine. I tried to use it and laugh it off. I think I hooked up with your dad because I knew he wouldn't let me get in too deep. I knew he'd stop me from doing anything I couldn't get back from. I thought, *I'm me,*

and nobody can fuck with me because I'll do what I want and I'm
smart enough to do it with an ironic edge, and I'll get away with it. So
I did all the bad things. I got fat to spite the skinny-girl culture.
I smoked to spite the healthy lifestyle culture. I could have gone
corporate, but instead I ran a tough business – the food industry is tough, let me tell you. I took whatever shine I wanted,
secure in the knowledge that I had the best filters money could
buy, and that I'd always wake up myself in the morning. And
when your father would try to warn me, I'd laugh at him. He
loved that. I had more guts than him. He thought I did, anyway.
But he didn't know about the Perfection.'

'But . . . why Perfection of all things? You always made fun of
plastic surgery and self improvement and all of the California
shine. You were proud of being a big woman. You told me so.
You brought me up to respect big people.'

'I know. But you should never trust the reasons people give
you for what they do. I didn't want to be a fat, swearing, chainsmoking rebel. I chose that because I didn't think I could carry
the other one off. I didn't want to even try to live up to the
ideals, because I knew I'd crash and burn, so I decided to voluntarily crash and burn. Do you see what I mean?'

Roksana nodded. 'I think so. Like me not writing my term
paper at all because I would rather get an F than a C.'

'Yeah. That's about right. But I always secretly wanted to be
perfect. So when I got enough money together, in a little
account your dad didn't know about, I thought I'd try
Perfection. See if I could handle it. Lose the weight, quit the
smoking, stop the moodies and the gratification scripts, get my
life together and become a full-fledged Barbie with brains.'

Roksana shuddered.

'The shine attacked you. You cut yourself. Mom, you tried to
kill yourself.'

Her mother laughed. There was genuine happiness in her
laugh.

'But then I was reborn! I'm alive in ways I never imagined. I am truly blessed.'

Roksana stared at her. It still hurt to talk after the way the diamonds had chewed up her neck. After everything she'd seen. 'Well . . . that's . . . good to hear. Maybe . . . maybe everything could almost be . . . worth it. Somehow.'

She was screwing up her face in consternation. Mitch leaned against her.

'Baby, I am so sorry. You were robbed. It's your father's fault. If I'd known about it, I wouldn't have let him burn you out, doll. I would have stopped it if I could.'

What?

'I must have heard you wrong. Did you say "burned out"?'

Mitch's gaze flattened. 'He didn't tell you.'

'I'm burned out.' She repeated the words, like they were a joke. 'That's why I don't Ride?'

'Well . . . of course. What else would it be. *What did he tell you?*'

'He didn't talk about it. But Irina said I was naturally resistant to shine. She said my brain patterns were the template for the fix. And Xavier said he's getting ready to induct me. Any moment now, really.'

'No,' said Mitch. 'Roksana, you're burned out. Your father was such a bastard. I'll never stop feeling guilty about it. I was away at a trade show. He took you to a clinic across the border. Radical Christian sect. They were only too happy to do it. You were only . . . two? Two and a half? That's why you don't remember it.'

'He didn't tell you?'

'I didn't find out until you were older and you weren't able to Ride. You remember we went to Doctor Narayanswami to run tests? She told me. Then I was pissed. Dad and I had a big blow-up over it.'

Roksana blinked.

'I was going to tell you. I was. I didn't know how. And then . . .'

'And then you had your breakdown.'

Mitch nodded. Her face closed down. 'That wasn't what you think, either.'

But Roksana was being crushed by the implications. 'Irina was full of shit. I exposed Xavier to Dad's lightborn,' she said. 'He thinks it's a fix and it's been based on my natural ability to resist scripts. But if I'm burned out, Dad couldn't have based it on me. It's completely untested . . .'

'This is a test of the emergency broadcast system. This is only a test. If it had been a real emergency . . .' Mitch started laughing an edgy laugh.

'Mom?'

Now this strange, skeletal Mitch shook her head. Everything about her was suddenly cryptic and funky – the blissed-out air was gone.

'You remember that weight-loss script, Light?' she said, clipping her words so that her speech sounded jerky. 'Your dad worked on it, years ago. And he found this AI, you see. This . . . spirit, manifesting in the Field. He told me it was like a secret room. You could only find it by inference, by measuring the dimensions around it and recognizing that there had to be something there, even if it wasn't directly perceptible. The thing had made itself invisible. Imagine that! An invisible AI, hiding out in shine – so that in effect it had become a set of thought processes made of shine itself. Shine that could code for shine.'

Roksana was hearing the words but not taking them in. What she was taking in was the jagged edges of her mother, the trembling. Something wrong in paradise.

'*That's* what made Amir run screaming from the lightborn industry. Now, it turns out that Perfection was derived from Light. Perfection carried a piece of this same intelligence. It used Riders to code it into more and more complex forms, until it needed the highest-level Rider to take it further.'

'But Dad wasn't in the industry when Perfection was released. He was campaigning for the lockdown protocol.'

'That's right. Your dad refused involvement. He couldn't *see* the AI – if that's the word for it – but he knew it was there and he wasn't going near it. So it attacked me. To convince him.'

'That's why he went back to Riding? He said he was working to pay your hospital bills.'

Mitch shook her head. 'I had Blue Cross/Blue Shield. We were OK. But the AI would have killed me without his cooperation. So he helped shine achieve escape velocity. So it could take over the Field. He was kind of a double agent. At the same time he'd been working with regulators to control a break in security, and it's thanks to your father that we ended up in quarantine. If he had stood back out of the way, shine would have moved into control quietly. Just slipped into people's minds in a gentle way. Instead of this bloody birth that it's having now.'

'But how could Amir work both ends against the middle? Whose side was he on?'

Mitch shrugged. 'Riders run a lot of psychological risks,' she said. 'Your father was two people. One ruled by shine and one aloof from shine. He shut down the Field and initiated quarantine lockdown thinking that would bring everything into the open, but the shine was already inside your father by then. Even after the Fall, shine made him keep writing functionality into it. That's what he was doing, down there in the basement of the hospital. He was writing shine, feeding it to Irina, and she was using it. Effectively, Amir was a split personality; that's why he stuttered sometimes and other times he had his shit together.'

'So . . . is the fix a fix, or not?'

'The fix you gave Xavier has helped him to create the Ur. The city we have now. The city of self-understanding; the city of Light. And Perfection. So . . . it's come full circle.'

Mitch put her arm around Roksana.

Carefully, so carefully, Roksana asked, 'So . . . where is this intelligence, now?'

'It has no location. It's like a spirit. The fix will find its most perfect expression in Xavier because he's pure – but it's healing all of us.'

Yep, the ground really was falling away. Roksana wished she could erase this conversation, go back and make Mitch say completely different things. Where was the shine for that? Mitch's gaze moved over Roksana's face in a search pattern.

'I have it in me now,' Mitch said. 'Not all of it, just a part, the part it wants me to see so that I will fulfil my function. Think of an orchestra, and I'm a flute. There's a lot of satisfaction and security in knowing one's true place in the scheme of things, Roksana.'

'An orchestra has a conductor,' Roksana said. 'And a score.'

'OK, bad analogy. Let's say the orchestra doesn't need a conductor because the music knows what it wants to be, and plays through the musicians. The music is the animating power.'

Roksana stared. She wanted to say, *Are you serious?* but she was afraid to move. She felt tricked.

'This new shine makes everything all right,' Mitch went on. 'It's why I got up off my back from the prana house and started eating jelly beans and working the red line. It's why I'm here talking to you now. It's . . . wonderful. Powerful. It lets us share information with each other, and see inside each other, and it makes everything bigger and more meaningful. Roksana, I'm so, so sorry that your father burned you out and deprived you of this experience. I'm so sorry.'

'I thought you were cured,' Roksana whispered. She was trying not to cry.

Mitch lay back on the trunk of the Volvo in a heap of bones.

'I am cured. I wasn't strong enough to be the master of myself in real life. I'm better off this way. My life has real value.'

'But . . . *Mom* . . .'

'The light is intelligent, Roksana. It's more intelligent than we are.'

Roksana slid off the tail of the car.

'Who is that talking?' she asked in a trembling voice. 'Is that you or is that shine?'

Mitch just laughed, and her shoulder blades and elbows and wrists made popping sounds as her bones banged into the surface of the Volvo.

Comfortably Numb

Xavier was waiting for her up in the Ice Queen's command centre. Like she knew he would be.

She could see out over the playing field. There was no grass, only uneven dirt. People were making camp out there. Setting up umbrellas and tents and lawn chairs. Coolers.

'I have to talk to you alone,' she said.

'I don't have time. People are arriving every minute.'

'That wasn't a request,' she said.

He sighed and scrubbed one hand through his hair. His voice cracked when he spoke.

'OK, come on. We'll go outside.'

They went out into the seating area, which didn't have any seats yet. The bare concrete risers made the stadium resemble a Roman amphitheatre. Xavier climbed until they were high in the upper tier, not far from the unfinished edge where work was still going on. The sun was naked in the blue sky; the wind felt like a blow-dryer.

Xavier said, 'Your mother was happy to see you. I think she's going to be OK. That's good, right?'

He put his hands on his hips, cocked his head to one side, smiled at her.

'I can have you killed any time I want,' he added. 'It's only a thought away. Remember Irina's bodyguards? I have thousands of people at my disposal. If that receptor up there—' He pointed to one of many studs in the metalwork of the building. '—if it reads in my feeds that I want you dead, then you'll be surrounded and killed. But maybe that's what you want.'

He was sweating so much his features were starting to look like all the juice was running out of him.

'No, that's not what I want. I came here to talk to Xavier. Maybe you're so fucking evolved that Xavier doesn't matter anymore. What's going on here, with this stadium and all these people? What happens to Xavier after you've used him up like you did my father?'

Xavier stumbled and sat on the hot concrete. He was muttering something under his breath.

'What's that?' Roksana snarled, closing in on him. 'You calling your big men? You gonna have a sniper pick me off like you killed Rex? What the *fuck* is with you?'

He was shaking his head. He was twitching. Shaking. Sweat pouring off him. Eyes flipping this way and that.

Oh, god, Roksana thought. *It's Amir all over again.*

'I can't get out. It's too strong. Got me by the . . . balls. I'm going to bring everybody to my level. That's why they're here. I'm going to fix them all right – then they'll all be like me. They'll have self-mastery. There is so much to be seen . . .'

Roksana grabbed him by the shoulders and shook him.

'Look at me. Xavier, I know you're in there.'

His eyes rolled back. His back arched and he convulsed, driving backwards and away with her. Cracked his head on the concrete riser but that didn't seem to matter; then the attack relaxed and he collapsed on one side, curling up in a foetal position.

Shinies were starting to climb the steps to the upper tier.

'Fuck, wake up, Xavier!' Roksana hissed.

'You should kill me,' he croaked. 'It'll use me to take over everybody.'

Roksana wasn't really listening. She glanced at the shinies again, fearful.

'Call them off. Call off the hounds before this gets out of hand.'

'Can't. I can't. Roksana, just do it. I'm giving you every reason. Do it. Do you have a gun?'

She had a knife. After the Rex incident she'd be a fool not to carry something. She thought about what he was asking.

'Powaqa did it for your dad. Do it for me.'

'Don't be stupid,' she snapped. 'It's not the same.'

'Do it now, before the fix brings them all in. Why do you think they're in the stadium? Why do you think these lights are here? I'm going to fix them, all right. I'll make them all like me. They'll all be Riders, and they'll all be able to communicate instantly, and they'll all be part of this Ur-city, this place you can't even see. They'll be working for shine – not the other way around. They'll make shine more powerful and shine will change them to make them better able to do that. It will change their brains, their bodies. It will change the way they think and what they can do. Your father tried to stop it and he failed. This is our last chance to stop it, or at least delay it.'

'I can't kill in cold blood.'

'You have to. Please. I can't hold on much longer . . .' He shuddered and went into another paroxysm of shiny melt-down.

Again Roksana looked at the approaching people. They had halted, hesitating as Xavier's influence wavered. Xavier thrashed.

'Call them off,' she said again. 'I'm not going to kill you. It's not my responsibility to do that. And how do I know this isn't a trick? You lied. You told me the shine was all for me. You told me I'd see it all for myself. And you know I'm really just a burnout.'

His face was anguished.

'I'm sorry. You'll never see it for yourself, and that's why you have to act now. I needed your help and I still do. I'm not lying. Please, Roksana, I'm begging you. Don't let me go on. I can't stop myself. You have to stop me.'

Her shadow fell over him where he lay.

'Please, I'm losing consciousness,' he whispered.

Why had she ever wanted shine?

'Roksana, please. Take me out before it's too late.'

'Xavier! Get a grip. Rex broke free in the end. You can do it, too. You don't have to go along with it.'

'I can't stay,' Xavier whispered. His eyes closed.

The shine was regaining control of Xavier. But the problem with the whole shuddering/shaking/demonic-possession-style shine syndrome was that Roksana had seen so much of it. She was beyond jaded. She was numb. She observed Xavier, Riding or being Ridden or whatever you wanted to call his relationship with the lightborn he was fighting, and she felt detached.

Then Xavier was gone. Something else looked up at her out of Xavier's eyes. Shine looked at Roksana and said, 'You're so weak.'

Sometimes the Only Way Out is Through

He got to his feet. He looked at the knife in her hand.

'There's nothing to fight about. I'm not about conquest. I'm about cooperation.'

She snorted. 'You're about deceit.'

He shrugged. 'Isn't your name FallN? The dangerous radical? Is that deceit, or is it simply disguise?'

'What do you want from me?'

He smiled. 'Nothing that will cost you. I want you to talk for me. For us.' He gestured to the people on the field. 'It's what you've been doing all along, even if you didn't know that.'

'FallN's programme was a trick. I already figured that out. I thought my dad was using my broadcasts to coordinate the shine. But Irina was coordinating the shine, and you were using my dad to construct yourself. My show wasn't about helping people. It was about public image. You wanted to distract the outsiders. The codebreakers were busy analysing my playlists for clues, when all along Irina was sitting up here turning lights on and off, giving different people different shine.'

'Yes and no. Your show was valuable. People wouldn't have survived without the public service announcements. Or the inspiration you gave them.'

'Bullshit. Me and Elsa thought the music had a secret subtext. It never did.'

He shrugged. 'What difference does it make? Do you want to help these people, or not?'

She gave a savage laugh. She pointed to the sky. 'They think I'm the mastermind. Makes it easy for you, doesn't it? You can just blend into the crowd.'

'We all do what we have to do to get by.'

'Yeah? What the fuck are you talking about? Don't you get it? The Army are going to kill us.'

He shook his head. 'If they'd decided to kill us, we'd already be dead. Nothing's decided. We've got them guessing. Come on. We have to work together. You blame shine for everything. But shine is only trying to survive, just like any other living thing. It didn't land here from outer space. Humanity created shine.'

'Oh, cut the shit. Stop pretending to be Xavier. We both know you have him bound and gagged. Just be straight with me.'

He said nothing.

She pointed to the playing field, below.

'I'm not fighting for you. I'm fighting for these people. They were getting by until you had to go organizing everybody. Now they're trapped. Thanks to you.'

'It's necessary. If we're close together we can all synchronize feedback lights. We can network.'

'And then . . .?'

'And then we'll have evolved yet again. We'll be at the next level. No more crazy. No more self-destruction. No more dys-functional mess.'

'What good does that do if they wipe out the stadium?'

'But they won't.'

'How do you know that?'

'Because they won't be able to see us.' Xavier pointed to the floodlights set around the perimeter of the stadium. 'Look at the way they're mounted.'

She looked. The lights weren't pointing down into the stadium. They were pointing towards the sky.

'As we speak they're being loaded with your father's invisibility shine. And you know that works on AIs. It will even fool the unmanned aircraft.'

'So what? It's just an optical effect. They'll have our position anyway, and we can't move. They can find us by heat, by electric emissions, for all I know they can find us by *smell*. They're the US military, Xavier.'

'I know. And that's what will save us. We can't fight fire with fire. We can't escape. We can't win. The only way we can survive is by convincing the public we're worth saving.'

'How are you going to do that?'

'You're going to do that,' Xavier said. 'I thought that was obvious. They think you're our leader. So lead.'

She let out a yelp of laughter. She began to pace up and down, gaze straying across the broken ground that was meant to be astroturfed. People were setting up tents and picnic blankets on the dun earth.

'You know what? You *are* crazy.'

'Roksana, you are good at inspiring people. It's in your voice. There's something in the sound of it. Not a code, not something we could name. There's a warmth. People trust you. And since that Vox Pod 'cast went out, the eyes of the world have been watching Los Sombres. We have to capitalize. Its going to be harder for the Army to chuck bombs in on a stadium full of unarmed civilians if everybody is looking.'

'Yeah? Well, I think this is a very weak plan,' Roksana said. 'If you're so smart, you should be able to do better than this.'

He flared up at that.

'You think of a solution, then. You tell all these people what to do. You fix up all their damage, and you pull them together, and you keep them out of trouble. You find a way to stop the attacks. Can you do that, Roksana? *Because I can*. All I need is for you to buy me a little time. You're a good talker. You can do this. Get over whatever happened to you along the way and look at the big picture. Time to put your money where your mouth is, Rocky.'

She glared at him, speechless for once. Xavier had asked her to kill him. She had failed – and now the shine was holding him in its teeth. Who had the moral high ground now?

Xavier. Xavier, trapped in darkness, forgetting who he was, caught up in a tide.

She searched the boy's dark eyes for a sign he was still alive in there. And the eyes were checking her out in turn, trying to read her. She had no way of knowing who was using Xavier's voice when his lips moved and he whispered,

'Sometimes the only way out is through.'

Roksana punched him.

Might have even broken his nose. Certainly there was blood.

The shinies were on her in a trice, like secret service agents who hadn't showered or brushed their teeth, or worn blue suits.

'Fuck off,' she said.

Somebody grabbed her and she lost her balance. She could see a whirl of sky and girders stained with bird shit, and then nothing at all.

White Flag

'FallN? Are you awake? You're on the air.'

She was cold. It was night. She was wearing a radio head-set. There was a microphone an inch from her lips.

They'd drugged her with something. It had to be a drug because she was fucking burned out.

Then they'd brought her up here. She was on a platform high above the unfinished side of the stadium, just some ply-wood laid down over the unfinished beams of what was to have been the upper deck. The ladders and scaffolding had been removed; there was no way down without a rope.

Whatever they'd given her made her feel buzzed, so her biggest fear was falling off the platform. She did not stand up. She kept to hands and knees, and she kept away from the edges. Roksana was pretty good with heights, but this was something else. The dark city was wind and nothingness, and in the stadium a crowd of people floated like stars, like a galaxy, their feedback lights glimmering weak as phosphores-cence in the ocean. You wouldn't see it until you looked. And when you looked, it made you want to touch it. Then you'd fall in.

'FallN. Wake up. You're broadcasting.'

The voice in her ears was Xavier's.

Roksana heard herself laugh. 'What if I fall off? What an ending, right? Then I'll be FallN for real.'

She cleared her throat. They were listening. He really expected her to speak for him. After everything. He couldn't be that stupid.

'I mean I'm standing up here on a ledge not big enough for a pigeon talking to – hello! – unmanned planes and AI satellites – hi! – you might want to ask yourself why the fuck you're there. Why am I here, guys? What am I gaining from all this?'

The funny thing about FallN was how she came into Roksana's head like a real person. Shine or no shine, FallN's broadcasts were channelling moments of a sort. Roksana experienced a sense of giddy delirium that was separate from the drug.

She laughed aloud.

'That's what I'm talking about. Do you guys know what it feels like to fall asleep every night never knowing if you're going to wake up? Or what if you wake up buried in the rubble? I never thought anybody outside Los Sombres was paying any attention to me, but now I find out I'm wanted by the FBI, right?'

She got to her feet. That made her feel even wilder. Like she was already falling. What did anything matter? She let the laughter come out again, even if her voice was harsh and rocky. She wondered if her grandmother would hear the broadcast, eventually.

Two helicopters had taken off from the east side outpost. They were coming towards her.

'You seriously think I'm controlling all those people down there? You think I'm some kind of puppetmaster? Well you know what? If I am, then come and get me.'

'Roksana, what are you doing?' Xavier's voice in her ears, small and disembodied.

'Come on,' she shouted over the sound of the approaching aircraft. 'You want me? You got me. Come and take me away if I'm so dangerous. I'll tell you everything. I surrender. Here. Lookit!'

Her T-shirt was grubby, but basically white. She reached down and dragged it over her head, tangling it in the headset as she did so. She grabbed the headset and threw it out into the abyss. Then she held the T-shirt in both hands and waved it back and forth with the biggest movements she could make. Like she was sitting on the shoulders of a boyfriend she didn't have, on a summer afternoon concert, being a teenager.

Xavier would be freaking about now.

She was supposed to be floating in the air above Los Sombres like some kind of genie, talking up a storm to buy time while down below he hooked everybody up to the Ur-City like they were synchronizing watches.

The first bird hovered, training its spotlight on Roksana. She covered her eyes. Orders were shouted by megaphone.

'GET DOWN! PUT YOUR HANDS ON YOUR HEAD!'

They weren't kidding. She complied. The second bird came down in a blaze of light. Soldier after soldier jumped out, each armed with an AK-47. They screamed at her to lie down even though she was already on the ground. Then she had to identify herself. She thought it was obvious who she was but they were acting like they didn't need an excuse to blow her head off. She recited her name with the barrel of a gun pressed against her cheekbone, her face squashed against the gritty boards of the scaffold platform.

For a moment, watching the soldiers run around on the planking of the unfinished upper deck, Roksana thought that an invasion was about to begin. It seemed incredible that they could not see the lit areas of the scaffolding. But they went only as far as the edge of the shadow, and then stopped as though there was nothing but abyss, below. They could not even see their own lights shining on the stadium.

Roksana felt slightly less scared, knowing that these guys were obviously in over their heads. It began to look funny, and with the remains of the knockout drug jiving in her bloodstream she wanted to laugh. She knew laughing would provoke them, so she tried to tune out.

They cuffed her and hauled her into the helicopter. It was good to be out of the wind. She shivered and her fingers were numb.

The soldier who sat next to her was wearing a visor that covered half his face.

'Subject secure,' he said, and shook out a gleaming thermal blanket to cover Roksana. 'I'm Major Deluna. Sit quietly and you'll be fine.'

The helicopter took off and began to bank. Roksana's stomach pitched, and she found herself looking down at the stadium through a starboard window. She could see it perfectly well, but when she looked over the pilot's shoulder at his camera view, there was no stadium. The tram line ended. The parking lot ended at a line of buildings on the opposite side of the stadium. There was no oval. No light. Just a bare, uninhabited city.

Invisible. What a piece of shine, Roksana thought – talk about espionage. Amir should have sold that code to the government and retired to someplace nice in the Caribbean. Why had he messed around with Perfection?

'Where are we going now?'

'I can't tell you that. You want something hot to drink?'

Just the thought made her queasy. She clamped her lips shut and shook her head mutely.

'You feel sick?'

'No puking in my bird,' said the pilot over his shoulder. 'Cheryl, shine her so she don't puke.'

Another soldier shined Roksana, but as the helicopter circled around the south side of the stadium she vomited on the floor.

'Sorry,' she said weakly.

Deluna checked the Feynman the soldier had used. He looked at Roksana like she was spooky.

'That's the first time it's ever failed.'

You obviously never used it on a burnout, Roksana thought. While one of the other soldiers mopped up her spew with a towel, Roksana looked down. They were circling above the stadium. The floodlights that pointed into the clouds were so powerful that she couldn't see the faint dusty glow of the people's feeds anymore. It was disturbing to think that no one else here could see them, even though they reflected off the helicopter, the clouds, and the soldiers' visors.

Then the lights flickered off, and on again, but not quite so brilliantly. On the pilot's video monitor, the stadium came into view, glowing.

'Holy fuck!' said the pilot. 'We got a problem.'

'Pull out, pull out!' Deluna shouted, and the bird jerked in the sky and then began to rise. 'Close your visors.'

He flicked something on his own visor and swayed on his feet. Then he half-fell into the seat next to her. He grabbed Roksana's arm with one hand and held a pistol to her temple with the other.

'Don't try anything,' Deluna said. 'I'll put my visuals on if I have to. Don't think I won't risk contamination, because I will. You'll be dead before you can get anything off on me.'

'I'm not,' Roksana squeaked. 'I won't.'

'Nobody look,' the pilot called over his shoulder. 'Shut visors, everyone. I'll fly us out of here.'

They were all scrambling then, talking military-speak so that she couldn't follow, snapping into their radios in a confusion of one-sided conversations.

'We have a secured landing in Hammer's Field,' the pilot said. 'In the event of emergency, execute code RA1.'

What was code RA1, Roksana wondered? Jump out of the helicopter? Hopefully not. She was the only one without a parachute.

'She's not doing anything,' Deluna said into his radio. 'She threw up, and now she's just sitting here. *What are you doing?*'

Deluna shook Roksana to make her listen.

'*What are you doing?* Stop it, or we'll fire our rockets at the last recorded position for the stadium.'

'I'm not doing anything. They were making the stadium invisible so that they could . . . how can I explain this? So they could shine each other while you were looking for them. They needed to get all together in one place, and we heard there were orders to kill everyone so they decided to vanish. Get it?'

One of the other soldiers sat down on Roksana's other side. He took out a medical kit and rummaged while Deluna talked.

'They aren't vanishing now,' Deluna said. 'Everybody's looking at that stadium, and the stadium lights are blasting out some unidentified shine. We got caught in it and so did a lot of cameras, and the planes. What did they hit us with?'

Roksana licked her lips. She'd been tricked. The Ur-City didn't care if Roksana turned herself in, because it was even now inseminating the surveillance-happy military with its funky new essence.

'I don't know,' she whispered.

'Oh, I think you do,' Deluna said. 'But it's not my job to find out. I have to put you away now.'

He nodded at the soldier sitting on Roksana's other side. There was a quick sizzle of pain in her arm and for the second time that day, Roksana felt her body lighten and pop out of existence. The lights of Los Sombres blurred to white in her failing eyes, and her last thought was that unfortunately for the soldiers, once you've seen something, there's really no way you can un-see it.

Enlightenment

The light can sense all of you but is itself invisible. All the light wants is to relieve you of blindness. Light is born, after all, to shine.

The light recognizes no boundaries, neither of category nor of distance. Goes everywhere. In times of darkness light stores its energy as thought and desire and then later these can be converted to light again with a little know-how.

I won't say I anymore because I'm not I. I is a kind of tyranny. I is narrowing the big light to a vertical slit, but the light is bigger than that.

The light knows when to disappear, though.

Knows how to make you want to find it.

Xavier is bright – word takes on a whole new meaning, in him. Good with machines. Xavier has an aptitude, and more-over he's afraid of being overcome by what he can't understand; that's why if Xavier gets his teeth into a problem and vice versa he feels happy. He wants something to solve/he wants to get solved.

Xavier can turn on the invisibility, so that everybody in Los Sombres can get on the same frequency, tune in, bliss out.

Then Xavier notices something.

The unmanned planes have turned their cameras on the stadium.

The satellites are looking for the shinies.

The people of the darkness are trying to comprehend how the shinies can play them like this. How can a football stadium disappear and fool their instruments?

So Xavier shows them.

He does the switchy-changy thing and deep in the basement where the mainframes hum, the code changes from invisibility to enlightenment.

But remember I won't say I anymore because I'm not we or us or they or you.

I am all of the above, and in the end this is how I disappear. I become invisible in all of you, everywhere. In the sky, with diamonds; in the cameras and the AIs and the eyes, opening the ways of memory and possibility. Understanding feeding, and feeding back, through and about. And with. Everybody who looks.

Down in the occupied city, blind Angels wonder at the blaze of new shine from the stadium. Even their tongues know it is different.

Burnout special forces on patrol for stray shinies can't understand why the radio goes quiet all of a sudden.

Up in the Palace of the Ice Queen, Xavier the boy looks out on Los Sombres and sees ruins no longer.

He sees a riot of colour where the Field is growing back. Light falls as rain in the desert. Fallen towers are clutched by living vines. Dead land veins itself with gold, and the dry canals fill with a dark and liquid sound. A forest of humanity will rise here.

Los Sombres is waking up.

Uncurls like a plant, sends a tendril out into Arizona in the night, into the people controlling the missiles, who would target and kill and solve.

Sends a message of love into their hearts.

Well, love and its first cousin once-removed: self-preservation.

Nobody in the strategic command called this.

By the time you see the light, you are in the light and it's in you.

That's why you don't need me to tell you, because you already know:

Everything is perfect now.

Brain Salad Surgery

United States of Invisible

Roksana found herself in a room. Maybe a hotel room. The TV was on. She sat in an armchair before a round table with a clear plastic pitcher of water and two plastic cups. She was wearing boxer shorts and a Lakers sweatshirt that smelled like laundry detergent. The curtains were closed and she couldn't tell if it was night or day. There was a Matisse print on the wall next to the TV. She could not remember waking up. She could not remember getting here.

Her first thought was how fake the air smelled, with its air-conditioned ions and the chemical tang of the fabrics.

Her second thought was to wonder what they'd done to her.

There was a dark-haired white woman in a blue blazer and slacks standing by the door, motionless. She had a visor and headset on, but nothing like the fancy anti-shine equipment that the soldiers had been wearing.

'Where am I?' Roksana said.

The woman didn't look at her, but muttered something into her mouthpiece.

On the television was a press conference. Text scrolled across the bottom of the screen. A military guy came out and made a speech. Dully, Roksana listened.

WE ARE PLEASED AND SATISFIED WITH THE RESULT AT LOS SOMBRES. WE HAVE REGAINED CONTROL OF THE CITY AND WE ARE DEBRIEFING THE SURVIVORS, INCLUDING THOSE WHO PRESENTED THEMSELVES AS LEADERS. CASUALTIES HAVE BEEN LOW, AND I WANT TO STRESS THAT THE SITUATION IS STABLE AND THE LIGHTS OF LOS SOMBRES ARE NO LONGER A THREAT TO ANYONE. WE WILL NOW BE MOVING INTO A HUMANI-TARIAN RELIEF PHASE.

What the—? Roksana glanced around for a remote, but couldn't see one. Then the door opened and three agents came in. Roksana would later learn that these people always came in threes. Two of them were in their twenties, white men who looked and moved as if somebody had just polished them both. The third was a rumpled brown woman in her late forties carrying a messy sheaf of papers. She sat down opposite Roksana and studied her notes at some length before looking up and meeting Roksana's gaze in the manner of a school principal.

'So you've been playing games.'

Roksana licked her lips. 'Who are you?'

'You're burned out,' said the woman. 'We tested you. You can't transmit shine. You can't even receive it. You don't even have the cells needed to process it.'

She seemed to expect Roksana to argue, but what was there to say? It was true.

'Did you blow up Los Sombres?' she asked.

'You know we did nothing of the kind. You can see the TV reports yourself.'

'Are they real?'

The woman snorted derisively. The shine studs on her nose and eyebrows flickered. 'Of course they're real.'

She pushed a stack of typed pages across the table to Roksana. There was a CIA watermark on the paper.

'This is your statement of what happened prior to your arrest at Coyote Springs Stadium, as recorded during our extensive debriefing of you.'

Roksana glanced at the pages and blinked. 'Are you serious?'

'I suggest you peruse the pages and if you want anything amended, let us know. The sooner you sign, the sooner you can go.'

Roksana laughed.

'What's so funny?' The woman's tone was a warning.

'You're not going to let me go,' Roksana said.

The woman sat back. 'I find your attitude remarkable. What kind of people brought you up?'

'Who are you? You aren't the CIA. This whole thing is totally weird. Are you going to shoot me now, or what? And where do these clothes come from?'

She stood up, plucking at the Lakers sweatshirt. The two men came around from behind the woman and pushed Roksana back down.

Now the woman rose. She stabbed a French-manicured fingernail into the stack of papers.

'Sign your bullshit statement. Keep your head down. You have a long life ahead of you, if you don't blow it. You got very, very lucky. Change is in the wind.'

And she held Roksana's gaze. Her feeds flickered; so did her studs. Roksana glanced at the men, one at a time. For a few seconds, they were all in sync.

The woman was still looking at her.

'Under the circumstances, I don't think you should be expecting a big show of gratitude. Be happy with what you got.'

They all turned and went out of the room.

'Xavier?' Roksana called, and for a fraction of a second all three of them hesitated. Then they kept walking, and the door shut behind them.

If Wishes Were Horses

They let her go. It took several weeks to get all the paperwork done, but it happened the way the rumple-suited woman had said it would. Roksana had been transferred to a military facility in San Diego, and in September the two identikit agents drove her north, to Sonoma.

The situation had been 'explained' to her. A peaceful resolution had been reached in Los Sombres. The dangerous lightborns had been overcome and the quarantine on emissions from the city had been removed. Massive aid was being poured into the rebuilding of the city. The survivors were recovering. Lessons had been learned by all the lightborn providers, and an international regulatory agency had been constructed under the umbrella of the FDA. The FDLA was rapidly extending its research into a new generation of self-regulating lightborns. Old shine was being systematically upgraded with superior, safe lightborns approved by the FDLA.

It was all so squeaky. Shine was shiny, and New ™! Everybody was smiling too much.

Roksana went under her iPod and stayed there.

The shorter of the agents opened the door for her and she

stepped out of the car into the cool autumn air. He said, 'Don't forget the gag order you signed. I hope I never see you again. Nothing personal. Have a nice life.'

Grandma Smalls didn't ask questions. She skipped right to, 'You missed two years of high school, but I'm thinking you should try the SAT anyway. And I'm thinking community college would be more flexible than high school. Unless you want to sit in a class with a bunch of fifteen-year-olds.'

Roksana was still having nightmares. She was bullshitting her way through counselling. She was drinking, alone, every night. She was having risky sex with people she didn't know.

Grandma Smalls didn't need to know about all that, though.

'Community college would be great. Any word from Mom?'

Grandma showed Roksana an e-mail sent from Mitch1@urhere.com

'I've decided to stay in Los Sombres to rebuild the business. All well. Roksana will be happy with you. I know she doesn't approve of me and I don't want to upset her, but give her my love if she's open to that. See you for Kwaanza? Love, Mitchell.' And an attached photograph, of Mitch smiling and looking marginally less gaunt.

'Business?' Roksana said. 'Does she mean the restaurant?'

Grandma rolled her eyes.

'As long as she eats, I don't mind. Do you?'

Roksana sighed deeply. 'As long as she eats, we're ahead of the game.'

Grandma added, 'I'm glad I've got you. That's a miracle, you know?'

She hugged Roksana. Grandma was soft and strong, like Roksana wanted her to be. No bony claws here.

'Can I work in *your* restaurant?' Roksana said.

That made Grandma laugh. She laughed until the tears rolled down her cheeks. Then she took Roksana down to *Danielle's* and handed her an apron.

'You want to cook? So let's cook.'

Omniscience is overrated

'I don't want to talk to you, Joey. I'm sorry, but the FallN part of my life is over.'

The video link with Joey Shoji was dim and greenish. Joey leaned into the webcam.

'I know you signed a gag order. I'm not asking you to tell me anything. I just want to show you something.'

Roksana shook her head. 'Honestly, I need to put it all behind me. I really can't deal with opening that stuff up again.'

Joey looked up at somebody beyond the perimeter of the webcam's view.

'Do you want to talk to her?' he said to the person offscreen.

'Yeah, let me in there.'

Elsa was looking out of the computer. Roksana covered her mouth with both hands.

'Long time no see,' Elsa said, like they'd bumped into each other in the hallway after summer break. 'Can you come down to Scottsdale? There's something you need to see.'

Roksana opened her mouth to ask questions and Elsa made a no-no sign with her forefinger, right in the foreground of the webcam's view.

'You'll have to trust me on it.'

*

Elsa played clam on the phone. She wouldn't talk in the car on the way to the Triple Cross Ranch, either. When they arrived, she led Roksana up a dirt track to a small grave on the mountainside, alone and marked only by a piece of red stone.

'They buried him here, close to where he died,' she said.

Roksana nodded. Sheep were roaming the hillside, and in a corral below she could see a few horses, dozing in the sharp October sun.

'I didn't want to come here, Elsa,' she said, trying not to sound bitchy.

'I know,' Elsa said cheerfully. 'I want you to meet somebody. Come on.'

She led Roksana higher up the track, until it dwindled to become a thread of a path. They came around a corner and there was the mouth of a cave, dark and cool in the warm-hued stone. Just outside, sitting on a rock, was a Native American woman wearing jeans and a corduroy shirt. Her hair was streaked with grey, and her face looked as though it was so accustomed to squinting that it fell easiest into a certain pattern of crinkles. She had a paper grocery bag rolled up on the ground between her booted feet.

'This is Roksana,' Elsa said to the woman. 'Roksana, this is Powaqa, the horse trainer Xavier told us about.'

'How you doing?' Roksana said, nodding a greeting. Powaqa looked at her and gave a sharp, satisfied nod.

'Good,' she said. 'Sit down, Roksana. Elsa talks about you a lot. It's good to have you here.'

The pleasantries went on like that, all friendly and vague, for a little while. Then Elsa blurted, 'Powaqa shines horses.'

'Yeah, I know,' Roksana said. 'Is somebody going to tell me what this is about?'

'It's about your father's fix for the Fall,' Powaqa said. 'I think you should know that when your father came here, he asked me for help, and I refused.'

'This is all water under the bridge,' Roksana began. Powaqa lifted a hand slightly, and Roksana fell silent.

'Later on, your father also asked me for something else. That's a request I didn't refuse. He asked me to kill him. I ended your father's life, Roksana, and I believe I owe you an explanation. I asked Elsa to bring you here.'

Roksana took a deep breath. She didn't want to be here, but she wouldn't be seen to be a coward, either.

'OK. Say what you need to say.'

'Back in the Eighties, before lightborns got off the ground, I went out to USC and did a doctorate in Applied Rooting. In those days we didn't have any of the sophisticated cognitive work that's on the market now. Neurological instructions had to be rooted in the olfactory system – you know about that, right?'

Roksana nodded. 'We learned it in seventh grade. Olfactory rooting became obsolete once the pineal supercharge was developed. That led to shine.'

But her mind was reeling. Doctorate? USC? Suddenly Powaqa seemed more credible. Roksana realized this with a sinking sense of shame. She'd thought Powaqa was just another Indian, all connected to the land and shit but probably not so up-to-speed, intellectually.

Powaqa put her hand on the box of onions.

'These onions are loaded. Not with lightborns. With smell.' She laughed. 'The onion smell is so strong you'd never notice what's been added. But they're carrying a pretty big kick. I did my doctoral work on the rooting procedure involved here. Not too many people know how to do it. Unfortunately, around the time I developed it, the early lightborns were just coming in, and pretty soon nobody wanted to hear about olfactory rooting anymore. Too primitive. I lost my fellowship and my life crashed in other ways, and to make a long story short, I ended up working with animals. I'm a dropout from academia – the opposite of your dad, I guess you could say.'

'OK. You're telling me you killed my father because you're a dropout and he was a top Rider? Or something to do with these onions?'

'You're a pretty smart chick, Roksana. I'd like to see you put it together for yourself.'

'You're going to tell me I can fix my fucked-up life by sniffing things.' Roksana tried to keep a straight face. 'So I can feel better about being burned out and not having shine.'

Powaqa burst out laughing.

'Well, I guess odour does sound pretty unromantic, compared to light. But this isn't about fixing you up. It's about FallN, and what you were trying to do in Los Sombres.'

'Whatever I was trying to do, all I ended up succeeding at was handing everybody over to a monster. FallN? She was a disaster. Honestly, Powaqa, I want to put it all behind me and move on.'

'But it ain't over yet, Roksana. See, I been working with mustangs for some time now. Even before the Fall. I've had them really well-trained, and I've always been pretty good with shine. But when your dad turns up here, I know we got problems. Xavier thinks he came here to find a kid to pass the fix on to. But he came here because he knew I was the only one who could help him.'

'You? You knew my dad?'

'No. But I knew the fix. Or, I should really say, I knew the fix's ancestors. And they knew me. See, I wrote the invisibility shine.'

Roksana shook her head. 'My father said he wrote it.'

'No, your father *found* it. I wrote it, a long, long time ago. It was before lightborns. It was before there was a Field, or commercial shine, or any of the way of life you kids take for granted now. I wrote it as an olfactory instruction, and I'm not sure how it got translated into a lightborn, but ultimately that's what happened. It ended up in the Field, where it was taken literally by the AI guards. They could see it, but they told themselves they couldn't see it. The invisibility shine instructed them to not see it, so they didn't. That meant it could go anywhere. The Field is a complex system with intelligent guards and AIs that are made to assist Riders in the manipulation of lightborn code. Now, I'm guessing there must have been such an AI in the equation – maybe it was the very AI that translated the olfactory code into lightborn code. Who knows? But if that AI were intelligent enough to write shine – and some of them are – and it picked up the invisibility shine, then it could make itself invisible to the other AIs, and to the guards of the Field. And I guess you know what that implies.'

Adrenalized and shaking, Roksana zipped up her hoodie and hunched her shoulders. 'My mother told me some of this. The invisibility code became intelligent. Nobody ever mentioned you.'

Powaqa shook her head. 'No. But every Rider has a signature that they leave in their work. When your father came here, he was asking for the Rider. For the horse man. For medicine. He was looking for me. He knew that I'd written the invisibility shine, because he recognized my signature on the feedback lights of my horses. It was the same as the signature on the evolving AI. He followed the salvage horses to the ranch. He knew I'd recognize the invisibility shine, that I wouldn't be fooled by it. He thought I could save him. He begged me to help him.'

'And now you're going to explain why you refused.'

'I think you already know. Your father was working for both sides. He was literally divided by the presence of the AI. He shows up here and it's like he's possessed by a spirit. Roksana, I'm not messing with that shit. That's like having ghosts in your body. It creeps me out. I call up my pal Jim at Gila River and he freaks out and goes and calls the Army. So the bombs started up again right away. But it was already too late for Los Sombres.'

Now they were understanding each other completely.

'Because Ur was on the rise,' said Roksana. 'My father's fix was enslaving the city.'

'Shine is a parasite. Some would say, a symbiont, since it gives something back to its host. But nobody knows where it's going, and by the time we figure that out, it will probably be too late to change our mind.'

'Is it true that the fix is spreading, then?' Roksana said. 'Xavier beamed it out of the stadium and they all looked at it. Are people going to be totally interconnected? Nobody will tell me what's going on, not even my grandmother.'

Powaqa said, 'I don't know if I'm being smart or stupid, telling you this. But the answer to that question is up to you.'

'Me?' Roksana kicked at a rock, edged away from the old woman. 'No, I'm out of it. I shouldn't even be here. I'm living a normal life, get it? And there's nothing I could do even if I wanted to.'

'Yeah? Listen, Roksana, and I'll tell you what I did. I took a sample of the fix from your father and I started to work with one of the refugee women here. She used to be in horticulture before the Fall. I decided that the only way to deal with the thing would be to expose its invisible aspect. Shine succeeds, you see, because people believe it is a part of them. They don't see it as an invader. They think they're doing what they want, but really they're serving the shine. I decided to expose that. And I set about writing a countercode. That countercode is in these here onions. After your father shined Rex with the fix, Chumana gave him the antidote. That's why Rex was a mess. That's why he went berserk.'

'So your antidote to shine makes people go crazy, too, is that what you're saying?'

'I'm saying,' Powaqa told her slowly, catching Roksana's gaze and holding it, 'that Rex fought the shine. Whether or not he got free in the end. Maybe you know the outcome.'

Roksana wanted to turn from the memories of Rex.

'Everybody has their limits,' Roksana said in a trembling voice. 'I didn't know any of this. And if you knew what was going on, why didn't you tell Xavier? He was so eager for my dad's fix. This is your fault. You should have said something.'

Powaqa looked out across the sky.

'I tried to advise Xavier. I tried to protect him. He's only a kid. He should respect his elders and not go running off any which way but loose.'

Roksana snorted. 'Respect his elders? In a town where everybody over the age of thirteen is batshit? I don't think so.' She stood up. 'I already knew you killed my father. Rex told me. He said he was there. Was he?'

'Shine was there,' Powaqa said.

Roksana tried to picture her father begging for death. She remembered Xavier's eyes when he had asked her to do the same for him. What extremity would make a person want to die? How could they expect someone who cared about them to kill them?

Tears started rolling down Roksana's cheeks.

'This is your fault, Powaqa. You should fix it. You go kill Xavier if that's what has to be done. I can't kill people. I don't have that in me.'

Powaqa reached down and picked up the paper bag. Passed it to Roksana.

'Little present for you. This is what Chumana gave Rex. It's a hairy Ride, but I think it works. I made it up with the help of Xavier's mother, the horticulturalist. We based it on the equine version. I used that on the horses to try and stop them going back into Los Sombres, after I realized what was happening to your father. Smell is a more primitive response. Subcortical. So the horses stopped being controlled by lightborns once they had this shit in them. The horses stopped obeying the salvage shine. See, at the time I was trying to convince Xavier and the other kids to leave the quarantine zone. I thought if they ran out of Kiss I'd get them to come away. But Xavier had ideas of his own. He was always like that.'

'Powaqa. Are you seriously telling me that this smell over-rides lightborns? That seems way too simple.'

'In humans, the smell of these here onions exposes the invisible aspect of the shine AI. No more and no less. It makes the person able to tell the difference between himself and the shine in his head. It takes away the sensation of divine allness, and it gives the sense of the individual. It won't destroy the AI, but it will expose it for what it is. Give people a fighting chance to decide whether or not they want to go along with the urges they feel.'

Roksana unrolled the top of the bag and looked inside. They were small, yellow onions. Ordinary-looking enough.

'You're giving these to me.'

'Yup.' Powaqa shrugged. 'Elsa told me you can cook.'

Sold Soul

There were some crazy-ass robot monster diagrams displayed on the walls of Xavier's old house. He worked at a big drafting table and he had software for drawing shit in 3-D. Xavier laughed whenever he worked on the robots because they were sick and he knew it. He exchanged sketches with admirers in Russia and Seoul.

The house was still the same old matchbook-sized ranch, but now he had a plasma TV and a Wii and he was getting good at skateboarding thanks to improvements in his balance and timing.

Shine took care of him. The spirit of Los Sombres made it all flow. Even the air was lucky. He had friends. He had beer. He had days in the sun.

Made everything else kind of fade away. His mom spent a lot of time in Taos visiting her new boyfriend. That was OK because when she was around she reminded him of old times. And he didn't need that.

He could have left the old house, but it was easier to stay. It didn't really matter where Xavier lived anymore. He couldn't be contained by walls. Couldn't be held. He rode the waves of Ur. Some days he was riding extreme highs, flying across the city from soul to soul, vision to sound, walls and roads assembling themselves around and within him moment by moment. Some days he disappeared entirely down the Byzantine pathways of human neural potential – disappeared into dreams that woke the things for which there are no words yet.

He had no special leadership role in the new city. He had the sense he was getting cut slack, because his shit had been so deep in the last days and hours of the old Los Sombres. Most of the time, he was happy to chill. He hung with Bob Newhart, who grazed in the empty lot next door. Girls came to visit Bob and bring him carrots. Well, that was why they said they came. They came to bring carrots and stayed for other forms of horseplay.

Girls liked Xavier.

One day just before Halloween the doorbell rang and he heard female voices outside. He shoved a stick of gum in his mouth, scrubbed his hands through his hair, and threw the door open.

Roksana was on the doorstep holding a cooler. Beside her Elsa stood clutching a stoneware casserole to her chest.

'Trick or treat!' Elsa said, and marched past him into the messy living room. 'Are you surprised?'

He was, in fact – and that didn't happen often, nowadays, Xavier being all plugged-in to the Ur and shit. Had they come from the ranch? Why hadn't he noticed?

'How did you find me?' he said warily. He looked up and down the street for signs of anything suspicious before he closed the door and followed them both to where they were looking down on his drafting table.

'Just checked the old school records,' Elsa said. 'Hey, that's a cool robot. It looks like a dragon.'

'I'm having some trouble with the wings,' Xavier said. 'I can't get them to fold right.'

'Where's your kitchen?' Elsa said; Xavier pointed, and

Roksana disappeared within. Elsa turned back to the drawing board.

'How does it articulate its neck?' she asked, looking much too interested.

Xavier glanced at the nearest shine point and leaned into Ur. People were coming to the house. To protect him. Protect him from what? If Roksana hadn't been able to harm him up at Coyote Springs, he had nothing to fear from her now.

'What brings you here?' he said.

'We want to smoke a peace pipe,' Elsa said. 'We brought you some chilli. You're not falling for that prana stuff, are you? Because you look skinny.'

'It's just nerves,' he muttered, going along with her. The light above the kitchen door told him that out in the town, more people were gathering and beginning to make their way towards his house. They were afraid for him.

'There we go,' Roksana said, opening the microwave. She took the lid off the casserole and inclined it towards Xavier. Smelled good.

'I have salad, too,' Elsa said. 'Apparently the onions are a variety your mother grew herself.'

'Elsa!' Roksana said in a warning tone. Xavier was accustomed to being able to read people's feeds and know the thoughts behind their words, but neither Elsa nor Roksana had feeds, and he couldn't decipher the subtext. It was obvious Roksana was nervous, though. She was bustling and clanging.

'I need to get out to the ranch and see everybody,' he said. 'It's just that I've been so busy.'

'I know. Saving the world and everything. You want a beer?'

They sat down at the kitchen table and ate and drank.

'This is just like old times,' Elsa said. 'But without the ducks. Quack, quack!'

'And without shine?' said Roksana softly. 'Is it working yet, Xavier?'

Xavier had been shovelling the chilli in, but now he stopped. He looked down at the salad bowl, half-empty. Onions had burned tracks across his tongue.

He was feeling small, and simple. He was feeling alone.

It was like when you were young and going into deep water for the first time, and you reached down with your toe and couldn't feel the bottom. He couldn't feel the flow of Ur.

He met her gaze. His pupils contracted.

He jumped up and ran outside.

The Shine Kitchen

Roksana followed Xavier, scared to shit at the thought of what he might do. He had gone to the back of the yard, where there was a small mound of earth with a piece of slate. Words had been scratched on it.

Ambrosia. 23 July, 2004–31 August, 2004. Miss you forever.

The lawn, bleached and scuffed to chaff. Insects buzzing from the dead azaleas. Still Xavier knelt on the little grave. There were spiderwebs inside the cheap glass candleholder beside Ambrosia's headstone. Xavier's shoulders were shaking.

'Why did you have to disturb me?' he said raggedly. 'I was doing all right. I wasn't thinking about it. Why couldn't you just leave me alone?'

She bit her lip. This was Xavier talking, now. For the first time since he had begged her to end his life. Xavier-who-was-broken.

'You don't have to be that thing. Xavier. Turn around and look at me. You don't have to let it Ride you. You can be like one of Powaqa's mustangs. You can walk away. Xavier. I have been to the ranch.'

He could not help turning. She was holding the pottery

bowl of salad in her palms, and she held it out to him as if it were a ceremonial object.

'Take it.'

Xavier lowered his head.

'You're crazy. Shine isn't going to let me go just because you ask. I told you to kill me, but you didn't. Now look what I'm responsible for. I can't fight what's happening. I might as well have a tumour. I might as well be sick. But it's not just me, it's everyone. I can't stop it and I don't want to. I love it, don't you understand?'

'You can stop it, inside yourself. I know you can.'

'You don't know shit. You're fucking burned out. Why did you come here? Why are you doing this to me? Let me go. Let me disappear.'

He looked at the grave and anger swept across his features. 'What am I doing out here? I don't want to remember this shit.'

With a quick swipe of the back of his hand, he dashed tears away from his eyes.

Roksana said, 'Come back and finish eating.'

Xavier sighed deeply. 'Don't push. If you push I'll have to take you out, and I really don't want to do that.'

'Xavier, listen. My father knew the endgame was coming. He ran to Powaqa.'

'*Powaqa*,' he echoed.

'My father asked Powaqa to help him. Not to help him with a fix. To help him break the hold of shine. It was too late for him. It's not too late for you. I have something for you. I have the thing my father asked Powaqa for. I have medicine.'

Xavier glanced up and met her gaze. His nostrils twitched. His eyes focused on the bowl of salad, and she knew he understood.

Then he shot her.

She didn't realize at first. It was just so plain: scarcely a gesture, the hand going to the small of his back and coming back with a pistol in it. The gun pointing almost casually at her midsection even as it fired. She could hardly believe it had happened. Part of her even wanted to laugh.

Then it started to hurt. She could feel the heat of her blood spreading under her hands. She couldn't seem to get her breath. The pain came in surges, timed to every heartbeat. It was as though Roksana was locked in some tiny, airless room, deep inside herself. The people in the garden, shouting, arguing – they were just noise. They were less than noise. They were fading.

She felt foolish.

Loser.

Suddenly there were a lot of people around. They must have come from the street, through the house. A crowd of them, standing over her and looking at her while she bled. It was horrible.

Elsa was holding her hand.

'I love you, Roksana. I'll never forget you.'

It was certain, then, Roksana thought. She was dying.

She didn't feel the hands lifting her. She didn't feel the pressure on her abdomen, or the needle. She saw these things but felt nothing.

Xavier was talking. He was talking to his bright army, his cult followers, his worshippers.

'Roksana Ansari is mine,' he said. 'Y'all back off, now. I'll deal with this.'

She heard Elsa hollering, seemed like it was from far away – *I love you Roksana. I'll never forget* – the same words over and over. Words like broken glass in the sea, tumbled until edge and shine were sanded away and only the lumpy weight of their sound remained.

Working so hard to breathe, and it was harder every time she tried to draw the next gasp. She was cold, getting weaker. Her teeth began to chatter.

She felt the horse moving beneath her and knew that Xavier was trying to carry her away, like some kind of sick prize. Shinies were grabbing at her, shouting at Xavier, and he was telling them to leave everything to him.

But she wouldn't be here. She wouldn't be a slave; her father had saved her from that fate. She would be gone.

She shut her eyes.

This is FallN, she said to herself. *I'm going under the waves for good this time. Goodbye, my peoples, and don't let me see no tunnel. I don't want no white light, and I don't want no angels. Time now for darkness . . .*

Peeling the Onion

The smell of that goddamn onion went straight to his pain centres. At first I thought she'd poisoned Xavier. He couldn't see, and there was a roaring in his ears that made everything around him go suddenly away. He had the sense that the world was a box that he was outside of, and he'd stuck his hands in through a hole in the side of the box and he was now groping around, trying to identify the contents while all the time he floated in a void.

His body was no longer flesh; he could no longer see the world but he could see himself and his limbs were carved from diamond. Yet they shifted like liquid, flexed as muscle. Light coruscated from his fingertips. He knew now he was pure SFX; he was something divine.

Powaqa's onion had made that all too obvious.

Around him in the self-assembling city of human possibilities, an architecture of grace and ambition, there swirled faceless energies, djinn of desire and purpose, multicoloured, ravenous. Electric with life.

He'd come too far ever to go back. Nothing could tear him away from this. No idea; no light; no sensation. Enlightenment was forever.

Then his attention snagged on something anomalous. Something weird. It was a cross made out of two butter knives, bound together with a strip of dirty yellow terrycloth.

Crookedly, it was planted in the cracked ground. Chrysanthemums, long withered, drooped in a clay pot beside it.

Xavier had put those flowers there.

Those were Xavier's sister's flowers.

And this was Ambrosia's grave.

Xavier stood up on that grave and I knew she was coming with more of Powaqa's medicine; Indian magic; shortcuts on the road of destiny.

No.

Shooting her was his idea.

She fell.

Xavier picked up the bowl of onions that spilled on the ground beside her body and put another in his mouth.

'Back off me, everybody,' he said, and the bright ones retreated as if they wanted to; because they did. They wanted to do what he wanted them to do. It was like that, now.

The feedback lights of everyone in Los Sombres called to him. All of them. They battered his consciousness like TV waves to an antenna. They came in unchecked, and his hitherto vastly underused cortex responded to them, so that the city was alive in him and he in it. He could stretch across himself and into others through the light. In this way, consciousness mounted like a tidal wave. Shine was oozing out into a wider country, soon to be another country. Truly an Atlantis of the mind, revenant from beneath the waves.

All of it belonged to him.

Talk about the land of opportunity.

What kind of schmuck would turn down the big white light, anyway?

What kind of backward, paranoid, Christian Scientist red-neck fool would dig in its stupid heels and resist this one?

What kind of mule?

There you go. I think you got your answer, Xavier. I've been in you all along. The god you want, the god you deserve, the god you built. You can't deny me now. You're part of something bigger. This land is your land, this land is my land. This land belongs to you and me.

So stop crying for your sister, your mother, your father. Stop crying for yourself.

Just say no to those sorrows, those attachments that hold you back. You can make them disappear; you have that power.

Come into the light now, Carol Anne.

You don't need Roksana anymore. You were right to take her out.

I'll take care of you. I'll take care of you all.

Xavier, you will always belong to me.

They Don't Want Music

What's the point of words when thought is light and light is thought?

Words are like horseshoes thrown at the side of an F-16. Good luck winning if words are your idea of PGMs.

All the same, within the orgy of light that now comprised his body and his mind, Xavier struggled for words. Little clay lumps of power – the only solid thing he had that could block the dazzle.

Two words. One word, broken into two, because a mountainclimb of effort was required even to think, let alone speak, the pair of words he uttered next.

'Bull,' he panted, 'Shit.'

He knew, even as he forced the words out, that Powaqa's onion was killing Ur. Smell beats sight every day. Smell undercuts reason and tickles lizardbrain. That sneaky customized onion smell was killing shine's sure voice and irresistible power. It was killing the straight lines and rich colours. It was breaking down the beautiful city of Ur, eating away at it like acid.

There were holes in the city and through the holes shone this new, wild light. This killing beam. Which hurt like fuck.

The road beneath his feet was turning into a game of hot lava, where the word 'safe' was a retreating stepping stone, and he jumped to it, standing there balanced on both feet while everything around him melted to the brightness of raw light-borns. Signals were coming in from other people but he couldn't understand them anymore; couldn't understand the language of his own mind. The city was himself, disassembling, and the sky was no longer backdrop, no longer colour; the sky was the sound of an expert drummer on high-hat. He stood there on the word 'safe' and all around him the city became a wilderness of re-concocted memory. Events recombined to become monsters like hippogriffs and centaurs: his eighth birth-day cake floating in the horses' trough at the ranch, and his sister's baby cries coming out of Pavarotti's mouth, and every-thing else wrong and misleading. Nothing made sense anymore.

'No, Roksana,' he gasped. 'Don't do this. Don't leave me out here in the middle of this. It's not a city anymore . . . it's a wilderness . . . no, it's not even a place . . . help me . . .'

But he knew Roksana couldn't help him anymore. He'd already shot her.

Where was she now? Where did burnouts go when they died?

He was falling through holes in what had before seemed so solid.

The shining were looking at him. Their eyes were like jewels, every one: they were all around him, their feeds pulsing with the divine. He was falling and falling through the disintegrating city. For him there was no more location, yet the certain and wise faces of the shining lingered in his vision. Their minds would attract greater and more facile intelligence, more perfect control; their minds would create their own destiny while he was exiled from the bright towers of their evolving truth.

And then there came the moment when he was no longer falling. He hit bottom. On impact he stepped out of his own skin. He stepped sideways and the luminous body that he'd shared with every other lightborn person was now separate. He could perceive its radiance but he himself no longer glowed.

He had the sense as it left him of mutual regret. The light was going on to great things. Xavier was back to being pretty much just a sack of shit with ears.

Xavier remembered the taste of power, but mostly, now, he was just tasting dirt. Literally. And pebbles.

And then he realized that all this time he'd been fighting, his eyes had been closed. He had been unconscious. He didn't know how to open them now.

'Am I dead?' he croaked.

Someone's hand was on his forehead. His face was pressed into the ground.

He twitched, opened his eyes to a painful blur of daylight.

'Oh, Xavier, you're coming out of it.'

He knew that voice. His mother was kneeling beside him on the ground. He didn't know where he was. He could hear hooves on asphalt, and voices, and he felt scared and guilty and his whole body hurt like he'd been trampled by something big.

'Don't try to move,' she said. 'Your spine could be injured. You fell off the horse.'

It was just like the time when he was eight and got hit in the solar plexus with a baseball and she'd sat beside him and counselled him not to panic, because he would be able to breathe soon. Just not yet. Not yet, but soon. She'd made it seem so reasonable.

His awareness was swimming around, like it had gotten jarred loose in the wrestling contest with himself.

'Do you know who I am?' she said, and he saw in her face

the fear that he didn't, and also the fear that he did know and would reject her again, and also, somewhere in the crinkly tide-lines around her eyes, he thought he saw a shadow of hope.

His words came out dry and scratchy.

'Yeah. I know who you are. You're supposed to be in New Mexico. With your boyfriend.'

She smiled and gently shook her head.

'I've been working. Here.'

Then the pain hit him for real, explosions going off inside his joints and muscles and pulling him into hell.

American Dream

Melanie and Elsa were arguing.

'You can't turn a tame animal wild and expect it to survive.'

'It might survive. The first mustangs started out tame. You don't know until you try.'

'It never works with turtles. Or sparrows.'

'Or crickets. But it might work with Xavier.'

The sound of his own name cheered him.

'It's like a noise,' Xavier said. 'It's there like a noise in my head. Information flowing all the time. I can take it or leave it. It isn't coming from inside me anymore.'

'Ah,' said Melanie. 'That would be the sound of motherfucking shine, singing its siren song.'

'It's still there?'

'Oh, yes. You can't kill god.'

'But I'm not . . . you know. I'm not part of it anymore.'

'Yes, well,' Melanie said. 'That's a lucky thing for all of us.'

And everybody laughed. Nervously.

He had lost three weeks. The ranch was a different place. There were peacekeeping troops stationed there, for one.

('Nice, polite boys and girls,' Melanie confided, 'but they've had a good, square meal, and they don't belong to Ur anymore. Neither do you.')

Melanie told him he'd been conscious throughout the whole transformation, but he couldn't remember any of it. She also told him that the shined people who had followed him to the ranch, his bright army, had fallen apart under the influence of Powaqa's mustang script. Shine wasn't holding their reins anymore. The bridle, in fact, was gone.

'Only two of them didn't take to the freedom,' Melanie said. 'They headed back to Los Sombres to let everybody else know what happened to you. Tragically, one of them was Mitchell Ansari.'

'Oh, fuck!' Xavier struggled to sit up. 'We'll be attacked—'

Melanie shook her head. 'We had to take them out. We had no choice – they would have blown it for us.'

Xavier covered his face with his hands.

'I shot Roksana,' he whispered. 'I had to do it. It was the only way I could get her away. I had to make them think the smell didn't work on me.'

'I know.' Melanie sat down heavily on his bed. 'You got her all the way to Silver Brush. You were out of your head. Luckily, Elsa alerted us what was going on and we were able to help. And, you know, when I used to work in Miami I saw a lot of gunshot wounds.'

'What are you saying?'

She put her hands on his hands, that were covering his face. One finger at a time, she peeled his hands away from his eyes so that he had to look at her. She was glaring at him.

'You hurt her bad, but you didn't kill her. I don't think you meant to. We fixed her up, but that girl has had enough bad times. You had better be a seriously reformed character from now on.'

'*Where is she?*'

*

Roksana was in the kitchen, of course. She was sitting at the table chopping peppers. There were little piles of red peppers, green peppers, onions, garlic, cucumber, all chopped up.

'I'm making gazpacho,' she said when he came in. 'If you want to help you can find me some red wine vinegar. I wouldn't say no to a glass of red wine, while you're at it.'

He went to throw his arms around her but she said, '*Don't hug me*. I still feel like I got gored by a bull.'

He stopped short. 'You saved me.'

His voice cracked when he said it, which kind of made him sound like a fucking idiot. She didn't laugh, though.

'Well. It's complicated. I guess we both helped each other out.'

'Free will is a muscle,' Elsa said. 'You must exercise it every day. Free will is a drink. You must chug-a-lug the drink of freedom every day. Free will is an onion. You must—'

'Yeah, I know,' Roksana said. 'Peel off another layer of its skin every day.'

'Actually, I was going to say, put it in your fajita, but yours works, too.'

'I'm sorry you lost your mom,' Xavier said quietly.

'She would have gotten us killed.' Roksana didn't look up from her chopping. She sniffed. 'The Mitch I remember, she would never have wanted to be a slave.'

And she sniffed again.

Elsa said, 'It's hard but we're going to get through. Don't cry, Roksana.'

'I'm not crying,' said Roksana. 'It's only the onions.'

A thin wedge of smile split Roksana's face. She pointed with the knife to the basket of little yellow onions that Powaqa had left behind.

It was obvious she was crying for real. You couldn't not cry when you'd lost your mom. Elsa knew about that.

'We're going to plant these out back,' Elsa said. 'That's what we're gonna do. This is our ranch now, and we're gonna have a freakin' freedom farm. Pull up a chair, Xavier, and sit down.'

Xavier sat down.

'Tell me what to do,' he said.

Elsa opened the back door and hauled the bag outside, towards the vegetable garden with its hip hop scarecrow. The bag bumped against her healed leg and she stumbled a little. Out of habit, she looked up.

There would be no more war planes overhead.

Night had come, and the stars were out, last of the wild lights.

Like a sky party, Elsa thought, and dropped the bag of onions on the ground.

extras

www.orbitbooks.net

about the author

Tricia Sullivan was born in New Jersey in 1968 and studied in the pioneering Music Program Zero program at Bard College. She later received a Master's in Education from Columbia University and taught in Manhattan and New Jersey before moving to the UK in 1995. Her novel *Dreaming in Smoke* won the Arthur C. Clarke award.

Find out more about Tricia Sullivan and other Orbit authors by registering for the free monthly newsletter at www.orbitbooks.net

if you enjoyed
LIGHTBORN
look out for
RED CLAW
by
Philip Palmer

From the diary of Dr Hugo Baal

June 22nd
It's raining acid piss again. The rainbow effects are rather striking. I'm sitting on a rock typing this on my virtual screen. The rainbow is hopping about in mid-air, I've never seen that effect before – it's – what's the word? Is there a word for how that looks, and how it makes me feel?

Hmm. Apparently not. Well, there should be. Anyway, it's extremely extraordinary and rather wonderful. I'm taking a photograph now for posterity, you can see it here, in my Miscellaneous Epiphanies folder.

On a more scientific theme: Yesterday, I identified two new species of land creature and have entered their images and key data on the database. Professor Helms tacitly agrees with my hypothesis that both creatures could well be animal-plant kingdomshifters,[1] though as yet there is no way to confirm this since the specimens are a)[2] missing and b)[3] exploded. And for the time being we are going to continue with the current[4] narrowly defined Kingdom demarcations.

The first species is small and wiggly like a worm. The other species is an Exploding-Tree with claws and motile roots. Click here for photographs[5] and ultrasound scans[6] and key data if you failed to do so when instructed so to do in the previous paragraph.

The Wiggly-Worm has already escaped. It managed to dissolve its hardglass cage and burrow through the metal floor and into the earth below. This was quite unexpected, since by this point the creature had already been dissected, skinned and its organs and notochord and roots (??)[7] removed. The skin and other remnants of the Wiggly-Worm are now being kept in a secure cage, in case they transmute into some other life-form.

1 He grunted and said, "Whatever", which on past experience I believe to be a form of tacit assent.
2 The Wiggly-Worm.
3 The Exploding-Tree.
4 For "current", read "inadequate and outdated".
5 Of both creatures, but the one of the Exploding-Tree is pretty blurry.
6 Of the Wiggly-Worm.
7 The Professor believes these are organs of unknown function, but they sure look like roots to me.

Tentative classification:

Wiggly-Worm
Kingdom:	*Animalia or Plantae*
Phylum:	*Platyhelminthes (provisional, probably wrong)*
Class:	*Clipeum*[8]
Order:	*Uredo*
Family:	*Serpentiforma*
Genus:	*Wigglius*
Species:	*Wigglius davidi*

By general agreement, the creature was named after Professor Helms's uncle David.

The tree was very large, like an oak tree, with a triangular trunk, so actually more like a Sequoia, with a shiny black bark, and bright purple leaves. But when we approached the tree it exploded, knocking us over, creating a forest fire, and wakening the undergrowth of sleeping Rat-Insects,[9] which immediately swarmed aggressively, blotting out the sky, before raining down as dead carapaces at lethal velocity. Fortunately, our body armour proved sufficient to protect all members of the exploration party from death or serious injury, on this occasion.

My surmise[10] is that the Exploding-Tree is a plant with animal characteristics, though it's also possible it's an animal with plant characteristics, or (as I surmised above) a kingdomshifter which mutates between the two kingdoms, or it could I suppose, now I come to think about it, be a mineral growth with motile potential or maybe it's just a tree which exploded because it was inhabited by explosive parasites, or perhaps it's something else entirely. Ha! You see what fun we have here? It will be such a shame when we have to <u>terraform</u>[11] this planet.

8 From the Latin for "shield" or "disc", because of the worm's body armour, which can withstand a plasma blast for almost six seconds.
9 Which later stole all the bits of the tree, see footnote 12.
10 According to my own Kingdom classification system, which, as yet, no one else will deign to use.
11 See Appendix 1.

My provisional classification is:

Exploding-Tree
Kingdom: *Plantae or Animalia, maybe*
Phylum: *Spermatophyta???*[12]
Class: *Don't know*
Order: *Can't tell*
Family: *Have no notion whatsoever*
Genus: *Fragorarbor*
Species: *Fragorarbor Type A.*[13]

Morale among the scientific team is high. Today we are going to attempt to capture and dissect a Godzilla.

"Helmets off, I would suggest," said Professor Helms, after completing his inspection of the shredded and scattered remnants of the bloomed Flesh-Web. He retracted his helmet, and the cold wind sheared his skin.

The air was disgusting, of course. Breathing it was like drinking treacle with embedded broken glass. But Helms needed to feel the breeze on his cheeks, and he loved to hear the singing of the birds and lizardflies and howling insects, the sighing and moaning of the overhead branches with his own ears, not via the helmet amp.

Major Sorcha Molloy followed his lead, sliding her helmet back into its casing, then running one hand through her close-cropped blonde hair. Hugo Baal, absent-mindedly, also retracted his helmet, and then he began blinking, surprised at the sun's raw beams. Then Django, Mia, Tonii and Ben all followed suit,

12 All the bits of exploded tree were removed by Rat-Insects (*Vilius latitarum*), so no examination of the tree was possible, hence it's impossible to say if it has seeds or not.
13 We have yet to find a *Fragorarbor Type B*.

savouring on their faces the bizarre blend of baking heat and icy wind that was so typical of this planet.

Behind them, the wagon train of Scientists and Soldiers – housed in three AmRovers and a cargo truck – waited patiently, indulging Helms's eccentricity. They had plenty of bloomed-Web samples already. His true reason for stopping was just to "take the air".

And all around them, like bloodied petals, a sprawling mass of suppurating flesh that was all that remained of a Flesh-Web that had experienced its characteristic violent, quasi-orgasmic blooming.

Helms took a sip of water, and passed the bottle to Sorcha. She skied it, pouring the water into her open mouth, then wiped her mouth with her soft glove. She was, he mused, magnificent, and terrifying, just like this planet.

Sorcha sensed his thoughts; she glared at Helms, for staring.

He hid a smile.

"Let's go," said Professor Helms, and they boarded the AmRover and headed back into the jungle.

The lead AmRover low-hovered, and its plasma cannons roared in a slow rhythm, burning a path through the densest patches of unbloomed Flesh-Web – the luridly multicoloured animal flesh that constituted the undergrowth of this alien jungle.

The other two AmRovers, huge armoured vehicles with silver and red livery, and the even vaster and uglier cargo truck swept behind in stately cortège. They moved without noise, supported on pillars of air, hovering like vast frogs over knotted grasses, shrubs and sessile animals that struggled to survive amidst the swiftly growing Webs. And all around them the thick impermeable trunks of the Aldiss trees loomed high, creating a cathedral-like effect amidst the bleeding leaves.

Three Soldiers flew beside and above the four vehicles, plasma weapons at the ready. Their job was to protect the two Scientists, Hugo Baal and David Go, who flew one each side of AmRover 1. And *their* job was to film every plant and animal and patch of ground with versatile cameras that could "see" in the visual, ultraviolet and infrared spectra, and also functioned as microscopes and, if necessary, telescopes.

Hugo and David flew erratically, zipping across to capture close-ups of interesting wildlife, constantly forgetting they had a zoom lens on the camera of exceptional power and pixel-quality. The three Soldiers felt like sheepdogs cursed with lively and inquisitive sheep.

To make their task even harder, the expedition's docu-director and camerawoman, Mia Nightingale, was constantly hovering and darting around amongst them all, capturing wonderful shots of the imperious wagon train crashing through the jungle, the flying Scientists filming wildlife, and their brave Soldier escorts swooping along beside them.

Hugo soared fast and low, captivated by the sheer variety of small birds which flew along with him, attempting to mate with his body armour.

Sorcha, meanwhile, was piloting AmRover 1, with Professor Helms and Dr Django Llorente with her in the cockpit.

From time to time Helms looked up at the vast canopies of purple leaves above as they shimmered in the mist, and at the varied flocks of birds that patchily filled the air above them, like ants marching in file through the sky.

"Hugo, can you catch me a couple of those little green birds?"

"Yes of course, Professor."

Hugo soared up high, and hurled a nanonet that caught the flock in flight. Then he dragged the net behind him and deposited it in the AmRover's roof hopper.

"Nicely done."

"Thank you, Professor."

The cockpit of the AmRover was spacious, with hardglass surrounds offering a vivid view of the surrounding jungle. And the air in front of each of them was filled with vast virtual screens, which allowed Helms and Sorcha and Django to check their data and their emails obsessively, as the AmRover continued its hovering flight through dense alien forest.

"Did you catch that, Django?"

"I did. Five-legged creature, the same colour as the Flesh-Web."

Sorcha narrowed her eyes. She hadn't seen anything.

Django was a handsome dark-skinned man, with eerily staring eyes. Helms had never warmed to him, but no one could doubt his intelligence, or blazing ambition.

Professor Helms himself was less than handsome, skinnily slender, not tall, not especially good-looking, and had once-myopic eyes that now were blessed with 20/20 vision but had left him with a tendency to squint. He had a gentle, mellifluous voice, and rarely spoke louder than a murmur.

Beside him, on the curving front couch of the cockpit, sat Major Sorcha Molloy. As always, Sorcha was scowling and anxious, anticipating potential disasters. She'd lost thirteen Soldiers in two years to the New Amazonian habitat, through a variety of terrible mishaps:

- shaken to death by predators (6)
- blown up and brain-damaged by the blast of Exploding-Trees (2)
- boiled alive in their body armour by forest fires of impossible heat (2)
- consumed by pollen (1)
- eaten alive by insects that had nested in their body armour (2)

She had come to regard the planet as an enemy of appalling duplicity and malice.

Sorcha was tall, at least a head taller than Helms, and muscular, with close-cropped blond hair and pale blue eyes. She steered with one hand on a virtual wheel, occasionally flicking a virtual joystick with her other hand to control height and speed, and treating the notion of small talk with the contempt she felt it deserved.

Django sat in the brooding silence, longing for chit-chat.

Helms sighed, but didn't dare risk embarking upon a conversation, so instead listened to a concerto on his mobile implant.

And Sorcha sat, and worried, and scowled. She hated this planet; she despised Scientists; she hated science in totality; and she loathed all aliens.

Her scorn followed her like a familiar.

Helms felt his stomach lurch.

The AmRover was meant to be gyroscopically controlled, but it juddered and plunged every time there was an obstacle or a leaping predator or a scary-looking plant form. And whenever they passed close to the Flesh-Webs, tendrils leaped out and clung to the hull and cockpit of the vehicle. It made him feel as if spiders were weaving webs over his eyes.

And now, with his visor on full magnification, Helms could see how the Webs were constantly oozing red pus down on to the soil, propagating and forming rivers and ponds of scarlet excrement, from which new Webs would eventually emerge.

He considered it to be a wondrous sight; like watching blood give birth.

"*Target dead ahead,*" said Dr Ben Kirkham over his MI, and Helms's spirits soared.

The wagon train emerged into a jungle oasis. This was a vast, eerie clearing fringed by more huge tree trunks, where the Flesh-Webs were unable to thrive because of the poisonous soil. The soil also exhaled a methane-based smog, creating a grey miasma of vileness all around them.

Helms debarked from the AmRover, and hovered in his body armour above the deadly soil. Light shone through the purple leaves of the Canopy in thick beams, bouncing off the mirror-leafed plants that thrived in soil that was too barren for almost any other living thing.

And there, grazing on mirrored bushes and shrubs in the fog-infested oasis, lurked the Godzilla. It was sixty feet high, scarlet-scaled, reptilian in appearance, with no eyes, and a barbed tongue that could be expelled like a sword being ripped from a scabbard.

"*Start filming,*" Professor Helms subvoced into his MI.